DEAD MAN'S QUARRY

by

Robert Kline

This is a work of fiction. All events, locations, institutions, themes, persons, characters, and plot are completely fictional. Any resemblance to places or persons, living or dead, are of the invention of the author.

Copyright ©2002 by Robert Kline. All rights reserved. Printed in the United States of America

This book or any portion thereof may not be reproduced in whole or in part in any form or by any means without written permission of the publisher, except by a reviewer who may quote brief passages in a review. For information, or to order copies, contact:

> Galaxy Books, Inc.
> Post Office Box 1421
> Orange Park, FL 32067 or
> www.galaxybooksinc.com or
> Email info@galaxybooksinc.com

First Edition
Publisher: Galaxy Books, Inc., Orange Park, Florida
Cover Design: Graphics Ink Design Studio, St. Augustine, Florida

ISBN 0-9652682-3-3

Simply put,
"Thanks, Mom."

DEAD MAN'S QUARRY
by
Robert Kline

## DAY ONE

Four boys, recently graduated from Nepper Memorial Junior High School, paddled their oil drum and board raft across the water, the echoes of their misplaced paddle strokes and their adolescent voices mocking them, the veined granite walls holding them captive that early summer evening.

They approached the middle of the quarry.

Kurtz sensed motion in the air behind him and glanced up at the sky.

"Holy shit, here it comes!"

The boys stopped as one and looked at the roiling darkness which was nearly upon them. The raft glided forward, rocking slowly as water thunged against the oil drums.

The clouds rolled over themselves, building as they advanced. At first the air was still, but as the storm approached, the leaves on the bushes at the lip of the quarry moved restlessly and then turned, their silver undersides exposed to resist, flickering with the breath of the wind.

"I don't think this is a good idea." Alan Wasterly was close to weeping. He was the youngest and the weight of the storm touched him first, brushing against the backs of his hands and the scruff of his neck and then settling onto his narrow shoulders.

"Come on, you guys. Let's get out to the center." Ricky Cavenaugh, the tallest and the oldest boy, dug the end of his board into the water and began to paddle. Because he was the only one who did, the raft pivoted with him.

"Cut it out, we're just going in circles." It was Kurtz, irritated with himself and mad at Alan for being afraid.

Sitting at the front of the raft and opposite Cavenaugh, Alan realized that the raft had swung around so that they faced the landing. The young boy dug his board into the water and thrust backward, stopping the revolving motion of their craft and momentarily moving them toward the one low wall of the quarry.

Cavenaugh saw what was happening and quit paddling. He pulled his board out of the water, lay it at the side and then balanced his way across the raft to Alan, who was still working desperately, and now that Cavenaugh had stopped, was succeeding only in turning the boat in a circle opposite the one the older boy had begun earlier. Cavenaugh put his hand on Alan's shoulder and then lowered himself beside him.

"We won't go out to the center, Alan, we're out far enough." He paused and looked at the sky. "Let the storm come a little closer and then we'll go back to the camp—I promise."

Roger added calmly and without rancor, his comments only observations, regardless of their perceived criticism, "You know, you guys, every time we say we're going to do something, somebody chickens out. The high school kids come out here all the time, why do we have to be such wieners? I, for one, am disgusted with us."

Kurtz turned. "You never volunteer to go out alone. So how come? It seems a guy as brave as you would be out here every storm, charging his batteries, sucking up the juice."

Cavenaugh had not heard the others' remarks. He left his hand on Alan's shoulder and turned to the two who were arguing. He was about to speak when lightning appeared deep in the sky toward town. Each boy held his breath. They waited and silently counted.

A thousand one. A thousand two. A thousand three. A thousand four.

When the thunder came it was still only a mumble.

Roger stared at where the lightning had glowed in the distant clouds and then pronounced, "Rain, any minute—bet me."

"No shit?" Kurtz taunted, "I must have missed that class."

Lying in the center of the raft, Alan's retriever, Blacky, suddenly looked up to one of the surrounding walls of the quarry. He stood and stared for a moment more and then barked.

"Shut up, Blacky." Alan forgot the storm as he spoke. He tried to see what his dog was barking at, but couldn't until Cavenaugh pointed to his left.

"It's the Moron Squad out airing their brains. Head for shore, girls." Cavenaugh resumed paddling, advising the others that they would be smart to join him.

## Dead Man's Quarry

The quarry was boxed on all sides but one by granite cliffs, flat plains fluted with drill borings, rising perpendicular from the water. At the top of one of the walls two older boys yelled.

"Time to go home, losers, your mommies are calling you," a broad, angry looking person shouted down to them. Phillip Henshaw had no good reason to be mean. He had graduated two years earlier and held a good job as a mechanic, and since he was a clever mechanic, he always had plenty of money. The girls liked him because he was funny and because he was a traveling party. He had built up the sharpest and reputedly the fastest '49 Ford in town, and from its trunk Phillip produced a never-ending supply of beer and cigarettes. But somehow his popularity wasn't enough for him. When he wasn't around girls he was cruel and a bully.

"Yeh, we just got done screwing them." It was Junior Swift and he was referring to 'the losers' mommies. Junior was the owner of possibly two active brain cells.

"Wednesday is Ugly Hag Day. I'll be glad when it's Thursday," Phillip added, again referring to the young boys' mothers.

Kurtz yelled back to them, "Yeh, well you guys weren't born; your moms just popped a couple huge zits."

Cavenaugh cuffed Kurtz. "Come on, stupid, leave 'em alone."

As the boys above called, they bent and retrieved chunks of stone and started throwing them down into the water near the boys on the raft. Because they were thrown from a height of at least forty feet, the rocks hit the quarry pond with frightening speed, throwing off oblique geysers when they plunged into the water. Gradually, Phillip and Junior loosened their arms and improved their aim and the falling granite walked closer to the raft, until at last some of the splashed water was landing on the younger boys.

"CUT IT OUT, YOU MORONS!" Kurtz shouted.

"Oh good, be sure to make 'em mad, Kurtz." Roger was paddling in earnest and he was upset and scared. The other boys were, also, and they looked over their shoulders and up as they tried to get back to the landing. But as the younger boys progressed, their tormentors walked along the rim, continuing the bombardment.

"REMEMBER THE ALAMO!" Phillip shouted as he heaved another rock.

"REMEMBER THE MAINE!" Junior countered as he tossed his own slab of stone.

"REMEMBER TO WEAR YOUR RUBBERS TO SCHOOL, KIDS, AND BE SURE TO TAKE PLENTY OF TISSUE!"

Phillip heaved in another.

Both of the older boys laughed at Phillip's humor, Junior snorting as he ran off to find another rock.

They had all forgotten the storm. It was almost on them now and lightning flashed several times from cloud to cloud. The rumbling thunder closed in as the wind picked up again and a mist of rain began to fall. It was nearly dark and the boys on the raft were finding it harder to spot Junior and Phillip as they bent and rose with the rocks they were to throw.

The flooded quarry was shaped like an obese 'L' and the boys still had to pass around the interior angle before they could land the raft. They had almost reached the protruding point where Phillip and Junior now waited for them.

Cavenaugh shouted up to them, "COME ON YOU GUYS, SOMEBODY'S GOING TO GET HURT. YOU MADE YOUR POINT." As he finished, a large shard of granite hit the water barely two feet from him. Cavenaugh swore as the water washed him below the knees. "YOU BASTARDS!" He looked down at his jeans. "IT MUST BE NICE PICKING ON LITTLE KIDS, JUNIOR. I SWEAR SOMEBODY'S GOING TO GET HURT!"

Blacky had risen and was answering an inner voice. Following each splash he ran to the edge of the raft, his tags rattling as he skidded to a stop, his front legs propped in front of him. He kept running from side to side, drawn to the splashing water.

Alan was beginning to panic. "Stay, Blacky! Stay!"

And then for a reason he would never understand, Alan looked behind him and into the black water. Something, darker still—darker than the water, slipped by the raft, barely below the surface. A sliding, shadowy form, obscured below the viscous water and opaque and dark as thought, briefly violated the surface beside the raft and then passed beneath it. Alan watched it flow past, distending the lense of water as it dove.

"Oh shit, you guys!" Alan could not pull his eyes away from the path of the passing shape. "Oh shit," he repeated.

No one knew what he was referring to.

Another rock landed near the raft and Blacky spun around.

The boys at the top of the quarry called down, "GET IT, BLACKY! GET IT! FETCH, BLACKY, FETCH!"

Splashing water and shouted commands—it was too much for Blacky. He whined twice and then raised his head and leaped into the water. The retriever's body was swallowed as he paddled to the last splash, his head leaning forward, craning to reach the center of the spreading ripples.

"No, Blacky! Come back, Blacky! Come!" Alan called before he started to cry. "GET BLACKY, YOU GUYS! GET HIM! BLACKY!!" Alan crawled quickly across the raft and leaned out over the edge, his arm extended toward the swimming dog.

And then many things happened at once. Phillip and Junior picked up a huge rock between them, swung it together several times and lofted it over the quarry wall.

Of course, Blacky did not see it. He had turned and was swimming back to the raft, to Alan. At that instant, Kurtz and Roger looked up at the older boys. They saw the descending mass.

Cavenaugh ran over to help Alan, almost upsetting the raft when he did.

Alan called one last time, "BLACKY!!" and then pushed his arm even farther out to his dog. In the heartbeat before he could touch Blacky — in the instant before the falling rock hit Alan's outstretched hand — Blacky yelped and was dragged beneath the surface of the water. He had turned to Alan and the last thing the boy saw was Blacky's shiny nose disappearing in advance of the plunging rock.

"BLACKY! BLACKY!" Alan flew toward his disappearing pet, but before he could reach the water, Cavenaugh wrapped his arms around Alan and pulled him back. Alan fought the bigger boy, pounding Cavenaugh's arms, and then went slack with his sobbing. "Blacky! Blacky Blacky!"

"Oh, shit," Kurtz moaned when he realized what had happened, and then he too began to cry. Roger stood with a board in his hand and looked from Cavenaugh to where the rock had hit and then to the dark quarry wall.

Above them, the boys disappeared from the rim as the rain came pouring from the sky.

They had sketched the raft on napkins in the lunchroom at school and then built it soon after the last skim of ice left the quarry. For three days they had raided area construction sites, filching boards and nails where they could. The oil drums came from Wasserman's Salvage, somehow rolling away in the dark of night, clattering along Tucker Street and then bouncing out of control down No Brakes Hill. It was during the descent of No Brakes Hill that one of the barrels took an unexpected turn and smashed into a pine tree near the bottom. The dent and the small tear in the side of the drum gave the raft its rakish tilt for that barrel was slowly filling with water.

The boys lashed the barrels in place with Old Lady Brinks' clothesline. One bright morning she walked out into her back yard with her wicker basket loaded with sodden clothes, and then stood for a moment trying to figure out what was odd about the two cross t's which stood at the back of her lawn.

"My clothesline!"

She dropped her clothes basket, spilling laundry onto the yard, and looked back and forth as if she expected her clothesline to reappear. She then searched behind her and finally kicked the overturned basket. "Those boys!" she exclaimed as she shook her finger and then huffed back into her home and attacked the telephone.

She called each of the boys' parents; for she was certain who had performed the deed, but she suffered such a reputation as a busybody and a snoop that none of the parents gave credence to either her accusations or her lament.

The event was subsequently mentioned quietly at the dinner table in two of the boys' homes, was referred to with humor in another, and was darkly avoided in the last. The boys referred to it as *The Brinks Robbery* and joked about it as they cut the rope into quarters.

"I bet she yelled, 'Those boys!' " laughed Kurtz, running his hand over the quarter inch nub he called his 'buzz' haircut.

"And she shook her finger when she said it!" added Roger shaking his finger at the pieces of clothesline. "That old biddy finally got some excitement in her life — bet me!"

The boys, referred to as Nepper's Lepers, embraced the summer of '59 as their last as a gang, sensing that high school would bring more changes than they cared to explore.

Dead Man's Quarry was the stuff of legends and stories, some of them going back to the days of the Indians, when there were no white men and instead of a hole cut from the earth, there was a ridge of stone. It was a ridge the Indians had stood on and looked across thousands of acres of their wilderness. Two hundred years after the last Indian, the white man was poised to harness the evil that had ruled the land, ready to foist upon the growing nation the will of the paper laws.

The stone cutters drilled and cut their way into the ridge, carting off the stone they freed, until it was not a ridge anymore, but a man-made chasm. Ever deeper the cutters probed, punishing the hand drills with their mallets, hoisting out the monstrous blocks of stone to be sent south to build the courthouses and the customhouses and the jails. And finally, when the edifices stood in which the papers that controlled the land lived, and the cells were completed to hold the bodies of those who did not believe the power of the papers, then the granite was hauled to build the monuments to honor those who had championed the paper. The men whose fragile bodies had been ripped apart and trampled in war were glorified with granite, some of it carved or lettered, some merely stacked in tapered towers, blocks of stone piled one on top of the other forming great limbless trees, cold and never changing. Paper was king, but it rested on a throne of granite, and the cutters would have followed that pillar of nearly perfect stone to the center of the earth, violating the veins of water which pulsed through the few flaws in its metamorphic body.

The quarry at Indian Ridge was opened and worked for fifty years until a cataclysm at the height of the demand for granite resulted in its abandonment and a different series of stories. When the big boiler cooled and there was no more live steam and the massive flywheels of the Bowers and Chagrin steam pumps coasted to a halt, the clattering valves and cams became as silent as the dripping oil, and hundreds of seeping cracks in the stone walls bled water and the quarry slowly filled.

Yet, it would not be accurate to say that the site was abandoned. A relic of the era when the quarry flourished still lived there. He was an old man, some estimated him to be a centenarian, and he lived in the machinery building. It was built with walls of granite rubble, and if the entry to the door was any indication, they were at least three feet thick. There was only one window on the first floor and it was to the side of the narrow opening where the cables entered from the steel derricks. There was a rusted metal door on the opposite side of the building and two large metal doors which faced the quarry road. Above the double doors was a faded wooden sign which proclaimed, *The Klauber Stone Works,* and under it, *Granite to build America est.1854.*

The roof was made of sliced stone and there was a dormer which faced the quarry. A hexagonal cupola interrupted the ridge line of the steeply pitched roof and the lightning rod which topped the cupola was a strange forked affair of hammered iron.

In the woods behind the machinery shop was a small cemetery, overrun by blackberry briars and the home of an inordinate number of statues and ornate headstones. Almost all of them had succumbed to the ignominy of vandalism. To the side of the shop stood a water tank, tall on its webbed tower, a bent, metal ladder leading to its surrounding platform. The tank was the size of an inverted automobile and constructed of curved sections of boiler plate held together by intersecting armies of domed rivets — the old kind which looked like Chinamen's hats. A pipe ran up one of the legs of the tower, broached the top of the tank and then disappeared inside, and another, wider, descended from the center of the bottom.

The tower and tank were black, fading to rust, with a painted overlay of years and slogans. Currently, "Class of '59" and "1960 — the future" dominated.

A mountain of coal shouldered the back of the machine shed and a hill of clinkers and cinders ran into the coal. Concealed beneath the back shining pile was the coal trap and chute.

The old man who lived above the machinery shop was wounded, his back humped and the right side of his body stooped as if bearing a poorly distributed burden, and he was simple. He had lived at the quarry beyond anyone's memory and the town records showed him to be the owner, although no one could understand how that came to be. The National Bank was rumored to hold a trust account in his name which he had not drawn from in many years. Phineas Lathram, the bank president and sole stock holder, was the only one who knew the value and the particulars of the account. Anyone who tried to trick that information from Mr. Lathram encountered an Arctic chill and a stare hewn from the ancient granite of the quarry. The value of the trust could have been millions and it could have been next to nothing. It generated income sufficient to address the annual property taxes and the minor electric bills which were forwarded to the bank.

The hermit's name was Ezechial Flander, but the adults and the children called him The Doll Man. He was a dump picker and he invariably returned to the quarry with at least one discarded doll. He did not bring back the dolls which were modeled after infants — he would gently lay those aside. The ones he chose were older, with long legs and long hair and they were adolescent girls. Even if the doll were missing an arm or a leg he would carry it carefully back to the machine shed, cradling it as he walked.

Ezechial had a bushy beard and glazed, watery eyes, and he was the children's favorite monster.

But he was not a mean man and he did not approach anyone who came to the quarry. In fact, the only time he was seen was on his visits to the dump, and there, if an adult confronted him, he would stare toward their voice as if he could not see, and rarely, when a child addressed him, he would smile a crooked sort of smile at a spot about two feet to the right of the child who spoke.

A few children claimed they saw him peeking from behind the shuttered window of his dormer, but the children who said this often saw other things too strange to believe.

Once a month The Widow Orlap left a box a canned goods at his door, but it did not seem that could be enough to sustain him. The old lady told no one what prompted her generosity; she had been leaving packages since before the death of her husband, the Reverend, forty years earlier. It did not seem an act of charity and neither did it seem to come from love, much to the disappointment of the townspeople. "I do it," she would croak after a long silence, "because it must be done." She never said more and she was neither perturbed nor saddened by the question or her answer.

Some said he ate mice and squirrels and drank the water from the water tower, and they were partially correct.

The machinery shed was fifty feet from the edge of the quarry. A series of greased cables ran from a low oblong slit in the side wall of the stone shed and passed slack along the granite to either of the remaining derricks which stood at opposite ends of the quarry rim. The fact that the cables were greased did not seem odd to the children who frequented the quarry and dove from the wall at the base of the lower derrick.

An old sedan bumped along the back road to the quarry. Beth Wasterly sat in the back seat with Freddy Auftencampf and they both held onto the covered cord which stretched behind the front seat.

"Slow down, Will, you'll kill us," Freddy warned the driver.

Beth thumped her head against the roof of the car and laughed.

Will Duchamp slammed on the brakes and everyone slid forward.

"Is this slow enough, Freddy?"

The rain began in earnest and Will switched on his windshield wipers. The two cleared areas looked like mouse ears.

"Mickey Mouse©!" screamed Beth.

Beth and Freddy and Will then started singing together, "M-I-C-K-E-Y—M-O-U-S-E!"

In the front seat, beside Will and leaning against the door, Louise Kurtz looked with disgust at her companions. She was going to be a famous movie actress and she could hardly wait until she could leave these boring people, her boring town, and most of all, the boring state of Maine, and begin to enjoy her stardom.

Louise did not try out for the school plays or the church plays or any of the talent shows. It was just too depressing to think of the embarrassment she would cause everyone else. Let them pretend they had talent; let them make fools of themselves as they tap danced across the stage or shouted their lines at each other. She did not have to endure the mawkish costumes or the discordant music.

She knew she was special — Louise could feel her gift deep within her. It would require neither practice nor training. One day she would simply drive to Hollywood and be a star. They were waiting for her.

Presently, she did not have her own car. She didn't even have a driver's license, and she did not have any money. In fact, she wasn't entirely certain where Hollywood was, except that it was in the West and there was plenty of water near it.

But she would graduate next year, and she had the dream, and that was all she needed. She doubted that she would even write to her friends once she got to Hollywood. Let them write to her. Louise would answer their letters, eventually, when she had time, but she would not sign them. Why give away something so valuable?

Will looked at her as he put the car into first gear and started forward again. "Let me guess — you're in Hollywood and your adoring fans are reaching out to touch you."

Actually, Louise had just brushed their hands away and stepped into her chauffeured automobile. Yes, she would have a limousine. The studio would buy it.

"Good-bye, my fans. Good-bye."

She stared back at Will with disgust. "You are so common, Will, don't you have any plans? Are you always going to drive around on dirty roads in your dirty car?"

"With your dirty friends?" Freddy piped in and tried to kiss Beth.

"Gross! Get this sex fiend away from me!"

As Beth pushed him away, Freddy's hand brushed against the side of her breast.

Beth flinched and blushed. "I should slap you, Freddy Auftencampf. Don't ever try that again."

Will and Louise thought she was referring to his attempted kiss.

Freddy could have cared less. He could still feel her softness on the back of his hand. It was worth a slap.

"I'll never wash this hand," he whispered.

Beth leaned toward him and slapped his face. As she did, she felt his open hand around her breast.

"You animal!" She hit him again, this time harder and from farther away.

Will was watching in the rearview mirror. "Been to a foreign country, Freddy? Roman hands?"

Beth whacked the back of Will's head.

"Gheez, don't beat on me! My hands are on the wheel!" Will protested, when in fact his hands were now protecting the back of his head.

Louise moved the mirror so she could examine her lipstick. "Are the children done playing?" She looked back at Beth, smiled a cold smile and then rolled her eyes. "Can we listen to some music, now? Turn on the radio, Will." She twisted the knob before Will could react. The radio crackled and hissed and then began to hum.

They pulled up to the side of the quarry and parked before the radio warmed up and the music came on. The rain pounded on the roof of the car. The windows steamed and the four sat listening to Will's radio.

Freddy flirted with the idea of once again trying to kiss Beth but decided it was safer to hold her hand. He did like her.

They were parked on the side of the quarry opposite the machinery shed.

"What do you think The Doll Man's doing?" Louise asked.

The back of Alan's hand was scraped and covered with blood. It pulsed and stung but he didn't care. They were in the cavern of the quarry and the storm was directly over them. Lightning exploded again and again, drenching the sheer stone walls with white iridescent light. The artillery of thunder rode the back of the lightning and it too reverberated back and forth across the quarry. The boys' greatest fear was that one of the two derricks at different ends of the quarry would be struck. Each tower was nearly a hundred feet tall and guyed at the top with a circus tent of inch thick cable spreading to the ground around them, bridging the quarry and crossing and interlacing with the cable of the opposite tower. The wind had achieved such velocity that the rain no longer fell but swept by them, and the towers and cables hummed to the storm's crescendo.

Cavenaugh and Roger shouted directions to each other and Kurtz bent paddling madly with his board. He would not look up. With every thunder clap he rolled his shoulders farther to his ears and cried to himself. He would die soon, he knew he would die. Their parents would find all of them curled up on the raft, charred to a crisp and floating in the quiet morning air. The whole town would stand around the quarry and everyone would cry and say what good boys they were, and his sister — his bitchy sister — would then take over his room. Kurtz paddled harder than before.

They were beyond the corner beneath the derrick and moving toward the landing, struggling through the sweeping clouds of rain. The thunder and lightning storm passed but the showers became heavier. The mist from the rebounding rain kept the boys from seeing more than a few feet in front of them.

Alan sat in the center of the raft, huddled over his hurt hand, crying uncontrollably and repeating his lost dog's name.

At last they bumped into the side of the low quarry wall and Cavenaugh looked around and realized they were by the old narrow gauge railroad tracks, too far down from the landing.

"Pull us back up to the left," he shouted to the others as he grabbed the granite lip.

The rain slackened and the boys manhandled the raft back toward the landing. And then from the woods behind the landing they heard a bark. They heard Blacky's bark.

"Here, boy," Cavenaugh called, knowing the dog could not be Alan's, but unable to accept that it wasn't.

In a second the dog broke from the woods and was on the low wall beside them, barking and whining, his tail and body swashing back and forth.

Alan leaped up and ran across the raft. "Blacky!"

When Alan reached the wall, Cavenaugh lifted him up to his dog. Alan scrambled over the lip and grabbed Blacky as the dog licked his face. "Blacky!" he said again and then started crying harder than before.

Roger looked at Alan and the dog, and then to the others. He stood for a moment, rain drenched, his hair matted to his head. He tapped the end of his paddle against the wood of the raft and then looked back at Blacky and Alan. In silence he shook his head and then said softly, "I don't think I understand this."

Cavenaugh looked out through the rain toward the center of the quarry.

Junior and Phillip ran back from the edge of the quarry. When they stopped by the rain-shined coupe, Junior said, "That was one dumb, fucking dog."

"That is one *dead* fucking dog," Phillip corrected without emotion.

"I thought we'd see some blood or guts or something floating away. Maybe we didn't because it was so dark and everything. We must have driven him to the bottom of the quarry."

"Happy trails to you, little dog."

They climbed into the car. Phillip shook a cigarette from the pack on his dashboard and stuck it in the side of his mouth. Next he produced a stick match and flicked the end with his thumbnail. The match erupted in sulfurous flame and Phillip lit his cigarette. He did not offer one to Junior who sat and watched.

"You're one poor shit, Junior." As Phillip spoke the cigarette wobbled in his mouth. He took a deep drag and examined the remaining cigarettes in the pack. "You're one poor shit, but you're the best shit I know." He offered the pack to Junior.

They sat silently, filling the car with curling clouds of smoke.

As an afterthought, Phillip depressed the clutch and reached for the ignition key.

"Switches on," he mumbled.

"Clear in the front" was the reply.

"Fire in the hole."

"Contact."

The big engine turned over as if the battery were nearly dead. Twice it dragged through and then it caught and coughed briefly. To anyone who did not understand high compression, advanced timing and racing cams, it sounded like a limping tugboat or a clown car at the circus.

It then there was a miraculous recovery. As if clearing its throat, the engine expectorated and then roared. Phillip revved it twice and each time there was a snapping, growling, instant response. The needle on the tachometer on the dash flicked to the side and the coupe twisted with the torque.

WWUUUUPPP —— AHHHH

WWUUUUPPP —— AHHHH

Phillip crossed himself and chanted, alluding to the dangers of exploding racing clutches, "Thank you, Jesus, guardian of rip-ass engines and protector of scatter-shields. Save these legs from instant destruction."

Junior looked to the roof of the car. "And, baby Jesus, save these balls from disintegrating pressure plates." He cupped his groin as he spoke. "All the little girls thank you, baby Jesus, for I will bring them happiness. And if you have the time, baby Jesus, please make their tits bigger."

"Amen."

"Amen."

The engine settled into a loping, irregular idle, the tachometer needle bouncing around 2500, and Phillip listened carefully to every sound the engine made.

"We're making popcorn, fans."

He dragged the chrome shifter into first, depressed the gas pedal, and feathered the clutch. The wheels spun for a second on the wet granite and the car lurched forward to the edge of the quarry.

Regardless of the money he worked for and then poured into his car — the racing accessories, bloated competition tires, and custom paint — regardless of the weeks Phillip spent rebuilding the engine, and the endless time he wasted smearing on the haze of wax and then wiping it off of the midnight metallic blue finish, in spite of it all, he invariably rammed his car closer to the edge of the quarry than anyone else would timidly creep in theirs — closer than those who followed the guidance of someone outside of the car, closer even than those who crept ahead a quarter inch at a time.

Phillip's car would lunge forward and at the last millisecond he would lock the brakes, his car at the rim, the front tires finally depressed by the lip of the granite wall, the shining chrome bumper brushing the air of the quarry. And when he had too much to drink he was worse. He would race the Ford from halfway down the road, slide around the last corner, the tires spinning and throwing loose stones everywhere, and then leap across the flat granite plain surrounding the quarry, the engine roaring full bore. At the same instant everyone watching had cardiac seizure, the sparkling blue blur would slam to a stop as if against an invisible wall, all momentum shed, all movement arrested, the car hanging its nose above the distant quarry water.

Phillip often bragged that he could do it with his eyes closed.

He probably could. He was a madman, protected by saints.

So far.

They sat for a moment, the shining coupe bunched at the edge as if preparing to fly. Phillip switched off the engine and it seized when he turned the key. The header pipes ticked as they cooled.

They sat and looked across the quarry, the lightning dancing in the sky around them, the thunder rattling the door panels, the rain sluicing across the louvered hood.

"Oh my, do you see what I see?" Phillip had spotted Will's rusted sedan parked at the other side of the quarry, beyond the second derrick. He waited until his partner saw what he was referring to and then asked, "You know what this means, Junior?"

Junior studied the car with steamed windows, recognizing it as the 'Duchamp kid's'. He stared through the rain a while longer, imagining who else might be in the car and then answered simply, "Potato patrol."

Phillip left the car and went around to the trunk. He opened it and routed through the loose beer bottles and crumpled blankets until he reached a mesh bag of potatoes. He took one from the bag and tossed it to Junior. "Maine's finest, my son. Treat it with care; some poor bastard in Aroostook County worked his ass off to bring you this beauty."

Junior followed Phillip. They walked along the perimeter of the quarry, careful as they moved through the warm rain and the dark night, passing around the long derrick boom. They were close to Will's sedan. They crouched and sneaked behind it, smiling to each other when they realized the motor was not running. They leaned against the back bumper and listened briefly to the tinny wails from the radio and the occasional laugh. Phillip turned to Junior and whispered, "Stuff it, father — bless this car on a rainy night."

Junior took the spud and twisted it into the exhaust pipe, the rusty lip cutting into the potato as he pushed it firmly into place.

Phillip reached to Junior's soaked shirt and pulled him away, singing softly, "One potato, two potato. . . ."

They ran back to their car and drove it around to the other side of the quarry, leaving the headlights switched off. Phillip turned on the lights as they came up behind Will's car, coasting past it and then pulling in and parking twenty feet farther down.

The lights flashed through Will's car and Louise squinted toward them. "Another dirty little car on our dirty little road."

Freddy wiped the steamed window with his hand and peered through the darkness at the now-parked car. "It's anything but a dirty little car, that's Phillip Henshaw, party king and hero to the weaker sex. No doubt, Junior-No-Mind is with him."

Louise rolled down her window and looked. "I think he's cool, I don't know why you guys don't like him."

Beth leaned over Freddy and looked, too. She could hear the radio of the other car.

Louise was fascinated by Phillip's car. "Why don't you get a different car, Will? Yours is the pits. Aren't you embarrassed?"

Will didn't answer.

He turned off the radio and reached for the ignition key. "It's getting late," he said, trying to sound as if he had been preparing to leave, anyway. He pumped the gas and tried to start his car. The engine turned over but wouldn't fire. He tried it several times and then pounded the steering wheel. "Great!"

Beth looked at Freddy.

Louise sighed in disgust. "This is too much, Will." She rolled her eyes.

They saw the interior light come on in Phillip's car and then they heard the doors slam. Two figures advanced behind a bobbing flashlight.

Phillip walked up to Louise's open window and leaned in. He shined his flashlight at her, running it along her upper body and then he swung the beam to the back to Beth and Freddy. He studied Beth for a moment in the probing light.

"Are you folks having a problem?" He continued to look at Beth.

Both Freddy and Beth were uncomfortable with his attention and the light.

Louise spoke, "Yes, Phillip, we're having a problem. Can you start this junker?"

Will ignored their conversation and tried to start the engine again. Nothing happened.

"I'll take a look under the hood for you." Phillip was halfway around the front before Will gave up and sank back in his seat.

"Junior! Come around here and give me a hand."

Junior appeared at the side of the car and walked up to Phillip who was now bent beneath the raised hood.

"Try it now."

Will sighed and tried the ignition. Again, the engine slowly ground until there was no power left in the battery. Phillip closed the hood and he and Junior walked over to Will's door. Will rolled down his window.

Phillip put his hand on Will's shoulder "That mill's in terrible shape, don't you ever clean it?"

"Clean an engine?" Will was at a loss.

"This is a tough one, Will. I think your plugs are opening too soon. You're lucky the whole thing didn't blow sky-high. Just happened in Bangor last month — killed a mother and her baby. You were lucky." Phillip shook his head and then continued, "Look, I don't have the tools to really help you tonight, but I'll come out the first thing tomorrow morning and tow this jalopy into the shop. I'm sorry I can't help you now."

Will wanted to say, "I'll bet," but he felt too vulnerable and too stupid — he hadn't even realized spark plugs did anything but spark.

Louise turned back to Beth. "I don't believe this. *Now,* how do we get home?"

The flashlight was shining on Beth again. "I'll give you a guys a ride. My wheels never stop rollin'."

They all knew he was talking to her.

"Forget it, we'll find a way home." Freddy was now angry.

"How is that, Freddy?" Phillip pointed his flashlight in the boy's eyes and then across the quarry. The beam didn't travel ten feet through the suddenly increased rain. "Going to use The Doll Man's phone? Or do you want to stay there with him tonight? I bet he has a spare dolly for you."

No one spoke as they thought of how they could get home.

Louise opened her door and got out, heading for the other car. "You all can argue the rest of the night. I'm going home with Phillip."

Phillip looked across the car roof and called to her, "You and Will and Junior ride in the back."

Louise stopped dead in the center of a puddle. She twisted around so that she faced Phillip. "That is where I intended to sit, Phillip Henshaw." She stomped through the rain to Phillip's car and then threw the door open, thrust the seat forward, and climbed over it into the back.

"Lock the doors, you guys." Will pushed Phillip aside with his door and walked to the other car. He got in back with Louise. She moved far away from him and looked straight ahead. "Keep your cooties to yourself."

Junior waited. As Freddy and Beth got out Phillip shined the flashlight in Freddy's eyes again. Are you riding shotgun with Beth and me, or do you want to sit in the back with Louise?

Freddy glared back. He took Beth's arm and led her to the coupe. Phillip saw what was happening and ran ahead of them. By the time Freddy and Beth caught up, he had opened the door. "Ladies", he said and swept his arm, offering the seat.

Freddy made the beginnings of a move to get into the car first but he stopped and guided Beth past Phillip. He then climbed in and slammed the door behind him. Phillip walked behind the car, passing Junior. As he went by him he winked and whispered, "You be good back there, Junior. No fair throwing Will out. Yet."

Beth and Freddy leaned forward as Junior climbed in behind them.

"Thanks for leaving the door open for me, *Freddy*." He mocked the boy's name.

"My pleasure, *Junior*."

Everyone was soaked. Phillip started his car and then looked at Beth. He stared at her for a moment and then said to the others, "Who gets dropped off first?"

There was silence.

He engaged reverse and backed around. He turned on his radio and by the time they pulled onto Old Quarry Road, he was singing, pounding out the beat on his steering wheel. The car fishtailed as he accelerated down the muddy road and away from the quarry.

Will looked back at his car and tried to remember if Louise had rolled up her window.

Phillip leaned forward as he drove. He reached under his seat, asking as he did, "Anybody want a brewski?"

Beth felt Freddy crush her hand while Phillip gently moved his leg against hers.

"Great night for ducks," Phillip added as handed a brown bottle of beer back to Junior and then lit a cigarette. He ran his hand through his hair.

Louise glared straight ahead. Her hair was a wreck and her shoulders and back were drenched. She felt Junior and Will at her sides. *If either one of these cretins touches me,* she thought, *I'll kill 'em.* Hollywood seemed very far away.

The boys tied the raft to a scrubby tree and then Kurtz and Roger ran down the back road to the old forge. Alan walked slowly, carrying Blacky, and he seemed lost until Cavenaugh put his arm around his shoulder and accompanied him.

Kurtz pushed the door aside and stomped his feet as he went across to the mound of their packs and sleeping bags. He pulled a candy bar from his pack and tore off the wrapper. When Cavenaugh came in he went straight to the iron furnace and started throwing pieces of kindling into it. "Let's get this thing going, I'm drenched."

Roger and Kurtz helped, but Alan sat on the bundle of his sleeping bag, holding Blacky and drying him off with a green flannel shirt. He rubbed his hand over the dog's head and back. There didn't even seem to be a lump or a bruise. Alan cupped the dog's muzzle. "I wish you could talk, Blacky." Blacky yawned and thumped his tail on the wooden floor.

Once the fire was popping and roaring, throwing orange light around the room, Cavenaugh and the others retrieved dry shirts from their army packs. They tossed their wet shirts onto the edge of an upended table near the fire and then pulled off their jeans and added them on the pile. Cavenaugh draped his dry shirt over one shoulder and walked around straightening up the room, kicking broken bottles into corners and throwing loose pieces of wood and broken chairs into a pile by the fire. He was lean and he worked out some, and he felt pretty good about his body. He seemed totally unconcerned that he was wearing only his underwear.

Kurtz and Roger buttoned their shirts while they stood in front of the fire.

With the fire driving the dampness outdoors, the smells of old wood and metal tools and oil permeated the room. Kurtz tore a calendar from the wall and tossed it into the furnace. Mosquitos came in through the broken windows and hovered around the boys. Alan dragged his sleeping bag across the dirt and broken glass and mouse droppings and placed it to the side of the fire. He sat down again and called Blacky. The dog clicked over to him and lay down at his side. Alan continued drying Blacky.

The other boys unrolled their sleeping bags and dragged them close to the fire. Kurtz fished a soda from his pack and then pulled a metal chair up to the furnace. He sat down and examined the top of the bottle. "Did any of you wonder-boys bring a church key?"

Cavenaugh stood at the open door and looked toward the quarry. He ran his hand absently along the door sill after Kurtz spoke. "Bring it here, Kurtz, I'll get it." He took the proffered bottle and caught the edge of the top on a nail. He jerked downward and the top flew off and rattled across the floor. Kurtz accepted the bottle, scooped up the bottle cap and went back to his chair. "Lotta-cola hits the spot," he sang, "in your stomach it will rot. Looks like water, tastes like wine...."

Roger joined him and they finished, "Oh my god, it's turpentine!"

Kurtz took a swallow and then spit a thin stream through his teeth. It hit the side of the stove and ran down the side. "Hot fire, me hearties," he pirated to the others.

Roger, now lying on his sleeping bag, his face to the fire, watched the liquid on the side of the stove. "Smooth move, Kurtz, and a great show. Why don't you wait 'til it gets hot next time? It would be a little more impressive."

Kurtz flipped Roger the finger and propped his feet onto the side of the stove.

Up until that point everyone was avoiding talking about Blacky.

Finally Kurtz turned to Alan and the dog. "Blacky, you must have a hard head."

Blacky lifted his eyes and wagged his tail. He then turned to Alan and licked the boy's face.

Cavenaugh walked across the room to the steaming pile of jeans and shirts. He spread them out in the little space that was available. "Let's put a rope up and dry these. Do you have some, Roger?"

"I am not only thrifty, clean, brave, and reverent, I am also prepared." He rolled to the side and pulled a length of rope from his pack.

"Got any girl scouts in there, Roger?" Kurtz asked.

Roger looked back into his pack. "How about a Brownie, Kurtz? Just your speed."

Cavenaugh tied the line diagonally across the room and over his head. "We've got to talk about what happened out there, you guys."

"Hard-headed Blacky," Kurtz said, anxious to avoid serious conversation about something which scared him.

Cavenaugh ignored the younger boy. He finished hanging the dripping clothes and then put on his dry shirt. He found a broken wooden chair in a corner and brought it to the fire. One of the front legs was shattered halfway down. Cavenaugh carefully sat on the chair and then leaned back, lifting the good front leg from the floor. He put his shoes against the rim of the stove. "I know what I saw. And I think I know what you guys *didn't* see," he indicated Kurtz and Roger.

"*Didn't see?*" protested Roger, *"Didn't see?* I saw Blacky get smashed by a hunk of granite going a thousand miles an hour. I saw that dog," he pointed to Blacky, "get clobbered by about a ton of stone. What did I miss, Cavenaugh? We were all in the same peanut gallery, you know." Roger was irritated because he wanted to be thought of as knowing everything.

"Yeh, the old black fur ball caught a rock as big as a car and then did a backstroke back to shore. What's so odd about that? Did he swim in circles and make pretty patterns or something when we weren't looking?" Kurtz asked. He spit on the side of the stove and this time it sizzled and danced.

"Better," observed Roger.

Cavenaugh sat in silence.

Alan looked up at them. He stroked Blacky's head. "He didn't get hit, you guys — the rock never touched him."

"Oh, bull-fucking-shit, Alan. That rock hit right where Blacky was. You had your hand over his head. I saw it. Look at your hand." Kurtz reached to Alan's hand.

It had stopped pulsing but it still stung.

Cavenaugh stared into the fire. "That's right, Kurtz — the rock hit where Blacky was. But he was dragged under. Something pulled him underwater and maybe out of the way before that rock hit the water."

"No way, Cavenaugh. You're dreaming.' Kurtz was not as certain as before.

Roger turned to Alan.

They looked at each other and then to Cavenaugh. "He's right," Alan said quietly, "something got Blacky. But Blacky got away."

They were all quiet. The rain rattled the metal roof and dripped into the corners of the room. The fire drew the air from around them and a mosquito landed on Kurtz's arm. He watched it test his skin with its proboscis.

"Weird," he said finally. "Very weird. Maybe it was The Doll Man."

Ezechial ran the dirty rag over the hump of one of the cylinders of the steam compressor. He had climbed onto the side and was attempting to keep his balance with his bad hand. The storm crashed and banged outside, but he seemed oblivious. Blue light flashed through the cracks in the boards over the one window, and occasionally the dangling electric light bulbs dimmed, but Ezechial did not look up. He carefully polished the top of the cylinder and then stepped down. He used a rag-covered finger to lightly trace the line of the faded red pinstriping around the flywheel, dusting the old paint with the slightest pressure. At last he patted the huge spoked wheel, put the rag on an oil-soaked table and turned and went to the stairs. He pulled the string for the lights and the room went dark behind him. The old man felt his way up the stairs, hobbling and limping as he did, steadying himself with a hand against the uneven stone wall as he climbed.

At the top of the stairs he pushed the door open into the darkness of his room and entered. He stopped after closing the door, and carefully unbuttoned his shirt. He twisted around several times before he was able to pull his first arm free. He took off his shirt, swept the wall with his hand until he found the peg, and then hung his shirt on it. He loosened his pants and stepped out of them, reaching them with difficulty and then hanging them over his shirt. It was dark in the room and the wooden shutters were closed, but he could hear the rain on the window.

Ezechial walked unclothed across his room, sliding his hand along the foot of his bed as he passed it. He reached the alcove and dropped into the moldy chair by the window. After he was settled he stretched awkwardly and pulled the shutters in and open. The rain on the glass blurred the dark outline of the quarry and the two derricks. Ezechial leaned forward, at last sliding the window open and feeling the warm mist as it blew in. *It is a little storm,* he thought, *a baby storm.*

He had known worse.

The old man put his hand on the shelf beside the window and found an object wrapped in cloth. He brought it to him, slowly unfolding the covering as he cradled the doll in his lap. Ezechial threaded his fingers through the doll's hair and looked out the window. He heard a car start and then he saw a shadow drive around the road to the other side of the quarry. Ezechial sat in the darkness, watching. Another car tried to start but it could not. Later, he saw a tiny light and again heard the car trying to start.

When the first car finally drove off, Ezechial followed the paths of the red tail lights until they disappeared.

He stared at the abandoned car the rest of the night, wondering if there were any little girls in it and fighting the need to go and look.

He knew there was a fire at the old forge; he could smell it, but the car held his attention.

When his room began to lighten with the morning he saw that the sky had cleared. Ezechial closed the shutters and walked with the doll to his soiled bed. He placed it on the faded ticking and curled around it and slept.

The four boys lay in sleeping bags spread in a semi-circle around the iron furnace, each hoping they could fall asleep before the fire went out.

Roger ripped the candy bar wrapper, broke off an even square of chocolate and said, "I'm not putting even one finger in that water until we figure out what happened." He spoke quietly, at a loss because he did not understand.

Kurtz spoke softly also, nearly whispering, "I think I'll do my swimming at home. In my bathtub. With the light on." He was very serious until he added, "With Betty Wall."

The others chuckled.

"Yeh, she could pull me under." Kurtz had a dreamy sound to his voice.

Cavenaugh countered quietly, "Well, we know what she'd never find to pull you down with, Kurtz."

It was not funny because they knew that he was trying to cover his concern. It was strained.

Blacky lay facing the fire, his legs stretched in front of him, his head between his legs and his jowls splayed on the wooden floor. The flames played in his dark eyes and cast little shadows from the bits of dirt and mouse droppings on the floor.

Alan put his hand on Blacky's head. "Good-night you guys."

One by one they answered,

"Yeh."

"Yeh."

"G'night."

Three boys envied Kurtz when they heard his tenor snore.

Alan was the last to fall asleep. The morning birds were calling before his hand slid from Blacky's neck.

Phillip pulled up in front of the house. Will did not move, he just stared at the back of Phillip's head.

"You live here?" Phillip asked.

"Yes, I live here. You know I do," Will said.

"See ya. I'll call tomorrow about your car or you can stop by the garage."

Will got out without saying anything to Louise. He was about to speak to her before he shut the door, when Phillip spun the tires and the car shot forward, the door slamming with the surge. "Goodnight, Louise," he mumbled as he walked to the back door of his house. The garage doors were swung open and awaiting the car that had failed him. "I hope you had a nice evening."

Freddy knew he was next. And he could not bear the embarrassment of being deposited at his front step. "Let me out here," he said as they passed through town.

Phillip locked the brakes and slid sideways on the wet pavement. The car behind them honked and swung by. Freddy got out in front of the theater. He met Beth's eyes as he stepped away from the car and she raised her hand and waved, but he only shrugged his shoulders and turned away.

They were not fifty feet down the street before Louise said, "I'll take that beer, now." She drank the beer she was handed, tilting the bottle and not lowering it until the last foamy swallow was gone. She looked at the empty bottle and asked, "Do you always drive around with just one beer?"

Beth turned around. "Louise!"

Phillip handed her another beer. Louise spilled some on the front of her dress, drank half and then looked at the others and smiled.

Junior laughed as he took the beer handed back to him.

Beth turned to the window, lost for a moment as they turned onto a road that led out of town.

"I'm sorry, Beth, I can take you home if you want. It's just that it's still early." Phillip poured it on thick. "I don't expect you to drink or anything."

By now Louise had finished her second beer. Beth heard her drop the bottle to the floor. Phillip handed back two more beers and then tossed a church key over his shoulder. "Fight for it."

There were about fifteen beers under the front seat. Phillip downshifted and slid around a corner, and as he did his liquid cargo rolled and clanked beneath him and Beth. One bottle tumbled out at her feet. She did not see it, but she felt the bottle, cold against the thin sock at her ankle.

Beth trapped the bottle with the toe of her saddle shoe, then she slid her shoe forward so that it rested on the long neck.

The rain had let up considerably.

Beth sat without speaking as they drove past the town limits, the tires singing through the wet streets. Finally she turned and studied Phillip in the reflected headlights of the passing cars.

He was leaning forward, caressing the steering wheel, enjoying his car and thinking of the money he would make for pulling a potato from Will What's-His-Name's exhaust pipe. At last he sat back and looked over at Beth. She was still watching him. He smiled and she asked, "Do you have another opener?"

When he dropped her off there was no more beer under the seat. They had driven out to the lake and she and Phillip had talked quietly while Junior and Louise giggled and wrestled in the back seat.

Louise had staggered to her front door.

Phillip pulled up at Beth's house and then jumped out and opened her door. He walked beside her to the porch, keeping his hands in his pockets as he walked. He looked down at the ground and said, "I'm really sorry your evening didn't turn out so hot."

He walked back to the car before she could answer. She saw Junior crawl over the seat into the front and she watched as Phillip got into the car and drove away.

He drove slowly until they were out of sight and then he downshifted and he and Junior roared off.

"We're dangerous, Junior. We are fucking dangerous." Phillip pulled out a cigarette and stuck it in the side of his mouth. "Potato their cars and steal their broads. Hot shit." He beat on the steering wheel as he laughed and slammed his car through the gears.

"You know, Junior, we owe a lot to our parents. If they hadn't given us such a rotten childhood, we wouldn't have such a great line of shit to feed the virgins."

Junior laughed even though he didn't understand. He was wondering if Louise had fastened her bra strap before she went into the house.

Beth entered the quiet house and climbed the stairs to her room. She showered and combed out her hair and then sat on her bed and looked out her window. She wore the long flannel pajamas she hated. Every other girl in the world wore baby dolls, but her parents said they invited trouble and no daughter of theirs would wear them. If she wanted to wear them when she moved out, well, that was her business. But she would live in a Christian home as a child.

There was a street light in front of their home that she had grown up watching. It was her star and her moon but her father had complained to the town that it was too bright and that it shined into every window of their home and kept them awake until past when even the sinners went to bed. The town sent out a man with a ladder and a pail of paint and he blacked out the side of the bulb which faced their house.

Later, Beth's father wondered if the darkness didn't encourage Peeping Toms. "I have half a notion to ask them to put in an unpainted bulb," he said one morning over breakfast, "they should have known better. They should have told me about the darkness. It's not safe anymore. This town isn't ours. I saw a colored man working up at Hoprich's Garage. There's no need for that. There are plenty of boys in this town who can do that work. Let the colored stay in Portland or better yet, Boston."

Alan usually avoided all conversation with his father, but he could not resist. "We learned in school that almost all of the stone walls in this area were built by colored people. There was a whole town up north and they traveled around and cleared fields and stacked the stones so they didn't fall over. Our teacher said that if you see a neat wall it is probably one of theirs." Alan saw his mother's discomfort and the anger in his father's neck as he continued. "A messy wall is a white man's wall." He said it with finality and then waited for the tornado to whirl across the breakfast table.

"It's rubbish! We should have sent them to a Christian school, Ruth." Alan's father threw his napkin onto the table, nearly upsetting his coffee, then slammed his chair back and left the room.

The three finished breakfast in silence. As the children were leaving, their mother added, "Be careful what walls you bring to our breakfast table, Alan Wasterling. Your father means well but he is often misguided. Don't torment him. That isn't like you."

Beth listened through the screened window to the big trucks on the highway. And then she thought of Freddy and Phillip. *Why is it,* she wondered, *that I think of Phillip as younger than Freddy, and yet when I think of Freddy, he's just a child?*

She reviewed her evening, remembering Freddy's hand on her breast and his attempt to kiss her, and questioned what she would have done if it had been Phillip. It would have been different. It would have been very different. She thought of Freddy's hand as a glove and could not imagine it any other way. *If it had been his bare hand on my body,* she thought, *it still would have seemed like a glove.*

She thought of Phillip and she let him undress her. She let him slowly take off all of her clothing, but she would not let him touch her. He unbuttoned her blouse and he talked to her, and he reached behind and gently unfastened her bra, and still he talked. He told her of his parents and when he was young and how much he hated them and by the time he had finished telling her these things, she was naked and then he told her about what he thought of the world and life and the stars and she was in front of him without her clothes and he just looked at her body as he spoke.

Beth unbuttoned her pajamas and lay back on her bed and listened to the crickets and the summer night and let Phillip caress her body with his words.

Phillip dropped Junior off at his parents' home and then cruised through town one last time. Moths buzzed around the halos of the yellow street lights. At last he turned down Brookside and pulled into the lot in front of the Best-Yet Auto Repair. He stared at the tachometer needle as the engine idled, walked it slowly up to 4000 and then shut the engine off. He took an arm-load of beer bottles and tossed them into the gully beside the garage and then returned to the car and collected the empties from the back seat and pitched them also. There was a crumpled cigarette pack and a smashed cigarette butt on the floor.

"I'll kill him," he mumbled as he snatched the trash and pitched it too.

Phillip walked around to the side of the garage and unlocked the back door. The neon wall clock hummed. "Best-Yet Auto Repair" was written in script in the center of the clock and surrounded by a circular tube of red light. The second hand climbed to the 12, and as it passed, it fell down to the 6 where it rested for thirty seconds and then like a car on the roller coaster, was dragged back to the 12.

He watched the climb and descent twice and then walked by the three bays and into the back room. The sweet smell of grease and oil filled the air. Phillip opened one of the battered steel lockers and retrieved a wire hanger. He placed his shirt on it, carefully fastening all of the buttons before he hung it on a metal hook. He then pulled his belt from his pants and hung it on another hook. In the corner was a grey folding chair which he sat on as he removed his shoes and then his white socks. The shoes he buffed with the lower half of his socks and then set side by side beneath the chair. The socks he threw into a cardboard box in another corner. He took off his black slacks — they were so tightly fitted to his calves that he could not have removed them before he took off his socks.

Phillip padded across the narrow room in his bare feet. Sandwiched between his racing trophies was an alarm clock. He picked it up and cranked the winged knob on the back several times and then pulled out the alarm button and set the clock back on his dresser. The covers on the cot were pushed to the side. There was a car magazine by the pillow which he removed and tossed onto the floor.

Phillip lay with his hands behind his head and thought of Beth. Beth the kid. Beth the girl. Beth the virgin. He started to say, "Not for long," but he stopped himself. He looked back at the clock, the glowing green numbers whispering what he did not wish to know. *Three hours and Old Man Horvath is here.* "Shit."

DAY ONE, New York, New York

When he awoke and before he opened his eyes, he knew that he was trussed to a wooden chair. He was still. He absorbed his surroundings and listened. *I'm tied to a freakin' chair and my freakin' pants are gone.*

Actually they weren't gone; they had been pulled down. They were bunched at his ankles, and his feet were tied to the chair.

He opened his eyes.

"He is awake. I told you." It was the little one.

The big brother smiled to the other.

The man who was immobilized looked around. The light was dim, but he could see that he was in a brick room. Overhead, a bulb hung from a poured concrete ceiling.

"Good evening, my friend," the little brother said.

"I ain't your freakin' friend, Joe." His accent was Bronx and his attitude matched.

"Tough guy," was all the bigger brother said.

"You fucks are gonna kill me — fine — do it — get it over with. If you got the balls."

The brothers exchanged looks and smiled.

The smaller brother answered, "We aren't paid to kill you."

The man trussed to the chair spat at the one who spoke. "No fuckin' shit? Pardon me if I don' buy it."

He glared at each of the brothers.

"We're paid to be sure you don't live. That's all. We don't have to kill you."

"Oh yeh?" the tough guy answered.

He looked down at his hands. One was tied to the arm of the chair. The rope was knotted professionally and sparely. And it was tight. His other hand was midway across his chest. A yoke of rope passed over his shoulders, twisted around itself, and secured his hand from moving lower, while a rope passing from between his legs prevented him from raising it.

There was a pillow between his head and the wall.

*Well now, shit. That pillow ain't there to make me freakin' comfy. This is it.*

The brothers stood side by side and looked at him. They didn't speak, they just observed him.

*Creepy bastards.*

"Let's go," the taller brother said.

The other one nodded and advanced to the man who was tied. As he stepped forward he pulled a nickel-plated 38-Special from one of the oversized pockets in his pants.

*Here we go,* the man tied to the chair thought and began to sweat.

He flexed his anus.

*I may die, but these light-weights ain't gonna make me shit myself. No way, Jack.*

But the man with the gun took out a length of rope and methodically wrapped it several times around the handle of the revolver. He tied the rope in a double knot and let the remaining ends hang as two tails. Each was almost two feet long.

The man tied to the chair watched, fascinated.

*What the fuck?*

The brother advanced and poked the short barrel of the gun at the man's lips.

He ground his teeth against each other and held his lips tightly together. He twisted his head from side to side.

*No way, Jack.*

But the big brother came forward and gripped his head with both hands in a painful embrace and the brother with the gun reached across and pinched his nose shut.

*Oh, fuck me!*

He had to breathe, and when he gasped, he felt the cold metal forced past his teeth, nearly touching the back of his throat.

The brother smiled and quickly pulled the tails of rope back, looped them around the man's neck once and tied them tightly behind.

He swallowed, his Adam's apple scraping against the rope around his neck. He started to choke and as he did he tried to force the barrel of the gun forward with his tongue. The steel touched his uvula and he choked again.

*Oh sweet Jesus,* he thought, *these guys are freakin' nuts.*

He kept swallowing until he realized there was nothing left to swallow.

*Dry as an old maid's twat.*

Involuntarily, he attempted to swallow again. Each time his throat worked, it seemed the barrel of the gun crept deeper. The front sight dug into the roof of his mouth. He tried to push it aside with his tongue but he choked instead, tasting bile as he did. His bowels were roiling and he had to concentrate to stay puckered. He squeezed the cheeks of his ass together.

The little brother was talking. He had stepped back. The other brother was smiling — the big brother, he was smiling.

*How the fuck do I know they're brothers?* he wondered. *I've never seen these assholes.*

He tried to swallow.

The little brother reached behind himself.

*Somethin's in his waist band.*

His hand came forward wrapped around the biggest goddamn knife the man tied to the chair had ever seen. Fully an inch of the width of the blade had been lost to constant sharpening and it was *still* the biggest blade in town.

*Oh shit. Just freakin' shoot me.*

"We're not going to kill you. Like we said, we're not paid to kill you. We are paid to be certain you do not leave this room alive."

The brother looked at the man's bare crotch.

*Oh, Jesus and Mary.*

His penis retreated.

"That's right."

He began to feel the sweat running off his body. He forgot his asshole.

"What I am going to do is cut roughly," and he laughed at what he had said. He corrected himself, "No, not *roughly — exactly and smoothly —* I am going to cut one inch off of your prick. And then two inches. And then three . . . ."

He had moved toward the tied man as he spoke. His face was inches away.

"The trigger on the gun in your mouth is free."

He lifted the broad blade to beneath the man's nose, sliding it upward until it moved against the cartilage.

"Use it when you're ready."

And when the brother finished he lowered the bloody knife toward the man's groin, locking the man's eyes as he did.

He started to hyperventilate when he lost sight of the knife.

*Oh, sweet Jesus, sweet Jesus.*

But he felt no pain. And no thin, searing blade.

He forced himself to look down and he saw that the blade was under the rope holding his right hand down.

The brother turned the sharp edge outward, toward the rope, and the rope parted.

His hand was now free to reach upward.

To the gun.

To the trigger.

Foolishly, he tried to jerk his hand outward, to the brother with the knife.

The big brother smiled and so did the little brother with the knife who shook his head sadly and looked down to the chair, moving his hand with the knife deliberately as he did.

"OH JESUS, NO!!!!"

The words were not clear but the man screamed them past the gun in his mouth and choked as he did and then started to vomit, but not before he felt the knife between his legs.

The brother leaned back and reached low and forward with his knife-hand. He sliced off the first inch as easily as soft cheese. Warm blood covered his hand.

The man in the chair started to faint. He tasted his vomit and he fought it. He evacuated his bowels in a rush and before the hand could be lowered again, before the pain could impossibly increase, he reached up and grabbed at the trigger.

He missed it at first, his fumbling finger sliding in front of the guard and working against the immobile loop of steel.

And then he found it.

Before his body cooled they dragged a cloth bag forward and removed two new, butcher's saws. They took off his arms and then his legs below the knees and finally his legs at the uppermost thigh. The little brother cut off the head.

They hefted the torso into an over-sized garbage can and then stuffed the other body parts around it. As an afterthought the big brother located the penis head and flicked it in.

They pulled the heavy can toward the stairs but stopped before they were to them. The floor was clean where they stood. They removed their clothing and then took two large rags from a bucket of water and wiped themselves clean. They added the rags and their clothing to the garbage can.

As one dressed in fresh clothing the other fitted the metal lid and taped it around and around with packing tape. Then he dressed and they each took a handle and bumped the can up the stairs and loaded it into the back of the stolen van.

As the bigger brother started the vehicle, the other went back into the building. He soaked the brain-spattered pillow with gasoline, dumped the remaining fuel onto the floor and left the cool end of a burning cigarette at the terminus of a liquid trail.

He smelled his hands as he climbed through the passenger door.

"Gasoline. I've always liked that smell."

They drove through the warehouse district and merged onto the expressway.

The brother driving whistled softly, then said, "You follow me. I packed sandwiches for both of us."

Later, they pulled up behind the car. As the riding brother got out, his keys in hand, he said, "We drive North, have our 'talk', get the cash, dump the van with the body, and then three months at the cabin."

He was not being informative, he was saying 'good-bye'.

The brothers followed each other out of New York City, across the state and into Massachusetts. They stopped once for gasoline just inside of the Massachusetts border. As attendants filled both tanks, the brothers stood at the side of the van and ate their sandwiches.

"Not a bad night," the little one noted.

His brother looked around, more at the people than the night.

"No, not so bad. I've seen worse."

The little one finished his sandwich, wadded the waxed paper and tossed it at a waste barrel, missing badly.

The attendant pumping fuel into the van saw it fall to the pavement. He watched the wad roll and then stop beside the other vehicle. He kept pumping, but looked up and remarked, "Nice shot."

The little one didn't turn his attention to the waxed paper ball and he didn't look at the fellow pumping gas. But he did walk over to him. He rested against the side of the van barely inches from the gas station employee who had spoken.

"Like your job?" he asked.

There was no answer.

He lowered his voice and asked again.

"Excuse me, I asked if you like your job. . . ."

The fuel backed into the nozzle and switched it off. The attendant pulled it out of the filler, dripping gasoline onto the side of the van. He ignored it and reseated the metal nozzle into the side of the pump. Still, he would neither answer nor look at the smaller brother who had spoken to him.

"That's three dollars and fifty-five cents." He gazed at the buzzing neon light overhead. Moths circled, occasionally bumping into the bulb.

*New York plates. Smart ass. Who needs it?*

When he finally turned to the fellow who had been taunting him he was surprised to see that he was smiling.

"Three dollars and fifty-five cents — does that include the commentary and the spilled fuel on the side of my vehicle?

The attendant glanced at the side of the van.

The little guy counted out four bills and extended them in his hand.

The attendant took the money and then counted out the change, but before he could walk away, he was grabbed and pulled forward.

He felt a sharp point at his side and knew that he was close to being stabbed. "Wha-what do you want?" he stammered.

"I want you to wipe off the side of the vehicle and then I want you to hand me your driver's license."

He pulled a cloth from his back pocket and began to nervously wipe off the spilled gasoline.

"My driver's license? How come you want that?"

He was fumbling for his wallet and then rifling through it as he asked. He pulled out a soiled and wrinkled license.

The little brother took it and held it up to the light and read.

"Jeremy Toffner. 875 Waller Street."

He put the attendant's license in his trouser pocket.

"Well, Jeremy, you have missed an opportunity to make a friend. Instead, you have made an enemy. Now, I'm going to use your restroom and I'll leave your license there. But I want you to remember that I know who you are, Jeremy, and I know where you live. My suggestion to you is that you work on your manners. Do you understand me? Do I make myself clear?"

He walked off before the other could answer.

The bathroom was unlocked. The little brother dropped the license into the toilet bowl, unzipped, and then urinated on it. He rezipped his pants, washed his hands and combed his hair. He cupped the doorknob with a paper towel and opened the door. As he walked to the car behind the van he passed the attendant.

The attendant turned his head away from the smaller brother.

"Remember your manners, and by the way, I usually flush. Keep that in mind. I don't wish you to think poorly of me."

He nodded to his brother and they both got into their vehicles and drove off.

DAY TWO

---

The two brothers passed through Massachusetts and into New Hampshire. They drove along U.S. 1, saw the ocean and became embroiled in summer traffic. The highway curved inland and they stopped at a small park and bought sodas and ice cream cones.

The bigger brother stared at his companion.

"Well, Claude, one more state to go."

He pronounced his brother's name as 'cloud', which, while it wasn't how it was now spelled, was in actuality, his name — a part of his name. The brothers were Indian. The older and smaller brother answered to 'Fox', and it was assumed to be his last name or at least a nickname, but it wasn't. Their rule was that after the 'did a job' in the city, they would not use any names until they were two states and one day away. Fox marked the change when he addressed his brother.

The little one rested his hand on the barrel of a Civil War cannon. There were several pyramids of cannon balls nearby. Claude indicated one of the piles.

"Do you think they're attached, or just piled loose?"

Fox studied them for a while before he answered.

"Welded. Surely, they're welded together. Some kids would have rolled them off ages ago."

Claude nodded slowly in agreement. "I guess you're probably right. Welded."

They finished their ice creams, Claude discarding the now-leaking cone.

"I think they should serve these things in cups, but with the cone on top like a little hat. I hate it when they get soggy. But I like 'em dry. Crispy-like."

"You ever notice," Fox asked, "that you get strange for a bit after we start using names again?"

Claude grinned. "I think I'm getting used to being me again. I'm not a bad guy, you know."

Fox returned to the van. As he walked he thought of the over-sized garbage can in the back. He called over his shoulder, "You could have fooled me, Claude, but you'd never have fooled him." He indicated the back of the van. "He'll always remember you as a bad guy."

Claude laughed to himself. "Well, he swore a lot. I don't think he knew any good guys." He chuckled as he closed the door and started the engine.

They swung back onto the road, Fox leading in the van.

The roads were so full of other out-of-state cars, and the going so slow that in Rye they pulled off again at a string of roadside cabins.

Fox walked over to talk to his brother who had already figured out why they were stopping. Claude settled back in his seat and eyed his brother.

Fox wiped the sweat off of his forehead.

"Sounds like a good idea to me," the younger brother noted.

Now Fox smiled. "Okay."

They checked in at the office and rented number three.

They didn't look like typical tourists to the desk clerk-owner, but she really didn't care enough to give it another thought.

They drove around to cabin three, parked the vehicles side by side and went in. Claude collapsed on one of the hard beds and Fox stripped and went into the bathroom and started the shower.

"I wonder if he's ever been to New Hampshire before," he asked his brother as he adjusted the water.

Claude looked absently toward where the van was parked. "I hope he has — he can't see much of it now." He could hear the shower curtain squeaking across the rod followed by the random splashes as his brother entered and began to wash. "Most folks come up here for fresh air — I don't think he's getting much of that either."

Claude thought of the decomposing body and grimaced. "He cooks anymore in this heat and we might have a problem, little brother."

"Not as long as you drive the van from now on. It won't bother me at all. Anyway, it should cool off tonight when we get back on the road." He washed his hair and then added, "You could get some ice cubes and chill him down a little. I'm content to let him be."

Claude didn't answer — he was asleep.

The rising sun hit the tops of the derricks first, illuminating each spreading spider web of cables. When finally it touched the rock of the quarry and the remnants of the storm steamed into the warm morning air, there was movement in the old forge shed. One by one the boys crawled from their sleeping bags, walked gingerly across the wooden, glass strewn floor, and then stepped out into the day to relieve themselves

Cavenaugh walked around the closest corner of the shed. Alan walked halfway down the road to a large tree and Roger went to a low bush beside the building. Kurtz, the last to rise, ran his hand across his 'buzz' haircut and went to the doorway. He could hear Cavenaugh to his right, he could see Roger at the bushes to his left, and he saw a portion of Alan's back unprotected by a tree. Kurtz chuckled softly to himself and began to urinate onto the dirt in front of the doorway. As he observed the waving arc, he laughed again and then looked around to see if anyone was watching.

"You're such an asshole, Kurtz," Roger called from the bushes.

Cavenaugh turned and walked back to the door. He looked down at the dark stain at his feet and then jumped over it to the threshold. Kurtz managed to step out of the way before the older boy bulled through the doorway.

"Is this your 'mark', Kurtz? Peeing where other people have to walk? It's pretty sick, if you ask me."

"I'm glad you noticed, Cavenaugh, my man. It's my signature. A little weak on the crossing of the 't', but I only had one soda last night."

Cavenaugh tried to stop himself but he couldn't. He went back to the door. There it was in cursive, KURTZ. Not badly done, either.

Alan stood beside Cavenaugh. Roger joined the two after hopping into the doorway.

"Nice work, Kurtz," Roger said as if he were quite intently examining the signature. "But we can't leave it here."

Roger turned to Cavenaugh. "Got an eraser?" As he spoke, he grabbed Kurtz. Cavenaugh immediately understood and grabbed the struggling boy also. They lifted him out the door, each of the holders stepping to the side as they did, careful to avoid the wet area. Kurtz struggled and pedaled air, exactly the wrong thing for him to do. They lowered his windmilling feet to the dirt and before Kurtz realized what was happening he had obliterated the name on the ground.

"Oh, Jesus, you guys are disgusting. Thanks for nothing." Kurtz hopped away from the disheveled dirt jumping from foot to foot as if each were on fire. He moved toward the quarry. As he approached the water, he slowed. "Shit," he said as he remembered the events on the raft. "Double shit," he said as he tentatively lowered one foot and then the other to the quarry water. He skimmed the surface quickly with each while he kept a vigilant eye toward the water in front of him. There was a splash to the right and he jerked his foot from the water, nearly falling backward. "SHIT!!!!!"

Roger threw in another rock and called, "You move pretty fast for a little guy."

Kurtz sat down on the rock and the others came up beside him, Alan finally joining them, Blacky walking up last and standing back from the edge and whining.

Alan kneeled to his dog. "What did you see, Blacky? What's in there?"

Kurtz looked out across the still water. "Anybody for a swim?"

Roger and Cavenaugh looked at each other and then grabbed Kurtz as if they were going to throw him in. Despite the boy's earlier bravado, Kurtz was immediately in terror. "Oh, Jesus, stop you guys, please stop, don't do it!"

They released him, and all of the boys were embarrassed by Kurtz's display of fear.

"Fuck you guys, just fuck you all!" Kurtz was angry as he stomped back toward the shed. "Fuck your mothers too."

Blacky barked at the departing boy and then Cavenaugh called to him.

"Get back here, don't be such a whiner. Let's talk about this place."

Alan looked back at Kurtz. "Come on, Kurtzy."

Kurtz didn't want to leave and he didn't want to be mad. He stood for a moment with his back to the others and then slowly turned around. As he turned he smiled. "Fake out! You guys are sissies."

The boys and the dog sat silently and listened to the morning. On the high quarry wall to the right of where they sat a trickle of spring water seeped from a crack in the granite and flowed through the green mosses until it dripped from a small overhang into the quarry water. Each new generation of spreading ripples was accompanied by the 'plink' of the falling water. The semi-circles expanded in diameter and decreased in height until they smoothed mid-quarry.

To the left of the boys a ledge of stone jutted out forming a step. It ran the length of the quarry wall and was nearly twelve feet wide. It was overgrown with briars and tall grasses and beneath them the tracks of the abandoned narrow gauge railroad rusted. A third of the way down their length was the punctured and battered hulk of the engine which had once been the pride of the area. Because it had come to rest beneath an inexhaustible supply of rocks, it had suffered at the hands of several generations of vandals and curious children. The smokestack was tipped to the side and the top of the boiler was nearly crushed flat from the pounding it received. The roof of the cab was split open in two places and the remainder of it resembled a relief map of the rolling hills and hummocks near the Indian tanning grounds north of town.

Everything removable had been stripped from the engine and a few things which couldn't possibly have been blasted free were somehow pried loose. The manufacturer's disc, the gauges and doors and knobs and spigots, the levers and signs and, of course, the bell and whistle, all were missing. The handrails along the sides of the boiler were twisted around like long thin snakes in the grasp of rigor mortis and the inspection door at the front of the boiler was unbolted and swung open exposing a honeycomb of pipes and wasps' nests.

It was at the engine that Cavenaugh stared.

"Does anybody know how deep this quarry is?" he asked.

Numbers started flying as the boys guessed.

"I heard it is over two hundred," said Roger.

"Two hundred, my butt," said Kurtz. "My old man says it is nearly four hundred feet to the bottom. They followed three stacks of colored granite, side by side. One pink. One grey and one black. And a skinny red one that twisted through the others like a liquorice stick."

"I heard it doesn't have a bottom," said Alan as he tried to figure out why Cavenaugh was staring at the locomotive. "Why are you looking at the engine?"

"It's a Climax," Kurtz interrupted, inflated with his knowledge of the quarry and the train that had helped work it. "It was built for logging. That's how come it doesn't have big wheels. Just four little ones at each end. All drivers. It can go around sharp turns and stuff. My dad has the bell."

He stopped abruptly, realizing that his father had stolen the bell, but proud none the less. "It's junk — nobody wants it."

Cavenaugh ignored him. "I was just thinking. . . ." He looked out at the quarry water again. "We have to find out how deep this is."

"Why?" Roger felt left out. "Why does that matter? It's just deep enough so the bottom isn't at the top."

"That was funny. So funny I forgot to laugh," Kurtz chided.

Now Cavenaugh was irritated. "Look you guys, we need to know how deep it is. Once we know that, we figure out how to find out what's in there. Something is in there."

Roger looked at the water near his feet. "I'll tell you this, there is zero chance that you're going to find out anything about anything if it means I go down looking for it. I wouldn't look for my mother in there."

"If you had one," Kurtz added.

Roger cuffed the younger boy who had by now had self consciously moved his feet far from the water.

"If we're really going to measure it, Cavenaugh, we can use fishing line or weighted rope. The problem with fishing line is that at that depth, maybe a current or something could screw it up. Kinda suck it to the side somehow."

"Then it's rope," said Cavenaugh.

Kurtz put his hands on his hips and lowered his voice an octave. "Men, we must rid our neighborhoods of the threat of clothesline. They are dangerous. Tall kids could be strangled. Short giraffes killed."

Cavenaugh hit Kurtz on the shoulder. "Clotheslines, guys. We get 'em tonight. Who can sleep out again?"

Two boys nodded but Alan was still. "I don't think my mom wants me out tonight, guys. Really."

"You pussy, Alan. Are you sure you're not a girl?"

Kurtz's statement called attention to the fact that they were standing around in their underwear.

Roger started back to the shed. "You perverts can stay out here all morning if you want. The high school girls will be out soon to expose their gorgeous bodies and torment those of us kids. I don't think they're ready for the Fruit of the Loom Gang."

"Gee, Roger, I thought you liked fruits." Kurtz dodged the kick and ran ahead to the shed.

When the old man awoke it was past noon. The light from the shuttered window cast his room in dusty shadows and the air was old. The stone of the roof above him cracked as it expanded with the morning heat, and swallows rustled through the cupola, chattering and scratching as they flew in and out.

He carefully moved his feet from the bed and sat and regained a sense of his body and how to make it do what he wished. He rose and remembered the car from the night. He shuffled across the room to the window, but he did not open the shutters this time, it was sufficient to bring his eye to one of the slats and squint across the quarry.

The car was gone.

He thought about the car and pictured it parked at the edge of the quarry in the darkness.

*In his dream, the old man awoke in the middle of the night and went down the stairs in the skittery darkness of mice and solitude. Before he left the shed he scooped his hand into a bucket, covering his fingers with cool, soft grease. He walked carefully around the edge of the quarry and stood in the blackness of the night shadows and watched the car. It was cloaked in blue light and the windows shined darkness. He stood and watched until a little girl's face appeared at the back window and her hands pressed against the glass and her hair shone and her fingers tried to reach him. She was smiling and he went to her and both of his hands were good and he raised them to touch where she touched and then he leaned toward her face and she saw him and began to cry.*

*Then Ezechial took his greased hand and passed it against the glass by her face and she blurred but he could see she was crying harder and she was saying his name. The little girl cried and he covered the window, obscuring her with his smearing hand and then he reached down and he held himself and turned and walked back to his bedroom.*

*The little girl screamed, but he could no longer hear her. She screamed from the fall and she screamed from the cushioning bodies of her father and the horses and the crushing weight of her brother and their past.*

Ezechial went to his clothing and dressed. Downstairs, he topped off the long-necked oiler and walked around the compressor and the boiler and the hoists and pumps and ratchets and huge spools of cable, and the gears and levers. He oiled them all, working the ones he could, carefully covering the metal with the protecting oil. When he was finished he hobbled around again and pumped grease into the fittings and joints.

At last he took a long bar of steel from a bracket on the wall and went over to the outside flywheel of the compressor. The spoked wheel was taller than he and the flat of the rim — the part which would have rested on the ground if it were not on its axle — was perforated along its circumference with square holes. It was into one of these that Ezechial fitted the matching end of the steel bar. He slid the lever into the hole and when it was snug and secure — when the bar was now a part of the monstrous machine — he moved along the lever's length to the end. Ezechial leaned his body over the bar and slowly lifted his feet from the floor. The big wheel began its sluggish revolution, accompanied by clicks and taps from the contact points and then the slow, moist, sucking of the valves and finally, a chuff of compressed air blending into a wheezing rush.

The old man rode the bar until his knees touched the floor. He pulled the bar free and stood and fitted it into another hole, this one three holes above the first. Once more he applied his weight to the rod. He persisted until it was late afternoon and he could no longer control his shaking; his exhaustion from work and lack of food taxing his body's meager store.

He rested on the floor beside the machine and evened his breath while he rebuilt his strength. Outside, he could hear the children playing at the quarry.

At breakfast Freddy tried to get his father's car, suggesting that he drive him to work, but Freddy failed, suffering a lecture instead. "A man needs his automobile, Fredrick. I worked many years to be able to buy ours. I worked for it and I saved for it." (His father alternately examined the ceiling and then the boy's face when he spoke.) "Your mother and I went without many things so that one day we could. . . ."

Freddy stared patiently at the pulsing knot in his father's tie until he finished. He wished his father would take either a speed thinking or a speed talking course. It could all be communicated so much more efficiently — that's what he needed, an efficiency expert to teach his father how to speak. . . ."It is my car. You may not use it." *Simple. Done. I get the point. It is your car. It is your house. I am your son. Yes. Yes. Yes.*

Freddy rode his bicycle across town to Beth's.

A hot rod roared by and a group of boys shouted, "Rev it, Freddy!" "Wanna race?" "Burn some rubber!" and squealed around the corner.

*I'm seventeen and I'm on a bike,* he thought, imagining his bike to be half its size, with streamers and training wheels. *I'm on a stupid bike with everything but a stupid bell.*

His parents wouldn't allow him to take a summer job and neither would they loan him their car. Even his mother was no help. "Honey, you're still my baby. Enjoy your childhood. You'll have a car when it's time.'

*Enjoy my childhood?* he thought bitterly, *Yeh, I think I'll get together with my old pals, Howdy Doody, Spin and Marty, Beaver, Hopalong Cassidy, and all the rest of the gang and have just one swell time. One helluva swell time. We could play with Dale Evans. We could plank her. Cop a feel.*

Now he smiled as he pedaled and continued fondling her body. *Why sure, I could play with her cowgirl knockers. Get into her pants, even. Get a little Western nookie.*

Freddy stood up and pedaled faster, disgusted with his parents and then repulsed with what he had just done to Dale Evans. *She's a goddamned cowgirl,* he thought. *A cowlady! She's my mother's age! Next I'll go for her horse —* "*Excuse me, Roy, would you happen to have a small ladder there in those studded saddle bags? I'd like to throw the old pork to Dale's horse if you don't mind, or if you're a mite jealous, well say, pardner, your horse 'll do — just lead 'er over here — this sad buckaroo'll do the rest.*"

He passed through the shadows of the tree-lined street and swung into Beth's driveway. He knocked on the screened back door and saw as he did that she was leaning against the wall, talking on the phone. He turned and stepped from the porch and waited, trying to figure out to whom she was speaking, without appearing to be listening. He examined the hair on his arm.

"I'll call you back, he's here." She turned and smiled toward the door and then added before she hung up, "No, not *him. Freddy. Freddy's* here. See you later."

She came out and let the door slam behind her. She was summer fresh; her blouse ironed and her shorts creased. Her socks were folded down and as white as her blouse. "I like your car, Freddy," she said, looking at his bike parked against the tree.

Freddy indicated her bicycle in the garage, clean and propped on its kick-stand. "Yours is pretty sharp, too."

Beth laughed and tried to figure how she felt about Freddy. He was her friend — that was easy. He was good looking in a television-kid sort of way and he could be pretty funny, but something was missing. She saw the rolled towel in the basket of his bicycle. "The quarry?"

"Yeh, you wanna go? Pretty much everybody should be there by now."

"I'll call Louise back and see if she'll find out if Will got his car fixed yet."

Freddy looked at his bike. "Do that."

Junior rested on his haunches, beside the legs and feet protruding from beneath the car. The black electrical cord from the drop light snaked across the garage floor and under the car to Phillip. Earlier, during Phillip's morning break, he and Junior had driven out to the quarry where they removed the potato from Will's exhaust and flung it into the water.

The morning was already hot, the puddled rain evaporated, the air muggy and still.

"Follow me back and don't be a wise-ass and try to race," Phillip said as he tossed the keys underhand to Junior and then walked over to the coupe. He started it and waited until Will's low battery dragged the sedan's engine through a few times before it started in a barrage of coughs and blue smoke. Junior floored the pedal until the alternately sputtering and wailing engine sounded as if it would continue running on its own.

Phillip pulled out and watched the sedan back around and follow.

They were still on Old Quarry Road when Junior flew by in a storm of yellow dust.

"YOU ASSHOLE!" Phillip screamed as he tasted the grit in his mouth and saw the dirt settling over his car. "You mother fucking asshole!" he swore as he downshifted and went after Junior.

Junior looked in the rearview mirror and laughed. "The race is on, sports fans. Will, my friend, let's see what this jalopy of yours can do." He mashed the pedal and hunched over the steering wheel, waving one arm out the window at Phillip who was now closing the distance rapidly. Junior sawed the big steering wheel back and forth, kicking his car spastically from side to side across the dirt road. Pebbles and rocks raced in all directions from the rear wheels. There was no room for Phillip to pass.

*It seemed* there was no room for Phillip to pass.

A film of dust covered the hood of his car. Several times his front bumper nearly touched the rear of the car twisting in front of him. "I ought to ram you, you asshole."

He pounded on his steering wheel.

Phillip thought of the dirt all over his engine and wondered if the three chrome air cleaners were letting any of the flying dust through. He imagined the particles being sucked into his engine, scoring the cylinder walls, fouling the oil, turning it to liquid emery. He whited-out.

"YOU BASTARD!! he screamed so loudly that Junior should have heard it over the roar of the engines. Phillip ripped the mirror from his dashboard. He pointed his coupe toward a momentary opening and stabbed his car through it.

Junior saw what Phillip was doing and couldn't believe it. "Holy Christ!" he yelled and checked the swing of his car. As the coupe shot by him a mirror came sailing through the open window and hit the side of Junior's head. At the same instant the rear nerf bar of the coupe kissed Will's front fender.

Phillip felt the bump. He was no longer thinking. He was three car lengths in front of Junior when he locked the brakes and spun his car to the side. Before it stopped he was out of it and ready for Junior.

Junior was in shock. He stopped inches from Phillip, who had materialized with his fists at his sides, in the middle of the road. Like the settling dust Phillip was on his friend before he could protect himself. He dragged Junior from the car and beat him to the ground. He pounded the side of his face and pummeled his kidneys. When Junior curled into a screaming ball, Phillip stood over him and kicked him until he nearly lost his balance.

"YOU BASTARD! YOU BASTARD! YOU BASTARD!" he yelled, the blood vessels on the backs of his fists and along his throat and neck pumping. Phillip looked at his dust covered car and kicked the inert boy again. He then turned and pounded on the roof of Will's beat-up sedan. Finally, he screamed while he pointed, FOLLOW ME, YOU MOTHER FUCKER, AND IF YOU FUCKING COME WITHIN ONE HUNDRED YARDS OF MY MACHINE, I'LL KILL YOU." He went back to the coupe and drove off in a hail of flying dirt.

The side of Junior's lip was bleeding and his left ear throbbed. He stood up and slapped the dust from his jeans and wiped some from his t-shirt. "Nice fucking temper, *Phillip*," he said and then thought, *I'll get you someday. I'll get you when you least expect it*, and got back into the sedan and crept off behind his friend.

He kneeled beside him at the garage. They had not spoken since their confrontation on Old Quarry Road. Earlier, Junior had leaned over Will's car while Phillip removed the air cleaner and wiped down the carburetor and manifold with a gasoline-soaked rag. He cleaned the engine for about ten minutes and then replaced the air cleaner and drove the car back around to the front.

Junior left and brought back donuts and coffee. Phillip ate two donuts, smoked a cigarette and drank his coffee without saying a word.

At last Phillip spoke. "Hand me a three-eighths crescent." His hand appeared from under the car.

Junior rattled through the red drawers of the tool chest and placed the wrench in the outstretched hand.

The voice from under the vehicle continued, "I told Old Man Horvath that I fixed What's-His-Name's sedan as a personal favor during my break. If the kid comes in, head him off and tell him not to bring up price around the old man because we're working a special deal for him." Phillip's tone indicated that things between him and Junior were back to normal.

"Yeh, okay," Junior answered.

When Will called he asked for Phillip.

The beat up sedan swung into Beth's driveway. She and Freddy got into the back seat behind Will and Louise.

"He fixed it?" Beth asked as they drove off.

"He fixed *me*," Will answered. "Twenty-five bucks for new plugs and something else, and eight bucks for the tow. I don't have two nickels to rub together."

"You also don't have a car worth two nickels," Louise chided.

Will pulled to the side of the street. "Ya know, we discussed this, *Louise*. If you don't like it you can lump it. Ride with Lover-Boy Junior. He'd French kiss his grandmother, for Christ's sake."

"At least he knows how." Louise looked back at Beth and winked. "You are a child, Will, I'm not surprised when a *man* threatens you."

"A man? If he's a man, I'm a monkey."

"You said it, I didn't."

By the time they got to the quarry, Louise and Will weren't speaking.

There were six cars parked randomly, a crooked row of bikes, and a few scattered motor scooters. Will parked where he had the previous night and he and Louise got out and walked to the edge. Three boys ran past and screamed "Geronimo!" as they leaped simultaneously off the quarry wall. They waved their arms as they disappeared, their yells followed by three echoing slaps and then splashes.

There were blankets and towels spread near the lip and the radios of two of the cars, tuned to different stations, blared in opposition. The boys outnumbered the girls by at least five to one, but no one seemed to notice. There were a few swimmers clustered at the raft, hanging onto the sides and talking to two girls who sunned themselves in bathing suits with little skirts. A cacophony of shouts and jeers ricocheted off of the quarry walls. A trio of tough looking characters loitered against the base wheel of the smaller derrick, their jeans tight, the sleeves of their black t-shirts rolled up over their thin arms, and their hair a matching grease-black. Two were smoking and one was combing his hair.

Will tried to impress Louise by yelling over to them, "Kookie, Kookie, lend me your comb," but failed when one of the boys gave him the finger and the others laughed while the one fingering Will shouted, "Hey, dick-face. When I want to hear from you, I'll pull your chain."

"Yeh, sure," Will answered and wished he'd kept his mouth shut.

"You certainly have a lot of friends," Louise commented as she left Will and walked over to a group of girls.

Beth stayed in the back seat and pulled off her loose shorts. She unbuttoned her blouse, but left it on. Freddy stood beside the car and danced out of his pants, then lifted them with his foot and threw them onto the hood. He checked the drawstring on his bathing suit before walked to the edge and looked down. Will joined him.

"Does this thing keep gettin' higher or is it my imagination?" Freddy asked, sounding genuinely scared.

Will's car may have been a wreck and he may have been only a minor success with Louise, but he could dive. He ignored Freddy and dropped his trousers and took off his shirt. His bathing suit was brown plaid, his chest white, and his sun tan (his burn, really) started midway down his arms.

He turned and backed to the lip of the quarry, carefully brushing bits of rock and broken glass aside with his foot.

"It's Wild Will the Wonder Wiener," someone called from the water, respect merging into sarcasm.

Will kept inching backward until his heels were in the air. He gripped the gritty quarry stone with his toes and stretched his arms straight in front of him. More kids stopped what they were doing and watched Will. He stared straight ahead for a moment and then looked over his shoulder and down to the water, professionally judging the distance. It was roughly a thirty-five foot drop to the water. He looked at Freddy, rolled his eyes and took in as much air as his lungs would hold.

As he expanded his chest, it was Louise's turn to roll her eyes.

"Don't be so dramatic, Will." It killed her when he got all of the attention. She toyed with the idea of learning to dive.

Suddenly he dipped and sprang backwards into the rarefied air above the quarry. His dive was smooth and clean and he somehow managed to slow himself as he sailed through the air. Will rotated gracefully, his arms spread as if he were a glider, his feet together.

All of a sudden he seemed to pick up speed and race toward the water.

Will heard the air rushing by and saw the details of the opposite quarry wall. But things did not seem right. He could feel the water approaching him. It was reaching up to take him, to snatch him from the air. Will realized that he was still, suspended in the air, and it was the water which moved — it was coming to him, coming to take him. Something was very wrong. He did not wish to enter the water. He panicked. He willed himself back to the lip, back to the car, back to his home, but to no avail.

As a reflex, he swung his arms awkwardly to cover his head and brought his knees to his chest. The water hit the flats of his forearms, smacking loudly, sending spray nearly to the raft.

But Will's journey had just begun.

"What the hell was that, an inverted cannonball?" someone shouted, but Will could only hear his body racing through the water.

Will stayed tucked in a ball as he plunged downward. He was not falling through the water. His weight was not dragging him lower. He was being sucked beneath the surface. He was being pulled farther into the depths of the quarry water than he had ever gone before. Will felt that he was being taken to some place beneath the quarry waters — beyond the quarry waters. His ears began to pound.

*I'm dead*, he thought. *I'm dead and I'm going to hell.*

Will still did not slow down. He raced deeper. He would not open his eyes.

And then Will felt the water turn to gelatin and he lost momentum immediately.

*Oh God, get me out of here. Get me out of here.* It was a quiet, desperate request.

He opened his eyes and everything was black. He was disoriented.

*Think, you dummy, think. Up. Up.* Which way is up? He thrashed his arms and legs in all directions, pushing the thick fluid aside, and then something he had read in a book about submarines came into his mind. He blew out some of the precious air from his lungs and tried to see which way the bubbles rose. He could not see and in the darkness he began to give up hope, when he realized he had felt them brush past his face. He swam upward as fast as he could, the strangely viscous water slowing him, holding him. He felt as if he were clawing his way through a nightmare which had just begun. And then he came to believe something was chasing him. And he could not get away.

Will felt the water near him part as something moved by.

*Oh Jesus,* he thought and tried to get away.

He continued struggling upward. Something was moving closer. It was soft and it brushed across his back. Will flinched and swam more madly. And then it brushed again and this time it stayed with him. At first, Will froze. Whatever it was, it passed along him, keeping contact with the crawling skin of his back. It just kept passing. Then, no matter how he contorted, the pressure kept gliding across him. Finally, something rasped against his skin and the feeling was gone — except that Will could sense that whatever it was, whatever had violated his security, was now retreating to the quarry depths. He felt the water throbbing as it dove, the pulses undulating through his body.

When Will broke the surface, he screamed.

When the others pulled him to the raft he was shaking and incoherent. He would not look at anyone and he would not attempt to speak. They paddled the raft to shore and three boys walked him from the landing around and up the hill to his car. The others moved out of the way and watched, dumbfounded, as he passed. When they reached the car, Freddy came up and handed him his towel and Will crawled onto the front seat and lay shaking. Will would not look at his friend, and Freddy did not know what to say.

Some of the kids pressed against the glass and looked in at Will or craned into an open window and asked, "Are you okay?" "Can we do something?"

Eventually, Will stopped shaking and when at last he answered, "I'm okay, leave me alone," they did.

Freddy was leaning against another car, waiting, when Will sat up, started his engine, and drove off.

"I think he knocked himself a little cuckoo," someone said and laughed nervously.

Louise watched him drive away. "He was *always* a little cuckoo, if you ask me. That's one of the few things I like about him."

Junior washed Phillip's car twice and then he and Phillip drove out to the quarry. By the time they got there all of the younger kids had gone home for supper. The two had hoped there might be a few female stragglers but there weren't.

"Grab a couple beers, Junior," Phillip said and walked past the derrick to the edge.

Phillip always parked away from the others. He brought his coupe past the machinery shed and drove out to the point by the taller derrick. He didn't drive particularly fast since there was no one except Junior to see him perform, but neither did he slow down until there was no more granite to be seen in front of them. He set the brakes and they both rocked forward in an exaggerated fashion.

Junior got the beers and an opener. He checked the front tire as he left the car — it was about four inches from the edge of the lip. "Not bad for a beginner," he said and walked over to Phillip.

"I'll give you a fucking 'beginner'," Phillip answered and took out a cigarette and stuck it into the corner of his mouth.

The raft drifted idly below them and a few bottles glistened over by the landing, but the shadows had begun to fill the quarry and the water was dark and still. In the distance two doves called back and forth.

Junior took a long drink of beer. "Ya know, in all the years I've known you, I've never seen you swim here."

Phillip stared at the water below them. "You couldn't pay me enough to swim in that shit. I don't swim in nothin' I can't touch the bottom of and I especially don't swim in nothin' dark."

They were silent.

"I thought you said you reamed a colored girl in Boston, once."

Phillip blew smoke through his nose and laughed quietly. "You don't forget nothin', do you, Junior? Yeh, I had a colored girl. Boy, they know what they're doin'." He smiled to himself.

Junior watched Phillip as he continued with his story.

"They know what they're doin', but you have to be careful. Real careful. Colored people aren't built the same as us."

"What do you mean, 'you have to be careful'? You mean like 'careful you don't get slit by a razor or something?'"

Phillip laughed again. "That's the least of your worries when you throw the pork to a darkie. That is truly the least of your worries. It's the cunt lock that can get you in deep shit."

"The 'cunt lock'? What in the hell is a 'cunt lock'?" Junior was interested. Most of his knowledge of the mysteries of sex he had learned from Phillip.

Phillip settled into his tale. He told it as a story and he told it as if it had happened to him, when if fact it had not. It was a story he had heard from someone else. But so deep rooted was his prejudice and ignorance, he did believe it possible.

"I met a colored chick at a bar and she was a looker, Junior. She'd make you cry just to see her. Light skin. Thin face. Big tits. Tight ass — unusual.

"Well there was nothin' else but a couple white girls that looked like they'd been whumped for about an hour each with the ugly stick. Ugly club! They were disgraceful to the white race. The human race.

"This colored girl is sitting about three stools down and she smiles at me and I smiles back and she motions me to sit beside her, which I did. She noticed I was the best lookin' man she had ever seen and asked if I wanted to go to her place, 'cause she lived nearby and she was lonely, and bored with sittin' in a bar. I was a little scared, but she was sweet lookin' and I was kinda lonely and bored too, so we left.

"To make a long story short, I was slippin' her the ole slippery snake and she was goin' crazy — shoutin' and groanin' every second of it. She did love me. No 'wham-bam-thank-you-mam' from this guy. I took her every place she wanted to go and a few places she'd never heard of. Well, when it was over she smiles up at me and says, 'You did get yo twenty dolla's worth, white boy!'

"I coulda shit.

"So I says back, kinda jokin', 'Twenty dollars? I gave you that one for free!'

"And then it happened. Boy, don't joke with no colored girls when they ask you for money. She put her hands behind her head like she was really relaxin' and she gave me one of them big, colored girl grins and then her face kind of tightened up like she was either really thinkin' hard of somethin' or getting ready to take a big shit.

"I didn't know what was happenin' at first, and then, oh my god, Junior, I felt it begin. She clamped that pussy onto me like it was a Homing Number Ten Wood Vice. I thought I'd die. And then she started to really tighten it up! She screwed that mother tight and I couldn't move. She coulda squashed me if she wanted to.

She could have left me with nothin' but twelve inches of swingin' mashed potatoes.

"Well, I surely didn't care anymore about the twenty dollars, I just wanted to get out of there with my pecker intact.

"I told her, 'Okay, okay, you'll get your twenty dollars — I just thought we were friends', and she says, 'We's friends now, sugah, and when you put that bill in my hand, we's gonna stay friends.'

"She wouldn't let me loose' til I reached my pants and gave her the money. Honest to God, Junior, they must have muscles there bigger'n your arm."

Junior sat and thought for awhile about what Phillip had said and then added, "I once heard they have teeth."

Both boys were silent as they sat and contemplated the horrors of the world.

Ezechial attempted to take a deep breath and then rose and went to the stairs. He had been working and resting in the hazy bars of light which slipped between the cracks of the big swinging doors and the shuttered window. As he passed through them they highlighted his baggy pants, bunched at his waist by a cracked belt, and the stained brown shirt he wore. Ezechial put his good hand to his beard and idly combed it with his fingers.

Once upstairs, he kneeled by the nearly empty cardboard carton beside his bed. Most of the cans had been removed — long since emptied and pitched into the pile beside the water tower. The can he now held contained noodle soup, although Ezechial would neither look at the label nor pay attention to the taste of the food. He sat in the chair and ate, peering through the shuttered slats at the children playing around the quarry.

It was as warm as it ever got in his room upstairs — the stone building with its thick walls spent most of the summer losing the deadly chill of the previous winter.

Ezechial looked at the quarry and then something happened and he was not seeing the children of that summer day. The quarry was alive with the workers of a half century earlier. The sounds of their pounding and shouting, the milling of hundreds of men's voices — working men — strong men — harnessed men, bending to the back of the mother granite, violating her with probing hand drills, chipping and shaping her body into mammoth blocks of granite — these sounds caressed the old man and soothed him with the memories of his youth and usefulness.

There was wooden scaffolding everywhere and webs of ropes fell from the sides of the quarry walls into its depths. The walls were nearly sheer and from the machinery shed's upper room Ezechial could not see even halfway down the pit.

But the sounds rose to him and the clouds of fine dust wafted over the lip with the strange currents which dipped down to the workers and lifted the insignificant products of their toil — the powdered stone — into the air above them. The pole derricks surrounding the pit pivoted and strained as they moved the stone about. The teamsters yelled at their animals — the broad yoked oxen and the defeated horses — coercing them with the strength of a driven man's will of words.

Ezechial could sense the granite dying. He could smell its foul breath as it was torn from the earth and broken into unnatural shapes, the rising powder its parched blood. And he knew the sweat of men and the odor of the grit mixing with their sweat. He inhaled the garlic and the sharp spices of the Wops, and the sliced onions and beer and thick sandwiches of the Bohunks, and he was bathed in the sweet smells of the Frenchies. And all of the smells mixed as the workers ate and again later as they belched and bent once more to their work.

The granite was dying and the quarry was alive. The men's pride: their machine god, the shining locomotive, shunted back and forth along its narrow rails, its bell and whistle polished, the black paint shining in the sun, reflecting into the eyes of those who looked at it, blinding them momentarily with the brilliance of its deception. "*I am your future*," it said. "*I am the power you may use and I shall set you free.*" And the men could not see the lie, for it was more seductive than war, even.

The steam curled from the cylinders at its sides and bubbled and dripped and hissed from the fittings around the whistle and the pop valve. Dusted black cinders boiled rhythmically from its narrow stack and then bursts of steam shot in rushes here and there.

It backed out onto the ledge above the workers who wrestled with the ropes and chains securing the stone, and below those at the quarry top who guided the slowly rising blocks to the stone cars the engine pulled.

Different shouts came with the loading of the cars — short, guttural commands, carrying precision and danger and impatience and anger — and the men accepted their dominance because of the power of the stone.

Ezechial watched the engine drag a string of granite blocks away and he saw the foreman in a slouched hat waving to a group of men and motioning them to move to a different wall, to a different task.

Ezechial dug the bent spoon into the corners of the can and licked the remainder of the soup with his broad tongue. He watched the cars drive from the quarry one by one and the kids run a few steps with their bicycles and hop astride and ride off.

It was quiet outside and the dust from the departing vehicles hung in the air and Ezechial wondered if they had left any bits of sandwiches or cakes as they sometimes did.

When evening crawled over the day and the street lights came on and glowed, illuminating sanctuary for some, and danger to others, the boys paired off and spread out to gather rope. Yard after yard felt their denuding raids and the length of liberated clothesline increased. Roger wound around the circle of his hand and elbow the rope he and Kurtz collected, and Cavenaugh took what he and Alan 'found' and looped it cowboy-style.

Roger and Kurtz savored their cruelty as they lifted the new rope from Old Lady Brinks, untying the terminating knot and then lifting each length from the hooks screwed into the cross bar. Kurtz had climbed the pole at his end and sat with one leg wrapped around the support. He looked about briefly, savoring the eluding benefits of being taller.

It was as he lifted the eighth row that he found his hand entangled in thin string. He had not noticed it before and then he saw that it was secured to a knot in the rope he was undoing. He tugged at the string and was initially confused when he heard the clatter of empty tin cans at the old lady's back door.

Kurtz' realization of the nature of her alarm coincided with her screen door flying open and slapping against the siding of her house. Old Lady Brinks burst into the darkness of the back yard screaming, "I CAUGHT YOU NOW, YOU RAGGAMUFFINS! TORMENT AN OLD LADY, WILL YOU? I CAUGHT YOU NOW!"

"Holy shit!" Kurtz hissed to Roger and started to climb off of her laundry post, but as he did he caught a pant leg on one of the hooks, and the harder he pulled, the worse he became stuck.

Roger darted into the shadows by the bushes at the edge of her yard. "MOVE! MOVE! MOVE!" he shouted to Kurtz, careful not to use his name.

Kurtz tried to twist himself free as he watched the advancing, broom wielding, mad-woman. Already she has swinging it over her head, yelling, "CAUGHT YOU NOW! YOUR PARENTS WILL HEAR ABOUT THIS, LET ME TELL YOU!"

Kurtz knew she would never be able to tell who he was unless she stuck her face within inches of his. Unfortunately, he became so excited and so anxious to be somewhere else — anywhere else — that he pulled too hard and lost his balance and fell backward over the cross bar. Still, his pant leg was stuck and now Kurtz hung by one leg, upside down, swinging in the violent night air.

"HELP!!!!" he screamed just as Old Lady Brinks drew back and wailed him with her broom. "HELP ME!!!" he yelled again when she whacked his head and his shoulders and his pendulous body. The blows started to sting and then really hurt as he screamed for her to stop and for Roger to come to his aid.

It was the clamorous barking of the neighborhood dogs which finally shocked Roger into action. He sprinted through the darkness toward the excited old lady and her flailing broom, and as he ran he pulled his t-shirt over his head.

Old Lady Brinks did not hear him coming — did not imagine that there was anyone else around — and so when Roger ran up to her from behind and pulled his shirt down over her head and wrapped his arms around her, she was taken by surprise.

She struggled in silence for a moment, but the quiet had to end.

"RAPE!!!" she screamed at last, and then, "HELP! POLICE!!!! POLICE!!!!"

She had dropped her broom and was kicking backwards with her black, old-lady shoes into Roger's legs. He lifted her from the ground, surprised at how light she was and then as gently as he could, he lowered her to the pile of her own clothesline. He didn't tie her so much as he embroiled her writhing body in a tangle of rope and then ran over to Kurtz who now hung silently watching, his mouth open, his eyes as big as baseballs.

"My leg, it's stuck! Undo my leg! Undo my leg!" he begged, his voice low.

Roger tore Kurtz's pants from the hook and carried him off in his arms while Old Lady Brinks rolled around on the mound of clothesline, screaming, "RAPE! POLICE!! MURDER!!" The tugs and pulls of the rope as she turned made her think her assailant was still wrestling with her, probably at that moment either undoing his pants or reaching for the sharp butcher knife he had strapped to his leg.

Roger carried the rope from the other yards over one arm and both he and Kurtz ran as fast as they could after he had lowered the younger boy to the ground. The lights flashed on in the surrounding houses and the boys could see the outlines of families walking cautiously about trying to find the source of the commotion.

They sprinted halfway across town before they stopped, collapsing behind the school yard, their chests pumping, their breath coming in tormented wheezes.

"Holy shit," Kurtz finally said, "we were trapped!"

"*You* were trapped," Roger reminded him, "and if you hadn't been born so *short* you wouldn't have had to climb her laundry pole. Blame your parents; it's hereditary."

"Very funny," Kurtz answered and then said, "Do you think she's still fighting?" and both of them thought of Old Lady Brinks and began to laugh. Before they knew it they were out of control, rolling through the grass, grasping their sides, thinking of the stories the old lady would tell.

"Jesus Christ, you guys! What's going on?" It was Cavenaugh, and he and Alan were standing above the two who were laughing. "The whole town's out tonight. I've never seen anything like it. Why are you guys laughing? What's going on?"

Toward the end, Cavenaugh laughed a little also, the hilarity of Roger and Kurtz so infectious. Finally he sat down beside them and waited. "Come on you guys, one of you spill the beans."

When Roger stopped laughing and Kurtz was only chuckling occasionally, the older boy told them his version of their adventure, with Kurtz adding a few extraordinary details. All four boys laughed briefly.

They examined the rope they had and decided it was adequate. Later, they sneaked back to their homes and went to their respective bedrooms to wait out the night and wonder at and then dream of the consequences of Old Lady Brink's alarm and enforced immobility.

Freddy and Louise and Beth hooked rides back from the quarry with several kids they knew from school. Freddy asked to be dropped off at Will's and when he was, he saw the beat-up sedan parked in front of Will's house. Freddy shouted, "Will!" and then knocked on the back door. Will's mom answered and told him that Freddy was either in the back yard or the garage.

The table was an assortment of car magazines, greasy and worn, and a few torn copies of Readers' Digest. Under the pile was a phone book.

Phillip sat down and looked up her number. Balanced on an upended crankshaft beside one of the chairs was a black metal telephone which he picked up and dialed. He wasn't certain he had either read or dialed the number correctly in the gloom until he heard Beth's voice.

"Hello, Wasterly residence."

Phillip was momentarily at a loss, immediately aware of the various distances between Beth and himself.

"Hello?" she asked again.

Phillip had the phone halfway to the cradle when he changed his mind and brought it back.

"Yeh, Beth, hi. This is, uh, Phillip. Phillip Henshaw, and I, uh, was callin' to say 'hello'. Which I guess I already said. Sorta."

"Phillip — hi!" and then Beth took over, thanking him for the ride and with embarrassment thanking him for the beers, and then rolling into a conversation about what had happened at the quarry to Will.

Phillip couldn't believe it at first. He pulled the phone from his ear and stared at the voice coming from it. Beth was talking to him as if he were an old friend. He tilted his chair back against the wall and let her words absorb him, their cleanliness and innocence misplaced in the gloom of Horvath's garage.

"Yeh, well, I wouldn't go in that water, myself," he interjected. "I'm not real comfortable with swimming in something that deep and dark. I hear its over three hundred feet deep in parts." As he said 'dark', he remembered his story to Junior and smiled to himself, adding, "You just got to be careful not to get stuck," and laughed softly.

"*Stuck?* What do you mean, stuck, Phillip?"

*Shit.* He pack-pedaled fast. "Did I say 'stuck'? What I mean is, you're kinda 'stuck' if there's a problem — the water bein' so deep and all — and there's no real shallow part or nothin'. That's all I meant," he pleaded defensively.

"Mmm. Well *anyhows*, Freddy said that Will is really scared, but I agree with Freddy that he probably just flipped underwater toward the wall and scraped his back on something. He didn't take any warm-up dives and he probably just messed up."

Phillip did not want to agree with anything Freddy-the-twerp said, so it was with reluctance that he responded, "I don't know, Beth. I don't think anyone can say that nothin' lives in there. That water's deep and it's been there for almost a hundred years. Anything could grow in there in that time, plus, my old man used to tell me that it was a spooky kinda place back in the old days and that some old crazy Indian he worked with used to claim it was haunted one day and then say it was sacred-special the next."

And then a thought occurred to him. "Beth?"

"Yeh?"

"You want to drive out there tonight and look around? I mean, I don't really think we'd see anything, but you never know."

Beth was silent as she thought it over. She was uncertain whether the excitement she felt was because of the mystery of the quarry or because she was going to go out alone with Phillip — she knew she would have to sneak out to do it, and she had never done anything like it before.

"Phillip, I don't know." She hesitated, took a few breaths and then added, "It's kinda late."

He knew how to handle her.

"Okay, sure. I don't want to push you into anything, Beth," he said reassuringly and then was silent.

Neither spoke. Phillip listened to the neon tube around the clock hum. Beth looked out her window at the night.

"Pick me up at Grant and Tinker in fifteen minutes." She said it quietly and quickly, and fearing she would change her mind, she hung up.

Beth sat beside the phone and stared at it. She would not allow herself to think of the evening ahead.

Phillip took the case of beer from the trunk of the coupe and left it inside the garage door. He surprised himself when he also removed the blanket and placed it on top of the cardboard beer carton.

Beth said goodnight through her parents' bedroom door and moved quietly down the carpeted stairs. She didn't know if Alan were going to sleep out or stay at a friend's but she had no concern that he would seek her at night. It was as she slowly closed the screen door behind her and stepped onto their drive that her brother spoke.

"Where the heck are you going?"

He was sitting on the grass near the side of the house, Blacky's head resting on the boy's lap. Alan's white t-shirt glowed flourescent white.

Beth sat beside him and drew her knees to her chest.

"I'm sneaking out!" she whispered.

"The heck you are!"

It was impossible for him to think of his sister doing anything without an hour's worth of their parents' approval.

"I am, Alan. You get to roam all over the place and it's okay. Why shouldn't I?"

"Louise?" he questioned with hope.

"Never mind, Alan. What have *you* been up to?"

He forgot Beth and thought of the previous two days.

"The world has really become strange, Beth. Blacky almost died at the quarry. We were out in the raft and. . . ."

She knew he was about to take her on a twisting tale regarding his adventure and she didn't have the time.

"Alan, you'll have to tell me later. I'll come into your room when I get in. You are staying home tonight, aren't you?" She patted Blacky's head and then rose.

"See ya later," she whispered.

Alan was back at the quarry, reaching for his dog when he realized that he didn't know where his sister was going and with whom.

"Beth. . . ." he called, his voice low.

"See ya," she answered and was lost in the evening.

Alan wanted to follow his sister but he would not. It wouldn't be fair. She always left him alone and only gave him advice when he asked her for it. When they were younger they did a lot of things together but now it seemed they merely tolerated the same parents.

He went into the house, rattled dog food into Blacky's bowl and got an ice cream bar for himself out of the freezer.

The headlights of the big coupe died as it turned down Tinker and rumbled slowly toward Grant. Phillip would have killed the engine and coasted to where he could see Beth standing on the corner, but he knew that restarting the engine had the potential for awakening most of the neighborhood. He pulled up beside the girl and reached across and opened her door.

"Hop in," he said as she slid across the seat and pulled the door closed by the cloth strap.

"Hi!" she said and smiled.

Phillip engaged the clutch and they turned away from Beth's house and drove off.

They cruised out through town and turned onto Old Quarry Road before either of them spoke again. Phillip drove leaning onto his steering wheel and Beth was fiddling with the radio, seeing which stations she could get now that it was night.

Ezechial followed the chalk marks which lined the stone walls of the machine shed, marching along them until he reached the end and there adding one more mark, and with it, completing another set. He was pleased that he had, for they represented the passing of another quarter-year and with that event, Ezechial would do what he loved more than all that which was left in his world — he would spend the day preparing, and tomorrow night he would start the great engines.

While the townspeople turned in their beds, while the nocturnal animals stalked through the urban wilderness, and the big trucks raced myopically through the darkness, their tires singing a feminine song compared to the extinct bass thunder of steam locomotives, Ezechial would command the monsters of his shed.

Before he could start them, before he could awaken them, the machines would require his attention all of the next day as he drained the rust-smothering waste oil from the boiler tubes and primed the pumps and checked the settings before he could once again fill the boiler and then fire it, building its power slowly, coddling it back to life, nursing its slumbering strength into motion. He would adjust the levers and turn the great valves and then start the little fires, allowing them to grow, and then frenzy the water that finally metamorphosed into a head of steam.

Ezechial's machines would shift their masses in counter-motions, opposing forces revolving and sliding, the long connecting rods slugging back and forth, translating their iron urgency into the fluid revolutions of the huge flywheels, there storing the energy, spinning it in heavy circles, building the working forces of the compressors and pumps and cable lifts to do as Ezechial bid — to do as Ezechial could (but would not) bid — for he had no work for them now — he was as emasculated as they and as old and as useless and as trapped in the building of stone. It was really only a futile exercise, culminating when the old man eventually dowsed the fires and let the behemoths cool and finally resume their cast-iron sleep, embalmed once more in waste oil and grease.

But today that did not matter to Ezechial, for he was breathing anticipation, suckling his body with the coming sounds and smells and deep vibrations.

By the time Phillip turned off of the quarry road, a paring of distant moon balanced at the top of the taller derrick. Both derricks were outlined against the still darkening sky, and the buildings and bushes were black.

Beth caught her breath as the car lurched to a stop in what she feared to be the air above the quarry. She reached across and grabbed Phillip's arm, her fingernails digging into his skin. She could not imagine that any portion of the front tires rested on stone.

"Oh, please!" she begged and then hid in embarrassed silence when she realized they were not about to tumble into the water far below.

Phillip chuckled quietly and then switched off the engine and rested his left hand on Beth's. "We aren't going anywhere I don't want us to go, Innocent One."

He smiled at her as he spoke and Beth was reassured.

"Do you always drive like that — crazy and out of control?" she asked.

Phillip had taken out a cigarette, started to bring a match to it, and then pulled it unlighted from his mouth and flicked it out his window.

"No," he spoke quietly, as if thinking carefully of how he drove, "no," he continued, "I sometimes drive faster. And I sometimes drive crazier. But I'm always in control."

Beth waited a moment longer and then slid her hand from under his. She leaned forward and looked over the hood of his car.

"You know, Phillip, you could only do this wrong, once."

Again he chuckled and then answered, "Well, I guess you're kinda right there — I could only do it wrong once with *this* car, but you'll notice, that as crazy as I may seem, I keep my window open. I plan to be out of this rig before it hits the water."

"And what about me?"

It was an unexpected and tough question. He looked through the darkness at her and then looked at her closed window and then back at her, clean and pressed beside him. He raised his hand to his face and then rubbed his chin and cheeks as if testing a week's growth of beard.

"I guess I'd better be certain you roll your window down. I always figure Junior will get out somehow."

"Don't kid me, Phillip," she admonished, "you don't just come out here with Junior, and you and I both know that. The whole darn town knows that." She was peeved.

He had been watching the dim outline of her mouth as she spoke.

"Well, I guess I never thought about anybody else until you."

As he finished he realized the flaw in his statement and saw from Beth's look that she had also.

"It seems I had to ask you, Phillip. I guess you don't think about *me* either."

As soon as she finished speaking, Beth opened her door and stepped down to the quarry lip. She closed the door softly and walked over to the edge. She gave no indication as she did that she was angry or hurt, only that she was done speaking with Phillip in his car. He scooted across the seat after her, got out through her door, and then walked over to where she now sat, her legs over the edge. Both of them listened to the frogs croaking down by the old railroad tracks and to the crickets' high rasp all along the rim. Swallows and bats swooped overhead.

Phillip bent to the stone and picked up a handful of fine gravel.

"You ever hear bats get a toothache?' he asked and tossed the tiny stones high into the air and into the path of a bat. There were a series of little 'skrees' and the bat veered to the right and both Beth and Phillip heard bat-teeth grinding onto the insect-rocks.

"That ought to piss' em off," Phillip offered as he laughed.

Beth couldn't help laughing but then said, "That's a pretty mean trick, Phillip. Did you learn it from Junior?"

Phillip was at a loss because, in fact, *he* had taught it to *Junior*.

He didn't answer. He dropped the remainder of the stones from his hand and sat down on the ledge beside her. Had any other girl tried to put him down he would have left her sitting at the quarry wall. He wasn't certain if he were going to get even with Beth but he knew he was now involved in some type of game for which he didn't yet know the rules.

At last he said, "I guess I wanted to make you laugh," and rolled his shoulders forward.

"Well, I did laugh," she answered and then added, "but I shouldn't have. Some poor bat is probably spitting out broken teeth."

Phillip cocked his head as if he were listening for falling teeth. "Wait, I think I hear one now." He quietly flipped a rock through the darkness into the quarry. "Listen. . . ."

There was a splash in the water below and Beth laughed and Phillip felt better.

He leaned to look over into the quarry darkness. "Must have been a molar with a big filling."

Beth laughed easily. "I think that was the bat. He must have been like the jumping frog in Twain's story."

Phillip asked, "Who?" and then flushed in the darkness when he realized that he must sound ignorant to her.

"Twain — Mark Twain. You remember, you had to have read it in Mrs. Mayer's class. They bet on the jumping frogs. One got filled with lead shot."

A faint light glowed through his humiliation. "Oh yeh, yeh, the guy who wrote Huckleberry Finn, and Tom Sawyer, and a bunch of other stuff." He paused and then added, "I think I skipped too many classes."

Beth's voice came quietly from the dark, "I think you may have."

Phillip could not have been more uncomfortable were his pants on fire and his car floating through the air upside down. What had started as a seduction, to use one of the few nice terms he knew, had degenerated into a Sunday church bumble.

Neither the local police nor Mrs. Brinks were certain if she had been attacked by children or thugs, and the more she explained and embellished, the less seriously anyone else took the episode. When she finally confided that there were probably six or seven of them, and now that she thought of it, big colored men, 'darkies' she called them, the police closed their notebooks, left her living room and waited until they were in the police cruiser, driving back to the station, before they laughed.

"Well, I guess we now officially have a 'colored problem' here, Sarge," Sonny Turbetts said as he laughed and tossed his cap into the back seat.

"Keep your eyes peeled for a gang of blood-thirsty Negroes carrying a tangle of clothesline and lusting for dried up old ladies." Sergeant Wilminski chuckled and bit into a pretzel log.

"Probably goin' to strip her, tie those old wrinkled bones up, and then take her picture and use it to keep the cockroaches and rats out of the slums."

Both policemen laughed, Turbots because he thought of a sea of insects and rodents fleeing the rows of tenements, and Wilminski because he pictured Mrs. Brinks without her clothing.

Phillip sat so that the side of his leg brushed against Beth's.

"So what happened to Freddy?" he asked.

"Will," Beth corrected. "It happened to Will. He dove off of the quarry wall and something scared him so that he hit the water wrong and then he said he felt something touch him when he was underwater."

Both of them sat above the quarry and thought about the black water.

"I can't tell you I believe anything that guy says, Beth, but this place can be pretty spooky." Phillip stopped and looked around and then continued, "Ya know, it's not like the quarry itself gives me the creeps," he looked back over his shoulder toward the machinery shed. "The Doll Man, he's just some poor old fart who's barely hanging on to his last days. He couldn't hurt a flea — but the water, the water here gives me a definite case of the 'wanna-be's."

"'Wanna-be's?" Beth asked and then understood before he explained.

"Yeh, just thinkin' about that dark water makes me 'wanna be' somewheres else. I heard there's no bottom to this place, that a sort of cavern twists way below the bottom of the quarry."

Beth looked over the edge into the void. It was so dark the water could have been a thousand feet below them instead of thirty or forty. "I heard that the

Indians say this place is sacred. They have legends about it, that they once fought evil here."

Phillip moved the conversation away from Indians.

In a particularly violent fight he had heard his father accuse his mother of having some redskin blood in her, and his father, Irish and cruel, could think of nothing more demeaning. It was the reason Phillip hated his dark, straight hair.

"I wonder what's in there," he said, also looking down. "I wonder if there could be something like that slimy thing that's supposed to swim in Ireland."

"The Loch Ness monster? My brother did a report on it last year. That and the abominable snowman." Beth laughed as she said the latter, and Phillip joined her.

He looked at the outline of one of the derricks. "And this is a place where little green men from Mars come and hook up their radios!"

Beth was now looking up also. "Have you ever 'charged your batteries'?"

'Charging your batteries' was a particularly foolhardy stunt someone had dreamed up years before. A few of the high school kids claimed they had done it and all of the junior high boys wished they had the nerve to try.

Because the quarry stood on high ground and because the two steel derricks fingered the sky above the quarry, lightning often struck the towers, and when it did, it was said that anyone floating on a raft in the quarry would experience the most amazing light show known to man and that the experience would make that person invulnerable to old age or disease.

Phillip started to lie and then said, "No, I can't say that I have. I saw that tower struck one night when I was drivin' by, and I can tell you it scared the hell out of me. If I had been down there on a raft my guess is I would have either been fried or in need of a new pair of undershorts."

He laughed because he didn't tell Beth the story he often told Junior and because he felt relieved being honest with her and departing from his endless line of 'bullshit'.

"Anyway, Beth, I wouldn't recommend trying it. I think it's stupid."

Beth countered hotly, "You mean 'stupid' like driving over the edge of the quarry? 'Stupid' like risking your life and the life of anyone who's riding with you?"

Beth wondered why she was back on the attack and realized that it was because she had shown her fear and dependence so clearly when she grabbed his arm in the car.

Phillip was lost. One minute he thought he was getting somewhere with her and the next she had slammed him down on the ground and was jumping up and down on his pride. He toyed with the idea of telling Junior that he had planked her and that she gave him a blowjob that wouldn't quit. And that she was a nympho — she couldn't get enough. He thought of taking one of the nicer pairs of panties from his collection and telling Junior they were hers.

He was shocked from his revenge when she asked, "What are you thinkin' about?"

"You don't wanna know," he answered, startled.

Beth slid away from him and turned and brought her legs up from the quarry wall. She pulled her legs to her chest and leaned her arms on her knees and then rested her chin on her arms.

"Tell me, what are you thinking?" she asked again, this time more softly.

"I was thinkin' about you," he said with deceptive honesty. "I was thinkin' about kissing you, I guess," he lied.

"Then why don't you?" she whispered.

*Holy shit,* a voice screamed in his head, *where in the fuck am I, and who is this broad? What is wrong with me?*

He didn't move.

"Don't you want to? Is something wrong?"

She almost purred as she spoke and Phillip would actually have been content to just listen to her. For the next week he would hear those words, *Don't you want to?*

They held him gently and he could not remember being held gently.

*Don't you want to?*

Beth was not thinking when she spoke. The words just came out and she listened to them with Phillip. She could not believe the sensual tone she had used.

When he hesitated, when he did not reach for her, she withdrew them and stood above him. "It's really late. Please take me home."

Phillip sat and looked up at her. Now he heard "Please take me home," dancing slowly around with "Don't you want to?"

*I am one confused, mother fucker*, he thought as he got to his feet and walked behind Beth back to his car.

Alan wondered what Old Lady Brinks would say to his parents. He knew she'd blame him and Cavenaugh and Kurtz and Roger, and he wondered where Beth had gone. He had just finished speculating when he heard her on the stairs. He padded quietly to his door, opened it a crack, and waited for her. She had to pass by his room to get to hers and as she did, he hissed to her.

Beth moved as quietly as she could up the stairs. She had never sneaked anywhere in her life and she had to admit there was something delicious about the whole thing. She carried her shoes in her free hand and glided the other carefully along the banister, using it to take some of the weight from each step and to pull herself up as she stepped beyond the step that squeaked. She heard every clock in the house as they whirred and banged and announced the first hour of the new day. And then she heard Alan.

She stopped at his door and raised her shoes to her lips. "Alan, hush!"

He withdrew and left the door open as he did. Beth followed him into his room. There was a night-light in the far corner and the dial of his clock-radio glowed, giving the room a twilight look. Her brother sat on the edge of the bed, waiting in his undersized pajamas, the embarrassing spacemen with their big glass helmets easily seen.

"Well, Video Ranger, why are you up so late?" she whispered.

"Why am I up so late? I've been here in our house all night, where have you been?" He looked her over as he spoke, trying to detect a misbuttoned shirt-front or disheveled hair. That's the way it always was in the movies.

He couldn't believe his sister had actually sneaked out. Ordinarily, she wouldn't even sneak out a *library book!*

"Are you going to start wearing angel blouses and lots of eye make-up now?" he asked her , referring to the uniform of the 'loose' girls at the high school, the ones who smoked and swore and hung around with scuzzballs and hoods like Phillip and Junior.

She sat on his bed and didn't answer.

"Sorry," he mumbled. "I just can't believe you sneaked out and didn't tell Mom and Dad." He thought about what he had just said and then added, "You know what I mean. Are you changing or something?"

Beth smiled at Alan, so serious in his ridiculous pajamas. She knew he was worried about her but he hadn't asked a question yet which she felt she could answer. "Alan, somebody asked me out and I just went."

"Without telling Mom or Dad! You didn't just *went*, you *sneaked*!" Alan did not want to use the tone he had adopted. He did not mean to interrogate or to accuse Beth, but he was too confused by his anger to understand what was happening.

Beth whispered to him, "You don't always go where you say you're going — don't tell me you do. Plenty of times you say you're going to sleep out at the quarry and I hear later about you and your friends roaming around town in the middle of the night. How about when you visited Mrs. Brinks?"

She was referring to the other time — she hadn't heard about the adventure the old lady had just endured.

Alan thought about what she was saying to him. He couldn't deny that he went a lot of places his parents didn't know about, and in the middle of the night, too. "This is different though; you're a girl. Guys can do plenty of things girls can't."

"I was with a guy, does that count? We drove around."

That was not what Alan wanted to hear. Even though he had examined her clothes to see if they were recently adjusted, and in spite of the fact that he had spoken to her as if she had been with a guy, Alan was secretly hoping that she had gone to meet Louise. But by what she had just said, he knew the truth and he knew that she had been alone with a boy. A boy who drove, apparently. *Don't tell me they went to the quarry,* he thought.

The quarry at night. It was where every girl took off her blouse and where every girl eventually lost her virginity. The quarry at night was where mysterious things happened to good girls. He had once heard Junior say, "A good girl can lose her balance at the quarry in the day but she'll lose her cherry there at night."

He didn't understand the details of Junior's comment, but he got the message.

He was afraid to ask. He nearly gagged on his words.

"Where did you go?"

Beth hesitated because she knew what her brother would think. She looked down at the shoes she held and brushed some dirt off of the soles and then looked at her fingers, rubbing them together as she did.

"Will almost drowned there today. He thinks there's something in the water. Something alive."

Alan could barely believe the relief he felt. She went with Will. Now *there* was a harmless person. Will couldn't screw a cork and he'd probably get his fingers stuck in a bra strap.

"Is he okay?" he asked.

Beth had returned to the quarry and was temporarily lost by her brother's question. "I guess he's okay. I don't know."

"What do you mean you 'don't know'? I thought you said you were with him — at the quarry."

Alan was accusing again.

Beth stood up and turned toward the door. As she crossed his room she whispered over her shoulder, "I've already got two parents, Alan — a mother *and* a father — I don't need any more. Goodnight."

But before she pulled the door shut she turned again and smiled.

Phillip sat in the clock's light at the garage and chain smoked four cigarettes, lighting each with the last before it was ground out on the greasy floor.

Will struggled with his nightmares.

Beth idly touched her body as she looked beyond the folded pajamas and thought of her evening.

Ezechial removed his soiled clothing and hobbled out to the taller derrick and stood and showed his doll where the quarry train had run and where long ago the horses bolted and pulled the third derrick over the rim.

Old Lady Brinks clutched her covers and wondered who the young man was who had come with Edna Wilminski's son, the sergeant.

# DAY THREE

They drove through the early morning darkness, through the small coastal towns and along the dark stretches of deserted beach. Toward Portsmouth they turned inland again. There was no late freighter traffic and the bridge was down and passable over the Piscataqua River. The stars reflected on the van's windshield and the following automobile as they drove into Maine.

Both Fox and Claude noted their entry, Fox with the words, "Greetings my old friend," and Claude by inhaling deeply of the night air. It was the land of pine and lakes and of their ancestors. It was the land they had lost. Again they coasted through sleeping fishing villages and honky-tonk tourist traps, and as the horizon lightened they made their final turn inland, abandoning U.S. 1.

They did not go to the quarry first. It was already too light to do that had it been their intention, and neither did they proceed directly to the bank. It would not be open yet and they had preparations to make first, as they were not expected.

Always before they had dropped the body and the vehicle and then driven through the wilds of New Hampshire to the cabin. There would be food for them and within three days there would be an envelope with the money.

The money. That was the problem.

It was not enough.

True, it was what they had agreed upon, but that agreement had taken place nearly twenty years earlier, and the unsolicited increases were not enough. Not nearly enough. Now they wanted more. Much more. Besides, the first agreement had been made when the two Indians were much younger. They were two of the few who escaped the final debacle of the devil worshipers who met at the quarry.

And Phineas Lathram's influence had weakened until it no longer existed. He was their employer. That was all. His words no longer held them and his eyes were now rheumy with weakness. The two Indians detested him.

Even the quarry had lost most of it's power. It was the water — they had agreed — the water which smothered the blood-red stone and kept it cool, allowing the spirits of goodness to once more temper the dominating evil.

As planned, they drove an hour past the town, found an out-of-the-way motel, awoke the owner, and checked in.

Once again Fox showered while Claude fell asleep and, again, the younger brother slept fully dressed. They awoke at noon and Fox dressed and then he and Claude went out to the auto. The brothers now wore 'fishing clothes' — flannel shirts and heavy canvas pants, thick socks and laced boots. There were fishing rods and tackle boxes in the back seat of the auto, so they easily passed for a couple of out-of-staters on a fishing holiday. Dark fellows, to be sure — almost Indian-looking.

Half way to the car, Fox asked, "Did I dream you went out while I was asleep?"

"No, you didn't dream it. I took the van for a little drive and then I came back and showered."

Fox had no suspicions regarding his brother. If he felt he should 'take the van out for a little drive' and then come back and shower, that was fine. He knew he would learn why, when it was time for him to know.

"Oh."

They backtracked to town, stopping along the way at a birch-log restaurant where they ate a full breakfast and drank several mugs of coffee. By the time they reached the town and pulled in a block down from the bank, it was nearly two o'clock. The day was hot and even as far inland as they were, the roads were choked with tourists. The town itself was actually a little less congested; it seemed the vacationers headed inland were interested in lakes and woods, not the insignificant centers of commerce.

The bank was one of the few brick buildings on the main street, the others being the theater and the Pythian Block. The three story bank stood shoulder to shoulder beside a clapboard five-and-dime and a clothing store with aqua porcelain panels masking the first floor in an attempt to look 'big city'.

Fox followed his brother into the bank and as they entered, Claude brought a small package out of his pants pocket. Fox was surprised, but only for a moment. It probably had something to do with why he had taken the van earlier.

Claude walked over to the oldest teller, assuming she was the one in charge. He smiled and asked, "Could you please tell Phineas that some old friends have stopped by to see him — (he spoke as if what he was about to say had just occurred to him) and would you give this to him first?"

The old lady took the newspaper-wrapped package and went around the side and into an office door, attempting as she did to figure out what was in the package and nursing her irritation with their using Mr. Lathram's first name.

The package was very light.

She returned, closing the door as she passed out of the office, and said to Claude, ignoring Fox as she did, "*Mr. Lathram* is very busy this morning, but he asked me to have you take a seat, he'll be out as soon as he can."

There were no chairs to be seen.

She had barely finished speaking when the office door opened, and an ashen Phineas Lathram stood in its threshold, searching the bank for the ones who had sent the package. His eyes paused for a moment on the bank guard, One-eyed Ernest Lawler, and then discarded him with a glance.

Claude walked along the front side of the teller bar and waited to be invited into the office. Color had begun to return to Mr. Lathram's face and it was pumped by obvious anger. He motioned Fox and Claude with his head and disappeared back into his office.

The elderly teller watched and then she too looked over at One-eye. He was dozing on his feet as he usually did, one hand on a narrow counter which ran ten feet along the far wall, the other lightly touching the antique revolver in the drooping holster.

The town joke was that Mr. Lathram had once told him to 'keep an eye out' for crooks, and he had done just that before he realized it was just an expression.

But there was neither a joke nor humor as Claude closed the door to the office after his brother passed through.

Mr. Lathram had put the large desk between himself and the two Indians before he spoke. His anger had turned from red to white-hot and his voice trembled with the seething words.

"I have told you to never — NEVER — come to this bank — to this town."

His eyes burned at he looked rapidly from one to the other. It was as if he feared he might incinerate them before he had a chance to pillory them verbally.

"NEVER!" and he pounded on his desk. Actually, his fist thumping on the plateau of walnut was the loudest thing so far. He had been shouting at the interlopers, but it had been in a whisper.

He was sure to continue, for he appeared to be building to either an attack on the two or advanced apoplexy, but Claude stretched across the president's desk, stretched, and slid things out of his way and onto the floor as he did.

Fox followed the two, nearly disinterested, for there was an olfactory assault taking place in the office which the others seemed determined to ignore.

Claude spoke clearly and evenly.

"Before you raise your voice, Phineas, and before you injure your pitifully bunched hand once again on this fine desk, you shall be quiet." As Claude continued, he withdrew from his encroachment across Lathram's desk, lowering his voice as he increased the distance between himself and the bank president. The effect was to pull the Lathram forward so that now he was leaning across his own desk.

Claude bent so that their eyes were level.

"We are here, because we have been treated badly — without honor. We are not here to cause a problem and we are not here to discuss anything. We are here to tell you." He softly drew in his breath and finished, "We have been consistently underpaid. You owe us fifty thousand dollars and we will have it tomorrow. Large bills, small bills, marked or unmarked, it doesn't matter. We will be here at this time tomorrow to get it. After it is counted, we will dump the body and the van. If it is not here, we will dump two bodies and the van." He waited while Lathram built back to white-hot. "Call your local police if you wish — you're in it with us."

He paused and chuckled; Lathram *was* the local police.

"It's your choice, Phineas; try to kill us on your own — we would enjoy the competition — or pay us."

He withdrew and started toward the closed door. Fox turned also, his nose working.

Claude remembered and turned again. "It smells like decomposing flesh in here, Phineas — " he sniffed tentatively, "decomposing genitalia, I'd guess." He sniffed again and then seemed to be working the odor. "Three days old — four days, tops. Aren't you glad it isn't yours?"

They were a mile out of town before Claude turned to his brother, an indication that he could comment on their visit.

Fox chuckled. "'Four days tops'. You must have been in there up to your elbows. No wonder you took a shower after you got back."

"It wasn't pleasant, brother. Needle in a hay stack. I did vomit once. You know, once you've encountered it, that smell seems to cling to you forever."

They went to another restaurant, had dinner, and then drove to the motel, Fox checking from time to time to see that they weren't being followed.

They settled back into their room, Claude working on a crossword puzzle in the newspaper he had bought at the restaurant, and Fox cleaning the various guns and then honing the big butcher's knife they preferred.

They went to bed as soon as it was twilight.

"Interesting day tomorrow," Fox noted.

"He'll pay," was all that Claude said. It wasn't too long before they both were snoring.

Alan, Roger, Cavenaugh and Kurtz met at the box-bin behind Schoenburger's Grocery. Inside the cement-block room were the discarded cartons and cardboard boxes in which a mountain of grocery articles had been shipped. The room had the jungle smell of rotting vegetables, most notably lettuce, and the rough-textured aroma of discarded coffee grounds.

Each boy was settled onto a mound of crushed boxes. Kurtz had also covered himself with a corrugated carton about three feet square, a hole cut from the inside circle of the 'O' printed on one of the sides, and he peered through the opening, his eye blinking between the 'K' and the 'TEX'.

"Always thought the view from one of these would be better," Kurtz commented, his voice hollow, echoing inside the box and the room.

Roger couldn't contain his disgust. "That's as close to one of those as you'll ever get, Kurtz."

"Well, *Roger*, at least I don't *wear* 'em."

Roger jumped from his pile onto Kurtz's box, yelling, "At least I don't *eat* them!"

He had leaped from the top of a pile of collapsed and bound boxes, and from that height he crushed Kurtz and the Kotex© box when he landed. Cavenaugh started to laugh when he heard Kurtz swearing. Alan strode through the boxes as if through deep snow and piled onto Roger, shouting, "Wait for me, Wild Bill!" whereupon Cavenaugh completed the pile with the war cry, "Oh, Poncho!"

From deep under the struggling mass Kurtz yelled, "Oh, Cisco! — Now get the *fuck* off me you homo's!"

They wrestled around for a while, progressing to a cardboard box fight and then to a rotten vegetable toss. The fighting and yelling continued until the boys heard the all-steel fire door behind the grocery groan open.

"Old Man Schoenburger!" Roger warned.

The boys burrowed under the boxes, trying to get as deep as they could. Then, by an extraordinary sense, they knew exactly when to stop, remaining stone-still and silent. A few boxes settled and then it was quiet as Old Man Schoenburger unlocked the other door to the box room and stuck his head into the pale light of the 25 watt bulb.

"What is it — I have shouting rats now?" he said before he closed the door and listened from outside it.

"Rats?" hissed Kurtz. "Fucking *rats*?"

Alan shifted under the pile and the others mistook his movement for an advancing army of bubonic, crazed, rodents.

Alan panicked when he heard the others shout "RATS!" in unison and explode from their hiding places and wade toward the other door, the one that was never locked, the one opposite the door Old Man Schoenburger now stood outside of, laughing into his sleeve.

As Alan started to wiggle out from under his pile he felt something gnawing against his leg. "MOM!!" he shouted before he knew what he was saying, and then tore through the boxes. He was almost to the door when he heard Kurtz howling with laughter behind him.

"MOMMY!" Kurtz mocked as they both passed out the door into the glaring sunlight of morning. "MOMMY! MOMMY! MOMMY!" he repeated as they ran across the back parking lot and into the ravine behind the store. All of the boys slid down the dirt slope as if they were heading for home plate. At the bottom they caught their breath, gathered the rope they had collected and left there the night before, and started for the quarry, Kurtz still taunting Alan.

"Man, you guys should have heard our little 'momma's boy' here," he said as he pushed Alan to the side.

"Quit ragging 'im," Cavenaugh warned.

Yeh, don't *rag* him — *Kotex© Man*," Roger added.

And so the boys kidded their way out of town and to the quarry.

They stopped briefly at the bottom of No Brakes Hill, and gathered and ate blackberries, finally continuing when Roger said, "We're done. Grab your coat, *Tex*, and we'll mosey on down to the quarry."

Kurtz heaved a handful of berries at Roger, peppering his white t-shirt back with purple stains.

Roger contorted, and then twisted his shirt around so that he could observe the damage.

"Nice work, Kote-brain." He released his shirt and didn't give it another thought. In fact, it remained partially twisted around his middle the rest of the day.

Alan and Cavenaugh carried the two bundles of clothesline. Roger lugged an army knapsack with soda and donuts and a bag of pretzel logs stuffed into it. Kurtz carried a collapsible shovel on his shoulder and his pocket knife tied to a braided thong, the other end attached to a loop in his jeans.

It was still early enough that there was no one else at the quarry. Actually, most of the older kids were probably still in bed. Advancing adolescence seemed to attack them with the lassitude resultant of attacks by an omnipresent Tsetse fly — they wouldn't appear at the quarry until at least noon, and even then there would be a pervasive sluggishness to their actions until they dove into the water a few times. The boys would do that and then become animated. The girls rarely swam at the quarry and never dived, even from the lower 'pizza-slice' rock platform down by the landing. Consequently, the girls never really seemed to awaken. They just let the sun bake them further into a stupor as they watched the boys make idiots of themselves.

Alan had observed that it wasn't until his sister, Beth, returned from the quarry and showered that she emerged from her haze of cobwebs and half nods.

When he teased her about it she answered, "I get tan, I listen to music, and I wake up. What else is daytime good for?"

As they approached the lower derrick, Alan thought of Blacky. He really missed him but he was not ready to bring him back to the quarry. The big dog had whined and pulled at his chain when Alan left that morning. Even as Alan crossed the street a block down from his house he could hear Blacky's protesting barks.

A few cicadas rattled in the bushes and trees and the morning birds jumped from branch to branch and called to each other.

"It's gonna be hotter'n a bitch," Kurtz swore, and pulled off his t-shirt.

Cavenaugh crossed his arms and grabbed the sides of his t-shirt and yanked it over his head. He stuffed the top of the shirt into the back of his pants and wore it like a tail. Kurtz had his over one shoulder.

They walked past the parking area, raising little clouds of yellow dust as the walked, and went down the hill to the landing. They stood at the edge of the low quarry wall and surveyed the still water.

"Well now, *shit.*" It was Cavenaugh, and he was reacting to the fact that the raft was not tied to the landing, and further, it was not even in sight.

"Those fuckers." Kurtz was referring to the older kids who used their raft and then left it floating free in the quarry. Because they came late in the day and always swam to and from the raft, they didn't give a thought to where they left it at the end of the day.

Alan searched along the far walls of the quarry, still in the shadows of morning. "There's The Devil's Club," he said and pointed to the tree trunk and knob of roots that was floating near the far wall. It and the raft were the two hazards for night-diving. Three years earlier a group of high school kids had been partying on a moonless night and a drunk boy had dived into the darkness on a dare. The others, hooting and hollering and taunting him, had fallen silent when they heard his head and shoulder crushed as they smashed onto the log.

The Devil's Club was tied down by the landing for about a year after that, but someone had untied it, and now it moved slowly about the quarry, three-quarters submerged, awaiting the next child. Most night divers now took the time to locate The Devil's Club and the raft before they plunged into the darkness.

Each of the boys toyed with the idea of swimming out to the raft — it had to be hidden around the corner by the taller derrick and the machinery shed, but no one volunteered. That section of the quarry seemed to collect floating debris — the beer cans and bottles, the paper bags and pieces of plastic that either blew into the water or were thrown. In addition, the walls there were not sheer, rather blasted curves and angles that some of the kids climbed down to paint their names on the expanses of rock. Because the water was still around the heads and knuckles of some of the rocks that poked above the surface, it was brackish, with a skim of algae and slime.

Roger left the group and walked out along the ledge with the railroad tracks so that he could see around the distant corner. The others sat and watched him work his way out, climbing on and around the abandoned engine when he came to it, and then continuing along the track.

Kurtz waited until Roger was on the engine and then instructed the others, "70 ton Climax. Built in 1898. She could follow two lines scratched in the dirt and was a sweetheart to fire and drive. The quarry men named her Vulcana and used to take turns washing her. She was the only piece of machinery The Doll Man ever hated. My ole man says his grandaddy says The Doll Man could fix a steam machine by smilin' at it...."

"Kotex-Man©," Cavenaugh interrupted.

Kurtz pulled back from his recital and looked over to Cavenaugh. "Yeh?"

"Can you not tell us that story again? I'm a little pissed off about the raft and I know your stories by heart. Show a little mercy until we get the raft. What do ya say?"

Regardless of what he said or didn't say, Kurtz was hurt. As much as he and his father shared a mutual hatred, Kurtz wanted to be like him. His dad's stories were about all he had been given that he could use, and so he settled into them any chance he had.

"There it is!" Roger called from the end of the rail ledge. "It's against the derrick wall. We could lower a rock onto it and drag it around to the landing. Shouldn't be too tough."

Kurtz saw the direction Roger was pointing. He left the others and scrambled around that side of the quarry and out of sight. "Bring the rope, you guys," he yelled as he disappeared into the surrounding woods.

Roger watched Kurtz run off and knew what he was going to do. "Cool it, Tex — I'm the Spider Man©." He turned and tried to make his way quickly over the rusted hulk of the engine.

Kurtz ran across the granite plain by the derrick. He edged toward the rim and then looked down. Beneath him was the raft, nudging the jagged rocks.

There was a series of stair-step ledges Kurtz carefully jumped down. After them the quarry side was a convex slab of granite extending twenty feet, ending in a pile of rubble blocks that dropped below the water's surface. Kurtz examined the curved section of rock. There were random hand holds and a few inch-or-so ridges which ran along the surface. He carefully lowered his body down the granite wall, holding on by the tips of his fingers and pressing his body onto the cool, painted stone. He hadn't gone far before he wished he'd worn his shirt. Any time he slid to a lower hand-hold he scraped his chest against the rough stone.

He was resting, trying to find another place to move his hands, one foot on a lip of rock, the other pawing slowly along the stone, searching for an irregularity, when a length of rope went sailing past him.

"Look out below," Roger called after the clothesline slapped across Kurtz's back.

"Do you fucking *mind?*" Kurtz yelled up to him. "Why don't you just drop a few *rocks* on me?"

Roger wasn't listening. He was hurrying down along Kurtz's path, aided by the knotted clothesline. Before long he was beside Kurtz, holding onto the rope and leaning out from the rock.

"I'd offer you my rope, Kotex© Man, but I don't think it'll hold both of us. Grab it once I'm down."

With that, he rappelled below the stranded boy. It wasn't long before the rope fell slack against Kurtz's back. He had been studying the grey and pink crystalline surface of the rock in an attempt to ignore his predicament. He moved the rope off of his back with subtle shifts of his shoulders and finally was able to grasp it with one and then both hands. He chest stung as he lowered himself to the jumble of rocks beside Roger.

As soon as Kurtz made it to the rocks, Roger stepped out onto the raft. The other boy followed, and they hand-paddled the raft away from the wall and started their trip back to the landing.

At the top of the quarry wall, Alan pulled the rope up, looping it as he did, while Cavenaugh untied it from the base of the derrick.

"You didn't want to go with them, did you?" Cavenaugh asked as he joined Alan at the rim.

"I can live a little longer without sticking my hands in that water," the younger boy replied.

Cavenaugh put his arm on Alan's shoulder and the two boys walked back toward the hill descending through the woods to the landing. They could hear Kurtz and Roger splashing and cat-calling below them, the noise echoing back and forth up the quarry walls until it escaped.

"How's your hand? Cavenaugh asked.

Alan turned his hand over and examined the streaked scabs as he walked.

"It's okay, I guess. I don't think about it, really."

"Blacky okay?"

Alan stopped walking and so did Cavenaugh. They looked at each other for a moment and then to Alan's hand. Below them, Kurtz and Roger had started to splash each other.

The rising sun was behind Cavenaugh so that Alan had to squint when he looked at him. "Do you really believe me Cav? Do you really think I saw something?"

The older boy looked down at his friend. "Alan, if you told me the earth was on fire, I'd believe you. Yeh, I think you saw something, but I have to admit, I don't understand any of this, although I think we're gonna find out, one way or another.

"First we've got to find out how deep that beast is," he said, indicating the quarry behind him.

"Yeh, I guess we do," Alan responded and then turned and continued walking down through the woods to the landing.

Roger and Kurtz had the raft snugged against the landing wall. Both boys' hair was wet, and Roger's t-shirt hung soaked and sagging from his chest.

"We girls had a little water-fight," Roger informed Cavenaugh and Alan.

"No shit," was the older boy's response.

Alan headed toward the forge. "I'll get some paddles."

"And something to weight the rope down with," Roger added, running over to join Alan.

Cavenaugh placed a small rock on the granite by the landing and then paced off a distance and marked it with another rock. "Ten feet. Exactly." He turned to Kurtz, who sat on the low landing wall and steadied the raft below him with his foot. "Kurtz," Cavenaugh instructed, "tie a big knot in the clothesline, every ten feet. I marked it off here." The older boy indicated the distance between the two rocks.

When Alan and Roger returned they brought with them not only boards to be used as paddles but also a cast iron gear that they had found behind the forge building.

Alan hefted it to his shoulder. "This mother will drag the rope down."

Kurtz examined the rusty weight. "That mother would drag me down! Don't you think you maybe overdid it a little, there, Alan?"

"Hey, Super-Absorbent-Brain, all that dry clothesline will have a lot of buoyancy — sorry for the big word, Tex — we need a lot of weight."

The boys spent most of the morning helping to measure and knot the lengthening rope. Each took a section of clothesline and tied the marks into it before they joined it with the already knotted length. They drank soda and ate the donuts and pretzel logs they had brought along. Kurtz kept a length of pretzel stuffed in the side of his mouth and handled it from time to time as a cigar, crooking a finger over it when he used it to point.

"Good job, lads," he said when the rope was finished. "You're a fine bunch to work with."

Alan rolled his eyes and Cavenaugh and Roger simply ignored Kurtz as they piled the rope and the metal weight onto the raft.

The late morning heat had begun to penetrate the canyon of the quarry, the southern walls baking, those still in the shadows, yet cool. The doves were quiet, and an occasional cicada replaced the earlier cooing with an irritatingly high grate. The boys paddled cautiously away from the landing. Usually, at least one of them would be dragging a leg through the water as he paddled, but now all of the boys remained within the raft's perimeter, studying the water around them as they dipped the ends of the boards and pulled themselves and their friends forward. No one spoke until they were far from the low quarry wall they had left behind.

Roger searched the rim of the high walls. "Isn't this the part where The Moron Squad appears?"

Alan looked up. "Phillip should be at work, robbing the general public, and Junior is probably under a tree, picking his nose — "

"And eating it," Kurtz interjected. "Yum — moron snot."

"He could blow his brains out and nobody'd know until years later and he died and somebody did an alimony," Roger added, looking back at the landing wall.

None of the boys could relax.

Alan didn't really want to be the one who corrected Roger, but since no one else did, he said, "I think that's 'ortopsy', Roger. 'Alimony' is what a guy is fined when he dumps his wife."

Roger paddled a few strokes and then smiled at Alan. "By gosh, I think you're right, Mr. Professor. Score one for the little guy."

Alan splashed his paddle toward Roger who was working behind him.

"Hey, that was a compliment, you dolt," and Roger splashed him back.

Cavenaugh pulled his board from the water. "I think we're out far enough."

The others stopped and Cavenaugh took a folded piece of paper from one back pocket and a broken pencil stub from the other. He sited their location relative to the two derricks.

"Wait 'till we stop, you guys."

Kurtz was preparing the tethered weight. Cavenaugh drew an outline of the quarry's footprint and marked where they were with an 'x'. The raft coasted forward a few more feet and then rocked with the boys' movements. Kurtz dipped the gear into the water several times.

"Let it down slowly, Tex, and yell when you come to a knot," Cavenaugh cautioned as he stood poised with his pencil and paper.

Kurtz allowed the rope to slide through his hands to the first knot, singing as he did, "I'm Mike Fink, king of the river."

"Ten feet," Roger proclaimed.

Kurtz gave him a long dirty look and said through the corner of his mouth, "No shit, Wonder Child, your mommy have any children that lived?"

"Hey," Roger said, peeved, "my mom dropped me from between her legs, your mother wore you there," shutting Kurtz up for a moment.

He let another ten feet slide. "Twenty feet."

Cavenaugh marked the paper with little straight lines, drawing a fifth diagonally through the previous four as they progressed. By eighty feet, Kurtz asked to be relieved.

"Who else wants to have loads of fun?" he asked.

Alan wobbled over to him and took the eighty-foot knot in his hand. He was surprised as he did at how heavy the rope was. Kurtz laughed as he let Alan take the weight.

"Don't let it pull you in, little guy."

Alan freed a hand and gave Kurtz the finger.

"That your age or I.Q.?" Kurtz teased.

"It's your jock size in centimeters," Roger added, flipping his own finger to Kurtz as he spoke.

"Very nice," Kurtz said as he sat down on the raft and then lay backward, prostrate and staring at the cloudless sky. "I love being with my friends."

Cavenaugh interrupted the banter. "You know how deep that weight is so far, you guys?"

"Yeh, eighty feet," Kurtz said.

"Jesus," Roger said, looking up. "That's deeper than the tallest building in town. That's deeper than the tallest building in Portland!"

"Holy shit," Alan said, also imagining and looking up at the tallest building in Portland.

Alan began to lower the rope, hand over hand.

"Did you know they have 'hookers' in Portland? I saw one once," Kurtz said and the boys were silent as Alan continued playing out the rope.

"Ninety feet."

Cavenaugh made another mark on the paper.

"What did she look like?" Roger asked.

"Who?" Kurtz replied, savoring his information.

Roger smirked at Kurtz and continued, disgusted, "The 'hooker', you dip-shit. Who did you think I meant, your mother?"

Kurtz wasn't ready to answer yet. He knew there was time for one more smart remark before the others attacked him, possibly throwing him in. "Speaking of 'hookers', how is your mom, Roger?"

Roger started across the raft toward Kurtz, rocking the frail craft as he advanced. Alan sank to a sitting position and stopped releasing rope.

Kurtz laughed unconvincingly and said, "She looked like the snake-lady at the carnival. You know, all made up, with holes in her cheap-shit costume. Lotta hair. Pissed look on her face. If I ever met her in an alley, alone, I'd give her my money just to protect myself."

Alan released more line.

The boys thought about the snake lady and imagined themselves having sex with her.

Cavenaugh had her in a dark room in a big building in Portland. He imagined her writhing under him.

Roger sat on her and studied her body. He was convinced that all women, at least those who weren't fat, had gorgeous bodies. He laughed to himself when he thought of putting a sack on her head.

Kurtz took her in a flurry of uncoordinated, useless motions. He stabbed at a vague area between her legs and conjured up the feelings of masturbation.

Alan was at a loss. He apologized and left the room.

"One hundred feet," he yelled, trying to cover his impotence.

The knot at one hundred feet was larger than the others and allowed Alan a firm grip to hold as he rested his arms.

Kurtz looked at Alan and at the rope stretching rigid to the water. "You know what I think of when I see you there, Alan?"

Alan didn't answer.

"I think of the inky depths of water, and I imagine the creature from the black lagoon swimming around, pissed because he's so ugly. Mad because he's all alone and has been for a hundred years. I see him eating fish and leeches and scum and I see him swimming around and banging into our stupid-ass weight."

Alan looked over the edge of the raft into the water. He was becoming uncomfortable.

"Yeh, he bangs his head and then he gets tangled up in it, and boy is he pissed. He's *really* pissed! He grabs the rope. . . ." Kurtz was speaking rapidly now and he spoke as if he were a mad monster. "Yeh, he grabs onto the rope and he dives into the depths, dragging the weight with him, really pissed, angry as hell, determined to hurt whatever it was that just hurt him. Man, is he swimming fast and deep."

Then Kurtz paused for a moment and administered the coup-de-grace.

"Alan, the monster dives fast and jerks the rope out of your hands, but do you know what?"

The boy with the rope was mesmerized. He shook his head slowly from side to side, indicating that he didn't have the faintest idea what was going to happen with the monster.

Kurtz stared into Alan's eyes and then gradually moved his stare down the boy's body to his feet and the coil of line on the raft. Alan's feet were in the center of several loops of rope.

"Look at your feet, Alan." He waited until the frightened boy saw that he was standing in a ring of rope. "Good-bye, Alan." With his last statement, Kurtz rocked the raft.

Before Cavenaugh can speak, and before Roger can move to help Alan, the young boy thought he felt a tug on the rope and he yelled and did everything wrong. He screamed and released his hands from the hundred foot knot as if it were the carnival lady's snake.

"OH SHIT! OH JESUS!" he screamed and tried to dance out of the coil of rope before it tightened around his ankle. But the released line ate up the momentary slack as the weighted end bulled deeper, finally snapping it taut. The rope started to slide around Alan's feet and then the friction of the boy's jeans stopped it and Alan was jerked off of his feet.

Roger and Cavenaugh dove for Alan, grabbing him and wrestling with the rope at his leg.

"It's okay, it's okay, it's okay," Cavenaugh repeated as he freed the struggling boy's feet. Roger had Alan's arms pinned and was shouting, "CALM DOWN, DAMMIT, CALM DOWN! WE HAVE YOU, ALAN; IT CAN'T DRAG YOU DOWN!"

Once the rope was free from Alan's feet it played like a wriggling snake as it was pulled over the side by the submerged weight. Cavenaugh had inadvertently dropped it when he released Alan, and was now trying to catch the writhing line as it passed beside his legs and over the edge of the raft. Suddenly, there was a tangle in the coil and the remaining jumble dragged across the raft, between the boys, and then splashed into the water and disappeared in a flurry of bubbles.

All four boys looked at the rope's trail and then three of them caught their breath and started to swear.

"You fuck!"

"You shit — you scared me to death!"

"You Kotex©-brained ass-hole."

Kurtz stayed in a corner away from the others. "Hey, we know it's at least a hundred feet deep. A hundred and ten, probably, by the way the rope played out. What do we need, exact feet? Inches? Quarter inches? Christ, give me a break. I'm sorry. I thought it was a joke. I was trying to be funny. Shit."

And then Kurtz did something that threw them all off. He started to cry.

"I'm sorry you guys. Shit, I really am. I can't do anything right; my old man's right. I'm sorry." He sat down on the corner of the raft and hid his face in his hands and couldn't stop crying.

Alan started to cry too, and Cavenaugh looked at the two and balanced across the raft to Kurtz. He kneeled beside him and put his hand on his shoulder, shaking the crying boy gently. "Hey, hey, it's no big deal. You're right. Relax, it's no big deal. We're all fuck-ups, man. You're with your friends; don't worry about it. You were just trying to be funny. Hey, a quarter of the rope was yours anyway."

Kurtz stopped sobbing and roughly wiped his eyes with the back of his hand. He gave a couple of very wet sniffs and then asked, "Anybody got somethin' I can blow my nose on? A Kotex© or somethin'?" and everybody laughed.

Cavenaugh rose and stood apart and wrote something on his paper. The others went to their corners, picked up their boards, and waited for him to finish, then they paddled back toward the landing.

They were nearly halfway back when Roger bent to the water and retrieved an object. He put it beside him on the raft and examined it as he paddled.

"This is strange, you guys," he said, nudging the object

Kurtz was closest and looked at what Roger had retrieved. "Roger, if I weren't already in the doghouse, and trying to change my ways, I'd say you picked up a big brown turd. What the hell is that?"

The others craned to see what was on the raft. Roger laughed and picked it up. "It does look like a 'floater', you guys." And then with a rare brush with visual humor, Roger was tempted to take a bite out of it to gross the others out. Instead, he said, "It's a potato. With a strange hole in it." He tossed it to Cavenaugh. "What do you make of it?"

Cavenaugh caught the spud easily and turned it in his hand. "Looks like it's been jammed on a pipe. I can't figure it. Maybe somebody stuck it on a short pipe to throw it. Like we do with apples and sticks." He pitched the potato underhand to Alan. The young boy missed the catch but plucked the bobbing object quickly out of the water.

"I think you're right, Cavenaugh, unless somebody kinda ate out the center, or tried to."

Roger searched the surface of the water for additional potatoes and then said, "Nobody ate anything, Alan; the core's still there.

"Oh yeh," Alan said and rolled it to Kurtz.

Kurtz picked it up. "Boy, I'd hate to shit that mother." And then as an afterthought he added, "My oldest sister says that having a baby is like shitting a watermelon."

They momentarily forgot the potato.

Roger looked up to the taller derrick and saw that the sun was just above it. "'Shit a watermelon' — lord, I'm glad I'm a guy."

A flat rock skipped across the water near them, sending skittering splashes as it made its hops.

"You guys havin' fun?" It was Freddy Auftencampf, one of the few nice high school kids the boys knew, and he was standing at the landing. "Thought I'd come down a little early and see what's going on."

Cavenaugh answered, "Everything's goin' on, and nothin's goin' on. We're as confused as usual."

When the raft smashed into the quarry wall at Freddy's feet, Kurtz flipped the potato up to him. "You're older, what's this all about? We think it's been stuck on a pipe. Any brainstorms?"

Freddy examined the wet potato half heartedly. "Well, I think you're right. Maybe somebody stuck it on lawn marker or something."

Kurtz couldn't stay serious any longer.

"Maybe some guy with a hollow schwanz was bangin' the spud instead of poundin' his pud."

Everybody ignored him as they climbed off of the raft.

Cavenaugh walked over to Freddy and stood beside him. "This place is getting strange."

Cavenaugh, with interruptions by Alan and Kurtz, told Freddy what had happened to Blacky, and why they were trying to measure the depth of the quarry.

"You don't happen to know how deep this is? You could get me out of a lot of trouble", Kurtz pleaded.

Freddy was far away for a moment, looking through Kurtz as he spoke. "Hey, you guys were out here the night Will and I were here with your sisters," he said, indicating Alan and Kurtz. "It was the rainy night and Will's car wouldn't start and we had to get a ride back with miraculously appearing and unusually helpful Phillip Henshaw and Junior Swift."

Roger took the potato from Freddy's hand before he finished speaking. Roger ran his fingernail along the rim of the circle in it, and then he began to laugh.

The boys waited until he stopped. It was rare for Roger to be amused with anything.

He shook his head. "You guys got had by the oldest trick in the book." He savored his knowledge as he continued, "Let me guess — Will had Phillip fix the car — he *paid* Phillip to fix that old sedan!" Roger looked around at the others, incredulous that no one had figured what he was getting at. "The *potato*, you guys, Phillip and Junior *potatoed* Will's car. Of course it wouldn't start. Then, later, they remove the potato, and presto, Will's car is fixed."

"Yeh," Freddy added, "thirty-some bucks worth of *presto!*"

"And they pitched the potato into the quarry after," Kurtz concluded, laughing as he did. "Those guys are some sneaky."

Freddy moved his shoulders forward. "It gets worse — they dropped Will and me off and then went and partied with our girls."

Alan looked up sharply. He saw his sister sneaking out of their house. "That fucker," he muttered. "I may be little, but I'll kill him if he touches my sister."

"He can *have* my sister — that is, if he can catch her before she runs away to Hollywood." Kurtz was moderately serious. He didn't really relish the idea of Junior Swift pawing his sister. He thought about it for a moment more and then joined Alan. "Let's kill them both. Rid the earth of slime."

Cavenaugh had walked back to the edge of the quarry. "Seriously, how can we find out how deep this is? We lost our rope."

Freddy repeated, "We lost our rope," without comprehending the connection. "I've got a whole bunch of old cord I used to practice knots on when I was a Boy Scout. There must be five hundred feet of it. Stop by my house, you're welcome to it. In fact, it's under my dad's workbench in the garage. Take it."

As he finished, two cars appeared at the top of the quarry. A cloud of dust drifted over them and then the doors jerked open and a group of kids from the high school spilled out.

"See you guys," Freddy said. "I'm supposed to meet Will at his house." He wheeled his bike toward the hill. Before he was around the corner he turned back to the boys. "Will's gonna be real happy about this," and he held up the potato.

After he was gone, Kurtz questioned, "And what's Will gonna do? Beat up Phillip? I don't think so. It'd be his *funeral.* "

Cavenaugh thought about Kurtz's remark. "Those two morons couldn't be *that* tough to outsmart. Don't sell Will and Freddy short. If they get mad enough, I'd put my money on them."

The only one who shared Cavenaugh's faith in underdogs was Alan. He had already begun to plan.

Junior stopped by the garage at noon with two cheeseburgers, two orders of French fries, and two chocolate milkshakes. He and Phillip sat on a discarded car seat behind the garage and chewed their food and stared into the woods.

Phillip watched Junior eat a half of a cheeseburger in one bite. "You know, Junior, if you didn't try to stuff the whole fuckin' thing in your mouth at once, you wouldn't have to chew with your fuckin' mouth open." He shook his head in disgust and then added, "Do you realize how bad that looks? It's like watchin' one of them washers down at the Laundromat — the ones with the glass windows in the door and you can see all the clothes and soapy water slosh around — only it's filled with garbage and lasagna and shit — and I gotta tell ya, sport, it makes people look at your mouth, and them teeth of yours aren't gonna be on no Ipana commercial."

Junior continued chewing, and spoke as he did, pushing clumps of food aside to make room for his words. "I'm sorry, mother, if my fuckin' manners need a little fine tunin'," and as he finished his statement he started pushing the food out of his mouth so that the dripping mixture fell down the front of his shirt. He looked down at the accumulation in his lap and feigned surprise. "Well, excuse me, where the fuck did this come from? Looks like cow afterbirth to me." He scooped the mess from the front of his pants and shoved it back into his mouth with the rest of his food. "MMMMM, *tastes* like afterbirth, too. Yum." He smacked his lips and wiped his mouth with the back of his hand, then he licked each of his fingers noisily.

"I'm real sorry I brought it up," Phillip said and threw the rest of his French fries into the woods. "I kinda lost my appetite."

"Speakin' of appetite," Junior said, "when are we gonna get some pussy? Charlene cut me off after she heard we was puttin' the make on Louise and Beth." The girls' names ignited one of the many flammable corners of his imagination. "Say, let's call and see if they want to do somethin'."

Phillip was interested, but he wasn't certain he wanted to drag Louise and Junior along. "Why is it you always want to tag along, Junior?"

"Now that's a tough question — when are you gonna help me get my car fixed? It's only been about three months since you said you'd help me."

"You get the fuel pump?" Phillip asked.

"I got it a month ago. I told you that."

"No way, ass-hole, you didn't tell me, and I don't believe you coulda scraped together the money, anyway. How'd you do that?" Phillip tried to think of where Junior could have stolen one. Every car shop in the state locked up every loose item when either of them walked through the door. Somebody usually escorted them around while they looked. Two shops in town wouldn't even let them through the door.

"Hey, I got it. Don't sweat the details. I'm sure it works, too."

Now Phillip was intrigued. At last he had an idea. "Okay, who's gonna have trouble startin' their car?"

Junior laughed and smiled like a retarded elf. "Well," he said, still grinning, "I really can't believe Ole Lady Brinks would park her car on the dark side of her house like that. And hey, she's too old to be drivin' anyway. You ever see her? She sights under the steering wheel and then kinda closes her eyes and hopes for the best. I saw her run over the curb down on Brown Street and wipe out two garbage cans. Helluva racket. I did the town a favor." He was pleased when Phillip laughed.

"Jesus, Junior. Maybe I ought to stop by and offer her a free tune-up — discover a problem or two that needs fixed. There's good money in fuel pumps." Phillip smiled to himself as he thought of the money and then he remembered

Junior's earlier suggestion. "Hey shit, yeh. Let's take the girls some place. I got a feelin' I'll be comin' into a little extra money soon. What the fuck, let's see if they want to drive down to Old Orchard. Maybe get 'em drunk, ride the rides, go for a walk on the beach. . . ."

"Screw their eyes out," Junior interrupted.

It was exactly what Phillip was going to say, but coming from Junior it angered him immediately. He whacked the boy on the side of his head with his open hand.

"No fuckin' class, Junior. You think with your balls. Let's just go and have some fun."

On his afternoon break Phillip rumbled over to Mrs. Brinks' house. He combed his hair in the new rearview mirror and buttoned his shirt to the neck. He saw that she was on the front porch as he stepped from his car.

"Mrs. Brinks, good afternoon!"

He walked on the sidewalk up to her steps. He stopped and looked down at the flowers that surrounded the porch.

"Mrs. Brinks, I've never known anyone who could grow such pretty flowers." He bent and acted as if he were smelling them.

She was delighted. "Why hello, Phillip I haven't seen you for a while. How are your mother and father?"

"Oh hey, they're just fine," he answered.

Only Old Lady Brinks would be unaware that his mother had run off with a salesman and that Phillip and his father had fallen into a drunken fight several years ago and hadn't spoken since. She studied his shiny car. "Phillip, I think that automobile of yours needs a new muffler. It's awfully noisy, don't you think?"

"Oh, yes mam, that's the darndest thing! I think I hit a rock or something last night. I plan on fixing it later today."

Mrs. Brinks' face clouded. "Phillip, you're so fortunate to have the touch with machines. That automobile of mine is broken again. I swear I wouldn't own one if we didn't have those terrible winters."

"Broken? Your car's broken?" Phillip's voice oozed concern and disbelief. "Why hey, that won't do. Not at all. Why not have it fixed down at the garage. We're not real busy now." He knew the direction of her answer.

"Oh, Phillip, Truman Horvath is just too expensive for his own good! He thinks we're all just made out of money. I have to be careful, you know." She patted the pocket book she clutched in her lap like a captured cat.

Phillip twisted his wrist so that he could see his watch and showed astonishment when he read the time. "My gosh, Mrs. Brinks, I'm late already. I've got to go." He turned and started to leave and then stopped as if a wonderful thought had just that second blossomed before him like a stand of sun flowers.

"This may not sound like a good idea to you, but, say, I could swing by here after work. I bet I could have that automobile of yours running like a top in no time!"

After the horrible night she had endured, she couldn't believe her good fortune. "Oh please, yes, Phillip, if it isn't too much trouble." She was so excited she rose and shuffled to her screen door. She rested her hand on it and turned and called out to her savior, "Phillip Henshaw, I'm going to bake you some cookies right this instant!" and she went into her home, picturing Phillip as thirteen and scrubbed with a tight little fistful of flowers for her.

She sang to herself as she opened the cupboard doors in her kitchen.

When he got back to the garage, his boss wasn't around, so Phillip slipped into the used-parts-and junk room and took the fuel pump off of an old Plymouth engine he had failed to tell Junior about. He dumped the pump into a coffee can filled with gasoline and let it soak while he finished putting the brakes on an old station wagon.

After work he went to Mrs. Brinks' house, ate cookies, installed the fuel pump, and took twenty dollars in quarters from the old lady. Before he left he showed her a copy of the bill Old Man Horvath had presented to Mrs. Odenwolfe for the same work two weeks earlier.

Mrs. Brinks handled the copy of her friend's bill as if it were a pornographic photo involving librarians and Shetland ponies. She frowned as she read and digested, finally reading again to be certain.

"My land, Phillip! Why, that's twice what you charged me," she said, stabbing at the bottom figure.

A smile realigned her wrinkled and spotted skin. "You are a dear boy, Phillip Henshaw. Here," and she handed him two more quarters.

"Poor Elenora!" she exclaimed and then laughed devilishly, confiding to Phillip, "She can afford it. Buried two husbands, both well-to-do. A widow's money is best spent!"

Before she could continue, Phillip finished wiping his hands on a red mechanic's rag, picked up the sack of quarters, and started toward his car.

"Sure glad I could help, Mrs. Brinks."


Ezechial drained the waste oil from the boiler and flushed it twice with fresh water from the tower. He then dragged out a short-handled shovel and used it as a rake to move some of the smaller pieces of coal toward the fire door, building them into a roughly circular mound. After he completed the pile he transferred larger hunks of coal one at a time from the coal chute to the other side of the boiler.

He now was leaning against the stone wall, staring through the dim light at the gauge indicating the water level in the boiler. It was almost full. The needle creeped toward the safe operating level mark. He reached out to the two oversized spigot wheels and began to close them, keeping his eyes fixed to the gauge as he did. He allowed the needle to rise well into the safety zone before he gave the wheels their last tightening.

Everything was ready for nightfall.

Tired and filthy, Ezechial hobbled around the compressor, running his good hand over every lever and knob. He did the same thing at the cable hoist and then patted the big flywheel as he passed it to go up to his room.

He stopped midway up the stairs and sat briefly on one of the steps. His breath rattled into his constricted lungs, stayed only momentarily, and then escaped, foul and hot. Ezechial ran his good hand through his beard and thought of the machinery in motion.

*They brought the machines to the quarry strapped to the backs of three railroad cars. Ezechial and his sister watched the men from Boston and Chicago and marveled at their clean confidence. They bossed the workers and they bossed the foreman, and every bit of advice the local quarry men offered, the men from different states shunned like country clothing. They were as magnificent as their machines, for they supervised the groaning hoists and the dusty teams of oxen, and the unloading, and transferring to the big wheeled gerrymanders, and never broke a sweat or soiled a cuff. These were giants who moved mountains of iron by chewing on cigars and swearing. The two men laughed together, looking over their shoulders in suspicious supervision. They always stood apart from the locals.*

*Ezechial came to know them as the Boston Boiler Man and the Chicago Compressor Man. And they were gods.*

*After only a month their machines were bolted to the stone of the earth and connected to one another with long wide belts passing over iron wheels, and contorted pipes that traveled in pairs or more from the boiler, disappearing into the darkness under the splayed feet of the monsters or rising to the ceiling and hanging until they dropped to the side of a fat-lunged compressor, or to the geared but still empty spools of the cable-hoists. A few escaped the machinery shed, climbing to the new water tower or racing out of sight to discharge near the valley behind*

*The machinery shed had been rapidly built around them and before long they were left alone in their cave, alone in the stone darkness, crouching through the quarry night, poised, cold and immune to all but their masters.*

*Young Ezechial had hung in the shadows and listened to the incantations of the Boston Boiler Man and the Chicago Compressor Man as each led their charges around the machines, pointing and watching as they indicated levers and wheels, flicking them open, pulling them shut, adjusting them with a doctor's aloof precision.*

*One day it was late before Ezechial and his sister got back to the quarry, and Ezechial knew the machines had come to life before he heard them, or smelled them, or felt their pounding, revolving madness. The Boiler Man stood outside of the machinery shed and studied the volcanic explosions of black smoke and listened to the sound of the vented steam. Inside, The Compressor Man dabbed the sweat from his face and drew strength from the steady, thunderous spinning of the giant flywheels of his machine. He shouted soundless commands and those near him nodded and ran here and there, some with oilers, others with huge wrenches, twisting and torquing as they were bid.*

*Ezechial marveled as one of the Irish quarrymen, muscled and stupid, backed to within inches of the flywheel. The Compressor Man reached out and plucked him easily from the spinning death, treating his act with more contempt than the boy had seen ignorant men use on dumb animals.*

The boys ranged through Freddy's garage, finding the cord not under the workbench but in a corner behind the push lawn mower and a deflated basketball. It was thicker than the boys expected, nearly that of light rope, and wound into a large ball.

Roger tossed the cord ball as he walked.

"Do you guys want to go out again now?"

"I gotta check in at home," Kurtz said, shrugging his shoulders as he spoke. "But I can get out later. Wanna camp out?"

Cavenaugh trotted ahead and then turned to receive the tossed cord. "No problem here."

Alan wasn't anxious to spend a night at the quarry. "I probably can't, you guys."

"Since when can't you sleep out?" Kurtz challenged.

"Since always, Tex. I have to ask. I'll ask, okay? No big deal. I just have to ask first, that's all I said." Alan continued with his defensive ramble until no one was listening.

Kurtz had run ahead of Cavenaugh, waving his arms for the older boy to toss him the cord. Roger sprinted beyond Kurtz, yelling, "Going out for a long one, but can he make it, fans?"

Before Cavenaugh could choose a catcher, Kurtz turned toward Roger and charged.

"Tackle!" And he threw himself at Roger's legs, succeeding in snaring only one foot as his encircled arms slid down the retreating jeans. Roger hopped once and went down. Cavenaugh came running up, spiked the ball onto Kurtz's head and then jumped onto his struggling friends.

After the fight, and as they neared their homes, the boys made their plans for the evening.

Cavenaugh ran down the list. "Roger: sodas, flashlight — a good flashlight, Roger, not some fairy little glow-worm."

Roger flexed his skinny arm. "More powerful than a speeding locomotive — brighter than a carnival spotlight — able to leap through the darkness in a single bound — LOOK!" and he pointed to the clouds, "UP IN THE AIR! IT'S A BIRD! IT'S A PLANE! NO, IT'S SUPERLIGHT!"

Then he deflated his oratory as fast as he had thrust it upon his listeners. Solemnly, he concluded, his hands now on his hips, "Yes, Cavenaugh, I'll bring a good flashlight. And the sodas will be real, with bubbles and everything." He turned from the boys, shook his head, and started across the street toward his house.

"Bikes!" Kurtz shouted after him.

Cavenaugh resumed, nonplused, "I'll bring the cord, candy, and a spare flashlight. Kurtz, you bring a mountain of junk to eat. Alan — you're coming, whether you know it yet, or not — you bring matches, soda and junk, and Blacky."

"No way! Blacky stays home." Alan said it with more power than anyone expected from him. "No way," he repeated to be certain there was no doubt. "I guess I can get out again, but Blacky would just get spooked. He's been real strange since the other day — he growled at me yesterday for nothin'. Go buy your own dog if you want one."

The boys had stopped in the middle of the street. A breeze argued through the leaves of the trees bordering the road, and a blue jay 'shranked' as it flew by. Cavenaugh scratched his head and Kurtz massaged his short haircut. Alan arranged street pebbles with the toe of his gym shoe.

At last, Cavenaugh spoke. "Does that mean you're not bringing Blacky?"

Kurtz laughed and Alan smiled.

"Meet you guys at the swings behind the school," Cavenaugh said and jogged off.

"Don't forget — bikes," Kurtz added again. "I'm tired of walkin'."

Cavenaugh nodded in agreement as he ran.

Phillip closed the folding wood and glass door to the phone booth. He rested his hip against one of the walls and propped his foot on the seat. Before he dialed he flipped the switch which turned on the ventilating fan, and dropped a filed metal slug into the phone. As he dialed he scanned the girls at the soda fountain behind him. Two were cute. One he thought was too disgustingly ugly to be allowed in public, and one was a little overweight but had a large chest. She turned in profile, whispering into her girlfriend's ear. Her friend looked at Phillip in the phone booth. He smiled. She smiled and wiggled her fingers in a wave. The girls giggled. The one with the massive chest had a chiffon scarf around her neck and her friend had a matching scarf tied to the shank of her ponytail. The other girl had a scarf tied around her wrist.

Cute, Phillip thought and sucked on the stick match he had in his mouth. "Why does every fucking broad try to be cute?" he mumbled and ran his hands through his hair.

"What? Hello, Wasterly residence," a confused voice leaped into Phillip's head.

He stood up and dropped his foot from the wooden seat. Phillip remembered where he was.

"Yeh, Beth. Hello, I mean 'hello', yourself."

"Who is this?" Beth asked, placing the voice but trying to figure out what he had said before she spoke and to whom he had been saying it — it was something like, "try to be cute — or buy to be cute," or something that sounded like it.

"Oh sorry; it's Phillip Henshaw. It's Phillip."

Beth agreed to call Louise and see if she wanted to double with Phillip and Junior to Old Orchard Beach, but even as she hung up she kept hearing the teasing word, 'cute'.

Beth hung up the phone and went into the living room. She picked up a cushion from the rocking chair and hugged it to her. The phone rang again and she tossed the pillow onto a t.v. tray and ran back into the kitchen.

"Wasterly residence," she said, wondering why Phillip was calling back, but glad he did.

"Beth, hi, it's me."

It was Freddy. Beth looked at the clock on the wall. She pulled a chair away from the table and sat down.

"Yes, Freddy, what is it?"

He couldn't believe her tone. "Don't sound so excited, Beth. I didn't mean to bother you or anything."

He waited for her to contradict him and when she didn't, he plunged ahead. "Do you want to go for a walk or something tonight? Maybe go to a movie?"

Beth surprised herself when she didn't bother to hedge.

"No Freddy, I don't. Not really."

"Are you sick? Do you feel okay?" Freddy asked, unable to accept such a flat rejection. Usually she would put him off with small talk for awhile if she couldn't go.

"I'm okay."

"World's shortest answers," he replied and waited.

Beth was silent.

"Well, hey," he finally said. "I was just askin'," and hung up.

Beth sat with the phone buzzing in her ear. She didn't care that Freddy was hurt. She didn't even care that she didn't care. She stood back up to the wall phone, depressed the chrome cradle and dialed Louise.

When Louise said she guessed she'd go, Beth wanted to hang up and call Phillip at the garage, but since girls didn't call guys she listened to Louise whine about how dull life in town was, how boring being young was, and what a horrible place Maine was to be trapped for seventeen years.

Finally, Beth became annoyed and said, "What do you want, Louise?" and Louise answered quickly, "I want to find a guy who will get me out of here. I swear, Beth, I'd marry my uncle if he said he'd take me to California."

Then Beth told the first dirty joke she had ever told in her life.

"Louise, do you know why Maine guys don't want to marry virgins?" Louise couldn't believe her ears.

When she didn't get an answer, Beth continued, "Because they think,'if she's not good enough for her own family, then she's not good enough for me'."

Had anyone else told the joke, Louise would have laughed. But Beth didn't tell dirty jokes and Beth didn't kid about sex and Beth never said, 'virgin'. Louise stared at the telephone receiver.

"What's on your mind, girl?" Louise asked.

"Nothing, it's a joke. You said you'd marry your *uncle*. I just told you a joke about it. It was supposed to be funny."

"Where did you hear that joke?"

And before Beth could answer, Louise knew.

"Aren't we growing up!"

Beth was trapped. It wasn't just a joke. She *had* been thinking a lot about sex, and particularly about virginity.

"*Louise*! You talk that way every chance you get!"

For the first time, Louise felt a kinship to Beth. For the eight millionth time, she was jealous of her friend. Phillip preferred Beth. *She* was stuck with Junior. Not bad to look at, but no brain, and far worse, *no car*.

Ezechial slept in the chair by the window, the summer sounds of the quarry and the shouting children cradling him. He saw his sister and he dreamed of their last days and he twitched and whimpered and held two dolls in his lap. His soiled clothing lay at the top of the stairs. An empty soup tin and a half eaten cracker were on the shelf beside him. He had noticed that he was nearly out of food, but he knew there would be a new carton soon. He had never run out. Years ago, a younger woman — a girl, actually — had left the food. Now, an old woman came with it. Ezechial did not understand that they were the same person, for to him they were mother and daughter. Both of them kind.

As he slipped in and out of the past, he was vaguely aware that he was disappointed more often than not when he looked for the arrival of the girl. Her visits were infrequent and unforeseeable. The older woman was more dependable, although she never stayed to speak with him or to allow him to show her his machinery or his dolls.

Of course, they were not dolls to Ezechial. They were his sister.

Paper wasps bumped limp-legged into the panes of glass before him, hovering at the periphery and occasionally landing and walking across the window, casting scratchy shadows within. A fly cruised through the bands of dusty light and a spider dropped beside the old man, moved across the floor and fell victim to The Doll Man's jerking foot.

Downstairs, rivulets of cool water ran silently down the sides of the boiler and puddled on the fine dirt of the floor. A single drop of oiled amber hung streamlined from a lever base, and the brass rimmed gauges caught the light from around the two large doors. Their round glass faces shone blank in the glare.

Three bicycles rested against the clapboards of the school building. Alan stood on the seat of a swing and thrashed the two chains back and forth while Cavenaugh sat with his arms hooked, his feet together and his head lowered, examining the rut below him. Roger looked up and squinted.

"Here comes Wonder Boy."

Kurtz pedaled standing up, his body rigid, the undersized bicycle waving from side to side as he pumped forward.

"GOOD NEWS!" he shouted as he approached.

When he was almost at the swings he threw himself into a burst of acceleration and then locked his brake and slid his bicycle sideways through the dust. Just before he stopped, his front wheel hit a rock and stopped and the rear wheel raised into the air and Kurtz was bucked onto the ground. He broke his fall with his outstretched hands, his fingers splayed. His legs were still tangled in his bike.

Roger watched his performance and then commented, "I'd work on that if I were you. It's a little rough."

"Fuck you!" the injured boy yelled and rolled to the side and examined his hands. "I can't believe I ever called you a friend."

"Can't say that I remember that," Roger replied and laughed.

Kurtz sat and picked little pebbles out of the skin on the palms of his hands and then brushed his hands across his pants. There were several streaks of blood. He looked at his bicycle.

"Bikes don't like me."

Roger wouldn't let it rest. "Who does?" he said and then felt guilty for saying it. He remembered Kurtz crying on the raft. He pulled a candy bar from his pocket and threw it at Kurtz.

"First prize."

Cavenaugh stood from his swing. "By the way, Kurtzy, what's the good news you were shouting about?"

Kurtz sat with his knees drawn to his chest. His hands had begun to throb and one of his knees ached. "Oh that. The good news is — I'm here. You lucky dogs," and he tossed a handful of dirt onto Roger's new tennis shoes. "Nice shoes. You goin' to church?" he laughed.

The boys mounted their bikes. Cavenaugh had his sleeping bag and supplies strapped to his seat and his back fender as did Roger, on his own bike. Alan had everything in the large wire basket on the front of his bicycle, a reminder of his short-lived career as a paper boy. Kurtz, as usual, had his knapsack on his back with his sleeping bag tied to it. When he had fallen it had come up over his head and rolled across the ground. He retrieved it, brushed a little of the dust from it and put it back on. The higher center of gravity it created was one of the reasons he fell so often when he was performing.

"Follow me!" Kurtz shouted and burned ahead of the others.

Roger and Cavenaugh and Alan watched the boy pedal off.

"Follow him?" Roger mocked as the three pedaled off slowly in Kurtz's low cloud of dust.

They rode out of town, stopping at the Dairy Wonder to buy 'skyscraper' ice cream cones. For twenty cents each boy got a mountain of frozen sugar and cream. Kurtz took three bites and a few licks from his but as he got back onto his bike he tipped his 'skyscraper' too far and it tumbled from his cone.

He looked at the glob of ice cream at his feet and then at the laughing boys. "Mother-fucker!" he said loudly, and Irma Wilson shouted from inside, "Watch your mouth, young man. If you are going to be obscene you just leave these premises!"

Kurtz ignored her. Roger was laughing too hard, so Kurtz scooped up his melting ice cream and meteored it at the side of Roger's head.

His aim was perfect.

Roger wiped the mess from his face. "You little fuck!" and threw his own cone at Kurtz.

Kurtz saw it coming and ducked and picked up more of his ill-fated cone.

Mrs. Wilson yelled. "Leave this instant! You boys are not welcome here!"

Kurtz nailed Roger again, this time on the side of his white t-shirt.

Alan threw his cone at Kurtz and as his ice cream started its flight, Cavenaugh pedaled by and pitched his cone to Alan's lap. All the boys were laughing and shouting and swearing when Mrs. Wilson came boiling out the side door of the Dairy Wonder with her broom — the big one that the blind man made and his children sold door to door.

By the time she got out to the parking lot where the fight had occurred, the ice cream spattered boys were halfway up the street. A car full of teenagers pulled in as Mrs. Wilson yelled, "And don't come back!" to the retreating bicycles. She turned and went back into the ice cream shop. As she passed the open window of the car she heard the older children inside laughing.

"Nothing but smart-aleck children," she mumbled. "No manners. Where are their parents?" and let the screen door bang behind her.

"Jesus, am I sticky," Roger said when he took a hand from his handle grip. It had stuck as he started to pull it away. "Smooth move, Ex-Lax," he said to Kurtz.

The four boys stopped at the top of No Brakes Hill and caught their breath. They stood astride their bicycles and looked down the hill. It was a long, downhill run, with a sharp turn at the bottom. There were several dangers associated with the hill — it was steep; the bicycles could pick up a lot of speed — it was long; so the bicycles could pick up even more speed — the turn at the bottom was not banked and blind — and worst of all; rain running down the long hill left an accumulation of loose dirt and gravel at the turn.

The boys loved it. The question was, who could get the farthest down the hill without using his brakes? — who had the nerve to hold off until the last second before he stood and locked his brakes and prayed? Narrow strips of shed rubber started halfway down.

The boys lined up their bicycles, side by side, and stared down at the turn.

There was one more hazard.

It was a right-hand turn and so the best path to take, the path which gave the rider the turn with the largest diameter, was in the left-hand lane, against traffic.

Some kids called it Suicide Hill or Devil's Bend.

"Together?" Cavenaugh asked.

Roger and Alan said, "Yeh," and "Okay," but Kurtz responded, "No, you guys go first. I prefer an audience."

Roger and Alan rolled their eyes to each other and Cavenaugh shook his head and asked the other two, "Ready?"

When they nodded he looked down the hill and also listened intently for a moment in an attempt to hear any approaching cars. When he was satisfied, he lifted his feet from the ground. Alan and Roger lifted theirs also and the three started a very slow roll.

No one started by pedaling. Everyone stopped dead at the top and let gravity perform the evil.

At first the coasting boys weaved as they picked up speed. Cavenaugh pulled ahead immediately, his weight an enemy. Faster and faster, all three boys went down the hill. They sat bolt upright to catch as much wind as possible to slow them down. Cavenaugh was pulling farther away. Roger was two and then three bike-lengths in front of Alan who was already thinking about touching his brakes a little.

Cavenaugh roared by the halfway skid-marks. The turn was approaching him quickly but there were still plenty of tire marks ahead, indicating those who had waited longer before they braked.

*I'm too young to die,* he thought with humor, and stood and slammed on his brakes. His momentum fought with his declining speed and tried to pitch him over his handle bars, but he held his arms straight and braced his weight against them, keeping his rear end as far back as possible to prevent his bicycle from tipping forward. He swung to the outside lane and blew through the turn, his back tire barely sliding on the gravel.

Alan felt his hair flying and his t-shirt pressed against his body, the ends of his sleeves rippling. His front tire began to wobble and he wondered about the patch he had put on the front inner tube. *Oh shit,* he thought, *I'm gonna die. Brake, Cavenaugh, brake!* he prayed.

As soon as Roger and Alan saw Cavenaugh stand on his brakes they followed suit. There was no predisposition for heroics in either of them. Roger passed through the turn at a respectable speed and Alan rolled around it on the inside lane, his heart pumping, his bicycle cruising comfortably.

Behind them, Kurtz had already started and was coming down the hill in the outside lane, hell-bent-for-leather. The other three ditched their bikes and ran back up the inside of the turn to watch crazy Kurtz.

No one thought to check for advancing traffic.

"He's insane!" Roger whispered, commenting on the fact that Kurtz hunched forward, his face just above his handlebars, his butt far back over the rear tire. The boy's stomach was flat on the seat. Only his knapsack broke any of his speed.

"Flying Quasimoto," Roger mumbled.

The three boys stood together off of the road, their attention sucked from them by their insane friend.

Kurtz was flying low. He had incredible speed and he had just rocketed past the first tire marks.

He gave no indication that he was considering braking.

"HIT THE BRAKES, YOU FUCKING IDIOT!" Cavenaugh shouted.

Actually, Kurtz was not yet at the point where Cavenaugh had braked, but Kurtz was going at least half again as fast.

"He must have pump started," Roger added, incredulously.

Alan looked behind them, around the corner.

"OH SHIT!" he screamed. "A TRUCK!!"

And it was. A squatty, overloaded dump truck approached in a cloud of dust.

Alan waved his arms wildly at the truck. The driver honked his air horn and waved back.

Cavenaugh and Roger screamed to Kurtz, jumping up and down as they did, pointing crazily behind them to the unseen road and the climbing behemoth. Black smoke now belched from its stacks.

"Oh Jesus," Alan said and began to cry.

The wind ripped tears from Kurtz's eyes as he tore down the hill. He knew he was going too fast. He knew he couldn't brake in time. And he knew no fear.

"You mother-fucker," he quietly cursed. "I'll take you, you miserable fuck," and he convinced himself.

He hunched lower in preparation for the turn.

His three friends at the corner were going crazy. It did not occur to him that they might be trying to communicate something to him.

And then he saw the dump truck nose around the corner — in his lane.

"Oh shit-fuck!" was all he had time to say.

The trucker saw the boy and swerved harder into the turn to give him room. The outside rear tandem wheels lifted from the road and the top-heavy truck tipped toward the other three boys. The driver slammed the truck back toward the boy on the bicycle, forcing his rising load down. He saw the boy's face flash by and below, as grim and clear as if the boy had his nose to the broad windshield.

Kurtz raced by the truck and felt its heat as he passed. He made it two-thirds of the way through the turn and then his bike completely lost traction on the gravel and he corrected and steered off the road. He hit the small berm and was airborne, tumbling as he flew. He pushed his bike from him and tucked his head and instinctively pulled his arms over him. He drew his knees to his stomach and tried to remember if there was any glass in his knapsack.

For all of the bad things about the inadvertent design of No Bakes Hill, there were a few miraculously placed advantages. First, the turn itself was not at the dead bottom of the hill.

Kurtz was sailing through the air, losing altitude and approaching the foliaged, sloping, continuation of the hill. He hit the leaves and low bushes and rolled through them. That section of the hill was always mucky because water running down the road never even tried to make the turn. It just flowed along the same path Kurtz was taking, percolating into the soft soil where it could.

The straps on the boy's knapsack ripped free and the contents flew out.

He rolled through several more low bushes, partially rolled and partially slid through the muddy stream at the base of the hill, and rolled part way up the other side before he stopped.

Kurtz lay still for a moment and then he opened his eyes and he could tell that he was on his back, head downward, with his arms and legs spread. He stared at the sky and listened to Alan and Roger and Cavenaugh come crashing down the hill he had just finished flying over.

"Oh shit. Oh shit. Oh shit. Oh shit," he heard Alan chanting as he stumbled ahead.

At last they stood above him.

"Is he dead?" Alan whispered.

They watched his eyes.

They didn't move.

Kurtz couldn't see them very well since he was staring straight up and he didn't care to move his eyes so that he could.

The boys were transfixed, their mouths agape.

He blinked.

"HE BLINKED!" Alan yelled.

A smile crawled across Kurtz's face.

"No shit," he murmured quietly and started to laugh.

At first the laughter was nervous and then the other boys joined in and it became insane. They howled and laughed until they couldn't stand. They clutched their sides and fell to the hillside beside Kurtz. Everyone laughed until they cried and then they laughed harder.

A deep bass voice came from above them. "I'd like to know what the hell's so funny. That boy almost got hisself killed, an' me an' maybe you with 'im."

A man who looked more like a farmer than a trucker stood above them. He was a big man with faded bib overalls and a washed-out red t-shirt. His arms were bigger than any of the boys' thighs and his hands were rough and his fingernails were black and serrated.

"Is his back broke?" he said with anger.

"It could be broke, you know," he added softly as he stepped closer.

The boys stopped laughing. Panic flushed across Kurtz's face. He willed himself out of the forgiving loam and tried to sit up. He could and he did, and then he regained his feet.

He smiled. "You can't break a Kotex©." He looked at all of the scratches on his arms and felt them on his face. Through a v-tear in the knee of his jeans he saw more torn skin. "Might get a little bloody, but. . . ."

The farmer scratched his head and looked back up the hill to the turn. He chuckled quietly. "You ain't gonna believe this, but my brother and me did the same blamed thing when we was pups like you-all." He smiled at each of the boys and then was serious again. "But he broked his right arm in three places. Never could use it real good again. Became left-handed, just as quick as you please. They called him 'New-lefty' the rest of his life."

He looked off away from the boys.

"Lied about his arm. Lied about his age and was killed somewheres in Germany in the last war."

A sadness embraced the man and settled on the boys.

"I'd best be goin'," he said and turned away, hiding his face. "Seein' you kids down here reminded me of when we was kids." He spoke without looking back at them. "I'd best move that truck. Have to creep up that ole bastard hill in first gear now. Might hit the top by dark."

The last thing the boys heard him say was, "Devil's Bend," and then, "Some devil."

They watched him disappear around his truck and then they heard the door slam. The dump truck's engine raced and the truck bucked forward several times and then crept up the hill, the engine roaring, the transmission whining and great clouds of volcanic smoke shooting straight up from the exhaust stacks.

Kurtz was wobbly when he walked. The boys stayed close to him as they picked up the knapsack and sleeping bag and retrieved the various articles strewn through the woods.

"Where's my bike?" he asked.

When they saw it they all fell into uncontrollable laughter again. Both wheels were now oblong and the handlebars were bent back so far that they nearly touched the seat.

Kurtz pushed his bike for a while, the eccentric wheels causing the front and back of the bicycle to raise alternately. He leaned on it as he pushed and it was obvious to the others that while he had suffered no breaks, he was in pain. Finally, and unexpectedly, he swore loudly, lifted up his bike, and threw it into the woods.

"Fuck you," he said, "you let me down when I needed you most."

The other boys were silent.


Freddy went to Will's and they drove out to the quarry.

"We do nice work," Will said as he drove slouched in the seat, his arm out the window. "We lost both our girls to the village idiots."

"With a great car, plenty of beer, and loads of money," Freddy added.

They drove in silence until Freddy turned to Will. "What do ya think our *girls* are going to lose?"

"Yeh, I already thought of that. Junior tells Louise he'll take her to Hollywood and she'll have her clothes off before he finishes the sentence."

Freddy pictured Louise ripping off her clothes.

Then he thought of Beth. And Phillip ripping off her clothes. It wasn't humorous anymore.

"That jerk will lay it on thick with Beth — she doesn't stand a chance. He could tell her he's an orphan and if he doesn't get married within a week the doctors say he'll die of a brain tumor and she'd buy it. And if he doesn't have sex before morning he'll grow an extra eye and all the old ladies and kittens in town will die, too. He could tell her anything as long as he doesn't laugh while he's doing it, and she'll believe it. The sappier the better."

Will smirked. "You're right; she'd believe it," and he thought of Beth crying and taking off her clothing, folding each article neatly. He nearly drove off the rode when Beth leaned forward, reached her arms around behind herself and unfastened her bra, whimpering, "Those poor kittens," as she did.

They drove for a while without speaking.

Will pounded on his steering wheel. "You know what peeves me off?"

Before his friend could answer he continued, "You know whose money they'll be spending tonight? Mine. Because this stupid rust-bucket breaks down and only Lover Boy and his faithful companion are there to fix it. That *really* peeves me off."

Will hit the steering wheel again and then he looked at Freddy, who was laughing to himself.

"What's so funny about that? Your girl's with 'em too."

It was a sobering thought to Freddy.

"You don't want to know what I was laughin' at, Will. You don't want to know. It would give 'peeved-off' new meaning."

"Worse than their spending the money they made fixing my car?"

"Yeh, 'fraid so."

"Great. I can hardly wait."

"Your car wasn't broken, Will."

Will absorbed the thought, kicked it around, and then slammed on his brakes and swerved off the road. "WHAT?" he screamed. "What do you mean, 'my car wasn't broken'? You were with me — it wouldn't start. It was broken," he concluded with finality.

"Freddy. . . ."

"Yeh?"

"They must have sneaked up on us before you tried to start it. They jammed a potato up your exhaust."

Will listened intently, visualizing the episode. When he had it firmly established in his mind, he reviewed it once more. Then he turned red. Freddy thought he was going to rip the steering wheel right out of the car with his trembling, skinny arms.

"THAT DIRTY, SLIMEY, ROTTEN, BASTARD, MOTHER-FUCKING ASSHOLE!! HE HAS MY MONEY! THE MONEY HE STOLE FROM ME, AND HE HAS MY GIRL!!!!"

He was so angry he had begun to confuse who was with which girl. Freddy didn't bother to correct him.

When he calmed down some he said, "I know your first reaction is going to be that I'm kidding, Freddy, but I'm not. Think about what I'm saying before you tell me, 'no'."

Will hesitated for a moment, allowing Freddy time to prepare for his unbelievable idea.

"Let's kill him. No, let's kill them both. I'm serious."

Will turned to Freddy.

Freddy sat silently, as he had been asked to do. There was some appeal to Will's idea.

"We can't do that, Will, but I'd like to."

Freddy started to laugh and then Will joined him.

Will said through his laughter, "Don't think for one minute that because I'm laughing I've ruled out doing it," and they both laughed harder.

Phillip and Junior washed and waxed the coupe. Phillip took off each of the three chrome air cleaners and polished them, setting them on the front seat after he was finished. Junior took a whisk broom and swept out the front and back floors and ran a cloth over the upholstery and the side panels. While he did that, Phillip polished the chrome, finned valve covers and the chrome fuel block. By the time Junior was done, he had also buffed the chrome generator cover and the chrome handle to the oil dip-stick. The shining metal contrasted nicely with the bright red engine block.

Junior asked from the back seat as he swept, "If you had to, which would you choose, your car or the most gorgeous girl in the world?"

He was surprised when Phillip didn't answer right away.

Phillip wasn't thinking of 'the most gorgeous girl in the world', he was thinking of Beth. "Very weird," was all he said because he didn't shout out, "My car!" as he always did.

Junior thought he was talking about him and laughed. "Not too weird, just sex starved. I'm getting in Little Louise's pants tonight."

Phillip answered absently, "Think they'll fit?"

"Will what fit?"

Phillip snapped the rag he was using to shine the chrome. The end cracked where a fly rested on the louvered hood, sending fly parts into the air. He examined where the insect had been. "Just goes to show ya — sit on your ass and think for too long and you get your ass blasted. You gotta keep movin'."

He blew moist breath onto the spot and then polished it.

"What time we pickin' 'em up?" Junior asked.

"Later."

He climbed out from the back seat. "Thanks for the info. Just thought I'd ask."

Once again the sleeping bags and most of the supplies were mounded in the forge shed. It was now late enough that there was no one swimming at the quarry, and from the bottles and trash the boys figured that it had been a busy afternoon.

"Think any fine young tits fell out of their bathing suits today?" Kurtz asked dreamily.

"Remember when that happened to Penney Holter?" Roger said.

The boys were standing outside of the forge, watching as Cavenaugh tied a small piece of metal to the cord. He knotted it several times and then looked up at Roger. "You talk like you were there when it happened."

"No, but I heard about it. I heard it was great. Those big babies just flopped right out as big as you please."

Cavenaugh stood and put his arm on Roger's shoulder. "And you don't recall who told you about it?"

Roger answered, embarrassed, "Oh yeh, sorry. I forgot."

That *definitely* had Kurtz's attention. "You saw them? Wow! I'd give my left nut to do that!"

"You *have* a left nut?" Roger taunted. "You don't even have a *right* nut." He thought for a moment and then added, "I bet you look through the key hole and watch your sister undress."

Kurtz smiled. "I do. Boy, have her tits grown."

Cavenaugh turned away in disgust and started toward the quarry. "You are one perverted individual. "Do you watch your *mother* too?"

Kurtz was still smiling. "Well, I used to, but my dad put the key in the hole."

"I don't want to know how your father found out you were watching your mother," Roger groaned.

Kurtz wasn't finished. "I bumped against the door when I was spyin' on them one night."

"Doing it?" Alan asked, more incredulous than Roger.

"Doin' *somethin*: I can't say I know exactly what it was, but it didn't look like much fun to me." Kurtz looked at his listeners. "I could tell you guys *plenty*. But I'm gonna save it 'til tonight. Suffer."

He caught Alan's eye and added. "I can even tell you somethin' about your sister, Alan. Somethin' I *know* you don't know."

Alan glared at his tormentor. "Fuck you. Your mom wears combat boots."

"At least I have one."

Roger joined in with, "Well Kurtz, my boy, your mom sucks big donkey dicks."

"Yeh, Roger, well, your ole lady sucks herself."

The boys lapsed into silence, picturing the acts they had just heard described.

Alan watched Kurtz's mom, a skinny woman with frizzy hair, sitting beneath a donkey with something the size of a Louisville Slugger pounding in and out of her mouth. Then he remembered about what Kurtz had said about his sister. With effort he turned his imagination to Roger's mother. First he saw her lifting her own breasts to her mouth and then he had her contorted with her head between her legs.

"YOU GUYS GET THE CORD?" an older boy shouted from above, in front of the shorter derrick. It was Freddy and someone was with him.

"YEH, THANKS!" Cavenaugh answered. "WE'VE GOT IT WITH US," and he held up the ball of cord with the weight attached.

Freddy made a circle with his first finger and his thumb and held the sign aloft.

"I guess we got company," Kurtz added.

None of the boys would admit it but they were glad they weren't at the quarry alone.

"YOU GUYS SLEEPIN' OUT?" Roger called up to them and then was embarrassed because high school guys didn't 'sleep out'. They slept in.

Alan and Cavenaugh and Kurtz knew what the answer would be, but they hoped just the same.

"NAW, I DON'T THINK SO," Freddy answered.

"WELL YOU'RE WELCOME TO IF YOU WANT," Roger said, trying to escape his embarrassment.

"What are you, a homo?" Kurtz chided.

The two boys at the top of the quarry moved to the edge and sat, their legs over the wall.

Cavenaugh looked to the side and recognized Will's car. "HEY WILL," he yelled.

Will didn't answer, but Freddy did for him, "WILL'S A LITTLE DEPRESSED. I TOLD HIM ABOUT THE POTATO."

"SORRY," Cavenaugh answered.

Freddy cupped his hands around his mouth and called down to them, "HEY, IS THAT ALAN WASTERLY AND KURTZ DOWN THERE WITH YOU?"

"YEH, IT'S US," the two answered in unison.

Then, Kurtz, irritated that Freddy didn't recognize him, yelled back, "YOU EXPECTING IT TO BE KING KONG AND MIGHTY MOUSE?"

"VERY FUNNY; HOW COME YOUR SISTERS GO FOR THE DUMB AND GREASY TYPE?"

Alan flinched when he understood what they were alluding to, while Kurtz merely shook his head and muttered, "Take off her clothes and you got a great body. Open her brain and there's nothin'."

Freddy and Will watched the boys drag the raft down from the far end of the landing and then load the cord and paddles onto it.

"Do you ever wish you were a kid again?" Freddy asked Will.

Will was watching the boys, too. "Yeh, I wish it all the time. I don't know why I was in such a flaming rush to grow up." He thought about it and then continued, "I guess I pictured myself with some hot rod like Phillip's and a bunch of hot babes all over me. Ever since I heard that Durskin — you know the guy who was in our junior high home room — ever since I heard that after he moved he became really cool and the girls just killed to get near him, I figured there'd be hope for me, too."

Freddy laughed. "Dumpy Durskin got popular? I never heard that. Man, that guy deserved it. I never knew anybody more goofy lookin'. What'd he do, get in an accident and get a new face or somethin'?"

Will was serious. "No, his father came into a lot of money and he got some clothes and stuff and a car and everybody just started seeing him as an interesting guy, I guess."

Freddy laughed and thought about his father getting a lot of money. "My dad would buy me lots of Bibles and a maybe if I got lucky, a ticket to Disneyland."

Immediately, both boys started thinking about Annette Funicello.

When Will said, "Boy I'd like to marry her," Freddy knew exactly who he meant.

"Yeh, when she says, "Annette!" all I hear her say is, "Come to Hollywood, Freddy, I'm waiting for you!"

"Gheez, you sound like Louise."

Both boys sank back into their depression.

The raft bobbed in the middle of the quarry. Water occasionally lapped over the sinking corner and washed in a semi-circle across the parched boards. Kurtz stood on the low corner, his shoes off and lumped in the center of the raft with his filthy socks. The boys had stacked their paddles beside Kurtz's shoes.

Cavenaugh was untangling the weighted end of the cord. "I forgot we have to knot this."

Roger stared at the ball. "There's got to be an easier way." He turned his gaze to Kurtz. "How tall are you?"

"Fuck you." Kurtz did not like his height discussed.

"No, seriously, I need to know."

Kurtz answered with surly resignation, "Five foot. Exactly."

"Looks more like four-eleven to me, but what's an inch?"

Cavenaugh understood the concept before Roger had a chance to explain. "Good idea. Kurtz, stand over here by me."

The short boy advanced across the raft to where Cavenaugh stood. Cavenaugh's corner started to sink and he noticed and ordered, "Shift" and moved to the center of his side.

Roger abandoned his corner and moved opposite Cavenaugh and Roger. The raft ducked back and forth a few times and finally steadied. Cavenaugh tossed his folded paper and the pencil stub to Roger.

"Mark every ten feet like I was doin' before. Five foot marks would fill the paper in a minute."

Cavenaugh let the weight slide until it touched the water. He held the string at Kurtz's height, dipped with the string to the water and proclaimed, "Five feet." He went to rise and realized there was no way to do it and still keep track of the string.

Kurtz laughed. "Plan B." He pulled a wrapped knot of bubble gum from his pocket. "I bet it marks the line." He handed it to Cavenaugh, smiling stupidly as he did, saying, "Saved by the boy on the flying bike."

Cavenaugh started the process again, this time nicking the line with the edge of Kurtz's chewing gum. Sure enough, there was a thin pink line on the cord. Cavenaugh looked at the line and then Kurtz. "I like you, Kurtzy, I really do," and began measuring and calling out.

The light line wasn't nearly as tiring as the rope with the heavy weight had been. It wasn't long before they passed the one hundred foot mark and were halfway through the next hundred.

"One-fifty," Alan sing-songed. "Break time."

"Amen," Kurtz answered. "'The yard stick is tired of standing." He sank to the raft.

Cavenaugh took the paper from Roger and examined the marks while Roger moved to the side of the raft and kneeled, cupped his hands, and peered into the water.

"Anybody home?" he asked.

"Just us monsters," Kurtz answered in a gruff, monstrous voice.

"Real funny," Alan said and shook his head. "If it's so funny, stick your foot in and leave it 'til we start measurin' again, Kurtz."

Kurtz crawled quickly to the edge and jammed his foot in, wetting the leg of his jeans as he did. "Give me a real challenge next time."

The boys sat quietly, Kurtz waving his foot slowly through the water. "Movin' target," he mumbled and leaned back on his arms, his hands propped behind him. Just then there was a splash near them.

Kurtz jerked his leg from the water so fast he fell backward screaming, "WHOA, SHIT!"

The other three boys clustered in the middle of the raft.

Two seconds didn't pass before Freddy shouted down, "SORRY YOU GUYS, IT SEEMED KINDA FUNNY AT THE TIME."

All four of the younger boys gave him the finger simultaneously, shouting variously, "FUCK YOU! YOU SHIT! THANKS, SHIT-HEAD," and another, "FUCK YOU!"

The boys went back to measuring, this time Roger dropping the line, Cavenaugh marking the paper, Alan worrying, and Kurtz remaining the reference point.

"Finally found something you could measure up to," Roger quipped.

"So funny I forgot to laugh," Kurtz answered and then went into a crouch.

"Knock it off, Kurtz," Roger ranted, whereupon Kurtz rose to his tip-toes.

"Probably closer to five feet," Roger muttered and went back to calling off numbers.

The shadows crawled across the still quarry water toward the boys. A cool breeze slid down the granite walls and puffed along, raising tiny waves as it did. The boys had a small 'whooping party' when they passed two hundred feet and then lapsed into solemn anticipation as they approached three hundred. At the three hundred mark, the ball of cord now the size of a tennis ball, the boys became frightened as each began to visualize how much black, cold water they were floating above.

One by one they whispered fearful remarks.

"Jesus H. Christ," Kurtz said with reverence. "I don't think this thing has a bottom."

A long, low, "Shit," was all Alan could say.

Cavenaugh spoke quietly, "I never dreamed . . ." and left his thoughts unfinished.

Roger was calling out the marks and his voice kept getting more and more quiet.

Finally, at three hundred and forty-two, he whispered, "That's it," and indicated the slack line.

Every boy said, "Wow," and lapsed into silence, awed by the limp cord, thinking of the weight so far below them.

Roger was the first to return to normal speech.

"I want you guys to look at something and tell me what you see." As he spoke he was pulling the slack out of the line. He stopped and the boys studied the cord.

"I'll be," Cavenaugh said, and Alan added, "I thought something was wrong when I looked at it before, but I couldn't figure out what wasn't right."

Kurtz was confused. "I give up, Wonder-Minds, what's the deal?"

"It's the line, it's slanted," Roger said.

"It's slanting toward the landing wall,"

Phillip laughed. "Naw, I want that soft, giving flesh."

"Mmmmm," Junior agreed. "Yeh, I'd like a big fat titty," and held his hands up and moved his fingers as if they were squeezing breasts.

Phillip didn't say anything at first. He attempted to come to terms with the anger he felt toward Junior. It had flared within him as he watched Junior pretend to touch bare flesh.

"You make it sound so goddamned crude, man. Don't you have any feelings?"

Junior stared at Phillip. *He's not my friend,* he thought. *He used to be, but he's not anymore. I'm sick of his shit.*

"Yeh," was all he said, then, "I'm gonna go clean up. See ya later," and turned and walked away.

Phillip watched Junior swagger off.

He coiled Old Man Horvath's hose, closed the coupe's doors, looked one last time at the gleaming car and went through the back door of the garage to the concrete block shower stall that he used. It was between his room and the office and it was about two feet square with a moldy curtain and grey muck growing in the corners and climbing the walls. The water was seldom more than tepid and the floor was covered with a slippery film. Above the showerhead Phillip had stuck a pin-up from a magazine. He had named the girl Lu Lu.

He undressed outside of the stall, then reached in and adjusted the water. He waited until a thin cloud of mist escaped above the shower curtain. He stepped in and examined Lu Lu. She was puckered from the months of showers she had endured; her bottom half nearly dissolved. She smiled down at Phillip, her eyes following his as he washed his body.

"Tell me, Lu Lu, am I goin' to get anywhere with this *girl?*" He surprised himself when he didn't say 'broad'.

"I mean, is this clean young thing gonna fall for me, or is she gonna wake up to the facts when I open my big mouth an' say somethin' stupid again?"

He washed his back and then picked up a scrub-brush from the floor and scoured his hands and his fingernails.

Lu Lu admired his body but kept her mouth shut.

"You know, Lu Lu, you got a great body, but that ain't everything."

He examined her from the waist down. She had one hand over her soggy pubic area and one leg tilted inward.

"I got bad news, Lu Lu. I think you got crotch-rot. You should get out in the sun more often."

He reached up and tore down her picture. It came easily, the wet paper separating beneath her nose. Phillip balled up the mess and threw it out over the curtain. When he looked back up he realized she was still staring at him. "Sorry," he said to the top of her head and finished his shower.

She watched his ass as he slapped wet-footed across the garage floor and out of sight.

Beth stepped out of her evening shower, took her robe off of the porcelain hook and slipped her arms into the sleeves. She wrapped one towel around her head and took another thick towel and dried her face and her legs. The terry robe absorbed the water from the remainder of her body.

"Hurry up in there, honey, I'm cleaning today," her mother called and Beth answered, "Clean the bathroom downstairs; I just got started."

"Are you going to Louise's, did you say?"

Beth lied easily, "Yes, mother, I told you that. She invited me last week."

She listened as her mother, apparently satisfied, descended the stairs.

Beth wiped a vertical swath down the mirror and examined her steamy face. Her robe parted as she bent forward and she felt the air against her body. Beth stepped back, allowing her robe to open farther.

She checked what she saw.

*Long neck*

*Small chest. Well, smaller than Louise's.*

*Stomach — youth flat.*

She put her hands on her belly. It was firm even though she did not exercise. She thought of her mother's body and wondered how long it would be before she looked like that.

*Yuck.*

She yanked her robe closed, but not before she looked below her waist. As she tied the robe she slipped her hand under it and brushed across the soft damp hair, wondering as she did if she would ever allow a boy to touch her there.

Louise had told her that it was like floating in a dream, but Beth couldn't imagine any of Louise's boyfriends producing dreams.

*They must have mechanic's hands,* she thought and then realized who she was going out with. She thought of Phillip's hands. They were strong, and in spite of the fact that he worked on cars, they were clean. His fingers weren't broad and they weren't too thin. And his wrists weren't blunt.

She had watched Phillip's hands the first night he had driven all of them home. He always moved them slowly, no matter what he was doing. He caressed the steering wheel, he moved his hand lightly over the shifter knob, and she had even felt him gently release the bottle opener when he handed it to her. At first she thought he was showing off, but after a while she realized he wasn't, and further, no boy would think to do it that way.

'Showing off' usually entailed some kind of destruction or crude remark. Freddy resorted to a sexual comment. Will would dive in the dark without checking for The Devil's Club.

Her thoughts about Will took her back to the quarry and she wondered what had happened to him the day he dove so poorly. Freddy seemed convinced that Will had imagined his problems, but she wasn't certain.

Last year, she spent an afternoon with Widow Orlap as part of a project for her church youth group and she found the old lady to be interesting, yet mysterious. She had heard one of her friends at school say that Widow Orlap was a witch, but another had disagreed, saying her grandmother told her that the widow had 'Indian magic' and that she was really an Indian — the only 'full blood' in York County.

Indians had once been common all through Maine, Beth knew that, but they had been decimated by diseases hundreds of years ago.

Beth was surprised to discover that while she was thinking these things her hand had lingered and that she was still moving it lightly over the inside of her legs.

Embarrassed, she took her other hand and switched off the light. Beth leaned against the bathroom door and her free hand stole deftly to her neck and then settled to her breast.

She stood and thought of Phillip and touched her body. She was older and Phillip was with her and they weren't in Maine anymore. He had on shorts and she smiled at the thought of Phillip Henshaw in short pants. *I'll bet his legs are beautiful,* she thought.

They walked along a beach on some island that was very warm and the sand wasn't the mish-mash of pebbles and brown quartz that it was in Maine. It was white and it was fine and it was hot under their feet as they walked. Overhead, palm trees stretched their fronds over them and the sky was crystalline. And the water — it was the green of young ferns and it was so clear that Beth saw fish shadowing through it.

Phillip spoke to her as they walked. He no longer sounded as if he were from Maine. He had the crisp diction of a hero and he laughed lightly at the things she said and he stopped from time to time and lifted her lips carefully to his. He smelled of the sun and his eyes were happy and his teeth shone when he smiled.

Phillip was strong and his body was tanned, his muscles sharp, hard ridges, and the hair on his arms bleached from the sun. The hair on his arms. She ran her hand over it and it was her hair and her hand was between her legs and her fingers were wet.

Louise was not in the mood to take a shower for a hick date with a local bozo. She changed her clothes, added a touch of perfume, and dropped into a comfortable chair in the living room, where she read of movie stars and waited to be picked up.

Phillip stopped in front of Junior's house. The boy was sitting on a case of long-neck Steelman's, finishing what Phillip hoped was his first bottle. Junior stood and brought the case around to the trunk of the car. By then, Phillip had the trunk open. Junior hefted the case in and commented, "We gonna potato some cars tonight? I thought we was goin' down to Old Orchard?"

There was a folded army blanket at the side of the trunk and beside it was the bag of potatoes. Junior assumed that Phillip would have left the potatoes behind. He was a nut about carrying anything in his car that he didn't need.

"Naw, I don't see us screwin' around with anybody tonight, but a potato can come in handy from time to time. You never know."

Junior gave him a confused smirk and went around to the side and got into the car.

"I watched you drivin' up the street. She looks sharp."

"Yeh," Phillip answered and adjusted his new rearview mirror. He ran his hand through his hair and pointed to the glove box.

Junior took his cue and got out a fresh pack of cigarettes.

"Mind if I have one, too?"

Phillip looked sideways at Junior. "What a mooch. You were at the store, why didn't you get a pack?"

Junior rolled down his window and blew his gum out. "Ya know, I *walk* to the store, buy us a *case* of beer with my last dime, *carry* it home, and *you're* pissed because I didn't have enough dough to spring for a pack of smokes for me. Nice. Sometimes you take the fuckin' cake."

Phillip had his hand out for the pack of cigarettes. When he finally felt them, he smiled. "Yeh, okay. Take a couple fags. You earned 'em."

He leaned over the steering wheel and banged the coupe through the gears. "I guess you don't have gas money."

Junior had taken back the pack and was shaking two, then four cigarettes out. He stuck three in the front pocket of his shirt. "You guessed right." He lit a cigarette and sat back in the seat, his arm out the window, the sill pressed against his bicep to make it look bigger. Junior assumed that girls liked flat distended muscles.

He whistled at a girl walking on the sidewalk. She smiled, but Junior could see that she was watching the car.

"This is some pussy-wagon."

Phillip laughed. "It's a pretty car for pretty people, Junior. We don't let ugly folks ride in it."

"Like Freddy and Will?"

"That was an exception — we were stealin' their girls."

"An' gettin' their money."

"Yeh, an' gettin' their money."

Junior launched into what was bothering him. "Ya know, *we* potatoed the car, *we* brought it to the garage — I did, actually — and *we* pulled off a big one together. *So*," he drew in a breath, "how much did *we* get?"

They rode in silence.

Junior cleared his throat.

Phillip downshifted as they pulled up to Louise's house. He stopped and stared out through the windshield.

Junior didn't move.

Phillip chewed on his lower lip for a moment and then gave a slow look to Junior.

"We made ten bucks each."

He was lying, Junior knew that, but it was also about twice what he thought he would ultimately get — if he got anything.

"Hot shit!" and he smiled.

They continued sitting in the car.

At last, Phillip turned to his friend. "Aren't you forgettin' somethin'?"

Junior was genuinely puzzled. He checked the zipper on his pants and then he rubbed under his nose, finally tilting back and facing Phillip, asking, "Big green hanger?"

Phillip laughed. "No, you dumb shit. *Louise.*"

Junior looked at her front door. "She's not here yet. I guess she's not ready. We got time."

"Go fuckin' *get* her, you moron. This is a class act tonight. You don' let a broad walk down to the car alone, you *escort* 'em." As he finished he made a sweeping motion with his arm as if to indicate his hand on a girl's shoulder.

"Yeh, yeh, yeh."

Halfway to the front door Junior turned back to Phillip who leaned across the seat to see what he wanted.

"Does this mean we use *clean* rubbers?"

He didn't wait for Phillip's reaction. Laughing, he continued toward the door. It opened before he got to it, and Louise stepped out.

"Aren't you the gentleman."

She ran lightly up to him and grabbed his arm. "Let's have some *fun* tonight."

"Yeh, let's." *Your mouth and my prick. Sounds like fun to me.* Junior chuckled as he opened the door for her. "Slide across, we'll get in the back when we pick up Beth."

She slid across the seat, farther than she really needed to, and put her hand on Phillip's leg, squeezing it as she said, "Hi, Phillip. Aren't you all dolled up."

She took the sleeve of his shirt between her fingers. "Fresh t-shirt and everything."

Phillip flushed. He wanted to push her right out of his car past Junior, onto the ground, and then roar away in a cloud of burning rubber.

"Fuck you," he mumbled.

Louise smiled, moved her hand closer to his crotch, squeezed again and turned to Junior. "Boy, is he grumpy tonight. I'll bet Beth can fix that."

Junior had his arm out the window.

Junior couldn't look at Louise or speak, he was pissed about her hand on Phillip. Then Louise scooted closer to him and put her hand on *his* leg. "Let's drive to Hollywood. Let's really get away from here."

He muttered, "I'm ready."

"But you don't have a *car.* You have to get *more* ready, Junior. You have to get *really* ready."

She was working wonders with her fingers as she spoke and before Junior knew what had happened, he was *really* ready. And then, as in a nightmare, they stopped to get Beth and she was already at the curb, waiting nervously.

*Well now shit, how do I hide this throbbin' monster?*

He snatched Louise's purse and said, "I'll take this for you. Let's get in the back."

He held her purse in front of him as he passed Beth and Phillip and climbed over the tilted seat to join Louise.

"My oh my, Junior, you *are* excited to be a good boy," she mocked and took her purse back after she and Junior were settled.

Both Phillip and Beth watched the two.

"What don't we know?" Beth asked.

"Plenty," Phillip responded, guiding Beth into the car. He closed her door and ran around the front to his side.

He revved the engine twice and they were off, the rear tires spinning and shrieking.

"Don't! Don't! Don't!" Beth pleaded. "We're right in front of the Andersons — they know my parents really well."

Phillip eased off the gas and a police car turned onto their road two blocks ahead. As it approached, Beth shrank down in her seat. "Phillip, they can't stop us, they just *can't.* "

Her plea wasn't completed before the policeman in the cruiser turned on the red light in the center of his roof and motioned for the coupe to pull over.

"Safety check," Junior told the girls. "Don't worry."

"Don't worry?" Beth hissed. "We're *one* block from my house." She turned back to Junior and gave him a filthy look.

The policeman was at Phillip's window.

"This being an older vehicle, sir, I'd like to be certain that it is being maintained properly."

He looked at each of the four in the car, his attention drawn to Louise and Beth.

"Turn on your headlights please, and when I walk to the back of your vehicle, please depress your brake pedal twice."

A car passed them and Beth swore softly, "Shit," and then corrected herself, "I mean 'shoot', that was the Cassidys. Did they look, you guys?"

"No," Louise answered, "everybody just drives right by police cars with flashing lights. It's really kind of boring."

In spite of her apparent attitude, Louise was relieved that it had not happened near her home.

"Horn, please."

The policeman was back at Phillip's window.

Phillip jammed the horn and let it blare.

"That's enough, *thank you.*"

The officer looked in again at Beth and Louise.

"I am going to give you a verbal warning, Mr. Henshaw. I believe I saw you operating this vehicle in an unsafe manner, earlier. If that happens again, we'll impound this vehicle and give it a thorough inspection. Do you understand, Mr. Henshaw?"

Phillip glared at the policeman. It was Thorton Pikes, two years older than Phillip and a professional asshole. A bully when he was younger, and then when everyone else had grown taller than he, a whining tattle-tale.

"I gotcha," Phillip answered, trying to sound offhand.

"No, Mr. Henshaw — *I got you.* "

No one in the car spoke as Pikes went back to the cruiser, switched off the red light and drove off.

"Can we get out of here, Phillip?" Beth asked and added, "Please — and drive slowly."

They made it to Route One without an incident, Phillip quiet as he nursed his temper. Louise talked non-stop and Junior relaxed and looked at the scenery. Suddenly Junior sat forward.

"I don't believe it."

"What's that?" Louise asked.

"We've been in the sex-mobile for half an hour and no one has had a beer."

Phillip pulled over without speaking and got out of the car. He walked around to the trunk, retrieved an armful of bottles, and brought them back. He handed them around and finally, to Beth's relief, he smiled.

"Let's drink to my very good friend, Officer Thorton, Asshole, Pikes."

"And to his girlfriend, ole man Griffin's pony," Junior amended.

"And ole man Griffin's sheep," Phillip joined.

"And Mrytle Mirrata," Louise said, referring to the fattest girl in the high school.

"And The Doll Man," Junior added.

They drove to the beach, toasting every misfortunate within twenty miles, including all those with brain-damage, acne, thick glasses, bad luck, advanced old age, and halitosis.

"I think Gina Meirs eats dead rats," Junior said, holding his nose. "But here's to Gina — and her rats."

Beth's contributions to the expanding list were always inane. She toasted dust kitties, nose hairs, mud puddles, and knot holes.

Louise consistently rolled her eyes when Beth spoke.

Freddy and Will left but said they'd be back later with various 'supplies'.

The younger boys went back down to the forge. They spread out their sleeping bags and ate what was left of the candy. Cavenaugh sat in the broken chair and Alan and Roger reclined on their respective sleeping bags. Kurtz sat on his and examined his increasing collection of scrapes and scratches.

"I think I'm runnin' outta blood," he said as he pulled at a scab on his elbow.

Roger ignored Kurtz and turned to Cavenaugh. "Okay, we have a pretty good idea of the depth, now what do we do about it?"

Cavenaugh tilted the chair farther back until it touched the wall. He rested his head on the boards behind him and clucked with his tongue. "Well, nobody's going to swim down that far, that's for sure. And I think we'll be old before what's in there lets us see it. *If* there's somethin' in there, that is."

Kurtz looked up. "Maybe there was somethin' and now it's gone. It went away. Swam away. Flew away. Who knows."

He was still not considered a part of the discussion.

Cavenaugh slammed the chair forward. He had forgotten about the broken front leg and when the chair pitched to the side, he landed on top of Alan.

"HOMO!" Kurtz screamed and laughed. "Homo attack in the forge shed!"

Cavenaugh rolled to the side. "A picture. We need to take a picture."

"Yeh," Kurtz said, "we'll just send down a yearbook announcement and wait." He pretended to be reading the invitation. "Pictures will be taken Monday through Thursday of this week. Please wear your best dragon skin and comb your scales." He laughed at his own humor.

"We build an underwater camera!" Roger exclaimed.

"Right," Cavenaugh responded and rubbed his ear. "Will has a darkroom. He takes pictures for the high school newspaper. I bet he'd help us."

Alan wanted to be involved but he hated to bring up bad news. "You guys, I think he quit the newspaper."

"And I bet he threw away his darkroom and completely forgot how to make pictures," Kurtz taunted. "You're a dumb shit, Alan. Do you practice?"

Through the early evening Roger and Cavenaugh tried to come up with a simple way to build an underwater camera. Alan made suggestions but they were usually too far beyond the boys' finances.

"Film is expensive enough, you guys. We gotta keep it cheap," Cavenaugh told them.

Finally, Kurtz couldn't stand anymore of the discussion. "I say we wait until Freddy and Will come back. They probably have an idea. In the mean time, let's talk about sex."

"Hey wait." It was Roger. "Before you start bullshitting everybody, look at this."

He reached into his pack and pulled out an object that impressed the others immediately.

"When did you make that?" Kurtz asked.

It was a pipe gun. Roger had taped a pipe, threaded on one end, to a pistol grip he had obviously made from a piece of scrap wood. The 'barrel' was held snuggly to the wood by a wound mass of electrician's tape. The threaded end of the pipe was at the butt of the gun, and there was a metal cap screwed onto it. Drilled into the center of the cap was a hole the width of a pencil lead.

"Does it work? Have you fired it?" Kurtz asked, not waiting for the answer to his first question.

Roger basked in the glory of his gun. He retrieved a smaller bundle from the pack and unwrapped it. There were assorted firecrackers, about a dozen ball bearings and a wad of Kleenex.

"We do it like so," Roger answered the unasked question, taking one of the small firecrackers.

"Don't use a 'ladyfinger'," Kurtz begged, "use that cherry bomb."

Cavenaugh had not seen the large red firecracker with the stick-like fuse. It was the size of a large, malted milk ball. "Holy shit, Roger, won't a cherry bomb blow up the pipe?"

"I don't know. That's why we're going to use one of these little guys."

He threaded the fuse of the small firecracker through the hole in the end cap which he had unscrewed and now held in the other hand. Twice the fuse bent and then it passed smoothly through. He grabbed the protruding fuse, snugged the firecracker up to the female end of the cap and then guided the firecracker into the threaded end of the pipe. When it was in, he secured the cap, tightening it firmly with one hand while he held the wooden grip in the other. Then he put the weapon gently onto his sleeping bag and picked up a bearing. He wrapped it carefully with one layer of tissue.

"Makes a tighter fit and the ball won't fall out if you accidentally tip the barrel down."

The others watched in awe. Kurtz was so jealous he could barely stand it.

The inside of the pipe was a little larger than the diameter of a pencil.

Kurtz studied the barrel and then looked at the cherry bomb. "Hey, you couldn't fit the cherry bomb in if you wanted to."

Roger didn't answer, but he did hold up an extension. It was a short joint which widened considerably in diameter on the end of which was a screw-plug. There was a hole drilled in its center also and the hole was large enough to accommodate the thick fuse of the larger firework. Once screwed onto the butt of the existing gun barrel, it appeared that the extension would do the job, holding the cherry bomb snuggly.

"Oh," was all Kurtz said.

Roger smiled and tamped the covered bearing down into the barrel of the gun, using a smooth stick he had brought along. He stood and held the weapon as if it were a real pistol, pointing the foot-long barrel at a window.

"POW!" Alan shouted.

"You have matches?" Kurtz asked.

Roger smiled and went out through the door.

"I got a bottle," Alan shouted and ran back in to get his just-finished soda.

Roger led them down the dirt road by the railroad tracks to a talus pile. It was approximately ten feet in diameter, made up of chips of granite and five feet high. Alan set his bottle up in the center.

Roger said, "Wait a minute," and searched the area. "Isn't there an old sign around here somewhere?"

Alan ran off and came back with a stop sign.

"Put it up there behind the bottle, Alan. Prop it up. I'm not sure how accurate this beast is gonna be."

Roger paced back ten feet from the sign and bottle. The others crowded beside and behind him. He took out a small box of matches and handed them to Cavenaugh. "When I say, 'okay', you light it. Okay?"

Kurtz laughed.

Roger ignored him and continued with his instructional lecture, "'The important thing is to hold your arm straight and turn your head away after you aim so it doesn't blow shit in your eye from the fuse hole."

Kurtz laughed again. "Great idea — then you only blow out your eardrum. You're some brilliant, Roger."

Roger turned the other side of his head toward Kurtz so the boy could see the wad of tissue jutting protectively from that ear.

"Big deal." was Kurtz's response.

Roger looked at Cavenaugh. The older boy had a match in his hand, poised.

"Ready?"

Cavenaugh nodded.

"OKAY!"

Cavenaugh scraped the match against the side of the box. The match flared and he moved it, cupped, to the fuse at the end of the gun. As soon as it began to fizz and spark, Cavenaugh stepped back from Roger and the hissing gun.

Roger closed one eye, sighted as well as he could down the barrel lumped with black tape, and then turned his head to the side. At first he turned his unblocked ear to the gun, remembered, and turned quickly to the other side.

At the instant the burning fuse reached the end of the metal cap and disappeared inside, a chipmunk stuck his head out from a shadow in the pile of granite. He was a foot to the right of the sign and sightly below it.

Alan saw the animal and yelled and threw himself at Roger's arm.

"DON'T!"

The firecracker exploded and smoke poured out of the gun. A thin trail wisped from the fuse hole.

Alan had knocked the gun out of Roger's hand. Roger swore and turned to Alan.

The bottle was untouched.

The young boy ran to the pile of rocks. He started digging madly where the chipmunk had been.

Cavenaugh ran up to him but he kept throwing rocks aside, burrowing into the granite.

Kurtz examined the sign. "You can stop the 'preserve nature' act, Alan. He hit the sign here," and pointed to a fresh chip and a dent near the top of the 'P'.

Roger and Cavenaugh ran their fingers over the dent.

Roger smiled.

"Not bad," Cavenaugh said.

Kurtz looked closely at the pock-mark. "Especially for a whimpy firecracker. I bet it would go all the way through with a cherry bomb. Can I shoot it?"

Each of the boys took a turn with the gun and a series of small firecrackers. Cavenaugh missed the sign completely, but Kurtz took two last-second steps forward and shattered the bottle with his shot. Alan was last and by the time he did shoot it was almost dark. He insisted that while he aimed the others throw rocks at the pile so the chipmunk would stay hidden. After his minor explosion they found a dent at the corner of the sign.

Cavenaugh carried the gun and turned it over in his hand as he walked. "You know, this pipe isn't real thick. I bet a cherry bomb would split it open."

"And blow off your fingers so there's nothing but bloody, oozing stumps. They'd never heal, just get pussy and gross. Every now and then a bone would poke through. And then how would you make the girls happy?"

After he finished with his description, Kurtz ran around in the last, weak light with one hand in the air, the fingers bent to hide them, screaming, "MY FINGERS! MY FINGERS!! THINK OF THE MILLIONS OF UNHAPPY GIRLS!!"

Cavenaugh watched Kurtz run in and out of the gloom. "I think he's right — about blowing off your fingers."

He handed the gun back to Roger.

Freddy and Will pulled in by the forge shed. Will honked the horn twice and raced the engine before he shut it off. The boys inside the shed had seen the approaching lights but they weren't sure who it was until they heard the horn.

"It's them," Alan told the others, his voice betraying his relief.

"Really, Alan? I was afraid the monster had learned to drive, stolen a car, and was coming here to run over us." Kurtz shook his head but no one saw him since they had switched off their flashlights when they first saw the headlights.

The boys spilled out of the shed to meet Will and Freddy. The two older boys were at the sedan's opened trunk. They were wrestling out two bales of hay.

"Hey!" Kurtz yelled to them.

"Yeh, hay," Will answered.

They took turns carrying them and dragging them around and up to the side of the quarry where they knew Phillip would park if he came out. Alan and Kurtz followed the others with their bale. They collapsed onto it when they reached their destination.

"Holy shit, that's heavy," Kurtz said, his breath coming in wheezes.

"Shut the fuck up," Roger whispered. "Do you see where we are?"

Actually Kurtz hadn't thought about it until he saw the bulk of the machinery shed near them.

"Sorry," he whispered back to Will and Freddy. "Fuck you," he turned and whispered to Roger.

The boys crept away from the vicinity of the machinery shed and regrouped at the landing. The raft was still there, flush to the wall.

Phillip and Junior and their girls walked around the honky-tonk section of Old Orchard Beach, riding the rides, shooting at balloons and trying to win Kewpie Dolls and stuffed animals. Junior nearly got into a fight when one of the roustabouts running the ferris wheel winked at Louise. Phillip and Beth pulled Junior away while Louise stood off to the side and watched.

"No fights here, Junior. Anywhere but here. The cops are real assholes and there are some bad gangs of slimeballs that come down from Boston lookin' for trouble. Cool your jets tonight; we're here to have fun." Phillip put his arm on Junior's shoulder when he spoke, and he massaged some of the anger out of his neck as they walked away from the ride and the leering, muscled, worker.

"Are you two queer?" Louise asked and laughed. "If we can't ride the Ferris wheel, can we go back out on the pier?"

Beth didn't want to go back to the bumping, jostling crowd. "Let's drive down to a stretch of beach where there aren't any people."

Junior looked at Phillip and grinned.

Louise said, "Fine with me," and they went back to the car. Twice, groups of guys with leather coats bumped into either Phillip or Junior and each time there was nearly a fight.

When they finally got back to the car, Beth hugged Phillip quickly and said, "Thanks, I know without us girls here you guys would have fought them."

They drove through town, the crowds on the sidewalks admiring the coupe, a few younger boys shouting, "Nice car, man," or "Crank that thing!"

Occasionally, Phillip would rev the engine, but usually he ignored them, pulling Beth closer to him and looking straight ahead as he drove. They were fairly far down the road behind the little cabins lining the beach when a car came up behind them with its bright lights on, illuminating the interior of the coupe in glaring surgical light. The car inched closer until it was on the blue coupe's tail. Phillip kept looking into his mirror, getting nervous and swearing, "Get the fuck off my ass, punks. Wish I had a truck bumper, I'd give 'em a fuckin' brake test."

Finally and in one motion he downshifted, floored the gas, popped the clutch and raced ahead. He barely had time to pull away when he heard the sound of a roaring big-block Chevy with the header pipes open. A '32 chopped sedan blew by Phillip and his friends as if they were parked.

Junior was saying, "Nice fucking car," when he saw three guys stretched out of the sedan's windows, flipping him the finger. "Full 'a assholes," he amended.

"Massachusetts plates," Beth added, thinking somehow it made it less embarrassing to be lunched by an out-of-stater.

Phillip turned down the next t-street leading to the beach. The big coupe rumbled one last time and then was silent after he flipped off the ignition switch. He sat and looked over his steering wheel at the luminous waves cresting at the beach. "Ya know, I *really* don't like this town. Maybe someday it'll drown in its own grease."

He and Beth got out of the car on his side and Junior and Louise followed. They stood at the back of the car and took off their shoes and socks, tossing them into the trunk, then they waited while Phillip reached in to get the blanket and more beer. Just as he was opening the beer case, headlights flashed across the barefoot group.

Louise saw the plates and recognized the car before the others. "It's them."

The chopped sedan revved its engine twice and it was sharp and deafening. The engine died and in the momentary silence Junior went to grab a beer bottle.

Phillip grabbed his arm.

"Not a broken bottle, Junior. We'd end up in jail for sure. Let's see what's botherin' these assholes first."

The doors of the sedan swung open. The headlights were still on so all that they could see were four very large individuals unfolding from the car.

"Well now, shit," Junior said quietly. "I guess we got company. Big company."

The four sauntered over making a semi-circle around the back of Phillip's coupe.

"Pretty car," said an oversized simian. "Kinda slow, but pretty. Which one of you girls owns it?"

He directed his remarks to Beth and Louise.

Another of the intruders saw the beer in the trunk. "You gonna offer us a beer before we beat the shit outta ya, or do we wait until we step over your bloody asses and get it ourselves?"

Phillip scanned them one by one. He turned to the trunk. "Yeh, no problem. I'll get it."

Junior turned to the trunk too. He watched Phillip, amazed. "What the fuck are you doing?" he whispered.

Phillip deftly took two potatoes from the bag and dropped each into a different sock. "Do what I do," he told Junior, sliding him a potato-sock. As Phillip turned back to those awaiting their beers he kept the hand with his creation behind him. He stepped toward them and Junior did also.

"I've thought about it, you guys, and there's just not enough beer for all of us. You'll have to go and get your own."

Phillip had barely finished before the biggest one started moving for him, his fists curled.

Phillip waited calmly, resignation dripping from his demeanor.

The big one reached out to grab him, but Phillip moved to the side, whirled the loaded sock over his head and brought it smartly down onto the other's forehead. The big guy's knees buckled and he dropped without a sound.

Junior couldn't believe it. Now he was excited. Quiet death — it had instant appeal. He brought his potato sock around and advanced on the remaining three. He was awestruck when Phillip dropped another of the punks as easily as he had the first.

"Hey, give me a chance, too," he said, and as he moved to the attack, the two still standing turned and ran back down the street.

"Oh god, are they dead?" Beth begged, sick to her stomach.

"Not likely," Phillip answered and bent to his first victim. "He's okay." He went to the other. "So's he."

He stood and called Junior who had given chase.

Beth said, "Let's get out of here," and went back to the driver's-side door.

Junior came back laughing. "Those guys are runnin' back to Mass.!"

He whistled as he passed the chopped sedan, saying, "Some beautiful," and reached to the exposed spark plug wires and ripped out a handful. "You need some a these?" he asked.

Phillip pitched them into the trunk. "You never know," and indicated to Junior and Louise to get into the back seat of the coupe.

Louise had been observing in wonder. "You guys can be fun to watch."

Phillip backed around and then pulled onto the street. In the shadows he saw the two from Massachusetts returning. He steered toward them and mashed the accelerator. They dove to the side as he flew by.

"Wanna see what The Doll Man's doin'?" Junior asked, laughing, still exhilarated from his brief run.

"Sure," Phillip answered, "the evening's young."

Phillip drove the big coupe through the night. By the time they turned onto Old Quarry Road, the four had emptied the case of beer and subsequently emptied each bottle. Louise had drunk enough to take her beyond the realization that no one was listening to her stories of Hollywood. Beth consumed more beer than she had ever thought of drinking, and Phillip and Junior drank to keep pace with their expectations regarding the tail of their evening.

Junior smiled at Louise and cradled her head on his upper chest. His arm drooped across her shoulder and his hand cupped her breast. He was just drunk enough to neglect kneading and mauling her. Instead, he kept constant, gentle pressure with his fingers.

His hand may have been on her breast but his mind was between her legs. He moved his other hand to her thigh as she told him of the movies she was going to overwhelm.

"Only romances, Junior. Romantic romances with handsome men to play opposite me. Really, really handsome men, Junior, but not 'pretty' handsome." She leaned her head to the side and tilted it so that she could look up at him. "You know what I mean don't you?" And before he could answer, had he been listening, she continued, "*pretty handsome* is kinda like if a guy is better looking than a girl."

Junior had just drifted back to her last words from his imaginary parting of the seas of flesh. 'Pretty guys' was the topic he found himself rising to.

"Faggots — you're talkin' about guys that shine their fuckin' hair and polish their teeth. Them guys that like guys. Fuckin' faggots."

Junior settled back into the silence of wisdom. Louise thought about what he said. Simple thoughts from a matching mind, but in her condition, they took a moment to grasp. Finally, she tilted back to look at him again and as she did, he was unable to keep his hand secured to her.

"You're right, Junior, a guy prettier than a girl is a guy who likes guys, not a guy who likes girls." And then the euphoria of discovery flowed across her features as Louise solved one of her oldest mysteries. "Junior! That's why Rodney Ball doesn't like me! He's queer — he likes GUYS!" She burst into relieved laughter.

Junior didn't know the boy but he definitely would have agreed with Louise if he had. Therefore, his lie was marginally smaller.

"That guy's a flamin' faggot, Louise."

And then when he saw her interest, he couldn't stop himself. "I've SEEN that fairy with another guy. If his tongue had been any longer, he coulda reached out that guy's asshole and shined BOTH their shoes."

The image Junior had just conjured, in combination with the satisfaction Louise was feeling knowing that the guy who was not interested in her was gay, tipped her into hysteric laughter. Unused to being considered humorous, Junior responded with a dippy, nervous laugh.

Phillip had one finger looped around the neck of a beer bottle, the remainder encircling the 'passion knob' on the steering wheel.

That knob, a clear plastic knot which was banded to the wheel, had cost him a small fortune, for it had been custom made. The uniqueness lay in the fact that Phillip had sent a photograph of his coupe to the manufacturer and they had mounted it under the plastic.

At first he found Louise and Junior's laughter irritating, but as it continued, he found himself chuckling. Beth followed the others and laughed with them, but quietly.

She pressed against Phillip's side. The alcohol had overwhelmed her from the beginning. Now she was afraid to speak because she sensed that her words would be anything but clear. Eventually her induced euphoria overrode her inhibition.

As yet, Phillip had made no untoward sexual advances — his attentions were strictly along the lines of conversation and warm company. She had feared earlier in the evening that he would take advantage of her attraction to him, and then later, as they both drank more and he still did not, she began to wish he would.

Those wishes also went through stages — from hoping he would try so that she could at least know he wanted to before she stopped him; to hoping he would try so that she could see if she actually would stop him. Most recently, the temptation to initiate action on her own danced drunkenly through her thoughts.

Phillip was in control and he knew it. She wanted him, he could tell that. Sure, she would resist for the sake of her debt to her parents or church or whatever, but after that he sensed that she would advance beyond him, actually *taking* him.

In some ways it would have been sweet for him — a goody-two-shoes asking for it. Little Miss Snow White dancing with the devil himself. But those thoughts and their pleasant associations were not long-lived. He *liked* her; he enjoyed just having her near him and he didn't even care that Junior and Louise were in the car with them. It was actually kinda fun, even though the term 'double date' was ridiculous to him, somewhere along the lines of 'honor roll' and 'square dancing'.

When she laughed with him it made him wish to drive past the quarry, to keep the evening at its current level. They could drive until it was time to take the girls home — why not? The car was a marvel, its throaty purr calming, the cluster of gauges registering good news in the engine compartment, and the shifter knob in his hand, a direct mechanical connection, confirming where the needles pointed.

But in the back seat, Junior's needs were different — he really wanted to get Louise away from the others. If he could use Phillip's blanket, he would take her around to a different part of the quarry, out of sight of the coupe, and he knew she would be ready for him. Take off her clothes? TEAR off her clothes, and she'd probably help. The girl was hot.

He had noticed earlier that they were nearing the quarry. They had taken almost every round-about road so far, and that had been alright with Junior, but now Louise was ready — they were both ready — so Junior kept watching out the corner of his eye for the last turn to the quarry.

"Turn comin' up, man," he noted when they passed the split pine.

Phillip saw it too and had made the decision to pass it by when he heard Junior's declaration. It angered him immediately, robbing him of the mood he was enjoying.

"No fuckin' shit, Junior. You think I mighta forgot where it was?"

Louise felt the grate of Junior's remark on Phillip. "My, my, aren't we a little jumpy tonight! You and Beth having a lovers' quarrel?"

Beth was confused with the byplay and wished they'd all shut up so she could ride with Phillip, listening to the discordant drone of the radio for the rest of her life. "Everybody just shut up, okay," she managed to say.

Louise mistook Beth's pique, thinking it was directed at Phillip. She was happy there was a problem. To a degree, her reaction was the result of her disappointment in herself for being sexually attracted to Junior. It smacked of being in his control, and while she wouldn't have minded had it been Phillip, the ignominy of being with 'Backseat Junior the Mindless Loser' was too much.

Junior felt the situation deteriorate. "Jesus H. Christ, all I said was, 'turn comin' up.' Will you guys give me a fuckin' break?"

Beth saw some humor, finally. "No, Junior, you never said, 'will you guys give me a FUCKING break until just now. So you weren't quoting yourself, you were merely saying what I just quoted."

Her observation and subsequent verbalization had taxed the limits of her sobriety.

Phillip was delighted to comprehend an addendum. "Actually, he never said, 'fucking', he said 'fuckin'."

Then Phillip added, "I don't know what the fuckin' difference is *called* but I do know there's a fuckin' *difference*."

Junior wasn't following — he was pissed.

Beth continued, "It's a contraction, Phillip, — F-U-C-K-I-N, and then Junior left off the final G — he dropped it. A contraction!"

Phillip felt himself to be an intellectual giant. "Gotcha — he left off the last G in the word he said that he didn't even say until the end when he said it." Phillip was laughing hard as he finished.

Beth giggled and fell into his lap. To her chagrin, she felt that he was hard, and rather than be upset or shocked, she was glad she was having an effect on him. "Gee, Phillip," she said and bumped her head onto him.

Phillip knew what she had discovered and the realization followed his delight with his crude experience with verbal repartee. "Is that the G you were talking about, Beth?"

"No, that was a soft G, this is a hard G."

"What are you fuckin' guys talkin' about?" Junior interrupted. "Do you fuckin' mind sharin' the joke?"

Now Louise laughed. "What's on *your* mind, Junior, it's not too hard to figure out. Not too *fuckin'* hard!"

Phillip had stopped the coupe in front of the turn-off for the dirt road at the machinery shed. "I guess we're here, fans. Pinch your assholes, we're gonna make a run."

But before he engaged the clutch he lifted Beth from his lap. "Would you *roll down* your window, miss? Just in case it gets too wet in here."

Louise burst in to hysterics, screaming, "I think it already is, you dummy!"

The *dummy* part bit Phillip, but Beth's embarrassed smile soothed him. She was pleased that he had asked her to open her window, and she giggled because she had never heard sex so openly joked about before.

Phillip floored the gas pedal. "Hang on, we're off!"

The engine ripped to life and Phillip popped the clutch. The coupe slid sideways as it clawed through the gravel and dirt, dragging itself violently toward the quarry. Phillip pounded the shifter into second and the needle on the tachometer momentarily dove and then flew back to 7000, where Phillip kept it hovering as he feathered the gas and slewed the steering wheel from side to side as they fish tailed forward.

They screamed past the machinery shed, the girls adding their voices to the howling engine, and Phillip wrenched the vehicle through a violent power slide as they reached the granite plateau at the lip. Tires bit into hard stone and started smoking as their rubber lost in the abrasive contest.

Junior leaned forward across the back of the front seat. Louise clutched his knee and screamed louder and Beth reached for the door handle on her side.

Phillip ignored them and squinted desperately into the darkness above the quarry, attempting to be certain his headlights were not deceiving him. He waited a split-second longer than usual and then he stood on the brakes. He drove his weight onto the pedal and the brakes locked on each of the four wheels and the coupe slid across the stone.

Ezechial was downstairs by the compressor when he heard the riotous, advancing automobile. It frightened him initially and he stood nearly upright. Then he scuttled across the shed floor to the light string. He pulled it and moved through the new darkness to the window toward the quarry. He caught sight of the tail lights of the roaring coupe heading in the direction of the quarry and a very long drop.

The six boys were half dozing on the other side of the quarry, slumped beneath the shorter derrick. At the sound of the coupe, Kurtz jumped to his feet and pulled himself over the bull wheel at the base of the tower.

The wheel was approximately twelve feet in diameter and formed the base of the derrick. It was parallel with the ground and cables extending around it were pulled to pivot the derrick and boom. The boom alone was at least eighty feet long and now rested at an angle away from the quarry wall. A swag of ten cables slumped from the pulleys at the peak of the tower and passed around corresponding pulleys on the far end of the boom.

Kurtz clambered over the metal wheel and climbed a few feet up the derrick. The tower was built with a zig-zag ladder of internal bracing, a sort of giant Erector-set© model, and so Kurtz had no trouble climbing the ladder-like diagonals.

"It's gotta be them, and, *holy shit*, are they haulin'!"

Kurtz was attempting to yell and keep his voice low at the same time — which was a ridiculous precaution considering that Phillip's engine would have masked a covey of Sherman tanks.

The headlights speared to the left of the boys on the tower as the coupe's wheels dug into the granite at the end of its path.

Alan remembered his sister and prayed for the fate of the metallic blue coupe.

"Oh God, please let it stop in time. Please let it stop."

Kurtz was fascinated with the thought that his bitchy sister might soon arc into the quarry. *A nice Hollywood ending,* he thought, then worried.

Had there been any loose gravel or sand in the path of Phillip's coupe it would not have postponed its trip to the depths. But the rubber grated along the small imperfections and ridges in the granite and the coupe ground to a stop.

The engine noise was ringing in Beth's ears as she realized the car was still at the top. Phillip had switched off the engine and was now letting out a low whistle.

Junior coughed lightly and then spoke.

"Anybody bring a spare pair of undershorts?"

Relieved, Louise smacked his shoulder. "You are such a *pig*, Junior."

Junior laughed with her but then became serious.

"You know, Phillip, some day you're gonna get us all killed. I know you drive good, but there's a fuckin' limit, ya know? I mean, I can swim okay, but I got my doubts about swimmin' up from the bottom of the quarry. No tellin' how many slimy things I'd have to swim past."

Phillip turned to him. "Well, Junior, my man, if you don't like the ride, you can always walk."

Junior shrugged off the barb. "Yeh, yeh, yeh — it ain't so much the fuckin' ridin' or even the walkin' that gets to me — it's the idea of flyin' that makes me nervous."

Junior turned to Louise to see if she appreciated his humor. She was serious.

"I just can't help but wonder if you're this exciting in everything you do, Phillip."

She smiled sweetly at Beth who was now twisted around staring.

Louise shrugged innocently and batted her eyelashes. "I was just *wondering.*"

Phillip put his hand on Beth's leg. "Let's take a walk."

Before she could answer, Phillip swung his door open and was out. Beth followed and moved to his side. She slid her arm around him as they walked away from the coupe and the machinery shed, retracing the coupe's earlier path.

Junior nearly called out, "Fuck her once for me," but Louise had begun to run her fingers around his ears and he decided not to risk a problem.

"Should I get us a couple beers?" Phillip asked.

"Not really, I'm kinda out of the mood right now," Beth answered, most of the residual drunkenness gone. "Do you mind if we just walk?"

Phillip wasn't listening. He put his arm around her and led them away.

The night was quiet except for the frogs in the quarry shallows and the crickets. It was a clear night and the stars shone brightly in the country night, reflecting on the shed windows and on the coupe and on the quarry water, far below.

Phillip and Beth heard Louise laughing back at the coupe.

"I think they're enjoying themselves," Beth teased.

"Yeh, I kinda think they have the same idea about fun. Junior's needs are pretty simple."

"How about yours?" Beth held her arm tightly around him as she spoke.

They walked on for a while before Phillip answered.

"I don't know, Beth. I really don't. I guess I need my car and my job, and in a funny way, I guess I need Junior around me — he's kinda like a personal cheerleader or somethin'."

They walked quietly until Phillip continued, "You know, it was a sorta shock when I got out of school — quit school, really — an' all of a sudden, there was nobody around. I mean, you look aroun' and you're the only one in sight under a hundred. I sure don't want to get old. I can't see myself all wrinkly and fat with my hair fallin' out and stuff."

Beth laughed. "Maybe you ought to marry Junior while you're both still young. You wait too long and you might get wrinkly and he might not want you anymore. Then who would cheer for you?"

Phillip turned to Beth and smiled, but he was stumped. He had missed a chance to tell her she wasn't just another girl to him — or was she? It didn't take him long to confirm that she wasn't.

And when he thought of it, he knew *why* immediately. All of the other girls he had known — dated — screwed — whatever — were for maybe one night and that was all.

They liked his car, sure, and he had all the beer they could drink, and he could always make them laugh, but it ended there. When he took them home or just dropped them off and then went back to the garage, it was their bodies he thought about, and the conquest which commanded his attention.

He smiled to himself when he thought of Judy Stamler — that girl had tits the size of footballs, but Jesus Christ, she wore a bra with at least two hundred clasps on the back. He had spent half an evening just getting them a quarter undone.

But Judy was always game.

"At the rate you're goin', it's gonna be morning, and I got school," she had taunted him. And when she took over — when she reached around and undid the others herself — he had lost interest. They were too big he remembered, too much like giant balloons filled with dough, and he had become sick of himself and his pawing attacks on her body.

"What are you thinking about?" Beth interrupted.

Phillip laughed. "Do you really want to know? I mean, you won't hit me or anything if I tell you?" He waited for her to nod. "And you have to let me tell you the whole thing, okay? Do you promise?"

"Yes, Phillip, I promise." Beth held up her hand and raised the proper fingers for the Girl Scout salute.

"Well, I was thinkin' about Judy Stamler's tits. One n. . . ."

Beth cracked the side of his head and then drew back and punched him in the stomach. She danced to the side and hit his head again.

"Stop, stop, you promised," he begged, but she kept hitting him. "Beth, dammit, you said you'd let me finish!"

Wham! Slam! She hit him again and again.

"I was thinkin' how *different* you are!"

And then she *really* hit him.

"No, I don't mean *that* — or *them* — or whatever!"

He ducked and covered his head and tried to get himself out of the dangerous mess he was in.

"Beth, dammit, I was thinkin' of how you're different, like I *like* you, like I *care* about you, and I haven't done that before. I never cared. I just thought about *bodies.*"

She stood over him, ready to belt him again, but she paused.

"Really? You're not just saying that so I won't beat you up?"

Phillip straightened up but kept his fists in front of his face, protecting it.

"Beth, in the first place, I don't have to take this beating. . . ."

"Oh really? Got another *potato*?" and she whacked him again.

"Would you *stop* it? I don't have to take it 'cause I could always run away — I *know* I'm faster than you!"

"Yeh, I'll bet!" Beth answered, "You probably run away from a lot of things." She said the last part softly and Phillip answered in the same tone.

"I guess I do, Beth. I guess I do."

They had stopped walking and now they were standing looking at one another. Beth looked up at Phillip and at first he could not meet her eyes. Then he did and he and Beth stood silently. He moved his hand to below her chin and lifted it carefully as he bent and brought his lips briefly to hers.

He kissed her and then pulled away.

"I'm not gonna run from you, Beth. You can try and chase me away if you want, but you'll just be wastin' your time."

Before she could respond he took her hand. "Come on, let's walk some more, I'm too serious. It makes me nervous."

She pulled him to a stop. "Were you telling me the truth?"

She planted her feet and Phillip pretended to tug at her.

He couldn't resist the joke.

"Yes, Beth, I'm telling you the truth. Stamler's chest is huge!!"

Then he ran ahead of her, backwards, saying, "A joke! A joke! I'm sorry!"

She came at him with clenched fists.

He held out his hand like a policeman stopping traffic.

"Okay, Beth, one more time — and seriously — yes, I meant what I said. You're really special to me. There — I said it again. Would I give up my right arm for you? Yeh. Would I give up the *coupe* for you?" There was a long pause. "Yeh. Now give me a break!"

She passed him, walked ahead, then slowed and took his hand at last, playfully pulling him after her.

"I'm satisfied, Phillip — for now."

Kurtz stood with one arm hooked through the bracing of the tower and a foot wedged at a slant on a diagonal of rusted steel. He had one hand over his eyes as if shielding them from the non-existent sun or somehow improving his vision.

The coupe had not flown into the water, that much was certain — there had been no arcing headlights and no splash. But the engine had died as if shot and the lights were dowsed.

Now Kurtz strained his ears with the same concentration he had used with his eyes moments earlier. He thought he heard a door squeak open — no that wasn't what it was. Actually, his attention was divided. Earlier, as the coupe fired ahead and just before it had turned toward the quarry lip, he had thought he saw a window light at the machinery shed. It appeared to be an outline of faint yellow around the shutters — but as he tried to see more clearly, the twin beacons of the coupe swung around as it turned, momentarily blinding him.

"What do you see?" Cavenaugh asked. He had climbed the opposite side of the tower.

"I can't see anything and I can't hear anything."

"Sounds like you're in the dark to me," Cavenaugh chided.

"Yeh, kinda," Kurtz answered, missing the humor and amazed that Cavenaugh was only now realizing that it was night.

More murky forms scrambled over the bull wheel.

"Whoa, SHIT!" Alan yelled as he lost his grip and flipped back to the ground. He landed on the hardest earth he had ever experienced, which was not surprising since there was less than an eighth inch of soil overlaying a few thousand feet of granite.

"Shut the fuck up down there, klutzo!" Kurtz called.

"Hey junior birdmen, is this as quiet as you normally operate?" Freddy said, definitely pissed at the performance of the 'kids' he had somehow ended up spending the evening with — while a hundred yards away, some moron was putting the make on his girl.

Will's thoughts were identical. "How much do we get paid for baby sitting tonight, and is there food and soda in the 'fridge?"

Roger didn't need the abuse and he saw the flaw. "Excuse *us*, our grown-up friends, but aren't you supposed to be mad at the guys over there — the ones who stole your girls?"

Will responded feebly, "Hey, they're *your* sisters."

Kurtz quickly jammed him with, "Yeh, but *we* don't want to date 'um."

The towering group lapsed into silence as they stared into the darkness and listened for sounds which didn't occur.

Ezechial listened to the silence. His ear ached for the car to go away. *Not tonight,* he thought. *Not tonight*

He wanted to be alone. Alone with his machines so that he could start them and feel them and absorb their smells and mechanical essence. The exhaust and the heat and the throbbing.

It happened so seldom. He spent so much of his life waiting, caring for his machines, preparing them for the next time and waiting — waiting for the time when he could suckle them out of their cold hibernation, injecting them with tempting oils and then violating them with steam. He wished to awaken the next morning with the smell of coal in his lungs, grit in his mouth and the loving smears of oil on his body.

He craved it all — the power, the pulsing strength, the massive wheels spinning through the air, the blazing, raging fire in the bowels of the boiler, and the white-hot water whipping through the pipes, driving the pistons, torturing them until they fled and then were forced backward to be punished again. It was a feast for the old man. A feast of iron and coal and smoke and steam and power and strength.

He could live alone. He could live alone with his 'sister dolls', and he could wait. He could leave life out there. Life could embrace the quarry — new life — children and automobiles — not men and machines and granite dust. All Ezechial needed was bound in walls of stone.

Ezechial knew life as few others. He knew the coming of power, the slow dance with the machines which led to the deaths of the horses who had earlier led the deaths of the long teams of oxen. The machines — the cast iron and the oil, and the grease and the heat — and the cold. The sleeping monsters — all of it — it seemed he alone knew.

The others could walk in their sleep-dreams while he, Ezechial, murderer of his sister, tempter of his sister, lived with the machines — the very machines which had brought it all to an end.

The quarry was done. The men were gone. All of them. Every nationality, every race — all gone. And the steam powered drills — silent. The steam grinders — silent. The roiling smoke — gone. Even the train and its devilish engine was silent — doomed — crushed — rusting now on the ledge beneath the little derrick.

Ezechial willed the car away with all of his heart, but it did not good. The coupe squatted at the edge of the quarry, settling into the darkness and the brief silence, mocking the old man on one of the few nights remaining of his tortured life.

Kurtz heard the door slam before the others could place the sound.

"Door slamming — bet me."

"Well now, shit!" It was Cavenaugh.

"Let's get over there now, and worry about who's still in the car later." Freddy said, below Cavenaugh and Kurtz who had climbed still higher. "Let's go get 'em you guys!"

They fell from the tower in pairs, Roger coincidental with Alan, followed by Freddy and Will, and finally Cavenaugh and Kurtz. As they rested momentarily on the ground, Kurtz said, in awe of the massed strength, "Would you look at us — we have a whole fucking *ARMY* here. I think we can deal with the world-famous Siamese Moron Twins."

The six boys loped in silence around the quarry, forgetting as they did that at least one occupant of the coupe had opened the door and possibly left the immediate area.

They regrouped in the blacker shadow of the machinery shed and made their final plans and observations.

Junior and Louise were entangled in the back seat. After Phillip and Beth had departed, the two remaining laughed about their friends, and started falling into kissing embraces. Junior worked his hand into Louise's blouse and with surprising deftness lifted her bra. The resultant treasures kept him humming at the doors of paradise until Louise became uncomfortable and finally unfastened her bra. Soon after, she unbuttoned and pulled off her shirt. Her bra tumbled to the coupe floor.

In the hazy darkness Junior worshiped his twin goddesses and answered Louise's probing tongue with his own. Before long he felt her hand on his jeans and her teasing fingers grasping him through the heavy fabric. He reached around her and pulled her down onto him as he lay back on the seat.

"Beth and Phillip?" Louise mumbled when her mouth was free, but she said it more as an obligatory observation than in anticipation of company. There was no guilt.

Junior stretched forward and locked the door on his side, and Louise took his cue and did the same on hers.

"Fuck 'em," Junior noted.

Louise moaned and pushed him back onto the seat. Junior again caught her breasts and fell back under her. Her nipples were small and hard and he locked them with his fingertips, squeezing and pinching as he moved his open mouth over hers.

Awkwardly, she managed to spread her legs, nearly pitching him onto the floor when she did. He arched up into her and she wished her shorts and panties into the front seat. But wishes weren't enough, and she refused to take her hands from the hair on the back of Junior's head. She levered forward and smothered his mouth with her own.

Junior wasn't certain if it were the alcohol or the thrill of Phillip's ride that had turned her on, but he wasn't stopping to question. He had never heard anything about her except that she was daffy on Hollywood; if she were the nympho she now appeared, he thought he would have heard it from someone.

She started mumbling and whispering, and at first he couldn't understand her, but then he made out, "take me" and Junior was never more ready. He moved his hands, first sliding them under her shorts and onto her cool, smooth bottom. While holding her served to excite Junior even further, it did not get him any closer to where he truly wanted to be. He soon pulled his hands out and started to work at her belt.

"I will, I will," he moaned.

Louise started to laugh through her kisses and squirms, and Junior raced his mind over what he was doing, trying to figure if perhaps he were tickling her. He wasn't, but she laughed harder, and he continued to struggle with the buckle on her pants while he looked to the windows to see if someone was peering in and making faces or something. The windows were blank.

He pulled his hands from between them and lifted his head away from her long enough to ask, "What's so fuckin' funny?" but she pulled his mouth back to hers. Her tongue was in his mouth and she was breathing heavily through her nose, but still he could tell that she was barely controlling her laughter.

Junior felt his humiliation growing. He pushed her back once more. "Tell me, goddammit!"

Louise laughed openly for a moment and then responded, "When I said, 'take me,' I didn't *mean* what you *thought*. I was talking about Hollywood. I want you to take me to Hollywood."

Junior shook his head in disbelief, saw the outlines of her breasts and the shadows of her nipples and was bathed in forgiveness.

"I'll fix my fuckin' car," he said as he rose to her chest, his mouth seeking first one nipple and then the other.

"I'll fix it," he mumbled, his mouth full, one leg raised so that she rode it.

Roger cut the twine surrounding the bales and each boy took an arm load of hay. They crawled stealthily on their knees and forearms to the quarry lip and the dark coupe and began their work. With six of them distributing the straw, it was finished quickly and efficiently. They wormed back to the deeper shadows and regrouped.

"Fire when ready, Gridley!" Roger whispered.

"I wish we had a potato," Freddy added.

Whereupon Will concurred, "I can't believe I didn't think of that!"

Alan smiled and added, "You'd need two — dual exhausts."

Kurtz rose to a half crouch and concentrated. A smile fractured his serious demeanor. "Anybody got a hanky they can spare?"

Freddy reached into his back pocket and so did Will.

Kurtz reached for them.

"Hey, what kind of shit are you up to?" Roger demanded.

"You may be dumb, but I think you got the idea," Kurtz answered and disappeared with the doomed handkerchiefs.

The boys waited in silent disbelief, listening to Kurtz's groans and efforts from the bushes.

"Fire one!" he whispered in tangible relief.

"Fire two!" he amended.

When he reappeared they shied away from him, his noxious cargo cutting through the darkness.

"You are one sick individual," Freddy said.

Kurtz didn't respond, he just moved off toward the coupe, bent nearly double and gingerly carrying two cradling handkerchiefs and their waste torpedoes.

"That kid may be sick," Roger whispered, "but I kinda like his style."

When the young boy returned he carried the unmistakable aroma of defecation.

"Messy work. Anybody got some soap and water to spare?"

Unfortunately for Alan, Kurtz went straight to him in the darkness and before Alan knew what was happening, he felt hands being wiped on his jeans.

Without thinking, he struck out and caught Kurtz on the side of his head with a reasonable right, but before a real fight could ensue, Will said, "I'm gonna do it now, you birds — get ready to scatter."

Phillip and Beth walked down the dusty road a short distance and stopped. There were blocks of granite scattered all around the quarry site and it was against one of the larger blocks that Beth and Phillip rested. They paused and then climbed.

They settled onto the top and sat with their backs to the quarry and searched the night sky. Phillip had his arm around Beth and they talked about the stars.

A meteor shushed silently overhead.

Neither spoke as the disintegrating trail glowed and seemed to fall in a thousand sparks to earth.

"I love to look at the stars," Beth whispered.

"I guess I really haven't," Phillip answered. "I guess there's a lot of things I haven't done."

Beth pivoted, intrigued by the glow in the direction of the coupe and the machinery shed.

"What's that?" she asked, initially with minor curiosity but then adding with alarm, "Is that a fire?"

"Holy shit!" Phillip yelled and jumped down from the slab of granite. He sprinted out of sight, leaving Beth to find a way to climb down unaided off of the block.

The boys had spread a horseshoe of hay and straw around the coupe. They were careful to keep it a constant six feet from the vehicle so that the effect would be more of shock than danger. The straw was mounded almost a foot high, and when the flames spread its length, it was an impressive display, from in or out of the car.

Junior noticed the glow and the flames before Louise. He sat up so quickly he slammed her against the side of the car. He saw the fire and thrust the front seat forward and grabbed for the door handle. He jammed it open and crawled out over the tilted seat.

The flames were higher than when he first saw them, but he could see that there was no real danger to the coupe and Louise. He looked around until he saw the boys nearby.

Kurtz and Roger and Freddy and Will and Cavenaugh and Alan stood and watched, incredulous and illuminated by the orange flames. They were unable to run. But it was not the fire which held their attention.

Junior had exited through the opposite door, and as yet they had not noticed him.

But there in the back seat, clearly visible through the various windows, was Louise. Her eyes were wide and there was terror on her face. And there below her fear was a pale chest and her orange-tinted breasts.

"Holy shit," Alan whispered, "I never knew they were so beautiful." He had never seen a girl's body before and the image would for a short time dominate his fantasies.

Louise seemed unaware that she was exposed. In fact, she seemed unaware of everything. She stared blankly out the window at the shadowy forms.

The others stood with their mouths dropped.

Junior raced around and was on them before they could react. He brought both Roger and Freddy down with his outstretched arms.

Phillip saw the flames around his coupe and jumped through them to his door. He almost ripped the handle off trying to open it.

"Open the fucking door!" he screamed, unaware that Junior had left the car and was now doing battle.

Louise came out of her trance and reached forward and unlocked the door.

Alan remained mesmerized as her breasts hung and seemed to sway in slow motion when she moved.

Phillip was in and cranking the engine which wouldn't start.

Alan and Kurtz saw the need to move — Junior was scrambling to bring them into the pile with Roger and Freddy. The two younger boys raced behind the coupe.

The exhaust plugs — the impromptu *human* potatoes were not as secure as their vegetable brothers. And the exhaust stroke from Freddy's engine was like mouse gas compared to the hurricane of the coupe's souped-up mill. Consequently, the big engine fired and first one and then the other turd shot from the tail pipes like mortar shells.

Kurtz's timing was poor enough that he caught the first missile on his thigh and one step later, the second, on his neck. Each impact was accompanied by a relieved roar from the engine, thus masking in the blast of sound, the import of what had happened. He didn't know until later.

Phillip crunched the shifter into reverse and set the tires spinning as he peeled the big coupe backward, through the flames, and then spun it out of danger. He killed the engine and prepared to join Junior, whom he had finally noticed wrestling and punching at least two kids.

As he pushed open his door he glanced back and then stared at Louise. She was still bare-chested and she was watching Phillip.

He looked at her and then outside at Junior and the fight, as if deciding.

He shook his head slowly.

"Nice tits, Louise."

He smiled to her, turned, and leaped out to help Junior.

By the time Beth got down from the granite block and returned to the coupe, Phillip and Junior were pounding on three boys. She did not recognize Roger, Freddy, or Cavenaugh. The other boys were rallying near the action, active at the periphery, attempting to find an opening to throw themselves through which didn't promise instant pain.

Alan was the last to enter the conflict, and he ran unnoticing past his sister to do it. He jumped onto Phillip's back. Phillip was over Roger, alternately kicking him and lashing out at Freddy, whom Junior had in the crook of one of his muscular arms.

Phillip shook off Alan and bent and landed several hard punches on Alan's upturned face. Beth started screaming, not because she recognized Freddy or Alan, but because of the brutality. Children — she could tell that much — were being mauled by Phillip and Junior.

Louise was in the coupe struggling to find her bra and then get it on, when she saw a hunched shape pass along the side of the machinery shed. She immediately recognized the dragging gait as that of The Doll Man and mistook the long-necked oiler in his hand for a huge knife.

She too began to scream. She interjected a few words with her terror.

"IT'S HIM! OH GOD, IT'S HIM! THE MONSTER, THE MONSTER! THE DOLL MAN!"

And then when she thought she had a few persons' attention, she warned, "A KNIFE! A KNIFE! HE HAS A KNIFE!"

Junior heard 'knife' and yelled, "Let's get the fuck outta here!" to Phillip and then violently threw Roger and Will onto the ground. He kicked Alan and Kurtz for good measure and raced back to Phillip's coupe.

Phillip disengaged himself and seemed to back-pedal to the coupe as he continued windmilling his fisted arms.

Alan and Roger and Freddy were too stunned and damaged to do any more than watch in shock as their assailants disappeared, and Will and Cavenaugh and Kurtz alternately swore at the situation, their own injuries, the back-fired plan, and their tormentors.

Of all of the boys, only Cavenaugh and Will appeared to have marginally requited themselves. Cavenaugh had caught Junior squarely in the eye, just as the over-sized terror was heaving Roger and Will, and Freddy had knocked Phillip twice on the side of the head before he had been so shamefully discarded.

The big coupe exploded into life and raced off, leaving the boys crying and cursing.

The Doll Man remained in the darkness, undetected, and listened to the boys' laments.

Most were sitting in a ragged circle where they had fallen, with only Cavenaugh and Freddy standing above them.

Kurtz chanted, "Mother-fuckers, mother-fuckers, mother-fuckers, mother-fuckers," as he explored his injuries. Alan's ear had been pummeled and the side of his head kicked so badly that all he heard was a ringing as he sat with his head down saying, "Hello? Hello? Hello? Hello?"

Will had his head tilted back in an attempt to stop the bleeding from his nose and asked, "Anybody got any other bright ideas?" before he shut up.

Roger rotated his right arm slowly as he massaged the joint at the shoulder while Cavenaugh started probing the air with his nose, asking, "Did one of you guys shit yourself?"

It was an interesting question and each of the boys took a break from his self examination to sniff the air. Before too long, five alarmed and disgusted noses were aimed at Kurtz.

He looked quickly around at the others and exclaimed, "No fuckin' way, Jose, I'm the guy who shit earlier, remember? My guts are hanging in me like a long, empty balloon."

But as he spoke, Kurtz realized the intensity of the shit-smell and coincidentally remembered the two objects which had hit him as he had run behind the coupe — *just as it started!*

"Oh, shit!" he exclaimed with accuracy as he wiped at the smears on his pants and brought his fingers to his nose.

"Oh, fucking shit!" he exclaimed when he realized something remarkably turd-like was resting inside of his t-shirt, above the bunched cloth at his belted waist.

He tore his shirt free and danced around until a black shape the size of a giant tootsie-roll plopped onto the granite and rolled briefly toward some of the seated boys.

"Live grenade!" Roger shouted and dove out of the way.

All the injuries and pain and humiliation were forgotten as the boys climbed over one another to escape.

Kurtz was no less animated as he ripped his shirt off and then discarded his pants, also. He stood in his undershorts and struggled with how to cope with his soiled and odorous body.

A week earlier he would have leaped the long dive into the quarry, the Devil's Club be damned, but fear of the unknown kept him earth-bound.

After the boys were certain they had escaped the dark peril, some of them began to laugh. The situation disintegrated into a lunatic howl as the tension and fear and pain released itself, at last finding an acceptable voice.

Kurtz laughed the hardest, but neither he nor the others were quick to reunite.

When finally they exhausted themselves, Kurtz trailed them back through the woods to the landing, each carrying within himself the dejection of a defeated nation.

At the landing, while Kurtz nervously and tentatively immersed himself and quickly washed, the others stood guard.

It wasn't until all six were back in the forge shed that anyone bothered to tease Kurtz. But by then it was too long after the fact and the circumstances didn't ring humorous any longer, probably because the boys were once again aware of the bruises and dried blood which covered them.

They talked quietly for a while about what had happened, each boy trying to interpret the altercation in a manner which left him a modicum of dignity, but by the end of the discussion they were more depressed than mollified.

It was Cavenaugh who signaled an end to the posturing when he asked, "Hey, Will and Freddy — will you guys help us make an underwater camera so we can find out what's in the quarry?

The two answered that they would, and then Will took them back one last time to the events of the evening.

"I hate to bring it up again, but. . . ." he paused and looked at each of the boys, "any of you guys interested in *really* getting those bastards?"

He paused and then continued before anyone could do more than nod. "I've got to tell you guys that I'm not messing around with them any longer. What I'm thinking of is definitely not kid stuff, so if you're not really serious, don't waste my time."

To Will's credit, he had imparted the seriousness of his plan with his tone.

There was no doubt to any of them that their 'kids war' had just taken a huge step toward adult retribution — criminal retribution.

Each boy thought it over before he answered. Not one of them doubted that someone could get very seriously hurt next time around. Someone could possibly die.

Roger answered first, "I'm there."

Then Freddy, "I guess I'm sick of being the wimp who gets pushed around."

Cavenaugh, "Yeh."

Alan had doubt in his tone but he answered, "Okay here."

Kurtz concluded "I think the shit's already hit the fan," and nobody laughed, because he wasn't kidding.

Junior got into the back seat with Louise, who was once again dressed, and Phillip sat behind the wheel and started the engine. Beth was beside him, and she wouldn't stop asking who they had been fighting.

Junior ignored her and went through his punch and counter-punch description of what had happened.

"I threw one of the little fucks about a mile," Junior bragged, and Phillip interrupted, "Yeh, me too — a little pisser landed on my back like a giant fuckin' mosquito. Shook him off and did a dance on his fuckin' sides — he'll pee blood for a while."

Phillip knew as he spoke that he was exaggerating, but the exhilaration was still pumping through him.

Junior was a pool of adrenaline also.

"I caught one of the big ones on the mouth — I think I lifted him with the first punch and then kinda carried him back with the next — hope he had flight insurance — he's gonna need it in the morning."

There was an unspoken understanding between Phillip and Junior that they would not mention who it was they had pounded. Few girls were impressed by the pummeling of little brothers and past boyfriends.

At first Beth refused to come to terms with what she feared had happened. But the obvious was too persistently coming to her thoughts — who else could it have been? The only thread she had left was the anonymity created by the darkness and the fact that no one had yelled or in any way identified themselves. It had been an ordeal from a silent movie.

But tacit agreements not-withstanding, Junior could maintain the co-operation between tongue and brain for just so long.

"When I see that little fucker, Kurtz, he gets another knuckle sandwich. The little prick bit me." He examined his left fore arm as he spoke.

Everyone remained silent as the implications of Junior's mistake settled and then grew.

Louise was the first to react. She turned and hit Junior in the face with her fist.

"You're talking about my little brother, you moron."

Beth started to cry and then she demanded, "Stop the car, I want out. Stop the car Phillip, I just want out."

Phillip wouldn't stop for her, but he did drive directly to her house, crashing stop signs the distance. At the rate Louise was building and Beth was falling, he couldn't get there any too soon.

Beth was sobbing and accusing, "You knew it was Alan and his friends all along. You knew and you didn't have the guts to say, just like you didn't have the guts to pick on someone your own age. They're kids — little kids who played a prank on you. But that's too much for you to take. They got near your precious car. This stupid, piece of junk car," and she kicked forward hitting the underside of the dashboard, "And you two losers had to beat them up — to show off for your girlfriends. You make me sick!"

She turned to her window. "Just stop the car and let me out. You make me want to throw up."

Junior said defensively, "Hey, they coulda started the coupe on fire — it could happen, ya know."

He was cut off by Phillip who said angrily, "Shut the fuck up, Junior. Just shut the fuck up."

They rode in silence.

Phillip wanted to be angry with Beth but he couldn't; she was right — he was a loser. And he was a bully. He pictured her little brother and he thought of Kurtz and Roger and it made him sick to think of actually hitting them. Who did he fight? Who had he hit? His answers made him want to puke.

And worse, she had said he was showing off for his *girlfriend*. She had said, *girlfriend*. And of course, he had fucked it up.

He stopped in front of her house. He had both hands at the top of the steering wheel, and he gently rested his head against them. He knew she was going to go at him again. In a way he wanted her to. It would probably be the last time she spoke to him.

Beth stared straight ahead for a moment. She was overwhelmed with disappointment in Phillip. He was exactly the way everyone said he was. He was a loser and he was cruel and he was stupid. And he had hurt her little brother. He had actually hit him — thrown him around. My God, Alan was a baby, a little kid — how could he do that?

She looked over at him as she reached for the door handle. She studied him as she pushed the door open and stepped out of the coupe.

Louise squeezed out from the back seat, momentarily blocking Beth's view of Phillip.

Before Beth turned and walked away, to be followed by Louise, she leaned in and spoke quietly to Phillip.

"You're pathetic, Phillip. You're a pathetic human being. I think you should try to get some help."

Ezechial stayed crouched near the wall of the machinery shed. Following the violence, the automobile drove off and the group of children huddled together, unaware of his presence. He heard them speak and he could tell that they were angry and full of bravado, but it was of the defeated, and Ezechial understood that too, for he had known defeat.

He found tremendous comfort in his invisibility, the first he had felt in the presence of others for as long as he could remember. These were young boys near him and he recalled when he was young. These were boys who ran with boys, and he had never done that. It had always been him and his sister, the two of them in the shadow of their father, the three of them in the pall of their mother. He and his sister had lived beneath their father's commands, but in the comfort of love and trust and strict observance of his rules.

Ezechial loved his father and he had killed him and he loved his sister more than he loved his father and he had killed her also. He had killed nearly everyone for whom he felt love, and if he counted the death of his mother when he was born, then he had truly killed them all.

His sister had been under him, just as his father had been under her. Yet even in his father's death he had somehow been over Ezechial, over him as he had been all of his life — but not threatening — teaching and showing — passing on his knowledge of animals and his love for his horses, his teams.

His father had been a man who spoke to animals and watched for their answers. At first Ezechial shared his love.

Together they had managed the quarry teams, over a hundred horses, and neither had minded the mountains of feed and the torrents of water or even the never ending piles of manure. It was not foul, it was just there, to be moved, just as when the feed bins were empty, they were to be filled. And the horses —

massive and tormented by flies, and slowly brimming with power and life and dumb trust.

They just stood. That his how he remembered the horses. Standing — waiting.

Standing in the rain or the heat of summer, surrounded by flies as big as your thumb, and standing in winter in the falling snow, their breath bursting forth, belying their strength.

They pulled and they dragged and they moved the granite from place to place, but to Ezechial, mostly they stood — huge statues of strength. They were monuments of power until the machines came, and until the day that the machines were dragged to the quarry side, Ezechial shared his father's reverence for the horses.

But with the machines, boy and man were drawn apart. Ezechial was lured away. He began to smell the horses for what they were and he began to resent their dumb power and their constant demands.

He was sullied and then weaned in the cigar smoke of the Chicago Compressor Man and the Boston Boiler Man. Those two, who never saw the spreading teams of horses any more than they saw the brooding men who did their bidding, took Ezechial away from the animals and from his father.

At first, when the huge machines chuffed into sight, silent on the backs of the rail cars, he was merely curious, not resentful as his father was. But then all of the men turned to the outsiders, and all of them did what the two bid and Ezechial began to respect the machines.

But it was the steam, the steam and the fires which welded him to the machines as surely as if he had been one more part forged in a distant city and appended with burning metal.

The day he rounded the corner with his sister and smelled the coal burning and saw the smoke, the day the quarry shelf pulsed with their rhythm, he was theirs.

His father had yelled at him after that, had shouted because Ezechial neglected the teams, walked away from them once and never really returned. He was at the machinery shed, always at the machinery shed, listening and learning and dreaming of the day when the brutes would respond to his hand.

Not that he had ever doubted who was really in control. He saw it when he was young and he never doubted it from the beginning. He would always be the skittish trainer, and they the beasts, never tamed, never broken. Only trapped, trapped and bolted to the earth, to the hard granite. Trapped, but ready to rip off an arm or a finger or to pulp a man without slackening speed — he had seen it happen more than once.

Punish them? Punish them because they had caught the Frenchy dozing and had snagged him by his loose shirt sleeve and snarled him into the revolving gears, nearly liquefying the hand he had used moments earlier, reducing it to meal and gristle? No, they didn't even shut the boiler down until nightfall, then wiping out the gore and balming the gears — balming the gears themselves! — the very gears! — with extra oil and grease as if to be a reward for a job well done.

The Frenchy had cursed the machine surely, had cursed it while he cradled the stump, cursed it all the way on the jarring trip to the doctor, and cursed it finally and quietly when gangrene set in and ended the cursing once and for all.

Ezechial knew the machines and he feared them. He kept his sleeves rolled and his hands away. He could use the beasts — he could fire them and make them boil to his command, but it was always from an arm's length until they cooled.

Perhaps their inbred violence was why they accepted him after he killed his sister and his father.

The boys did not know he was near, for he was quiet and they had not heard Louise shout. They left the taller derrick and the machine shed and went to the landing where Kurtz bathed.

Ezechial would not start the machines that night. He wished to, for he had the coal ready and the water set, but he feared the proximity of the youths. The machines were *his* and he had kept their dormant life secret.

He went back into the machinery shed and wiped down the machines once more, careful to avoid the water puddling at the foot of the boiler.

Beth did not speak to Louise after she turned to her house. The coupe drove off and she walked to the back door and went in.

Louise watched her and then started toward her own house three blocks down. She wasn't as angry as Beth — her little brother was a hellion who deserved most of the trouble he often found himself in. But the night had ended badly and the thought of Junior hitting her brother still grated against her.

As she walked through the small town night she thought about Junior and wondered if he could really get his car running.

Beth climbed quietly up the stairs to her bedroom. Her parents were asleep, in bed at least, and of course, Alan was not home. Blacky was tied in the back yard, and he had whimpered and wagged his body back and forth when she appeared out of the darkness.

She went to the bathroom at the other end of the hall, far from her parent's bedroom, and studied herself in the mirror before she began to undress. The night before, she had wondered if this would be *the* night, and she had half believed it would.

Her feelings for Phillip were basically unchanged, although she had been very angry. She knew he could be cruel, she knew he had no control over his temper, and she knew he was insecure enough that he would act long before he took any time to analyze. And in a way, she did too.

'Firing a parker' as it was called, was a dumb stunt and could be dangerous under the wrong circumstances. Alan shouldn't have done it, though she suspected he had out of some sort of protective feeling for her. He didn't care for Phillip, he had made that clear. In fact, not many people did.

Phillip's friends, the few he had, were carbon copies of Junior, and Junior wasn't someone it made a whole lot of sense to copy. They were all losers, she had been correct, but then again, who was a 'winner'? Freddy? He was a good kid, but he didn't really have any life in him. He just was. Will was the same. Louise? They had been friends for more than ten years, but she actually seemed to be getting younger, less mature. Her Hollywood 'thing' was truly born in an adolescent stupor, the kind a small town in Nowhere, Maine, induced.

So who were the *winners?* Her little brother had about the best chance of anybody she knew. He was a sweet kid, and he was going to be cute when he grew up — and he was sensitive, his treatment of Blacky showed that — but then maybe that was how Freddy was when he was younger.

Beth had been staring into the mirror without seeing herself. She stopped thinking of the others and focused on her reflection.

*And who are you?* she asked, *Are you a winner? Are you really any better than the rest of them, Junior even, or Louise and her ridiculous dreams.* She wondered about her own dreams and realized she didn't really have any.

She pulled her hair back and held it as if it were a pony tail. Her eyebrows were dark and full and her eyes were also.

*What's wrong with me?* she thought. *Maybe I'm just some kind of a mindless doll. Maybe there's nothing to me, either.*

She toyed with her hair, letting it fall forward. She shook one side so that it covered her eye, then she lowered her head slightly and looked up at herself. She wet her lips and pouted and liked doing it. It felt dirty and it felt sexual —- more sensual than when she touched herself. She could pretend then, she could lose herself in a fantasy and be someone else, somewhere else, but now in front of the mirror she was herself, at night, alone, in her home.

Beth stared into her own eyes and she saw another person looking back. The girl looked at Beth and her smile was small and secret and sexual. They stared at one another.

Beth tilted her head slightly to the side and lifted her hands from the bathroom vanity and as she did she straightened her back and slowly unbuttoned her blouse. Really, she unbuttoned the blouse of the other girl, the girl in the mirror, and it was very sexual to Beth and it was because it was another girl she was undressing.

When her blouse was unbuttoned, Beth reached behind and unfastened the girl's bra. She had not noticed before how gently it pulled apart and how her breasts moved down as she did — not far — but as they did, her nipples rubbed along the inside of her bra and her nipples hardened.

Soon her blouse was on the floor — the girl's blouse — and Beth felt the bra slide down her arms and then to the floor also.

At first Beth would not look at the girl's breasts, only into her eyes and it seemed to be a contest between the two of them for neither would look down. She drew in her breath and blew it softly at the mirror, smiling slightly again and turning her head further to the side.

Beth was wet and she knew the girl was too. They were very wet. Beth knew the girl was moving her hands to cup her breasts and she felt her breasts circled. She teased her nipples and then cupped them as an offering. Neither could stand it any longer and they lowered their eyes as if on cue and saw — really saw — another woman's breasts for the first time.

Beth had needed another woman to teach her about a woman's body, about her own body, and now she was learning.

She realized it would have been a mistake, a horrible mistake, to have left it to Phillip or any boy. They would not know, could not know — they would all touch her with gloves and they would all enter blindly.

She backed out of the bathroom, naked from the waist up, and as she did she moved her eyes from the other girl's eyes and to her hair and then to her hands holding her breasts. As she moved away Beth saw the color of her skin and the darkness — the pale darkness of the girl's nipples and wished she were holding them, and then — with delicious wickedness — Beth wished she could put her lips on them and gently kiss them. It was her dream.

She took the other girl into her bedroom and they finished undressing and went to Beth's bed and pulled down the covers so there was only a sheet — a sheet on a raised platform — an altar — and the two took each other to the bed and Beth and the girl fell in and out of sleep and spent the night learning to love their bodies and each other.

When Beth awoke the following morning she was not embarrassed, but strangely fulfilled and never more confused. Her confusion was something she felt she would not lose, just as she would never lose the girl she had gone to bed with — the woman she had awoken with — and when she realized, she knew she would someday take Philip and it would be less than she had experienced, but she would make it more.

Phillip returned to the shop and tried to keep his frustration and anger centered on Junior. He didn't attempt to understand or explain it. Junior was responsible. It was his fault.

The front of his shirt was spattered with dried blood and his knuckles were bruised and covered with small cuts. He undressed in total depression in the garage and went sullenly to the cinder block shower laced with mold. He cleaned himself and avoided Lu Lu's eyes.

"Bitch," he muttered as he went back to his room and put on his last pair of clean underwear and lay on his bed. He didn't allow himself to think of the evening. Instead, he thought of the coupe and the shiny engine and how he would tune it tomorrow evening and fiddle with the timing and adjust the progressive linkage on the carburetors.

He would hide in the midnight blue coupe as he had hidden in it for years — the years he had owned it, and those when it was only a dream. His car. At one time the fastest, but now, with the big blocks drifting up from Massachusetts, wearing more money internally in roller- bearing cams, high compression heads and competition lifters, and externally in direct-port injection, blowers, and brushed aluminum, than he had in his whole car.

He was a little man, all right — he was a little man with a dated car and a shitty job. He spent his days up to his ass in grease, hyping old ladies and kids who didn't know a universal joint from a hamburger.

It had been the little kids at Old Orchard Beach who had waved to him — the preteens who were pre-zit and even pre-driver's license. He had impressed them.

Phillip lay as he always did, his arms behind his head, and he listened to the sounds he always listened to — the humming of the neon halo in the clock in the waiting room, and the clacking refrigerator motor in the Coke© machine, and he smelled the smells he always smelled — the grease and the hand cleaner and the spilled hydraulic fluid and oil.

He lived in a fucking garage like a hermit — like The Doll Man — and when he thought about it, about The Doll Man, he began to explore the existence, the reality, of another human being. He thought of The Doll Man and he thought of their lives and he rose and dressed and went back to the coupe and then the quarry.

When Junior went to bed he was upset. He was angry and only when he brought his finger to his nose and smelled the sweet youth of Louise did he begin to calm down. He wondered what she would be like.

He was too slow to believe he could do anything which would make her stop going out with him. Sure, she was pissed, but when he got his car running, if he called her and told her he was ready to go anywhere she wanted, he knew she'd go where *he* wanted first. No contest.

And he was right.


Each of the boys was embarrassed because he felt he had not done enough in the altercation with Phillip and Junior. Only Kurtz seemed to warrant bravado, but his run-in with his own shit kept him more quiet than usual.

All six of them were in the forge shed, arranged variously on sleeping bags and broken chairs or leaning against a wall. Will and Freddy were initially silent, allowing the younger boys the chance to re-establish themselves with those older.

Alan was beginning to think of his sister and wonder where she had been during the fire and the fight.

No one spoke of Kurtz's sister, Louise, unwilling to risk a problem with her brother, but those who had seen her half naked in the coupe returned often to the thought of her. She would be the foundation for a series of fantasies which would endure for years. The excitement, her bare chest, her movement, and the subsequent disaster were enough to star her in a recurring loop of erotic action, complete with burning color.

It was early morning before the two oldest boys exchanged ideas quietly and then presented to the others a plan of such audacious brilliance and presumptive danger, that once discussed, none of the boys could deny the appeal, except Roger and Cavenaugh, who loved the plan but questioned the odds of survival for Phillip and Junior.

The coupe, without a doubt, was doomed.

Phillip thought of the old man as he guided the rumbling coupe through the night. He didn't doubt that The Doll Man was awake and at first he was sure he would get into the machinery shed to talk to him.

Actually, Phillip didn't imagine himself speaking with The Doll Man. It was more an imagined sharing of something — and the more he thought about it, the less certain he became, until his confidence vanished just before he turned into the quarry yard.

Before the last corner, the big coupe's engine shuttered and then was quiet, and the night sounds engulfed Phillip and his idea. He massaged the shifter knob and beat a silent tattoo with his fingertips on the steering wheel.

He opened the door quietly and then let it swing back to the latch as he stepped away, the door barely ajar, the engine ticking as it cooled, the water gurgling and draining through various tubes of the cooling system.

The coupe looked black and it looked like traveling evil. Phillip still loved the car, wanted to work on it, and lived to drive it, but it seemed less a part of him now. The chrome caught the light from the stars and reflected it, and the glass was peppered with points of white.

He walked up the dusty road, the first time he had actually walked into the quarry since he had been a kid. It was strange to him to leave the car and cover the distance on foot, and he was fascinated by the sounds around him. He passed where he and Beth had sat on the granite block earlier that night, and stepped over the charred oval of burnt hay. As he did he saw by its circumference that the fire had never been close to the coupe, that it had been a well planned prank, relying on shock effect, and he was embarrassed by this knowledge.

He rethought the evening and imagined himself running from Beth and confronting Junior before he had a chance to fight with the boys — he saw himself reasonable and good humored — calming — seeing it all as a joke. The kids were young, real young, and they were just playing.

And then he remembered that Will and Freddy were involved and that didn't jive with his 'young kids theory', until he thought of potatoing Will's car. They had probably found out somehow and had possibly instigated the whole thing. *'Small potatoes' revenge*, he thought.

He leaned against the bull wheel of the larger derrick and thought about the potatoing incident and was sorry he had remembered. Once more he plumbed the sleaziness of his own world — how he used others — the things he did to steal their money — and then Mrs. Brinks offered him another cookie and he believed he could not sink any farther.

He smelled the spent fire and looked into the quarry, barely making out The Devil's Club floating near the center. It appeared larger to him, but he hadn't really paid much attention to it lately and so he dismissed the inconsistency. The shorter derrick rose and spread its cables and he looked at them, tracing each as it disappeared into the darker horizon of trees and rock.

He nudged a stone forward with the toe of his shoe, finally booting it into the quarry air. He heard it reach the water and it reminded him of his joke with Beth regarding bats, and when he peered into the quarry to see if he could make out any of the ripples, he realized that they seemed much larger than they should have from such a small rock, until he saw The Devil's Club was gone.

Phillip moved closer to the quarry lip and he still could not locate the floating stump. It was as he strained his eyes to find it that he heard a metallic scrape come from the machinery shed behind him.

He turned to the direction of the sound and then looked back one last time into the quarry. There was The Devil's Club again, but this time it was at least forty feet to the right of where it had previously been, and perpendicular to its old axis.

"What the fuck?" he whispered as the stump produced a small wake and then disappeared. The skin on Phillip's forearms and the nape of his neck crawled and then rose to goose bumps. "Well fuck me," he breathed quietly then added, "I know you will," and as he contemplated what could have happened there was a loud clang from the machinery shed and Phillip moved away from the quarry, anxious to pursue the new focus for his attention.

He walked until he was within ten feet of the machinery shed. He stopped and stared through the darkness at the stone building, imagining the interior and what had happened to produce the sound he heard.

The certainty he had experienced earlier regarding The Doll Man was replaced by discomfort and then fear.

Phillip had never given credence to the stories about the old man, but now, alone at night, and ridiculously, far from his car, his cocoon, he was frightened. He imagined the previously unimaginable and he was unable to move. Perhaps it was because of the unsettling vision of The Devil's Club propelling itself around the quarry, but whatever the cause, it now centered on his confrontation with The Doll Man.

Yet, as much as he wished to turn and slink away, run away, really, Phillip felt as if he had an audience of every person he had ever bullied or lorded over. They watched him, ready to mock if he did anything but advance.

It was to his own surprise that Phillip found himself before the side door to the machinery shed. It was metal and Phillip believed that when it opened and he entered, he would never leave.

He stood at the door and imagined The Doll Man performing every disgusting act of which a human being was capable. He saw blood and viscera, and copulation with over-sized dolls. He saw children performing fellatio on the old man and each other. He saw acts of cannibalism and sodomy and every form of lechery. And in the midst, he always saw The Doll Man.

Phillip remained in front of the door, mesmerized as he exorcized from his imagination every loathsome act he had read of, heard of, or teased Junior with.

And then it was all ridiculous to him. He was standing in the shadow of nothing more than his own creations. It was dark. He was alone. He was reveling in the ludicrous.

Phillip felt the hard door against his bruised knuckles. For its bulk, the door sounded as if it were hollow and the noise it created was far louder than was reasonable to expect. Phillip knocked again and then took a step back.

His arms hung at his sides and his hands were open and useless. The only threatening aspect of his demeanor was the simple fact that he was there, at the door, in the middle of the night. The earliest part of the morning.

As Phillip waited he felt as if he could see the children from that evening. He could see them in the forge shed and he could hear them planning, and he was glad.

He would react differently this time. He would not lose his temper and he would be reasonable and he would see the joke for what it was.

Will and Freddy? He'd fix the old sedan for free — for nothing — he'd tune it up, make it so it had never run better. He could lift enough parts from Old Man Horvath and really give that dead engine the works. 'Lift the parts,' Christ, would he never stop? *Buy* the fucking parts. *Purchase* them. Lay out his own money for them. Could there be a greater surprise?

Yes. In front of him.

He became aware of The Doll Man at the door. Beneath him, really, for he was so much smaller than Phillip, so much more frail and crippled than Phillip had ever imagined.

The Doll Man was in front of Phillip and all Phillip could do was stand with his mouth open. *When* the big door had opened he didn't have the vaguest idea.

Surely, it must have scraped and groaned — and how could that little man have opened it anyway?

The old man had been upstairs. When he heard the noise he was momentarily confused — first thinking it was daytime and then believing that perhaps the girl or the old lady (Widow Orlap, old, or Widow Orlap, young) had come with another carton of food. His supply of stores was nearly gone and the old man had been thinking in terms of a visitor.

But it was most unusual for her to make a sound — the morning after a visit he often stumbled over the packages she left, but occasionally he would confront her — blunder into her presence, just as he did her deliveries, and then when he saw her, they would look at each other and after a moment she would inquire as to how things were for him and did he feel well and were his teeth all right — did they hurt, and that sort of thing — and he would smile because he was happy to see her, and he would say nothing because he feared he would upset things — go so far as to kill her perhaps, as he had his sister and his father.

The Widow Orlap — old or young — would examine him as she prattled, and at those times he felt as if he were one of the horses his father had cared for and it was his father before him pulling back the horse's lips and poking at its teeth or searching for something in the animal's eyes, or possibly probing a boil or a canker somewhere else on its body.

The Widow looked at him like that and he never minded except that he tended to think of his father then and that always made him unhappy — eventually — even though it might not at first, and if she did it long enough, he would really think about the horses — his father's favorite team and wonder if perhaps he was remembering it all wrong and maybe he had killed them too — been responsible for the fall in the first place.

He could not imagine how that could have been no matter how he contorted the situation and his guilt. It had been the explosion or the snake, either one; it could not have been young Ezechial. He could not have started it *all*, regardless of how bad he was, regardless of what he had done with his sister — to his sister — that night on the island.

When he pulled the big door inward and looked out, his first surprise was that it wasn't daytime at all. It was night at the quarry. It was the time, outside of the bitter winter, when he was alone with the stone, alone with the machines, and alone with the past and the evil and the horror.

The second surprise was that it was not the little girl, and so he was additionally disappointed, but even in the gloom he was soon to discover that it wasn't the old lady either.

But before Ezechial realized that it was someone else entirely, he thought it was a dream and he was asleep and he had opened a door which took him back to when he was a boy, for before him stood a young mechanic — Ezechial could smell that — a lad who loved machines, and who could make them work — he could smell that, too.

It did not seem quite the pure love that Ezechial equated with machinery, but Ezechial discarded his first concern, for this boy was Ezechial. He knew that he saw himself and he didn't know how to proceed — was unaware how one actually *decided* to do things in a dream, so Ezechial stood his ground and stared and waited for the dream to take them where it would.

The problem was that the dream didn't take them anywhere. It didn't seem to be working or something and so the old man stood and did nothing and continued waiting.

Phillip was entranced and all he did was stand immobile, lost in his own plan.

And then it became wrong for him and he knew he couldn't speak to the old man even though the smell of the massive machinery in the darkness behind the old man was a lure for which he had known no match.

There in that dark room were machines more powerful than any that Phillip had handled — his were toys, play things when compared with the strength of the essence alone of the brutes he felt poised in the darkness, waiting.

And they weren't broken machines. They hadn't been neglected and left to rust. They were not leftovers from another era as he had always assumed. They were still alive. He knew they were alive and that they breathed and were more seductive to Phillip than the warmth between Beth's legs or the heat of her approval.

Phillip and The Doll Man danced the mute, slow dance of each other's embrace until the sadness and the defeat and the guilt of Ezechial compounded those same feelings in Phillip. Each of them peered into themselves at different stages and initially they were unable to do more than they had.

It was The Doll Man who broke the contact. First he looked down and to each side, searching through the darkness to his stoop, searching for the packages he knew would be coming soon, brought by the young girl or the old lady, or perhaps by this permutation, this strange variation of the two, who could be either the old lady's son or the young girl's lover — her boyfriend — no, her brother — and when he realized that it could be her brother, he was afraid for her — afraid that this brother would love and violate her and then kill her, as he knew brothers could — did.

The Doll Man stepped back into the deeper shadows of the machinery shed and Phillip watched the big door swing shut in front of him. He confronted the door. He did nothing more than stand in opposition to a sheet of metal, hinged and locked and older than he.

Phillip walked back to the coupe, oblivious to the six boys a few hundred yards away who were thinking of him and capable of transcending their childhood.

What could have been the vanguard of a storm front passed quickly over the quarry with the uneasy wash of morning light. The clouds were grey and massed in small stacks, in total, a miniature version of the storm of days before.

But it was lanced by the rising sun and the golden arrows robbed the clouds of their fury. The clouds and the storm and its hints of power passed rapidly overhead and then hurried on. Only those who rose with the earliest morning — the milkmen and paperboys and various delivery folk saw the storm, for before the rest of the town awoke, it was gone, leaving a clear summer morning.

Beth awoke and went back to sleep, awoke and again slept.

The boys — the four boys (Will and Freddy had driven home before the first light, before the storm that wasn't) gathered their sleeping bags and piled the trash from the night.

Each of them, bruised and dirty and hung-over from the excitement and defeat, buoyed only by his hazy thoughts of plans for that day, wrapped himself in the armor of a soiled shirt or a musty bedroll and mounted a bike and slowly pedaled off.

Kurtz jogged heavily beside them, and from time to time someone loaned him their bike and took his place on foot. Just outside of town, Roger let Kurtz sit balanced on the front of his bike, squashing the front tire as Roger stood and pedaled them the rest of the way to their homes.

They passed the Dairy Wonder and each boy glanced at the mucky ice cream stains on the pavement and thought of the fight and before that, even, when they were back at the swings and Kurtz was riding up to meet them and they were clean and untorn.

Each boy went back to his house and half of them showered and all of them slept until early afternoon.

## DAY FOUR

Fox and Claude had a late breakfast and then returned to their room. The smaller brother assembled his fishing gear and went behind the motel and made a morning of toying with the trout stream. At one point the owner walked around and joined him; recounting the impossibly large and numerous fish he had pulled from that very spot years before.

Fox listened, aware that he was being victimized, but also certain that his companion could not dream of the fish Claude's and Fox's people had routinely netted hundreds of years earlier. And probably near where they stood.

It was past eleven when Claude came around and joined his brother.

"Well?"

"Nothing, yet." Fox lifted the empty creel.

Claude looked through the pines at the blue sky. He lost himself for a moment and then commented, "Let's go get a sandwich and then take the long way back to town. Storing nearly two hundred pounds of not-so-prime beef is not my style. I'll be glad when we're rid of it."

"I like the van, though, I'll hate to see it go, although I do get a charge out of the splash. Fox stopped speaking and thought of the various vehicles they had ditched in the quarry waters. "Remember that old Plymouth sedan? That trunk sure held a lot of air. I thought it would never sink." He saw the vehicle bobbing, trunk upward, a harvest moon illuminating the quarry water, leaves scattered over its surface. "I still think I lost my watch that night. I wonder if it was really waterproof."

Claude smiled as he too remembered past jobs. It was just like his brother to think of the sinking cars. *He* always thought of the deaths. Always clever. Always perfect. It was great work. The blood never bothered him but he thought he'd never get used to the evacuated bowels. No matter what time of day they died, it seemed they had just walked away from Thanksgiving dinner.

He heard the last part of his brother's sentence.

"— until we tipped it in."

Claude shook his head. A few years back a Studebaker with two bodies in the back had stalled and gotten hung up on the quarry lip. Usually, one of them would drive the car toward the edge and then step out at the last minute.

Usually, it worked.

They had had to push the other car over, nicking the chrome on their front bumper and causing more noise than they cared to — squealing tires and all. Tire marks on the granite. They had been a nuisance to cover — two trunk-loads of sand. It had been a long night.

Claude didn't like thinking of the problems. They had solved them. They were good at what they did.

"Let's go get paid."

Fox reeled in his line and followed his brother.

They took the van, Fox driving, his brother riding with his arm out the window, planing the air with the flat of his hand. They were working again, and neither spoke. When they got into town Fox had half expected to see some sort of a stake-out, but if there was, it was pretty professionally done. That was unless the pregnant woman with the stroller and the three kids running across the street were undercover.

Fox parked directly in front of the bank and Claude got out and went in. Fox watched him go to the same woman and through the glared window he could see her grimace. Claude walked out of Fox's field of vision.

A police cruiser rolled down the street. Fox watched it without looking, following its reflection in the windshield and then the quarter window. Fat and dumb, or skinny and dumb. That was the way they hired them in small towns. Sometimes mean, but always dumb. Fox shook his head.

He was startled when the side door opened.

It was Claude. With a big package.

"He's going to have a heart attack one of these days — you mark my words."

Fox was surprised that his brother had spoken. All he could figure was that things had gone very, very, well indeed. It appeared to be the case.

He pulled out and into the flow of Main Street.

Claude tossed the parcel to the floor at his feet. Fox knew he would do that. Claude was the last man to grasp money. He'd take it when he could, but he never gave it a lot of thought once he had it. He was always telling Fox that was where so many other professionals fouled up. "They concentrate on the money," he'd say, "when their lives are at stake."

He noticed that his brother rode with one hand in the cardboard box between the seats. It held a sawed-off Remington with enough ammunition to make hamburger of the police force, city council, local unit of the National Guard, and even a Girl Scout troop or two if it were necessary.

The tape around the lid of the garbage can let out a reminder of their job.

Claude shifted his body closer to the open window. "Next time, we get air conditioning. Or a refrigerator truck."

He was really relaxed.

"Next time?" Fox asked.

Claude chuckled quietly.

"Old habits die hard," he said and took a deep draught of passing air.

They spent the best part of the evening counting the money, and they were content to see that it was what they had requested. Later, they drove the car to the white-birch restaurant, ate a light dinner, all the while limiting their conversation to fishing and hunting, and then drove back to the motel.

Both brothers lay down and rested in preparation for the most dangerous part of their job.

"I wish we could somehow just vaporize them," Fox used to say, but through the years neither he nor Claude could think of a reasonable way to do it, and so finally, he quit bringing it up.

Claude set the alarm and said goodnight to his brother. As was his habit, Fox did not answer.


Alan awoke when his mother came into his room to tell him that Kurtz was on the telephone. He kept his bruised face away from her, talking into his pillow, telling her to please tell him that he'd call — no, he'd be over in a little bit.

"Are you alright?" his mother asked, anxious because her son usually leaped out of bed when anyone called him.

"Yeh, sure, I'm fine, Mom, I just had a bad dream or something, I'll be down in a minute."

Alan's mother rested her hand lightly at his door knob and waited, but when her son didn't say any more, she sighed loudly and pulled the door closed behind her as she left.

When Alan heard the door closing he listened carefully to be certain she hadn't come into his room and closed the door behind her. When he was sure, he pushed down the sheet and sat stiffly, propping himself on his elbows, deciding which part of his body ached the most.

He had washed the blood from his face the night before and bundled his bloody t-shirt into a back corner of his closet, determined to wash it himself one day when his parents weren't home. At first he thought of asking Beth to do it, but under the circumstances he was afraid she would tell him not only to wash his own clothes, but to mind his own business and leave her alone while he was at it.

Beth — she was a problem. He desperately needed to talk to her; to tell her about the night, to find out what she knew; to find out where she been when all of the action took place, but he couldn't face her rejection. He knew she was very upset with him — she had to be.

Then he wondered if she were angry with Phillip for beating up her little brother. Her little brother — little brother — little — -Alan said the words over to himself. Being 'little' — being thought of as 'little' — had always been a comfort for him, an identity to use and to hide in.

He could be protected because he was 'little'. He could be forgiven because he was 'little', and the older girls — Beth's friends — seemed to like him because he was 'little'. *He's so cute,* they said.

Alan the little boy. Alan the overgrown doll.

He wanted to puke.

Alan walked to the bathroom far from his parents' end of the hall. It was the bathroom he considered Beth's. The door was closed, so he tapped quietly, afraid his mother would hear and possibly come back up the stairs.

He edged the door open a few inches. There was no scream from an irate sister, no door slammed back in his face. He pushed it open enough so he could slide through. As he did, he kicked his sister's blouse. Alan levered the blouse up with his toes and then took it and tossed it into the dirty clothes basket. Her bra tumbled out of the folds of the blouse and settled back to the floor.

Alan stood and looked down. It was a snake ready to bite him. Finally, he reached and gingerly lifted it by the tag on the strap. 34C. He let it twist as he examined it.

He pushed the door softly with his foot so that it closed. Now, with the door shut, he tentatively put his fist into a cup and held the bra in front of him by his cupped hand. Alan studied it and then looked behind him at the door. He listened and when he was satisfied, he squeezed the bra cup which encased his hand.

Then as if he had been bitten, he flung the brassiere into the basket.

Kurtz's words haunted him.

*Yes, I watch my sister undress* — spoken as casually as if he were relating the tying of his shoes. *Yes, I watch my sister undress.*

It was unfathomable to Alan; his family took modesty beyond the extreme. He hadn't even seen Beth in her underwear, which she seemed to *live* in. She wore it during the day, of course, but she also wore it under her *pajamas* — to bed! He half expected to find it in the clothes basket, drenched after her shower.

He remembered a boy who had confided in him last year, telling him that he wished he had a sister like Beth. Alan had listened to the boy and reflected on his sister as a friend and a cohort, someone to help buffer the cold wall of their parents.

His thoughts returned to Kurtz watching Louise undress. It didn't really seem dirty to him when he thought of that way. Of course Kurtz would want to see her body — who wouldn't? He remembered Louise at the quarry — her breasts so clearly visible, so near, so three dimensional.

Alan showered, and while he did he kept returning to thoughts of his sister's body. It was as if her relationship with a scumbag like Phillip had made her fair game for *anybody*.

Something else had changed. Beth had never before left her underwear on the floor of the bathroom. A bra was a sacred thing. How many boys would give their right arm to be reincarnated as a bra? A beautiful girl's bra — for in pre-adolescent simplicity, beautiful girls had beautiful breasts — how could it be otherwise?

And ugly girls? No boy wanted to guess — wanted to know — the answer was too painfully clear.

Alan fixated on his sister's bra on the bathroom floor, fixated as he stood beneath the spraying water, his own skinny body naked, his own *little* body naked, his own awakened body, beneath the torrent.

Alan thought of her bra as he fought the other fantasy. He resisted thinking of her in her bedroom, because he knew the Beth who would leave her bra on the bathroom floor was not the Beth who slept in flannel.

Naked Beth. His naked sister.

Alan imagined himself walking down the hall. He had a towel wrapped around him — he was naked — no, he was fully dressed. He pushed her door open more quietly than he had ever done anything in his life, and there before him, there with the sheet pushed down to her knees, was Beth.

Alan's first erection was wonderful.

Phillip got into an argument in the first five minutes of his work day. For a change, it wasn't because Old Man Horvath was in a bad mood. For the first time ever, it was a fight precipitated by Phillip. Started by Phillip to punish someone, in all probability, himself.

"We need more rags around this place," Phillip had announced with annoying certainty, and Old Man Horvath had responded as Phillip knew he would.

"Before you came here, we had rags in every corner. You come here, Mr. Shining Car, and all my rags are missing. Rag man used to come once a month, took a box of old rags, left a band of new-clean rags. Now he comes at the end of the month and we have eight, maybe ten rags to give him. 'Where are the rest?'

he says, 'You eating them? he asks. 'Quilting a blanket?' So he sells me — *sells me* — a new band of rags.

"I tell you, Mr. Phillip, I tell you, if I ever find you stealing my rags, you will be walking — you can take a walk then — for if you steal my rags, you will steal anything. A thief is a thief, Mr. Phillip."

Alan washed himself, careful with his many bruises, and imagined his sister's body. He tried to compare it with the pictures in the magazines he had hidden in the loft of the garage. And he thought of her breasts.

How could any boy imagine anything else when every magazine had the girl covering her pubic area with her hand or holding a book there, or worse, have it lost in some photographic fuzz nightmare which always and only happened to that area of a girl's body?

An offshoot of his parents' protective-obsessive resistance to admitting that any of them had bodies was Alan's aversion to touching himself as he stood and washed, thinking of his sister.

But Alan's imagination walked him down the corridor of their hallway and pushed opened the forbidden door — the door to her bedroom — the door to where she dressed and undressed and slept — the room where she took off her pajamas — her innocuous flannel pajamas — and then her underwear (she had to change it sometime) and briefly stood naked, before she put on her clothes — before she put on a fresh bra — *put her breasts in her bra!*

Alan wondered what it would feel like to have breasts. He looked down at his skinny chest and imagined his sister's in its place. He thought himself a chest, trying the many sizes and shapes he had absorbed from the hidden magazines, and then added random nipples, all the while imagining himself to be his sister, or like his sister, and then it stopped — it reached a catastrophic end when he imagined them touched by someone else; for the only person he could think of, the only hands he saw reaching for his-Beth's breasts, were greasy hands, hands smeared with grime and overlain with grit, the only hands which sullied his perfect Beth-chest, were Phillip's — the same hands, when clenched, that had beaten him — humiliated him — driven home that he was still 'little Alan'. *Little Alan. Little Alan.*

And then two images wrestled in Alan's mind. First was the plan. The new plan was perfect. It was excellent. It was irresistible and only a fool would fail to see its lethal overtones.

It was a toss-up if Phillip — if Phillip and Junior — could survive it.

The other image was of Beth. Beth in bed. Beth naked in bed.

Beth had never slept in anything but her bra and panties and then an overlay of flannel. Plain flannel. Striped flannel. Flowered flannel. Always the coating, the protective wrapper.

It was exactly what he had hoped Horvath would do — call him a thief — call him a thief so he could tell him to jam his fucking garage — jam his grease and dirt in summer, and melting snow and wet floors in winter. Stick it all. Chuck it all.

Phillip had planned it to where they stood — his boss in opposition, accusing Phillip of being dishonest.

The problem was, that for the first time ever, it rang true. The old man was right. Phillip thought, *I am a thief. I am a thief and this man is an idiot to keep me.*

He stared at Old Man Horvath and finally saw him — a mechanic — a fucking mechanic, when every other Jew wouldn't get near anything dirtier than a fucking pencil.

At last he asked, "One question, Mr. Horvath. . . ."

It was the first time he had every addressed him as 'mister'.

The little Jewish man looked at him with the wariness of a mongoose confronting a cobra.

"Yes, one question, Mr. Phillip. What do you ask?"

'Mr. Phillip' did not have its usual ring of sarcasm.

"What do you ask?" he repeated.

It was early morning and no customers had come in yet to demand their unfinished automobiles. The shop was quiet — even the telephone was silent.

"Why are you here?" Phillip asked. "I mean, why are you *here*? I can tell you're a really smart man, Mr. Horvath. What I mean is, why aren't you working in a bank or something. Why don't you *own* a bank or something?"

The old man looked beyond Phillip. He looked into a past which Phillip could no more understand than he could a Martian dropping in to have his space ship tuned.

Cloaked in sadness, wearing a sacred robe whose fringes Phillip could hardly understand, he said, "Phillip, I have tried to work with people — *my people* have tried to work with people — and we cannot — it does not work.

"So I have turned to machines, my young friend. I have turned to machines," the old man looked away before he continued, "because they do not *hate*. They do not hate."

Phillip listened in silence and then his employer added, "and they do not steal."

The two stood in the presence of the automobiles and machines.

Will picked up Freddy and they reviewed their plan. It was incredible to each that neither showed signs of wishing to back out.

"The more I think of it, the better it sounds," Will said, defiantly glaring at Freddy, waiting for him to show any signs of altering what they had earlier decided upon.

But he was relieved and surprised when Freddy countered, "I was awake half of the night thinking about it and I think we have a winner this time."

Freddy watched Will drive and then added, "I think we can depend on the Kurtz kid — he's game. And I think Beth's little brother will come through too, although I don't think we really *have* to exactly match her handwriting. Frankly, I doubt if Phillip Brute-mind could tell hers from Ghengis Khan's."

"Frankly," Will amended, "I don't think Phillip Grease-brain can read."

"Then we're in trouble," Freddy said with feigned concern.

The Doll Man couldn't sleep. His schedule had been disrupted and then he had the confrontation with Phillip. He paced back and forth in his room, his clothing in a heap on the floor, a succession of dolls lifted, carried, set down, and then retrieved again.

It was as if Ezechial had everything he had ever depended upon yanked from him. Nothing was the same, and most important, the machines weren't running and they should have been. Not only that, but the old lady or the girl or someone should have left another package by now and they hadn't.

The brother-boyfriend-son had come — with nothing. He had stood there and done absolutely nothing.

Yes, *he* had shut the door. Yes, he had left him standing out there. The visitor had gone. Ezechial had shut the door, so he had to be gone. It was done. Finished. There was no more finality unless it was the tombs in the graveyard.

His mother.

His sister and his father.

Marked by his precious granite from his precious quarry. It didn't make sense to the old man. If they cut the stone and people died while cutting it, died while wrenching the granite free from the earth, then why cut the stone at all? Why die freeing a tombstone?

The machines were silent. They were silent for so much of the year, and now when they should no longer be resting, when they should be doing what they were designed to do, created to do, they were still silent and it was totally unacceptable to Ezechial. It was a pent-up scream in him. It was a taunt from the gods he could not answer.

He lived for his machines. He lived to care for them and to bring them back to life when he could.

Ezechial imagined he heard his machines. He imagined he felt them through the floor and that he smelled them spinning, whirling in the stone walls of the machinery shed. His imagination was more satisfying than the fact, for the machines did not move. They were ready; they had been prepared, but they did nothing but drip oil and water in the darkness.

The Doll Man knew he would start them tomorrow, regardless of the circumstances. He would light the fire, he would kindle it into water-festering flames.

He could not sit or remain still. He worried away the time, disturbing decades of dust. His room bore the tread of a nervous man times sixty.

Just when Ezechial made himself stop thinking of the brooding machines beneath him, he remembered the carton which had not arrived, and was perplexed anew regarding his friends who had not appeared.


Alan wrapped a towel around his waist and sneaked down the hallway to his sister's room. He left a trail of wet foot prints and dripping water, for he did not wait to dry himself completely. His hair hung in thin strands above his eyes and drooped along his ears, and his skinny neck craned forward, pushing his head in the van, forcing it to lead the way.

But as he got closer it was neither Kurtz's Louise nor the Beth of his fantasies he was stalking. It was his big sister after all, the one to whom he turned for help or advice.

He hesitated at her closed door. He studied its paneling and touched the cool knob. Turning it with the tips of his fingers, slowly revolving his wrist, Alan twisted his hand until there was a faint click.

He would not look. He would get her notebook — any of her notebooks — and steal away without even once looking in her direction.

Downstairs, his mother rattled around in the kitchen and then he heard her open the basement door — she was probably going down to the laundry room.

Outside, Blacky barked and then stopped.

The dog barked again.

Beth's alarm clock ticked on her dresser. She shifted in her bed and Alan heard the smooth rustle of the sheets.

He would not look.

He rose to his tip-toes and stepped soundlessly across her room, engulfed by the smells of Beth, the fragrance of his sister. He locked his eyes on her closet door and then her dresser.

The alarm clock ticked on her dresser beside a pile of change — quarters, half dollars, and dimes neatly stacked, pennies and nickels in an inter-mixed mound.

There was a row of perfume bottles, a few pieces of jewelry, and a china cup with *The Great Smokey Mountains* written in diagonal script on the side.

The mirror on the back of her dresser was castellated with postcards. Alan looked at them and saw that they were mostly from the trips their parents took together while Beth and Alan were in school. Those were the worst times, for then their grandmother came and stayed with them and she was more strict than their parents.

Her idea of a good time for a kid was to go to the library and write a report.

"But Granny, we don't *have* to do a report," they would protest, "our teachers didn't *assign* us a report. We're not supposed to do one!"

Their grandmother would smile triumphantly. "Then write one about something you want to learn about. Just think how impressed your friends will be — why you could have them over and you could read it to them. Or you could take it to school and give it to your favorite teacher to read. Oh my! Wouldn't they think you were cunning!"

Her other brilliant idea in the area of child care was the never-ending nap.

"Well now, children, I know you must have had an exhausting day at school and Thelma Watson just told me that the flu is going around (the flu always went around — at least for Thelma Watson it did. She used its presence as an introduction to her speeches concerning the state of her gastrointestinal tract — an apparatus which was usually blocked, bloated, gaseous, painful, or chock-full of diarrhea), so why don't you take a little nap upstairs until dinner time."

"But we're not tired, Granny," Beth would implore, having the same effect on the old woman as a sprinkle of rain on the Hoover Dam.

"Well, just rest your eyes a little. It won't do to have you ill when your parents get home. It just wouldn't do."

The old lady had finally driven Alan to switch his girlie magazine collection from the garage to under his mattress until his parents returned.

He hardly would have believed it possible, but he had taken so many naps he tired on occasion of the women who waited for him in two dimensional nudity.

With their clothes off — now there was the curse. Here was Alan in his sister's room, dressed in a wet towel, looking at the postcards on her mirror and thinking of naked girls. He tried to resist the other. But his eyes began to drift away from the cards.

He convinced himself it was different if he took a quick look through the mirror. Less direct. He wasn't really seeing her — just her reflection. A sexual bank-shot. Oblique voyeurism.

Alan drew in his breath when he saw her.

She was on her back, one leg drawn to the side, her arms spread and her head resting on the pillow, facing his back. The sheet — the top sheet — ran at an angle from her right foot to her shoulder, leaving a slash of flesh exposed.

Alan's mouth dropped open. His eyes went mad in the mirror.

There was so much to see — both of her breasts were there, one slightly to the side and a different shape than the other. And her legs — between her legs — he saw *her*. He saw *it*.

Actually, he saw her dark hair, the downy adolescent triangle, appearing strange and soft, yet missing something to his unaccustomed eye.

She breathed and Alan watched her chest move and thought he could see her heart beating, pulsing slowly under her pale skin.

He was mesmerized. This was different from magazines. Different from Louise, even, as he had seen her through the car window.

He didn't know if he would ever be able to move from where he stood. He hadn't realized it yet, so entranced was he, but like the man in mythology, he was beginning to turn to stone — partially.

Somehow his eyes strayed to her face, an unintentional act with so much else to see, but they did, and Alan saw how pretty his sister really was. Her face was relaxed in sleep and she looked so fresh and clean to him. Her cheeks were soft, her lips were slightly open and they were the same color as her nipples. Her eyebrows seemed perfect to him, and her eyes — her eyes were open and they seemed so dreamy as they looked at him.

HOLY SHIT!

Alan spun around. His heart dropped. He wished to leap for the door. He wished to be anywhere else in the world. He would take an extended visit with his grandmother.

He couldn't look at his sister after he turned, and then he did. She still watched him and Alan flirted desperately with the possibility that she was sleeping with her eyes open — Kurtz sometimes did. He prayed for a snore. Just a little one.

And then her eyes moved and Alan realized they were looking at the floor at his feet, at the towel on the floor at his feet, and then they rose to barely below his waist.

Beth smiled.

She spoke, and when she did the amazing thing was that she was still kind, loving, Beth, and still she made no move to cover herself.

She spoke through her sleepy smile.

"My little brother. Little Alan. I don't think I'll call you that any more."

And then she smiled at him and stared into his eyes and continued, "It looks like we've grown up, Alan. I don't think we're little kids anymore. What do you think?"

*How could she be so unconscious of her nakedness?* Alan marveled, standing unclothed before her dresser. He thought of her last question and something told him that he had better look while he still had the chance, so he did. He took her in from toe to forehead, pausing where he thought he should take the extra time.

And Beth spoke again and closed the door. "Hey," it was breathy when she said it, and it was as if she'd just gotten a great idea. "Hey," she had said, and then continued, "why don't you let me get dressed? Mom could come back up here, you know."

With the mention of their mother, the magic evaporated and there Alan stood naked in front of his big sister, and him as hard as a rock and her looking at him and then all of that compounded by the thought of his mother — the *image* of his mother standing in Beth's doorway, her hands on her hips initially, and then as she took in the situation, their flying to her face as she screamed, "HELP! POLICE! COME QUICK! MY SON HAS TURNED INTO A PERVERT!"

Alan left the room hastily, nearly tripping over the towel, but not stopping to get it. He raced down the hall as if chased, and barged into his own room, slamming the door loudly behind him and dancing around as he tried to get his underwear on before the church youth group came strolling through. "Gosh, I've never seen a real pervert before, Miss Lordenbacher — but I've read a lot about them."

He was determined to dress and get out of the house as quickly as he could. He knew what he would do then — he would find a quiet place where he could be alone and he would review his morning.

Again and again and again.

The last thought he had as he escaped his house was his grandmother appearing and calling after him, "Alan, honey, why don't you come in here and take a nap with your sister?"

Phillip and Old Man Horvath worked together on a particularly tricky cam installation and timing job, and it was the first time either of them had truly enjoyed the company of the other.

"You have good hands and a good mind, young man. You put in good honest work and long hours, and someday you'll have a shop of your own. You could have a shop of your own, Mr. Phillip, and you wouldn't have to answer to anyone."

He was proud of his garage. He was proud that he, a Jew in Maine, had worked with his hands and shown them all — shown them that he was a *man*, that he was a *craftsman*, a *mechanic*. And no one had noticed.

Old Man Horvath runs a garage — yes — so what? I always count my change.

No, not that he's *Jewish*, and he runs a *garage* — now what do you think of *that?*

Think of *what?*

Mid-afternoon, Alan and Cavenaugh and Roger and Kurtz rendez-voused at the school yard. Cavenaugh brought with him a pad of paper and a pen. Kurtz carried a vial of perfume he had stolen from his sister. Alan was supposed to have a sample of his sister's handwriting.

He did not.

They sat at the back of the school and Cavenaugh propped a pad of paper in front of him, on his lap. He turned to Alan who was ruing his request.

"Let's have it, my man."

Alan merely looked at him. Cavenaugh looked cock-eyed at Alan. "Come on, don't screw around, we don't have a lot of time. Fork over a note or something."

Alan turned to the others and responded defensively, "We don't need a sample. She writes all loop de loop with circles for dots on her i's and curves crossing her t's." He searched the eyes of each of his friends, knowing he had failed them and aware of the reason.

He had had sex with his sister.

And in his mind it was true.

You go out with a girl. You say really nice things. You take her to a movie. You buy her fries and a soda later. You kiss her. You kiss her again. Eventually, if you kissed her enough and said all the right things, she let you touch her. Or maybe if you are really lucky she let you look at them.

That was sex.

Alan's friends were confused by his behavior.

But before they would respond to little Alan's latest strangeness, he remembered that he wasn't 'Little Alan'. Fuck 'Little Alan'. He was Alan.

"Look, guys, she was in her room all morning. I couldn't get a note or anything. So, big deal. Besides, the macho-moron surely hasn't seen her writing, and tell me that if he has, he'll remember what it looks like."

The others were agape having witnessed Alan's graduation ceremony.

Kurtz was the first to speak. "Excuse me, but what happened to our old Alan? Is this the part where you flex biceps the size of sheep or do you just flop out a dong the length of a donkey's."

Roger laughed with Kurtz's allusions and said, "I think he has a point about Phillip. Let's just write the damn note and get it over with. We told Will and Freddy we'd get it done before three-thirty."

"And we don't want to disappoint Will and Freddy," Kurtz quipped.

Cavenaugh settled into agreement and started writing. "Okay, you guys, how does this sound?"

Phillip had just finished lowering the block back to the engine mounts, Old Man Horvath guiding it the last few inches, when the Old Man looked behind him.

He turned to Phillip and gave a confidential wink.

"Well look here, it's young Alan. What can we do for you? Your bicycle machine explode a piston?"

Alan raised a half hearted smile for Mr. Horvath and then glared at Phillip.

He burned his eyes through him as he spoke.

"My sister paid me to bring this down to you, don't think for a minute I'd have done it any other way."

He handed a folded note to Phillip and then walked off, departing with the words to Old Man Horvath, "I'll have a car someday, you wait and see."

The old man watched him stomp out and then grab the bike he had left outside of the garage door.

"You know, that lad doesn't appear too pleased with you, Mr. Phillip, but it sounds like he knows where he's going."

Phillip clutched the note in his hand and watched the boy pedal off. Then as if he had just heard him he responded to his employer's comment.

"Yes, he knows where he's going — and I know he sure as hell don't like where he's been.'

The old man observed Phillip's eyes as he spoke. He thought of the note and said to Phillip's relief, "That's special delivery, if there ever was, son, why don't you take a break and see what it says?"

Phillip opened the note as he walked.

*Son*, he thought, and he went to his room.

The old man sat and drank a soda, jumping when Phillip whooped, "HOT SHIT!"

Phillip ran to the waiting room and grabbed the phone. He made no attempt to keep his voice down when he reached Junior's mother.

"Yes, hello, hello to you — tell Junior I'll pick him up right after work — just tell him the girls want to see us." And then he whooped again as he hung up.

He nearly floated back to join his employer. The remainder of the day he did ninety percent of the work while Mr. Horvath observed in awe.

Will sat on the front fender of his car. Freddy rested against the other. The boys lounged nearby.

"Well, the wheels of fate have begun to spin, my friends. Let's hope all goes as we planned."

Will hopped down and went back to his trunk, opened it and retrieved a massive set of wire cutters — bolt cutters, really.

He held them aloft as if they were a prize.

"Kurtz, front and center."

Kurtz was prepared to march forward when Alan interrupted the proceedings.

"No, I'll do it."

Before Kurtz knew what was happening, Alan strode up to Will and took the tool from him.

"Show me what to do — it should be me — I'm the smallest."

Freddy watched and commented, "I said it all along, it should be him."

Will sized Alan, "I didn't think he had the balls."

Alan was already sliding under Freddy's sedan, saying, "Let's talk tomorrow — show me what to do."

Freddy and Will exchanged glances and then checked Cavenaugh. He shrugged his shoulders and grinned.

"Looks like a willing recruit to me."

Kurtz had remained silent as long as he could.

"Excuse me *girls*, but I think we need a man for the job."

Alan had rolled under the car and was grunting his way toward the back.

"I think we already have one, Kurtzy," Cavenaugh answered.

All of them, the boys and Will and Freddy, and Phillip and Junior would say it was one of the fastest days in their lives. Beth and Louise would say it had passed slowly, and the other kids who happened to be at the quarry, recalled it as the most exciting.

The coupe rumbled up to Junior's house. It had barely stopped before Junior was bounding across the lawn. He flung himself onto the seat beside Phillip.

"Bingo! Bingo! Bingo! Those broads need us, Phillip, my man, they fuckin' need us."

Phillip did not want to, but he had to smile in agreement.

Junior had to continue. Phillip had read the note to him.

"They have to see us at the quarry at five sharp — they *have* to see us."

He grinned at Phillip who was now massaging the coupe through the gears. It was fifteen minutes until five.

Junior as much as had his pants down.

"There's no controlling us; we're lethal studs."

Through Junior's tone, Phillip could sense the change. It was not Junior the follower. It was, at best, Junior the equal, with a maddening hints of Junior-the-superior. The feeling was confirmed with his next proclamation.

"Drive on, James, I have a meeting with a very important pussy — V.I.P."

He slugged Phillip's arm. "Get it? Get it?"

Phillip did not deign to turn his head.

"I get your fuckin' point, Junior."

But he couldn't stay angry. The girls wanted to see them again. They had forgiven them. Beth had forgiven him.

They roared out past the town limits and closed on the quarry.

Will and Freddy quizzed Alan for the eight hundredth time.

For the eight hundredth time, Alan responded perfectly: *First he did this, then he did that, and he was careful of this and the other, and finally he was really careful and did one more thing.*

*Stay low, be quiet, work swiftly, be quiet. Do it right, be quiet.*

"You can depend on me, you guys." Alan semi-boasted to them at last.

"Do you really think he's strong enough?" Kurtz challenged.

"It's leverage, Kurtz, simply leverage. Those cutters have handles long enough that my little sister could do it," Roger said referring to the sister he did not have.

And then, as the ways of fate would have it, Kurtz asked, "Speaking of sisters, Alan, you ever see yours naked? I guess we've all seen Louise by now, but how about old virginal Beth — you ever see those big floppers?"

It was with effort that Alan kept his mouth from dropping open. It was with even more effort that he restrained himself from glancing to his crotch to see if he had somehow betrayed himself.

He did react in the time honored and respected fashion. He flipped Kurtz the finger.

But for the plan, it was a normal, sunny, summer afternoon at the quarry. A normal *late* afternoon. By now the swimmers had left the water and had either gone home or were in groups around the various vehicles, talking, laughing, and listening to their radios.

The raft was snugged against the landing wall and The Devils Club was in the stills of a back corner, surrounded by flotsam and jetsam. The water was blue-green and its surface was roiled here and there from the light winds and the last vestiges of divers.

Freddy sat beside Will in the rusty sedan. It was parked — stopped really — in the middle of the road to the machinery shed. The boys were in the woods, hiding behind slabs of granite. Alan and Kurtz lay behind the block which Phillip and Beth had rested upon.

Kurtz was talking a mile a minute about everything in the world which didn't matter. Alan was on his stomach resting with his chin on his hands. There was a thin ribbon of red rock running through the grey granite which Alan traced with his eyes and then with the tip of his finger. As he did he lost track of Kurtz and where they were.

When the coupe rumbled onto the machinery shed road, Alan was the only one who didn't hear. He lay engrossed in the line of crimson stone shot red hot through the cooled granite.

Freddy climbed out of the sedan and walked around to its front. The hood was already up and Freddy leaned over the fender side, idiotically touching various parts of the engine, completely in the dark as to what they were.

Will grabbed the door handle and prepared to get out of his car. He was sweating so badly his armpits were soaked.

Kurtz shook Alan. "Get ready to move, hero, here they come. If you're gonna shit yourself, you better do it now, while you got the time."

Alan looked at him and was startled. Briefly, he had forgotten where he was and what he was about to do.

"Yes, I'm ready," he said but he looked dazed to Kurtz.

"You're real fuckin' ready, Alan."

Kurtz reached to the side of them and picked up the cutters. "If you were any more ready, you'd be home in bed." He shook his head, "Christ, are you sure you're up for this?"

With Kurtz's last question, Phillip's blue coupe thundered up to the granite block they were hiding behind.

"Now, asshole, now."

Alan snatched the tool from Kurtz and gave him a long, deathly stare. It unnerved Kurtz who had been thinking of Alan as a wimp.

"Excuse me, killer," Kurtz mumbled.

Alan moved on his hands and knees to the back side of the slab. He listened to Phillip boil out of the coupe. As they had anticipated, Junior was not a second behind.

While the two strode to Will's car, now blocking their way, Alan crawled out to the side of the coupe and then rolled easily under it. He worked from a back-down position, running his hand over the myriad of frame members, braces, bundles of wire, springs and other things which were as foreign to Alan as the tools for brain surgery. He scooted toward the front of the car, found what he thought was the correct thing and levered the cutters into place.

The copper line cut like chewing gum and liquid drained out of it. Alan rolled quickly to the other side and repeated the cut. More liquid.

"Shit fuck, shit fuck," he whispered to himself.

When he was finished under the front of the coupe he began to undulate like a restricted inchworm toward the middle.

"Too bad we don't have a tank," Junior swore. "We could ram this piece of shit out of the way — into the quarry — and I'm just the man to do it."

Phillip glared at his friend as they walked away from the coupe.

"*If* you had a car that ran. . . ."

"Fuck you. Help me fix it."

Each walked to opposite sides of Will's sedan. Will spoke first.

"Nice job fixing my car, Phillip. I heard about the potato trick, did you have to screw it up after you got my money."

Phillip stood at Will's window, his face void of emotion as he listened to Will's accusations. "I guess I owe you one," was all Phillip said before he walked around to the front of the sedan.

Junior had his head at the passenger side window and heard the exchange. He couldn't believe Phillip's tone. Before he joined Phillip he waited for Will to look at him. When he did, he sneered, "Fuck you, asswipe." and walked away.

Phillip was to the side of Freddy, who had dutifully gotten grease on his hands. He did not speak to Phillip, he just gazed into the engine compartment.

"What seems to be the problem?" Phillip asked, tentatively.

"How would I know?" Freddy responded, anger and sarcasm tempering his voice.

Phillip reached in. "There's your problem, distributor wire's half out. You're not gettin' any fire in there."

He jammed the wire in place and shouted to Will, "Try'er now."

Will stalled for a moment and then turned the key. The sedan's tired engine lurched to life.

Phillip walked past Will's window on his way back to the coupe.

Over the noise of his sputtering and coughing engine Will asked, "How much do I owe you for that little trick?"

Phillip paused and said, "Look Will, it's like I said; I owe you, okay? Let it go. It's on me, and probably a tune-up, too.

Of the three who heard him — Will, Freddy, and Junior — it would have been impossible to judge who was more surprised.

Junior shook his head and pushed past Freddy.

Freddy slammed the hood and went around to the passenger side of the sedan. As he got in he saw that Will was as incredulous as he.

Will looked in his mirror, "Did I just miss something? Did he lift my wallet or something?"

Freddy wouldn't turn around. "Maybe they've got the girls with them and once again the joke's on us."

"I don't think so," Will lamented as he pulled the sedan slowly forward.

Then Freddy spoke as if coming out of a coma, "Gheez, we're doing a personality profile on the town morons when Beth's little brother is crawlin' though the jaws of death. Is he done? Is he out?"

"My god, I haven't been paying any attention either. I guess he's crawled clear. What do we do now?"

"I guess we drive out of the way."

Phillip fired the coupe.

When he did, Alan nearly passed out from fright. The long-handled bolt-cutters had become wedged between the ground and the frame of the coupe as he shimmied back toward the rear of the car. He had only finished freeing them and was just raising the cutting tips to his mark when the coupe started.

"Oh fuck shit," Alan cried and grabbed a cross member.

Alan's choices were quite limited — he could *attempt* to finish the job and risk being dragged under the coupe — an uneven section of rock roadway would kill him in the crush — he could give up and roll out and perhaps be run over as he did — he could give up and let the coupe drive away and hope that it didn't snag him as it passed over — or finally, he could hang on and let the coupe drag him and hope that it stopped again so that he could finish the job.

It was really not a choice from Alan's point of view. He had two more cuts to make. He snipped the first. More liquid. He rolled to the side to attack the last section of tubing.

In his rush, Alan caught his shirt on a protruding piece of metal. He ignored it and stretched to make his last cut.

The coupe started to roll. At first Phillip eased out the clutch and drifted forward as Will pulled the sedan out of the way, the big coupe's engine throbbing and perking like a coffee maker.

Alan was being pulled with the coupe as it inched forward. He worked desperately with the ungainly cutters, trying as he did to lift his head from the passing road. His feet dragged at the heels and were dangerously close to the rear tires.

Phillip idled forward gently. Alan put all of his weight into the handles of the cutters.

The coupe was picking up speed. The engine, incredibly loud from the beginning, was gaining in volume.

"Shut-fuck. Shit-fuck. Shit-fuck." Alan feared they would be his last words ever.

Will's sedan was completely out of the way and Phillip could not resist the audience. He depressed the clutch and floored the gas pedal. Alan had his head within a foot of the cut-off exhaust pipes. The heat seemed ready to cook him if he didn't explode first from the noise.

The coupe was slowing down, momentarily coasting.

But not for long.

Phillip watched the tachometer needle leap to 4000. He slipped his foot off of the side of the clutch pedal. In an instant the screaming power from the engine had a direct mechanical link to the rear tires.

Fourteen inches of under-inflated butyl spun and howled and burned. The new sound — that of squealing rubber — brought Alan precariously close to cardiac arrest.

The coupe leaped forward the instant Alan cut through the last section of copper pipe. He dropped the cutters. He was ready to let the coupe drive over him, but that was not to be.

His shirt bunched with the lurch of the coupe and the roll of material had more than enough strength to carry his weight. It held as the coupe instantly picked up speed.

Alan screamed into the maw of the thundering exhaust. He heard "shit-fuck" rattling around in his brain.

All four brake lines were cut, Alan was certain of that.

And the coupe was racing hell-bent-for-leather toward the end of the quarry where Phillip *thought* he would slam on the brakes as usual.

"SHIT-FUCK! SHIT-FUCK! SHIT-FUCK!"

Phillip drifted the blue coupe through the last corner before he headed straight for the edge, and when he did, Alan's feet twisted closer to a still-spinning rear wheel.

He reacted and tried to draw his legs under him, but as he started to tuck them, his left tennis shoe toe was snagged by the racing wheel. There was an instantaneous fight and tug of war as the tire devoured more and more of the toe of the shoe and Alan tried desperately to pull it free.

Both won. The tennis shoe was inexorably shredded under the tire as the boy ripped his unclad foot forward.

Alan had both of his knees tucked to his chest as the howling coupe straightened and bolted the last fifty feet to the lip of the quarry.

Every child who was still at the quarry watched the blurred coupe spring for the edge.

Kurtz had scrambled out from behind the granite, as had Roger and Cavenaugh from their hiding places. Will and Freddy intuitively understood what had happened when they didn't see Alan.

There was no time for words.

"Shit !"

"Fuck!"

"Holy Christ!"

and a few others were still mid-throat.

The granite was biting into the bare skin of Alan's back. He was being pummeled as the coupe bounced, alternately thrown from the ground to the underside of the coupe and back.

Less than ten feet from the lip of the quarry, and the same instant Phillip stood on the brake pedal and felt it give as an over-ripe banana, Alan felt the final bath of brake fluid and the coincidental release of his shirt.

The powerful coupe roared away from him.

Phillip was determined to give them all a good show. It was an atonement.

Junior was ripping mad that Phillip had once more decided to risk both of their lives. If he had remembered two minutes earlier he would have walked the last stretch and let Phillip perform his asshole act alone. The instant he saw the panic in Phillip's features, he peripherally noted Phillip's foot jab *all the way to the floor.*

And then they were airborne. Arcing impossibly beyond the lip, beyond the hard granite, through the giving air.

Junior had time to shoot Phillip a killing stare before he clutched the dashboard with both hands and watched the opposite wall and then the water dominate his view through the windshield.

He yelled.

The desire to reach over and throttle Phillip wended through Junior's flirtation with the reality of his own mortality — his approaching mortality.

He was incredulous when he realized that Phillip had his own door open and was halfway out, his body contorted with the humor of weightlessness. The final seconds before the blue coupe became a submarine, Phillip hung in the air outside of it, one hand on the open door, the rest of his body in the position of a circus tumbler, hands and arms spread just prior to taking a bow.

The car hit the water nose first, and the louvered hood ripped backwards, and so doing, covered the windshield. Consequently, the glass did not absorb its full share of the impact and Junior was not given a glass face-lift.

The most natural and anticipated reaction for the boys and Will and Freddy would have seemed to have been to race to the edge of the quarry wall and observe what they had done.

But they didn't. No one moved.

Phillip's door wrenched free from the impact and by a quirk of trapped air, remained afloat. The coupe plunged downward. Junior was smashed into his door by the water rushing through where the driver's door had been.

Phillip surfaced immediately and oriented himself. Just behind him an incredible flurry of bubbles ruffled the broken surface. He swam through the turgid water and dove.

His shoes had been torn from him and it took him but a moment to kick his pants free from his body. The water was too disrupted for him to see anything, but he swam hard after the sinking automobile.

There was a deception regarding the coupe's rate of sink — while it did hit the water with respectable velocity, it pushed the water aside briefly and then actually rose momentarily from the mass of air trapped in the trunk and passenger compartment.

It hovered at approximately five to ten feet under the water and then as the buoyant air escaped, it resumed its trip to the bottom.

As the compensating forces of physics counter-played, Junior gained control of his body. He thrust himself against his door twice, staring stupidly through the water at Phillip's missing door as he did. At last he remembered to use the handle and the door swung away and he clawed out.

He struggled at swimming, immediately entangling his arms in those of Phillip, who was diving to save him. The two performed an underwater dance of the ridiculous until Phillip gained control and pushed Junior upward.

They broke the surface one after the other to the cheers of the children who had seen the flight.

Phillip roughly dragged Junior through the water toward the low quarry wall. Before he was halfway there, several boys had pushed the raft from the landing and paddled out to them. They pulled them one after the other onto the tipping raft.

Junior gasped and heaved, his chest inflating and then collapsing as he wheezed and finally retched over the side. Phillip stared back at where his car had hit the water, his eyes following the bobbing door as it drifted in the opposite direction.

By the time they reached the landing, Junior had unfortunately regained his breath. He was the first to climb over the low granite side, and after he did he turned to Phillip. Junior waited until he reached the granite plateau, the last seconds offering his hand to Phillip so that he could gain his feet.

Then, as the others left the raft, Phillip and Junior stood apart. There was a half smile of disbelief on Phillip's face as he turned from the floating door and looked at Junior. It was then that Junior caught him in the face with a double right and then a vicious crossing left before he knew what hit him.

Years of humiliation and groveling brought Junior's next blow up from the ground and solidly into Phillip's solar-plexus. Junior did not wait for the gasp, for he followed by a clip to the groin, and then as Phillip fell, a raised knee to the upper chest.

Phillip lay curled on the wet granite, his face bleeding, his breath gone and a noxious wave rippling continuously through his stomach.

He lay in his undershorts, his coupe gone, his body beaten by his friend, and in a final ignominious moment, he collected a broken tooth with his tongue and pushed it and an accumulation of saliva and blood past his lips.

He pursed his lips and pushed the piece of white enamel out far enough that he could take it with his fingers. As he did he moved to a sitting position and examined the broken tooth.

He probed with his tongue to find the remaining stub.

"Well, fuck you," he said and tossed the tooth into the quarry.

He watched it as it turned end over end and sank through the remarkably clear water.

By now Will and Freddy and the boys had gathered and decided to make a hasty and quiet departure from the quarry. They piled into Freddy's sedan, listening in anticipation as the old engine smoked to life, and then they breathed more easily as Will backed around and headed out the quarry road.

Phillip was still seated at the quarry landing when he caught the sound of Will's sedan. He tried to get a glimpse of it but couldn't, and then when he couldn't hear it any longer, he turned his attention to the door, still afloat, but now drifting past the corner of the larger derrick.

The ends of his bloodied mouth turned up into a painful grin and Phillip shook his head slowly. "Well, I'll be damned," he said, realizing what the boys had accomplished.

A sophomore with an acne problem kneeled beside Phillip and asked if he needed a ride home. Phillip accepted, more moved by the boy's clumsy attempt at friendship than by his diving coupe.

Alan and his friends were silent as they drove through town and one by one Will dropped them off at their homes. They had agreed earlier to meet behind the school the next morning. There they would move ahead with the construction of an underwater camera.

There had been no celebration, only momentary concern for Alan's cuts and bruises. It would be some time before he received the recognition commensurate with his hero status. As it was, each of the boys was in a state of shock regarding what they had accomplished and what they had narrowly avoided.

Beth was in the living room when Alan came home. She looked up from her magazine when she heard him, but neither of them spoke immediately.

Beth took in Alan's scraped face, arms, and hands, the torn shirt, the mangled shoe, and the covering of grease and dust. But he didn't look like a little boy. His injuries did not appear serious, but neither were they those of a child. Earlier in the week, Beth would have run semi-hysterically to him, but now she saw that he did not appear concerned, more resigned than anything, and so she let it go. He would tell her later, she knew that.

At last, Alan interrupted the silence. "Where's Mom and Dad?"

Beth gave him a look which communicated more than a month's conversation. Coincidentally, a voice called from the kitchen.

"Alan, honey, is that you?"

He rolled his eyes.

"Yes, Grandma, it's me," he answered with resignation.

"Well, listen dear, I'm starting supper now — why don't you take a nice shower while Beth and I work in the kitchen — there's time for you to take a little nap before we eat." She waited for Alan's protests and when they didn't come she attempted to mollify him, regardless. "You don't have to put your pajamas on just yet, just lie down and rest your eyes until we call you."

Beth laughed into her hand.

Alan gazed in his grandmother's direction. "Gee, grandma, I was kinda planning to do some work on a report. Is that okay?"

Brother and sister could hear the pleasure in her answer.

"Oh my, that's wonderful, Alan. Perhaps I could read it when you've finished."

Beth could barely contain herself.

Alan managed.

"Sure grandma, but it's awfully long and involved. Kinda technical, too."

She would not be denied.

"That's fine, dear. You could explain it to me. I'm awfully old fashioned — it's time these old bones learned a new trick or two."

Alan slapped his open palm to his head in mock frustration. He whispered to his sister, "Got any old reports I can borrow?"

Beth smiled. "How about 'The impact of the steam engine on the textile industry in Maine.'?"

"I'd kill for it."

"Good, I'll trade you for the answer to why you were in my bedroom this morning."

She gave him an impish smile.

"Deal?" she asked again.

"I don't think you want to know," Alan answered with enough conviction to set Beth up so that she demanded an answer.


When Phillip walked into Horvath's garage, a towel wrapped around his waist, his hair still wet, he passed Old Man Horvath without knowing it.

"That automobile of yours has gotten awfully quiet, Mr. Phillip. Don't tell me it's had a mechanical problem and you require a bit of expert advice."

Phillip stopped and located his boss, half devoured under the hood of an important Cadillac.

"Well, Mr. Horvath," Phillip answered carefully, "I can't honestly tell you how the engine's doing right now. I do think I've got a little problem with water in the gas. Any suggestions?"

"Well, if it's not too much water, we could add a little alcohol to your fuel tank. Otherwise, we should drain it. Do you know how much is in it? Approximately, that is."

Phillip took one hand from the towel he had wrapped around his waist, and tentatively scratched his head.

"I don't know, Mr. Horvath, but I'd guess at least a couple million gallons."

Mr. Horvath pulled out from the engine compartment and watched Phillip walk out of sight.

"I think we'd better drain the tank!" the old man called after him, matter-of-factly.

Ezechial rechecked the water level in the boiler. While some had obviously run on to the floor, it hadn't registered. He nodded in satisfaction and moved on to resume his inspection. What Ezechial didn't see was that the stream of water running silently past the broken fitting was far more substantial than it looked. The fact that it ran directly to a wide crack in the floor masked it's magnitude.

Further, the gauge had moved back a fraction, but it had hung up on the ectoskeleton of a long-dead spider, there arresting its further descent toward the red quadrant of the dial face. The water-level in the boiler was not yet seriously depleted, but there was now no way to judge its safety.

He had dressed after he was awakened by a noisy automobile passing by the machinery shed. Ezechial thought it a bit perplexing that he could not locate the vehicle when he looked, but there were other, more important matters to be addressed.

He ran his good hand over one of the spoked flywheels and then he hobbled around the huge compressor and fondled the other wheel. It was a consummate mating of form, function, and cast iron.

Had Phillip been there to share the experience he would have said, "It's truly beautiful, Ezechial — if it was a woman, I'd fuck it."

Ezechial savored the incongruous tenderness he associated with cold metal cast to perform in revolutionary power. The only woman he had ever touched was his sister, and she had been little more than a girl at the time, but he had transferred his memory of her flowing sexuality and sensual touch.

He had first realized it a half century earlier when as a boy he had sneaked into the hot, pulsing machinery shed. The machines were in motion, spinning, vibrating and hissing, and Ezechial had moved from one to the other, observing in awe the tremendous strength he saw spun in once-cold metal.

It was as he leaned against the railing protecting the unsuspecting from the revolving flywheel, that he experienced the vibrations traveling through his young body. The particular restraint he pressed against was barely below the level of his waist, and Ezechial had thrilled to the vibration before he could identify its source.

Here were machines which could not only lift mountainous blocks of granite and produce wild steam to drive the pumps and drills, but also generate forces which insinuated his loins. The machine brought to Ezechial a hidden erection.

Young girls' hands they had and they touched the young man and then carried the old beyond the constraints of guilt and murder and loss.

They would be there for him and they would wait patiently when they must.

Those hot days of emerging manhood, Ezechial made the only friends he ever had.

Ezechial and his machines. Ezechial and his machines.

The poetry and the love was all Ezechial had after the passing of his sister, all that he was to have until he came face to face with his youth.

Young Phillip. Phillip the bully. Phillip the brute. Phillip the imperfect.

The person he needed. The second chance for which he didn't know he longed.

The imperfect solution.

Ezechial moved about communicating with his machines and for the first time he began to sense that finite nature of their being. *Yes*, he thought, *they will live longer, but they cannot live forever.*

He walked through the only progression of time he understood.

Mother and father. Mother died. Sister and brother. Father and sister died. And all of it overlain with the coming of machines.

*Iron will not die,* he had believed. And now he had begun to wonder — to doubt. He started to think of his own life in terms other than murder. The machines could not live after he died. Who would care for them?

At the end of the two cylinder compressor the tappet rods spanned from the buried cam shaft to exposed the rocker arms. Each rod was more than three feet long and thicker than the old man's wrists. He grasped two of them, his bad hand holding imperfectly, and it was as if he held the bars of a prison.

Prison bars which held Ezechial out, not in, for he longed to crawl into his machines, longed to become part of them and forget the past and forsake thinking. He wanted to be. He would have traded his worn body and his bent and flawed mind to become any part of his fabulous machines.

Today he would start them. It was as close as he could get to a mechanical reincarnation.

After Junior and Phillip escaped the coupe, it had gathered speed as it sought the quarry depths. The dark blue coupe in the darker waters left an anchoring trail of bubbles, first from the interior and then from the trunk. They twisted upward, the bubbles themselves becoming smaller as less air was left to escape, until finally all that was left was the air trapped in the gasoline tank and it threaded past the vented cap in a fine row of spheres, one behind the other, each perfect.

The coupe came to rest near the center of the quarry floor, wheels down, hood torn upward, and passenger door opened as if awaiting a rider. It hit with no sound, settling with dumb finality.

In that black tomb, a form, long and thick, materialized, hovering above, and then circling the coupe. It finally glided through the opened door and out the other side, its distended length sometimes brushing against the steering wheel or the back of the front seat until it had almost completed its passage and the ragged tail followed and tore the upholstery it touched.

Each of the boys had his own nightmare regarding the retribution he would suffer at the hands of Phillip and Junior when they found out why the big coupe had turned short-lived airplane and then unsuccessful boat.

DAY FIVE

---

The alarm rang quietly and both Claude and Fox were instantly awake. Fox checked the shades and looked over their boxed arsenal one more time. There were enough weapons that the room took on the thin smell of gun oil. So preoccupied was Claude that he did not notice when his brother dropped a 22 caliber pistol to the floor.

"Toys — I always have trouble with the toys," Fox said to himself and retrieved the gun, wiped it off, and absently put it into one of his deep pants pockets. He took another small caliber pistol out of the box and handed it to his brother.

It seemed lost in his hand. Claude held it without seeing and then shoved it into the back of the waistband of his pants.

"Are you ready?" he asked.

Fox nodded and they walked lightly out of the room; Claude with a handful of fishing rods and his brother lugging the cardboard box. Fox angled the rods, handles down, from the back seat floor to the rear window of the car, a couple of red and white bobbers hanging conspicuously. Each brother wore a many-pocketed fishing vest and a hat resplendent with numerous feathered hooks.

Claude put the cardboard carton on the back seat beside the poles and pulled a green tackle box from inside of it. He handled it as if there were something other than fishing lures in it.

The crickets rasped away as Claude crunched across the gravel back to the van. The door squeaked as he opened it, confusing some of the nearer crickets and then the sound of the engine idling masked them all.

Fox started his car and backed around. He pulled out onto the highway and his brother followed a hundred feet behind in the van. Their taillights diminished and then disappeared down the dark tree-lined road, and the crickets resumed.

Several minutes later the owner walked outside in his robe and pajamas and peered down the empty road. He walked over to their room door, unlocked it, and opened it carefully. He swept the interior with his flashlight, saw the suitcase and the discarded clothing and quickly closed and locked the door and went back to his bed.

He had pegged the two for 'skippers' and was both pleased and disappointed that he had been wrong.

It was somewhere between late night and early morning. There was no hint that a new day would soon dawn just as there were no traces of the previous evening. They drove through the night, one behind the other, four headlights, four tail lights and two muttering engines.

Fox set an easy pace within the speed limit. He kept the car windows closed, warming the interior with the heater at its first notch, the fan slowly turning. He reached for the radio and then resisted. There would be plenty of time later to relax. He did a few mental exercises, teasing his mind to keep it alert.

Claude trailed the monotonous twin tail lights. *I hope he's on his* toes, he thought, concerned that his brother had not fully awakened. The car ahead of him drifted to the right and Claude feared that his brother was fighting sleep. He felt the front and then rear wheel hit the dead skunk, and realized what his brother had been doing.

The windows, both the driver's and passenger's, were open in the van and the cool night air was refreshing. With the skunk-bumps came the inevitable smell and Claude welcomed it. *Some sweet,* he thought, *too bad humans don't smell that way when they die.*

He called back to his silent passenger, "You get worse every day, you know that? If I smelled as bad as you do, I think I'd bury myself."

He glanced back at the garbage can, its front side reflecting the dashboard lights. Claude cleared his throat after he realized what he had been doing. *Here I am worried about Little Fox and I'm the one whose mind is wandering.*

*Little Fox — how long since he had thought of his brother as Little Fox?*

Claude swung through a left-hand turn with his brother. *I wonder if he thinks of me as anything but Claude? Stupid name if there ever was one.*

He looked at his reflected image in the windshield.

*Who would name a male-child such a thing?*

It was only at night and when he was either tired or tensed for a job that he thought of himself as different — as an Indian.

A cloud obscured a patch of stars as it traced the high winds. It looked more to be a sky of cold winter nights than mid-summer, and even the air seemed crackling with frigid crispness.

They cruised past a doe and a buck standing in a clearing, briefly illuminated and then lost in the darkness. Little Fox and Cloud That Walks bid them a safe night and silently thanked the animals' ancestors.

What should have been a good omen portended ill for Little Fox. He checked twice to see if his brother was still behind, somehow feeling he was no longer driving the van, that someone else was behind him now, following, making plans, ready to spring any moment.

Fox tapped the pistol in his pocket and then mocked himself.

*Woman.*

Alan awoke from a dream that had him wrestling with the wires and cables under Phillip's car. The more he struggled, the more entangled he became until the vehicle was alive and it grasped him and then hugged him closely. Alan kicked and tore the covers from his bed, fighting desperately to free himself.

The bonds softened and then they were arms and they were the arms of his sister, and Alan fought with himself to be released but a part of him didn't wish to. Finally, Beth became Phillip and then The Doll Man; but The Doll Man had a death's head with exposed teeth and gaping eye holes.

Alan lay in bed. He regained his breath and finally drove the cloying guilt and fear from his bedroom. He heard his grandmother downstairs, banging through the kitchen cupboards, withdrawing pans and kettles to start what Alan knew would be an enormous breakfast; one which would leave him heavy and sleepy, unprepared for the day.

He dressed quietly, made his way down the stairs and slipped out the front door before his grandmother was aware he had awakened. Once outside he inhaled the fresh morning, smelling those fragrances available only to the young. He topped his lungs with the damp air and then ran down the block to meet his friends.

Will awoke in the twin of the bed Freddy snored and tossed his way across. Will's fears were that the police would knock at his door and drag him off to court and then take him directly to the detention home. There had to be at least a thousand laws addressing what he had done.

*Willful destruction of blue coupes. Malicious dunking of town morons. Wanton submersion of chrome. And the misdemeanors of vigilante justice and naive participation in potential murder.*

He toyed with the semi-humorous list until Freddy snorted twice, said, "No, Beth!" and then stretched and with instant cognizance, tossed his pillow at Will.

"What are the chances he'll buy a new coupe? Faster, sharper, more intimidating?" Will asked, settling immediately into a conversation with his friend.

Freddy thought before he answered.

"He probably has one already." He faded into his imagination, his voice lowering. "I can see it now — candy apple red (color so deep you can't see the bottom), chrome engine — huge engine, covered with a million shining, expensive gadgets that we can't understand, let alone afford — fat, black, racing slicks, rolled and pleated interior," he paused before he delivered the death-blow. "And in the back seat, Louise. In the front, Beth."

Will groaned. "You can really make a guy feel bad, can't you. *Shit*!"

Freddy swung his legs around and set his feet on the floor. He scratched his head and ran his finger into the corner of each eye.

"Do you think people are *born losers*, or do you think they have to work at it?"

Will laughed before he answered. "Gheez, Freddy, it never seemed like we had to work too hard; what do you think? And Junior and Phillip; they seem to have cruised right up to major failures status without sweating a drop."

"Yeh, you might be able to call 'em major failures, but when you do, I think you must be forgetting whose girls they're with."

They thought of their girls — their past girls — and sank into depression.

Will shook it off first.

"Ya know, we must *work* at it. We just pulled off the best revenge of the century, really pulled it off, and we're still not happy. What do you think it takes to make us feel good?"

Freddy answered as if he had thought it through earlier.

"The way I see it, we sank the coupe — very big deal — I mean it was a big deal and all, because it's what we wanted to do and everything, but it was hollow. We're still the nerds on the block, *our* girls are still *their* girls, and here we are sleepin' in the same room, in our underwear. Doesn't sound too awfully successful to me."

"Well, is it because we're funny looking or somethin', I mean, I ask you, are we funny looking?"

The answer came without hesitation.

"Yes."

Near defeat, Will continued, "Okay, we're funny looking. How about personality? Do we strike out there, too?"

"Well now, *shit*," Will lamented, "you're not leaving us with much hope."

"You think *hope* would take the place of girls?"

And so their conversation continued while they rose and dressed.

The old school had the aura of a haunted house and it would have until school was back in session. There was a silence about the building which shrouded it in loneliness and spent evil. The boys were at the back play yard and went to great lengths to neither look at nor acknowledge where they were.

Roger dominated the conversation, reveling in his familiarity with science.

"At four hundred feet, the pressure is the same as the weight of four hundred feet of water."

"Pretty heavy, eh?" Kurtz offered in an attempt to enter the discussion.

Roger barely gave him a glance. "No shit. Do you really think so, Kurtz? I know you've done a lot of underwater research — playing with yourself in the bathtub and everything (Roger pretended to abuse himself as he finished his taunt) — but why don't you just shut up and let the people who know what they're talking about continue."

"You know, you don't have the corner on brains here," Kurtz added lamely, attempting to shrug off the insults.

Roger turned to Cavenaugh and then Alan. "You're correct for a change, little man. There *are* some with brains in this crowd. And you don't happen to be *one* of them."

He didn't wait for Kurtz's response. Instead, he turned his attention to the pad of paper in front of him, sketching something which appeared to be a cross between an oil drum and a poorly designed space craft.

He drew another view of it and it now resembled a wide eyed person with a very round nose.

"These are car headlights," he said, indicating the upper circles, "and this is a port where the camera sits. We need some really thick, really clear glass — I think that's going to be the hard part."

It was a challenge which sent Alan's and Kurtz's minds racing. Both were anxious to find a way to become involved

Kurtz excitedly interjected, "What about those glass blocks they use for building — you know, the ones they have over at Avenchey's — on the corner of the building?"

He realized his error as soon as he referred to the five and dime store.

Roger went on the attack. "Ooooooo yeh, Kurtz, we'll get lots of good pictures: ghosts in snow storms, wind in the fog, stuff like that. Personally, I think we should lean toward glass you can actually *see* through. But I have to hand it to you, they are pretty thick."

Alan was relieved — he was just about to suggest the same thing before Kurtz blurted it out. He smiled to himself and went back to his mental exploration of everything he had ever seen which was glass — and clear.

Junior hefted the fuel pump in his hand. "How hard can this be?" he asked himself. "I took the son of a bitch off without any trouble," and he thought of the circumstances. "In the fuckin' dark and in a fuckin' hurry, too."

He scanned the cuts on his knuckles and took a mental detour to his pounding of Phillip. "If that loser can do it, why can't I?" he questioned, equating sucker punches with mental prowess and mechanical aptitude.

He bent to the task and fortunately found himself involved in a relatively easy procedure requiring knowledge of the art of threading nuts onto bolts, picking up the gasket when it fell onto the ground, and slipping neoprene hosing onto the male end of the fuel coupling. He had broken the only hose clamp he had and tossed the pieces into the bushes, forgetting immediately that there had ever been one.

Junior ground the engine through, taxing the limits of his stolen battery, but his new independence was confirmed as the car grudgingly started. Blue smoke drifted skyward, signaling all who cared to look that he was at last a free man.

The new Junior was mobile.

No engine sounded sweeter than Junior's. He revved it tentatively and then stood on the gas pedal.

"Thank you, baby Jesus. Power me into Louise's pants."

He crossed himself and let the engine idle. The interior of the car appeared to be a trash receptacle. There were discarded lunch bags, beer bottles, cigarette packs and old magazines. Errant shoes peaked out from under the seat and wadded towels molded in the corners. The headliner drooped onto the back seat, obscuring any view through the rear window, and stuffing erupted from rents in the woven seat cover.

Junior surveyed it all with satisfaction. "Home at last," he said and grabbed his crotch. "Come to Pappa, Little Louise, come to Pappa."

He drove the auto to a dirt road, parked it with the engine idling, threw open all four doors and scooped the trash out and tossed it into the woods. Bottles sailed end over end and lumps of clothing winged into the ferns. Within fifteen minutes, years of junk was expelled from the car. After he had cleared the seats and floor, he took the whisk broom he had 'lifted' from Horvath's, and swept out the sand and cigarette butts and bits of paper.

When he finished, he stuck the small broom under the seat. Junior retrieved a wadded shirt from the woods, soaked it in a nearby stream, wrung it out and wiped down the interior, attempted to polish the windows, and took special care to clean the knobs and buttons of the radio which, miraculously, still worked. There was apparently a tear in the speaker, making any deep bass a raspy snarl, but the stations came in well, considering the coat hanger antenna, and Junior was in musical heaven.

His car looked better to him than Phillip's ever had. "She ain't much to look at," he offered, "but she's mine, she runs, and she ain't under a couple hundred feet of water. Fuck you, Phillip."

He spat into the woods, closed the passenger doors, and drove back to his home. It was easy for him to ignore the mist on the fenders and door, easier still to turn a blind eye to the frayed and holed carpet, and easiest of all to throw an army blanket over the ripped upholstery.

Junior parked his car, went into his house and dialed the telephone. Louise answered, paused for a few seconds after he questioned her, and then told him, yes, she would take a ride with him in his 'new' car.

"Mind if I bring my suitcase?" she joked and laughed with him when he responded, "I'd bring mine too if I owned one."

He picked her up an hour later in front of the dairy store a block from her home.

"You forgot your suitcase," he teased when she got in.

Louise's smile was short-lived, for she became serious when she said, "Junior, if you can get money for the trip, I can be packed in half an hour."

Junior looked at himself in the rear view mirror and thought of what she said. Both of them watched an elderly couple walk into the store.

Junior snorted and teased, "Don't want to end up an old lady in this town, eh?"

"I *won't* end up an old lady in *any* town, Junior. This girl has big things in store for her. Ride the tail of the comet if you dare."

'Riding tail' had a nice sound to Junior.

"I might just be able to get that money sooner than you think, sister."

Louise swept Junior with her eyes before she responded, "You couldn't get it too soon for me, *brother.*"

They drove around for a while, but Junior's mind wasn't on his passenger, it was on money and where he could get it. And once he decided, he was uncertain how soon he could accomplish the deed.

To Louise's surprise he said, "What the fuck!" pounded on the steering wheel, and drove her quickly home.

Phillip showered, conferred briefly with Lu Lu, and dressed. When he was finished he saw that his boss had finished the Cadillac and his office work, leaving a note by the back door for Phillip to see when he left.

He read it as he walked down the drive leading from the garage and then folded it and stuck it in his back pocket. *What's so important that he wants to talk to me about it first thing tomorrow?* Phillip wondered.

By the time he strolled to the end of the block it was more than he had walked in the three previous years.

*This ain't so fuckin' bad,* he thought to himself, feeling younger as he noticed the sounds of the birds calling to one another.

He turned down the street toward Beth's, debating whether to leave the collar on his shirt turned up or fold it back down. After he addressed that problem he worked on his speech and as he did he reviewed what he had thought earlier.

*'This ain't so fuckin' bad!' Christ, I talk like a fuckin' slime ball.* He mentally deleted the *ain't* and the first *fuckin*; then with self deprecation, the second.

His biggest fear wasn't that Beth would slam the door in his face, or tell him off, or even that she should laugh at his cut lip or his missing tooth. His concern was that either of her parents would answer the door, *particularly*, her father. Now there was a man who gave you the 'willies'.

When he could see her house midway down the tree-lined street, he stopped and stooped and retied each of his shoes, noticing when he did that while both of his socks were white they had come from different pairs. Phillip liked the look of pointed black shoes and gleaming white socks.

"Fuck!" he said, then corrected it with, "I mean, 'Shoot'!" And then, "Brother, it's like fu... like *talkin'* a foreign language."

He stayed crouched over one shoe and surveyed the area. It was a nice street, most of the houses recently painted, the lawns mowed, decent cars parked at the curb or in the driveways. Far from the rural poverty he had known.

Here was a dream world; one he had insulated himself from with layers of vulgarity and ignorance. A dream world where people worked at clean jobs and had dinner together and owned camps at lakes.

Phillip stared down the street, unfocusing. This was Beth. It was where she lived and it was what she believed in.

When he stood he came close to turning away and returning to the garage — this was too much. But he didn't return, he resumed walking the last yards to her home. He knocked on her door and before he could gather his wits the door was pulled open.

"Well hello, young man, how are you today?"

*An old lady* — Phillip struggled with his confusion. Had he gone to the wrong home? Were Beth's parents really that old?

"I don't believe I know you — are you one of the children's friends? Or are you collecting money for a church?"

*Collecting money for a church?* He cleared his throat. "Well, no Mam, I mean yes Mam, I *am* a friend of Beth's."

Beth's grandmother drew back visibly. "Well you don't *look* like a friend of Beth's." She appraised him doubtfully as if he were an insect wing in a bowl of jell-O.

Her *granny* — that had to be it. *Christ I'm afraid of her parents and I get this.* He shifted into the tone he used for elderly people when they came to the garage.

She didn't even seem to hear him. "How *old* are you, young man? Do you know Beth from school," she paused as if daring him to answer, "or *church*?"

She was building walls faster than Phillip could think of ways to scale them.

A saving voice came from inside the house.

"Grandma, have you seen my blue blouse?"

The old lady grudgingly retreated one step into the house but kept her hand firmly on the door knob as if expecting Phillip to attempt to bull his way past her.

"Hello, Beth," he called past the old lady, trying a verbal end-run.

She appeared at the door beside her grandmother.

"Hello, Phillip." she said in a manner which wasn't particularly friendly, but didn't carry with it the rejection he feared, either.

Now there was ice in Beth's voice. "He's a *friend* of mine, Grandma. You may not know *all* of them."

The old lady disappeared into the house, covering her trail with a string of mutterings. Beth now stood before Phillip and she extended one arm up the side of the door and leaned against it.

"I didn't hear you drive up — when did you get here?"

She scanned the road in front of her house and then before he could answer, she said, "Where's your car? I thought it was a part of you?"

Phillip appeared perplexed and then he smiled. It was that sort of a smile associated with private jokes and secret knowledge. He savored something momentarily and at last chuckled quietly.

"Well, I guess you could say that the old blue coupe kinda 'went off the deep end'."

Phillip laughed and then became serious. "I'm not sure you're gonna believe this, but your troop of friends — Freddy and Will and that Cavenaugh kid, and if I had to guess, little Kurtz and your brother, too — kinda evened up the score."

Beth was watching him as he spoke. She sensed there was much more to what he was saying than she could presently understand. Phillip saw her concentration and continued.

As the words left his lips there was an elderly gasp in the bowels of the house followed by a faint, "Nasty words — nasty mind."

"Grandma!" Beth shouted, "you are not involved in this conversation! Please do not feel free to invite yourself!" She surprised herself with her vehemence.

A distant door slammed.

Phillip picked up where he had been interrupted. "I've been. . . ." he searched for a more appropriate word and when he failed to find it he whispered, "an asshole".

Beth smiled for the first time.

"Oh you have, have you?"

Phillip began to feel even more uncomfortable.

"Yes."

Then, before she could pursue his admission further, Phillip told her why he had come.

"Look, Beth, there's a lot of things I want to talk to you about — to explain. Can you go for a walk with me? Now?"

"A walk?"

Phillip was convinced he was not going to get her to leave the sanctuary of her doorway, but as he wrestled with what he would say next she said, "I'll be right there," and then disappeared behind the door which she partially closed, and reappeared moments later, calling in over her shoulder, "I'll be back later. I'm going for a walk." They strolled through the town for several hours, Phillip pouring out all that had happened with the kids, his coupe, Old Man Horvath, and Junior. Beth listened intently and quietly, her hands behind her back, her head lowered as she walked and noted imperfections in the sidewalk.

Will and Freddy joined Alan and his friends, still discussing Roger's plans for an underwater camera. He had six or seven variations, but they were all stymied by the port-hole protecting the camera.

"I'm at a loss, you guys," Roger pleaded to the older boys. "If we can solve that problem, I'm convinced we can get this thing rolling."

Cavenaugh hovered one more time over the drawings and then handed them to Will and Freddy.

"Looks like some kind of a face," Freddy observed to the groans of the younger kids.

"Yeh, we already saw that," Alan said.

Kurtz readied a smart-ass comment and then thought better of it. He felt constrained in the presence of Will and Freddy. "Let's just build it and hope we find the glass," he finally added.

The others looked at him in silence.

Roger shrugged and said, "I think he has a point."

Kurtz smirked at Roger. "Thanks, Father."

Roger stood above them. "Let's go on over to my dad's shop — he said he'd help us. I told him it was part of a summer project us kids are working on."

"Like a summer report — are you related to my grandmother?" Alan asked.

His remark was so obtuse that they ignored it.

"Shotgun!!" Kurtz called.

Freddy shot him a withering, 'don't mess with the older kids' look.

They climbed into Will's sedan, Alan, Roger, and Kurtz in the back and Will, Freddy, and Cavenaugh in front. Will cranked the engine until it caught and vomited to life.

"Sounds real healthy," Kurtz observed, miffed that he was between Alan and Roger. "By the way, Will, could you drive fast? I'd like to get there before these homo's get any ideas."

Roger pounded Kurtz's arm at the shoulder and Alan slid away from him adding, "You're the pervert, Kurtz."

When they got to the machine shop, Roger introduced the older boys as 'my friends', and showed his father the plans.

The older man wore a welding apron and a tight fitting welder's cap. He tugged at the short bill of the cap as he inspected the drawing from different angles.

Roger smiled at his father. "It'll work and you know it."

His father smiled and went back to the drawing.

"What are these?"

"Car headlights. I think we can make them work under water."

His father smiled again. "I think you could."

Then he looked at the other boys.

"This is a pretty complex apparatus you're building. What grade are you in?"

Kurtz liked Roger's father. "We're pretty smart for our size."

He meant to say 'age' and when some of the other men in the shop heard his remark they laughed.

"They pack a lot of brains in them small fries these days, ayuh," a round machinist confided to his friend.

Roger's father reviewed the plans one more time and then sent the boys scurrying to different corners of the shop to retrieve the parts he thought would be needed. They piled them at his feet and looked on expectantly. He fired up his torch and the hull of the underwater camera began to take shape in a shower of sparks.

Junior ran through his plan again. Satisfied, he decided to burn his bridges. He would commit himself. There was a telephone in the basement. He found Louise's number in the phone book, tore out the page and held it as he dialed.

When she answered he hesitated and then said, "You better start packin'. I'll come around and pick you up late tonight."

There was an extended silence as Junior waited for her reply. He listened to her catch her breath.

Finally, all she said was, "Pick me up at the corner. At two a.m. Don't honk." and hung up. Louise had given no previous thought to the time, but two a.m. had a nice sound.

Junior stood with the buzzing phone in his hand. He chewed on his lip, scratched his groin briefly and then rubbed his face with his hand.

*"Two a.m.!* Holy shit, we're really gonna do it!" he whispered and went up to his bedroom. He rummaged through his drawers, throwing out a few pair of undershorts and a clean shirt. There was a jar of change on the floor by his bed which he hefted into his old gym bag. He looked around his bedroom to see if there was anything else he might be able to use. To his surprise he couldn't locate anything he cared about.

"What a mess of crap," he said as he stuffed his undershorts and shirt into the gym bag. As an afterthought he slid a crushed box of prophylactics from under his mattress and wedged them to the side of the change jar.

When he walked out of his bedroom he left the door open just as he did when he walked through the kitchen past the piles of blackened pans and food-coated plates and out the back door. His parents were alcoholics and terminally unhappy.

"Fuck you all," he said after he put the gym bag on the rear seat of his car.

Junior backed out of his driveway. He gave his parents' house a sideways glance as he drove off. He never saw it again.

Louise packed without thinking. What she packed didn't matter, for she would have all new clothing soon — dresses of silk which flowed with her success and clung to her body as would her fans, her admirers.

She knew the ridiculousness of her dreams as acutely as the others. She wasn't stupid. But she felt her talent, felt its power, and was confident in her knowledge of the those who had succeeded; those who were now the stars. They had all been regular people from hundreds of little back-water, dirty and semi-deserted towns. That was how it worked.

There wasn't a 'star-city' producing them. They were normal, they were all normal, no different from the millions of others except for the detail. The one detail. The dream.

They were people with dreams — dreams and the strength to pursue them. Every movie star had gone to Hollywood. It was so simple and so basic, and yet no one seemed to realize it. Talent scouts never came to Maine. Never went to Nebraska. Never walked the dusty streets of Georgia. Go to *them*. Go to Hollywood.

Dream your dream and then take it West. Take it across the desert and the mountains, and carry it safely inside of you. And it doesn't matter how you get there; there isn't a committee watching you roll into town, chug into town, walk into town. It didn't matter how you got there. Just get there. Don't sit at home, safely hidden in your tiny house with your unimaginative parents. Everybody did that. That wasn't how you got to be seen, to be noticed.

Louise grabbed a few of her prettiest dresses and threw them into the suitcase. She started to fold her panties and her bras, and then she laughed. You've got to be kidding, she thought.

Her dream was of arriving in a simple cotton dress with a suitcase in her hand. Plain pumps. A lot of dust everywhere and a hot sun. No underwear. You just stood in the middle of the street and looked around, kind of lost.

They'd find you. There was no question that they would find you before your arm got tired. Before you got thirsty. Before you were hungry.

They needed stars. They needed them because the rest of the country needed them. Try to make a movie without a star. Just try.

Try to make a movie without up-and-coming stars.

You couldn't do it. Movies were people. Plenty of people, and people were stars.

Louise tried to think of a special item she could take with her. Something she could talk about in her interviews — on the talk shows.

"Oh my, Miss Kurtz, you just left your home — just packed and walked out — how did you do it? Where did you get the courage? How could you just leave it all behind?"

"Well, it was so very difficult, but I brought my . . . I saw it there on the dresser, on the corner of my bed, tucked safely away in my closet, hanging on my wall, and I just put it ever so carefully into my suitcase, and it gave me the *strength*. It became my *dream*, don't you see."

Louise sat through the interview with her leg crossed high at the knee. She touched the lipstick at the corners of her mouth.

She picked up her jewelry box. *Forget it.*

She eyed a fan magazine. *No way.*

What did she have that she could take? What would *sound* good?

Frustrated, she grabbed her Shirley Temple doll, opened the suitcase, and mashed it in with her dresses.

*I just felt she would help me, kind of take care of me. She has always been such an inspiration. I've seen all of her movies dozens of times.*

Even Louise had to roll her eyes. *Oh, brother,* she sighed, hid the suitcase in the closet and then sat on her bed with a pile of magazines. *Six more hours,* she thought, torturing herself.

The boys helped Roger's father for the remainder of the afternoon. Each of them was excited as the apparatus took shape. They worked through dinner and then each of them was dropped off at his respective home.

Kurtz watched television until it was time for bed. He went upstairs, changed, and fell asleep immediately. He dreamed several dreams, tossed around for awhile, and then awoke. Something was wrong. He lay in bed a moment more and tried to figure out what was going on. That had to be his sister's door he had just heard open, and she didn't go by his room toward the bathroom. She had to have gone downstairs. On an impulse he looked out his bedroom window at the front yard.

"Holy shit!" he whispered. He saw his sister, suitcase in hand, briefly illuminated by the street light. "She's gonna do it — she's running away!"

He was out of bed in a flash, dancing into his jeans. He tucked a t-shirt under his arm, and took one dirty sock off of the floor. He pulled on the sock and then began to search frantically for his shoes. "Shit," he hissed when he remembered that he had left them downstairs. Instinctively he reached under his bed and pulled out a shoe box. He ripped the new sneakers out and jammed his feet into them, one foot with sock, one without. The shoes had their laces threaded from when he had tried them on at the store with his mother. School shoes. On sale. Don't wear them until September.

Untied, he slid silently down the stairs and out the front door. As he ran across the black lawn he stuck one arm and then his head into the appropriate holes in his t-shirt, finally working his free arm in also. There was Louise, standing a block farther down, on the corner.

"Holy shit!" he whispered again when a car pulled up beside her and she climbed in.

"Louise!!!" stuck halfway in Kurtz's throat — he realized at the last instant that to call out to her would awaken his parents.

He watched the car turn away from them. It wasn't heading for the highway. It was going the wrong way. And then it struck Kurtz and he turned and raced to his garage, slamming his knee into a car bumper as he grabbed his sister's old bike and dragged it out to the driveway. He pushed it at a dead run out to the street, hopped a pedal, swung his leg over the rear fender, and was on and pumping for all he was worth.

The car was gone, as he knew it would be.

"I've got to catch 'em. I've got to catch 'em" he chanted as he pedaled.

Kurtz knew were they were going and it made sense somehow; that they would go to the quarry before they left for good.

"I've got to catch 'em," he repeated and then thought of his sister gone forever and with that thought found himself crying a little at first, and then uncontrollably.

"Louise!" he called out through the darkness, through his tears as he headed toward the old quarry road. "I'm sorry," he cried again, "I'm sorry for everything. Don't leave me, Louise!"

Kurtz pedaled his sister's bike — a girl's bike — complete with fenders, bell and basket, and streamers trailing from the handle grips — down the deserted road.

Louise sat beside Junior and they both laughed.

"I don't believe you," Junior teased.

Louise shook her head and answered, "I don't believe me either, Junior, but it seems we're on our way."

Junior noted the road they were on. "Well, we're not on our way yet, but damn soon we *will* be. You bring a map?" He turned to Louise as he asked the last question.

"You've got the car, I thought *you'd* have a map," she answered defensively.

Junior was nonplused. "Well hell, little girl, once we really get started, I think we gotta just point this beast south for awhile, and then once we hit Mass., we just sorta drive west. Couple days of that and I think we can start to think of fine tuning. In the mean time, let's listen to some tunes."

He reached to the radio and turned it on. The initial static played havoc with the torn speaker.

Louise winced and then asked, "What do you mean, 'once we really get started'. Aren't we started now?"

Junior reached over and squeezed her breast. "I wanna give this town a good 'fuck you all' first. We're goin' to the quarry one last time, then we blow this hick town."

Louise thought of the quarry. *So they were going to the quarry first. Sounds like Junior wants the money in the meter before we leave.*

"Are you sure it's the town you want to . . . ." she couldn't say it. Not tonight, not at the beginning of her real life. Movie stars didn't swear. She looked coyly at Junior. He wasn't looking so bad. Probably the dim light. *"do?"* she finished.

Junior laughed. It wasn't too loud or particularly offensive, but it was a bit imbecilic for her.

"You know how much money I brought?" he asked her, immediately rekindling her interest.

"I'm afraid to ask."

"Grab my gym bag, it's in the back seat," he instructed her, pounding on the steering wheel in self delight as he did.

Louise reached around and took the bag by the handles. It was heavier than she anticipated, so she turned farther and reached it with both hands.

"Did you pack cannon balls or lead?

Junior laughed. "Worth lots more than either of those."

Louise unzipped it and probed around with her hand. She felt the large jar first and pulled it out. The change rattled and clanked as she did, and she experienced a sinking disappointment.

"You have got to be shitting me," she accused, forgetting that she was a movie star.

"Hey, there's a fair amount of money in there. More than you brought, I bet." He shifted the car and then continued. "Anyway, that's only part of it. Reach in there again. There's more."

Louise put the change on the floor and went back to the gym bag. She pulled out one old pair of undershorts and then another.

"This is disgusting, Junior."

She tossed them over her shoulder into the back seat and dug her hand into the bag again. This time she touched something which seemed to have more potential. She pulled it out, barely able to get her hand around it, and examined it.

It was definitely the right size. That is, it was the right size if it contained a lot of money. A whole lot.

It was a packet, about three inches by six inches by five inches, and it was pretty light.

*No cannon balls in here*, she thought as she unwrapped the red mechanic's rag.

"Oh my god, Junior. Oh my god."

She held the bound stack of bills up to her face and smelled it. There was an odor of grease, but it could not mask the heady perfume of the United States Mint.

"Oh my god," she repeated, turning the bundle in her hand. "How much is this?" she asked. "Do you know?"

And with her last question, Louise betrayed the fact that she knew it was stolen. She smelled it again and she unerring placed its owner.

"Oh my god, Junior, that old man will have a shit-fit."

She was coming back close enough to her stardom that she was aware that she had sworn.

She thumbed across the bills, trying to catch the printed corner numbers without seeming too mercenary. In the faint interior light she caught 5's and 10's and 20's flipping by — 5's and 10's and then 20's — they were in order. She skipped ahead to the last half of the wad. 100's.

"Oh my god, Junior," she repeated, in awe.

Junior had never felt more important.

"The beauty is, Louise, he won't miss it for at least three weeks. Phillip and I figured it out — he adds to it and then counts it once a month — like clock-work. Never fails. And the way I figure it, he just did it last week. Plus, he doesn't think anybody knows about it. He'd never dream it was us."

Louise didn't like the sound of 'us' — it was larceny, after all.

"What do you mean, 'us'? Is Phillip involved?"

Junior snorted. "Give me a fuckin' break. He's history. I mean you an' me. Us."

It took the weight of the money to keep her mouth shut. *Us.* It did not sound good.

"There's thousands there, little girl. Thousands and thousands. We're gonna hit California and I'm gonna buy you stuff like you've never seen before. Clothes, shoes — stuff — you know, fancy stuff."

It was sounding better.

Her suitcase full of dresses seemed a joke. She reached around again and opened it, pulling out Shirley Temple and bringing her forward.

"What the hell's that?" Junior asked.

"Let's give it to The Doll Man — let's leave it for him."

Junior eyed the doll.

Before she knew it, they had turned onto the quarry road.

Junior drove to the side of the quarry by the machinery shed, parking the car beneath the trees. He killed the engine and listened as the night sounds engulfed the car. Louise handed him the doll, hugged him and asked, "You wouldn't mind a whole lot if I wait in the car, would you?"

Junior smiled. "I figured you'd stay here. I'll be right back."

He got out, leaving his door open, and disappeared into the darkness. Junior jogged lightly to the back door of the shed. As he ran he took the folding knife out of his back pocket and performed impromptu surgery on Shirley Temple's face and then her arms. Laughing to himself, he propped the doll against the steel side door and loped back to the car. As he climbed in and shut the door he saw two sets of headlights passing on the quarry road. He watched until they suddenly went out.

"Strange mother-fuckers," he said to Louise who was also trying to see where they had gone.

"Let's have a look-see before we head out West."

"Are you really going to take me?" Louise asked.

Junior backed around, shifted into first, and answered, "You just watch me. Nothin's gonna stop us now."

In his mind, the night was young.

Claude and Fox had skirted the little town, taking the old wire road. The van had been bouncing vigorously on what was really no more than a rutted dirt path, the garbage can, securely roped shut and additionally tied to the inside rails of the van, thudding dully against the van's side. Claude slowed as Fox turned onto the quarry road.

Both drivers sat more stiffly in their seats, their eyes shifting constantly, their ears primed to hear what could not be heard. It was a short drive to the turn for the quarry. Fox pulled the car to the side and parked and Claude drove ahead, beyond the old stables, past the shorter derrick tower. Both vehicles had their lights switched off, and Claude proceeded cautiously. He had not been to the quarry from a little more than a year. As unlikely as it was, it was still possible that something might have changed.

The van bumped up onto the granite plateau surrounding the quarry and Claude stopped the vehicle some twenty feet from the rim. He walked with the tackle box back to the car parked near the road. He opened the back door on the driver's side, put the box back into the cardboard carton and then scanned the darkness once and walked past the van and to the edge of the quarry.

Junior kept the headlights out as he slowly drove the u-shaped road to the other side of the quarry. They had to be parkers he convinced himself but was confused when he and Louise bumped past the empty car. Junior saw that it had out-of-state plates and that the driver's door was open.

Satisfied, Claude walked back to the van, nodded to his brother, and climbed into the idling vehicle. This time he propped the door open with his left foot. He pulled the selector into drive and goosed the gas to get the vehicle rolling fast enough to propel both front and rear wheels into the quarry air. Five feet from the ledge, he did a combination jump and running dance out of the seat and onto the granite, barely keeping his balance. He appeared more the vaudeville performer, illuminated by the bright headlights, than a New York killer. The bright headlights. Fox had his gun out and was craning backwards in response to the approaching car.

"Strange," Junior mumbled to Louise as he reached for the headlight knob. When he yanked backwards the headlights flooded the quarry lip. It wasn't a car they saw — it was a van — a New York van, and it was driving toward the edge. At that instant Junior saw a man standing to the side and then the van door waved as a man jumped out.

It was like a movie. The van drove over the edge and dropped out of sight. Gone.

Junior slammed his car to a stop, threw his door open and was halfway to the one who had jumped out of the van.

"What the fuck's goin' on?" he demanded.

The last part of his question was submerged in the sound of the vehicle hitting the water below.

Junior hesitated. The fellow who had been standing to the side was advancing to Junior's door. The bigger guy was walking up to Junior.

Louise locked her door and then tried to stretch to close Junior's so that she could lock it, too.

The little guy was in the car with Louise before she reached the handle. He actually sat on her outstretched arm, forcing her down on the seat.

"My arm," she whimpered. She did not scream, although she knew they were in very big trouble.

Junior fisted his left hand and dug into his pants pocket with the other for the knife. He got it out and was fumbling with the blade when he caught the flash of a giant knife in the other guy's hand.

Junior turned back to Louise. He couldn't see her, but the little guy was in the driver's seat. The guy with the knife was on Junior before he turned back, and he was strong. Real strong. And quick.

Junior felt the hot blade cutting through his wrist. He went to raise his knife toward his attacker but his fingers wouldn't work. They couldn't hold the blade. It tumbled idiotically down his arm and fell to the ground.

Junior stared at the blood flooding from his wrist and then felt a big hand covering his mouth and nose.

In one stroke Claude nearly severed Junior's head from his shoulders. He arced the knife around and then plunged it into Junior's heart, twisting it as he pulled it free. He then jammed the boy's shirt into the wounds. Before Junior slumped into Claude's arms he was being dragged back to his car.

Louise saw the gun and heard the click of a trigger being drawn back. She went to hit at the gun with her free hand but saw the man move the gun to her forehead. Her arm froze in the air at her side.

"Car keys," Louise heard someone say outside of the car. The man in the car with her pulled out the keys and tossed them to the other man.

Louise would not allow herself to understand who the bloody face belonged to that was tucked in the crook of the man's arm. She stared out into the night as man and body disappeared. She heard the trunk hinges squeal and felt weight being added to the car. The trunk lid slammed.

Her door opened and she looked around just as a fist with something long and black in it came crashing down on her head.

A curtain fell over Louise's eyes and descended to her feet. For a second she felt as if she were a visitor in her own body, and then she felt nothing.

Claude ran back to his car, opened the trunk and took an unopened pack of clothesline out of a canvas bag. For a second he thought he heard something down the road. He was sure it wasn't a car and since they didn't have much time, he decided to ignore it for the moment, and ran back to Fox and the girl.

Fox had Junior's car running. Claude went around to the other side, trussed the girl's arms tightly together and then leaned in and looped the rope around the steering wheel.

He said, "No floaters," and then "Go," and pulled back out of the car, closing the door after he did.

Fox revved the engine and engaged the clutch. The car started forward, but it shuttered as it moved, alternately jerking with each cough of the engine. He had not given it enough gas. The car bucked two more times and stalled before Fox could push in the clutch.

He didn't swear; he reached for the key and restarted the engine. It ran briefly and then died. He tried again.

Junior was not as accomplished a mechanic as he had thought. The fuel line — the one he had installed without a clamp — had popped off.

Claude immediately smelled the spilling gas.

"Out. We push it over."

There was a car. It was parked at the entrance to the quarry. One door was open.

Kurtz let his sister's bike rattle into the bushes as he jumped off of it and ran up to the car and the open door. He was afraid he would see his sister making out in the back seat, but it was empty, except for fishing poles and a cardboard box.

"What the hell?" Kurtz said, confused, and then something made him reach in and grab the wrapped package on the front seat. He held it against his chest as he ran down the dirt road to the quarry.

As he approached the lower derrick he heard an engine cranking. He ran along the side of the road, protected by the high bushes. He stopped at the base of the derrick, dropped the package, and climbed up to see better.

Even in the dark he recognized Junior's beat-up car. He and Alan had played in it when it belonged to Mr. Mayer.

But he didn't see Junior.

There were two men and they were pushing the car toward the edge! Where was his sister?

Kurtz climbed higher on the derrick. The door to the car was open and the dome light dimly illuminated the interior. There was Louise.

Kurtz watched, astonished. It couldn't be happening.

It was a slight incline to the quarry lip. Fox bent his back into the moving car and Claude did the same. It was picking up speed.

*Faster*, Claude willed the car. It had to go faster or it would hang up on the lip. They'd have to push it in with the other car. *Faster.* Things were going wrong rapidly.

The front wheels went over and Claude and Fox drove their weight into the still moving vehicle. It dropped to the frame and slid toward the quarry. They knew it didn't have enough speed.

Kurtz heard the loud metallic scraping. He was flushed with panic.

The car ground to a stop. The front half of the car was in the air over the quarry. Without Junior in the trunk it would have toppled forward. It teetered once.

"I'll get the car."

Claude turned to run.

"No, wait."

Fox hopped onto the rear bumper and ran up the trunk. With arms outstretched he walked over the rear window and onto the roof. He turned and got to his hands and knees and crawled backwards down the windshield. The car began to tip noisily as metal gave.

It teetered and stopped.

Fox backed farther out on the hood, steadying himself by gripping the windshield wipers.

*She's a pretty girl,* he thought as he glanced through the windshield.

The car began to tip again.

Fox lowered a foot to the front bumper.

Claude ran around to the elevated rear of the vehicle. He kneeled and put his shoulder under the rear bumper and lifted.

"Fox!" he whispered forward as the rear lifted higher and the car slid forward.

It was going. The front of the car dropped.

Fox nearly lost his grip. He pulled himself back onto the hood, grabbing once more at the wipers. The right wiper came off in his hand.

The car was beginning to move toward a nose dive or a somersault.

Fox lunged across the roof of the car and pushed hard with his feet against the rear window and trunk lid.

The car was in the air. Louise fell forward and onto the floor, her arms still tied to the steering wheel. Something was wrong. She blinked her eyes. Something was very wrong.

Kurtz froze in his steps. A voice within him, a voice much older than he, told him that his sister was about to die.

Fox's front foot landed on the lip of the quarry wall. His weight was still far over the edge and he began to fall backward. He reached forward as he did, hoping to grab anything which might bear his weight.

Claude leaned as far out as he dared. He bunched the muscles in his legs and prepared. His brother's hand slapped into his and Claude wrapped his own around it and sprung backward. He pulled Fox onto the rim. They both tumbled one over the other.

Kurtz flew by them.

*Louise, I love you, I'm sorry for everything I every did!* accompanied the young boy's desperate leap. He knew Louise was in the vehicle which had just plunged into the water and he knew she was still alive. He didn't begin to think of Junior.

Kurtz sprang from the edge of the quarry, making no attempt to dive or clean up his performance. His arms and legs windmilled as he fell through the night. The wind whistled past the boy, taunting him as he fell.

A night dive.

*Where is The Devil's Club? The Devil's Club. The Devil's Club.*

He had nearly jumped over the two men at the quarry rim. The two who were trying to kill his sister. And then he thought of Junior. The two who must have killed Junior. Killed.

Kurtz was propelled so quickly into the world of homicide that he accepted it without thinking. These were killers. Louise could die soon. They were all facts which he processed as he passed through the night air.

He hit the roughened water just as he realized he should strip off his shoes and his pants. The water drove his bending body straight and smashed against his face, driving his eyelids back and forcing a huge draught of liquid up his nose. Kurtz ignored it and struggled to remove his shoes, but he was racing through the water so quickly that he could not force his body to bend. At last his descent slowed and he ripped off his shoes and then his pants. He turned several times in the water as if he were looking around.

It was blacker than night, blacker than death.

Kurtz began to panic.

A huge blister of rising air engulfed the boy and as it did it frightened him and he screamed and then inhaled. He drew in the escaping air and regained his self control.

Junior's car had sunk less quickly than the coupe, for its hood had remained latched and a significant amount of air was trapped there, in addition to the air in the passenger compartment and in the trunk with Junior.

In fact, Kurtz had almost smashed onto the automobile when he fell through the water, but he had initially leaped out farther than the path of the car and had actually passed it his first seconds in the water. The car expelled several large bubbles of air as it settled, the second of which Kurtz had robbed of some of its oxygen.

He dove toward the car, swimming in earnest, reaching forward with each stroke in the hope of touching the sedan. Once, he felt the a smooth expanse of metal and he kicked desperately lower, falling with it and struggling to find a hand-hold.

He grabbed the lower bead of the front fender, hit the bumper and then worked his way back toward the door. He could not see what he was doing, but he waved his hand in mad arcs in an attempt to reach the door handle. He grasped it on the third sweep and pulled himself to it.

The sedan was falling gently through the quarry water. Louise had been thrown about within the limits of her tethered arms and was now conscious, her head against the roof of the car, momentarily surrounded by the trapped air. The water had risen to her chest and was being forced into the sedan by the increased pressure as the it descended. She jerked her arms from side to side, but the rope was secure and she did not succeed in loosening it.

Kurtz braced his foot against the side of the car, turned the door handle and prepared to leverage the door open.

The compressed air escaped in a silent flood as the door opened easily. Louise felt the air hiss past and then the cold water cover her. She held her breath and tried to pull her arms free.

The young boy clawed his way into the vehicle, encountering his sister as he did. He grabbed at her soft body and attempted to pull her free. His lungs had begun to burn and the pressure on his ears seemed to be driving spikes into them.

She would not come.

Louise felt his hands and at first thought they were those of the killers, but she felt the desperate tenderness and then became conscious of their size.

*It is Timothy*, she thought. *My God, it is little Timothy.*

She wished to see her brother, to touch him, to look into his eyes and thank him, for she knew there was no way he could get her free. She tried to move closer to him but she could not.

Kurtz ran his hands down her arms and felt the rope. He fumbled for the knot, found several and worked furiously at them.

Very soon he would inhale. Very soon.

Louise allowed her body to become limp, thinking it might somehow help her brother.

Kurtz felt the change and feared for her. His hands automatically left the rope and sought her face. He held it in his hands and brought his face close to hers.

He could not free her. He could not save his sister. He knew that now and only wished to die with her.

In the blackness of the quarry depths, Kurtz pressed the side of his face against his sister's. He wrapped his arms around her and pulled her to him, and with that last embrace, and the last air in her lungs, Louise turned her head and moved her mouth to his ear saying, "I love you, Timothy, I'm so sorry. I love you, honey."

It was too much for the dying boy. He screamed his last air, screamed at the gods and at life and at this horrible ending to his sister's life.

He inhaled and struggled briefly and then was still.

Louise leaned into her brother and the water flowed past them and Junior's sedan continued downward.

She at last took in water and tried to expel it and then took in more. *It's like a movie,* she thought. *It's like a terrible, terrible, movie.*

The swirling water lifted Kurtz free from the sedan as it fell away from him. He drifted slowly upward, his body rising through the curtain of bubbles.

Fox rolled off of his brother and then ran to the quarry lip.

"What was that?" he asked and then amended his question, "Who was that?"

He thought for a moment and then spoke quickly to his brother.

"Take the car. I have the knife and a gun. I'll deal with this; you get the car out of here. Come back in one hour, I'll be out at the road. If I'm not there, try an hour later. If you miss me then, same time tomorrow. Same time as the drop. Get out of here."

Claude had risen and was standing listening to Fox. He nodded in the dark and then turned and trotted back to the car.

Fox peered into the white circle of water far below him. Bubbles still broke the surface. He stared at them and then looked around, orienting himself. At last he got to his feet and started in the direction of the landing.

The long form slid through the water disturbed by the two falling vehicles. It was repelled by the van and then drawn to the sedan, still coasting downward. It swam in an undulating, throbbing manner, sure and controlled as it circled the sedan, finally nosing in and touching Louise.

It backed its smooth head out and hovered, its long ophidian body coiling and uncoiling around itself as its head silently moved in a tentative circle. Finally it seemed to focus on something in the water above and it unraveled its length and moved toward the ascending boy.

Kurtz did not feel the slick bulk surround him, and was unaware when he was encapsulated by a small portion of its length.

Together, they rose to the surface, the thing at last pushing Kurtz into the night air and squeezing him gently as it did.

Overhead, the stars pulsed and sent their white darts of light from them. The wind picked up and tiny waves rose against the thing's wake. The advancing rain was almost over the quarry.

The young boy's head hung to the side and water ran from his hair. The thing constricted again and water and bile pushed past his lips. The thing flowed along the side of The Devil's Club, nudging it toward the landing as it did.

Fox crouched at the landing. Vaguely he could make out the floating, moving, stump and he did not know what it was.

The spirits of his ancestors awoke in Fox's mind and he thought the drifting log and its knot of roots to be one of them. Thousands of years of beliefs, hundreds of thousands of years of superstition and doubt and grappling with the unknown took him from the present, took him from civilization and white men, and set him squarely back into his Indian past.

It was moving toward him.

He was evil and he knew it and this spirit was coming to punish him. He had heard some of the legends regarding this area, and he had no doubt that good spirits were about, watching as best they could.

He reached behind him and pulled the knife free from its sheath.

Fox was evil and he would fight the spirit which came for him. If he must die it would be as a brave; he would not turn away, not now, not on the land of his fathers.

He would wait no longer. It was within an arm's length.

Fox landed on the trunk and jammed his knife into the wood, nearly to the hilt. He tried to withdraw it but could not. The thing was more solid than he expected and it did not move.

*Have I killed it so easily?* he wondered, his legs wrapped around the stump, his feet in the water.

And then he realized it was a floating log.

Humiliated, he sprang from it back to the landing granite. He looked around hastily to see who had seen his foolishness and then his attention was drawn back to the log. There was a sound. And a movement.

In the roots of the floating stump was a body.

Fox reached out from the landing and pulled The Devil's Club back to the stone wall.

It was a boy.

It was the person who had leaped past him and his brother.

Fox surmised that the boy had either hit the floating stump or had somehow swam to it and pulled himself to where he now lay. He looked at his watch and then surveyed the area.

Fox walked up the road from the landing, his knees aching from the weight of the dripping boy. He could feel the kid's small chest rising with shallow breaths and it annoyed him that the boy was alive and that he was forced to carry his soaked body back to where he was to meet Claude.

The car came down the quarry road and Fox waited in the bushes. The boy was gagged and bound by the remainder of the clothesline Fox had not used on Louise.

Claude pulled the car over and unlocked the door for his brother. Fox reached in and unlocked the back door and Claude watched as he heaved the boy onto the floor and then covered him with a blanket. One of the fishing rods fell out of the car and Fox picked it up and tossed it across the others. As soon as he got in beside Claude he saw that the package was missing.

Phillip tossed about on the cot and finally sat on its edge. *Beth. Beth. What is it about her that will not leave me alone?*

He reviewed their evening. It seemed they had walked half of the night, talking about everything. Most of the time Phillip apologized for one of the myriad of things he was sorry for having done.

*Potatoing.*

Beth had laughed about that.

*Charging Will for doing nothing.*

She didn't laugh.

*Hurting her little brother and the others.*

Beth had remained cloaked in the silence of anger as he beat himself over that. And then he had veered off and apologized for his life, his attitude, and his worthlessness.

"I've got to start all over," he said and Beth felt herself drawn to him. She would help him.

Phillip realized that what he consistently imagined and what he saw when he thought of Beth was not her body. It wasn't her legs or her chest, it was her eyes he remembered.

It was her eyes which looked through him; that went into his heart and searched for and then found the goodness that was hidden within him. She had seen it; she had located that part of him that he could feel good about and she had brought it out.

It was Beth that he loved and for the first time, he had begun to like himself.

*The automobiles! They were his curse!*

Every time Ezechial looked out at the quarry, there was an automobile. It was as if his life had become a mockery. All he wished to do was to start his machines.

He didn't wish to hurt anyone. He wasn't interested in bothering others. He simply wanted to be left alone to do what he needed to do, and he couldn't; for they drove in, they drove out, they appeared, they disappeared, and now it was nearly dawn. He clutched his bad hand with the good and wrenched it as he paced and willed them all away — to hell for all he cared.

And then the rain came in a deluge, pounding on the stone roof of the machinery shed, washing down its gutters, driving across the quarry waters below and the stone plateau around the granite-walled hole.

At first the pooled and drying blood resisted the rain and then it was battered and dissolved, finally flowing, trickling along the sloping stone until it reached the lip and ran down the stone sides, running along the granite, dripping from the myriad of tiny overhangs, sliding here, falling there, working its way to the water below.

It reached the quarry pool and was further diluted.

It had been Junior's blood, the most precious liquid he had ever owned, and now it was gone, indistinguishable, lost in the millions of gallons of already tainted water.

Ezechial listened to the rain and its sound began to calm him. Yes, he had lost another night. Yes, he *had* to start the machinery soon. He *had* to bring the fires and the heat and noise back into his life.

But he would not do it this night.

Once again he was delayed.

*Tomorrow.*

He dragged himself back up the stairs as the rain slackened and then ceased and the first birds of morning called to one another.

The rivulet of water ran unnoticed along the perpendicular pipe and through the crack in the floor of the machinery shed. It would take time, but it too would end its journey at the quarry below.

Fox felt along the floor of the car. "Where is it?" he asked.

Claude did not answer at first. He was thinking about the boy Fox had thrown into the back. *Why hadn't he killed him and tied rocks to the body? Why had he brought him along? There was too much danger. Too many things were going wrong.* And then he realized why they were driving away with the body. Fox wanted answers. He wanted to know who they had killed and he must have believed the kid would know.

He repeated his question. Calmly. "Where is it?"

Claude heard him and knew what he meant. "If you don't have it, then it's gone. It wasn't here when I drove off."

Fox stared into the night. *Another problem.* And then he remembered the boy. "The kid knows. Something tells me the kid knows."

Claude craned his head back as if to get an answer from the boy. *He can't talk now,* he thought. *But he will talk later.*

Fox remembered the man in the basement and then thought of the kid. *He'll tell us.*

# DAY SIX

Fox and Claude returned to the hotel room before it was light. They had decided how best to proceed. The plan was for Claude to stay behind at the motel. Get to a car lot somehow and buy a car. An old truck maybe. Then just keep an eye on things. Do a little fishing. Avoid suspicion.

It wouldn't do to have them check-out in the middle of the night.

Fox was to take the boy to the cabin. Take him to where no one would notice him. No one would hear him. Take him and have a little talk. Man to man.

And no one would find his grave.

Phillip rose early. He had lain awake through the rain storm and reveled in its violence. It was a beginning. It was a new beginning and the past was washed away. Phillip believed in his heart that he could start again, that there was a way for someone such as he to cleanse himself and bring a new focus into his life.

He was not certain if he was attempting simply to be a better person, or a better person for Beth. It mattered.

He shaved and showered and brought out a fresh pair of work pants and a shirt. There was a box of pressed blue shirts; work shirts which Old Man Horvath had made up sporting a dark blue patch with red script above the pocket.

*Phillip* it read.

He had refused to wear them.

*I'm no slave and I sure as hell don't need my name smeared across the front of my shirt,* he had thought in the past.

He tore the paper band from around one and then shook the shirt until it unfolded.

Phillip stood in front of the mirror and watched himself work with the heavy blue buttons.

*Phillip.*

In script, as if it mattered who he was.

He tucked the tail into his loose pants and then cinched his belt and pulled up his fly. There were two fresh pairs of socks left. He sat and slid his feet into a white pair colored at the top with red and black stripes, and then stepped into his shoes.

*Phillip.*

By the time the old man unlocked the back door Phillip had made a pot of coffee on the hot plate, first digging through various boxes until he found a jar of instant and two cups and spoons.

Beth stood at Alan's bedroom door and listened. It did not appear that he was out of bed yet and so she knocked lightly, hoping to awaken him. She waited and knocked again.

"Yeh?"

She pushed the door open and stepped into his room, wrapping her robe tightly as she did, leaving her hands clutching the terry cloth tie.

Alan propped himself on one elbow and rubbed his eyes with his fists. His hair was running in all directions and at first he seemed unable to focus on his sister.

Beth laughed. "Don't you think you ought to ask for new pajamas for Christmas?" she teased quietly.

He pulled his top outward and examined the pattern.

"Hey, spacemen are okay. These guys have been with me a long time."

He stretched an arm out and the sleeve barely extended past his elbow.

"I guess they're shrinking a little though." He looked closely at a bulbous, stylized rocket on the sleeve and chuckled to himself. "You aren't the new pj inspector are you?"

Beth smiled and sat on a large wooden toy box near his window. The top was covered with clothes and half of his sleeping bag, the rest of it cascading onto the floor at her feet. "I want to talk to you, Alan. About Phillip."

She continued before Alan could say anything. "I know what he did, Alan. I know all about everything he's done. I just want you to know that I'm still going to see him."

Alan frowned at her. He couldn't think of a way to respond. He was tempted to do something childish but her tone arrested him and he struggled to figure out why she would want to still see Phillip. Alan's relationship with his sister had changed and now it was as if they were equals and she was really confiding in him. Respecting him. He wanted to answer her on that level, as an equal, but the thoughts and the words would not come.

He just looked at her and finally she stood up again.

"I wanted you to know, Alan. I didn't want you to find out from someone else."

They observed one another, much as they had the previous morning, but things were very different now and still they were the same.

"Okay?" she asked and waited through his silence.

"Okay," he answered at last and then watched her leave, pulling the door closed behind her.

Alan lay back onto his bed and watched a dusty model biplane twist on its thread. Outside, the morning birds called from the trees and a warm breeze played through the leaves.

Mrs. Kurtz called up to her children. When neither answered she climbed the stairs, first stopping at her son's room.

"Timothy, it's time to rise and shine."

His door was open.

"Timothy?" she asked as she went into his bedroom.

She walked back out, calling down the hall, "Louise, did Timmy sleep out with the boys again last night? Louise? It's time to get up, dear."

She called Alan and Beth's house first. It was the most logical place to start.

Old Man Horvath smiled when he saw the shirt Phillip was wearing. He walked over to him and lightly touched the name tag. "I understand now why you never wanted to wear these shirts, Mr. Phillip."

The young man followed his employer's gaze.

"It's only half of your name. Only half and the last half at that. We should have had 'Mr.' sewn right on here," and he pointed to the space in front of the script 'Phillip'.

There had never before been banter in the garage, for Phillip worked well but he was always sullen around Old Man Horvath. He had resented his intelligence, resented his ownership of the garage, and absolutely bridled with the instructions he received regarding which vehicle to work on and when.

But this morning he did not see the old man as a boss or a threat.

He was a pleasant old man.

"Unless this big old nose is broken, Mr. Phillip, I would say you made us some refreshment. Let's get a cup and sit and talk."

Phillip followed Mr. Horvath over to the coffee pot, took the proffered cup and then walked behind him to the waiting area where they each sat.

"I am not a young man, Mr. Phillip, as I am sure you have noticed."

Old Man Horvath was launching directly into what he had planned to tell Phillip. There were, after all, many autos which needed repaired.

"And I have hoped for many years that our *relationship*," he said the word carefully, "would develop into one of trust. But that was not to be."

Phillip became wary for his employer's tone had chilled.

And as quickly, it warmed.

"Until now. Something has changed, my son. Something is different. I can only hope things stay as they are for you."

He cleared his throat and his listener started, so engrossed was he in the old man's words. Phillip shifted in his chair, leaned forward and noisily sucked in the top skim of his coffee.

The old man took a quiet drink and continued, "I wish to believe that you are to be trusted, Mr. Phillip, and so I am going to offer you some of my trust. I am going to let you know a secret and we shall see how much you have changed."

Phillip sat back in his chair. He was uncomfortable with the aura of confidentiality.

"Many people say we prize nothing but our money, Mr. Phillip; I am certain you have heard that, when in fact it is our secrets which we hold dear."

The old man set down his cup and spoke as he rose. "Mr. Philip, I am going to share with you where we keep our money and I am trusting you to tell no one."

Phillip's heart plunged. He already knew; it was no secret. Hell, even Junior knew.

But he wished to somehow rescue the moment. Mr. Horvath *had* to trust him, he *had* to see that he had indeed changed and that he was a worthy person.

"Mr. Horvath!" Phillip spoke more loudly than was necessary. The old man jerked to a stop and turned to face his confidant.

"Mr. Horvath, I already know. I know where you keep your money; I've known for a long time."

"So, then you show me, Mr. Phillip. You show me." There was irritation in his tone and fresh distrust and surprise. The young man could only have known if he had spied. If he had sneaked around like a thief and stolen one of the old man's secrets.

He was very angry.

Phillip saw the change and was desperate to rekindle the old man's confidence. Stupidly, he ran over to one of the steel lockers outside of Mr. Horvath's office, flung the door open and lifted out two fresh bands of rags stacked on its base. He then deftly lifted the steel bottom from the locker and set it on the garage floor behind him.

Phillip reached into the darkness and felt only air. Cool, empty, air.

The old man saw the look on Phillip's face and kneeled beside him. Phillip moved to the side and Mr. Horvath reached past him into the locker.

Phillip came close to vomiting as he watched the change in his employer's demeanor. It shifted from anger to disbelief and then to something like noxious pique.

Old Man Horvath retrieved his hand and stood above Phillip.

"We have a problem, Mr. Phillip. I hope you realize how serious it is."

He turned and walked away.

No one could find Kurtz and Louise.

The boys, Alan, Cavenaugh, and Roger, interrupted each other constantly for the first five minutes of their conversation behind the school.

"They wouldn't run away together."

"Maybe they're hiding."

"Do they have a grandma somewhere they may have gone to see to kinda get away?"

"Kurtz woulda told us."

"Louise woulda told Beth."

"Maybe Junior knows."

With the mention of Junior, the conversation ceased.

Junior.

Each boy explored the possibilities. Junior could have abducted them both. Raped Louise. Killed Kurtz. Junior could have fixed his car and taken Louise to Hollywood. Kurtz in the trunk. Kurtz hiding in the trunk. Kurtz finding out, threatening to tell if they didn't take him with them.

The boys pedaled over to where Junior lived. They cut across the field and approached his house from the back. An oil-soaked square of uncut grass and weeds stood near the trees.

The car was gone.

"Holy shit." Alan brought one hand to his mouth.

"Holy shit." Roger walked through the area where the automobile had been. He kicked a discarded engine part and bent and picked it up. "What's this?"

Cavenaugh took it and turned it over in his hand. "I don't know. It looks like some kind of engine part."

Had Kurtz been with them he would have added, "No shit, Sherlock."

Each of the boys heard him.

"Holy shit." Alan repeated, almost whispering.

The boys walked their bikes back to the school yard.

"What do we do now?" Alan asked.

No one answered.

"We've got to tell somebody; it's not like we're trying to get him in trouble or anything."

The others understood that 'him' was Kurtz and each of them was reticent to involve any adults in whatever adventure their friend was a part of. It had to be an adventure. There couldn't be any danger. There couldn't. That kind of danger didn't reach into small towns in Maine. Especially, not their town.

Cavenaugh stopped pushing his bike. "Let's give them a day. If they're not back — if we don't hear from Kurtz — then we tell somebody."

"Kurtz will get a message to us. He'll do something."

And then the trio discussed the different ways their friend would find to communicate with them.

They were at the back of the school again when Roger added excitedly, "Maybe he already did! Where would you leave us a message if you were Kurtz?"

Alan looked around him. "Here?"

"No you dummy!"

Cavenaugh interrupted Roger. "The forge shed."

"Yes! Yes! Yes!"

Alan shook his head. "Isn't that kinda far away for him? I mean, what if it was spur of the moment?"

Roger glared at him.

Alan shrugged his shoulders as he amended, "Okay. We check."

They pedaled out to the quarry. The rain from the night's storm was not yet evaporated and its vapor hung just above the ground. Even in their excitement they took No Brakes Hill carefully, each boy looking off to where Kurtz had made his flight.

Both Cavenaugh and Roger rode past Louise's bicycle without seeing it on its side in the woods. Alan was standing and pedaling and he had just cleared his throat and turned his head to spit.

"You guys!"

He skidded to a stop and pointed. "It's her bike! It's Louise's — streamers and all! I remember it from the bike parade last summer!"

Alan dropped his bike at the edge of the road and ran into the woods. Cavenaugh already had started up the side road at the quarry. He made a loop in the dirt and came back to join Alan. Roger propped his bicycle against a tree.

They stood in a semi-circle over Louise's discarded bicycle.

"It's definitely hers," Cavenaugh said. He nudged the front tire with the toe of his sneaker.

Roger walked around it. "It looks okay, why would she leave it here in the woods?"

"Maybe she met somebody," Cavenaugh answered.

"Maybe somebody got her," Alan whispered, concerned.

They left her bike and went back to their own.

"Keep your eyes peeled, you guys, let's walk in and see what we can see. Spread out." Cavenaugh took the middle of the road after he finished.

Alan moved up to Cavenaugh's right and Roger walked his bike to their left.

They didn't find anything as they pushed their bikes past the tower derrick and descended toward the forge shed. Once inside they quickly saw that there was no trace of Kurtz. Cavenaugh even walked around behind the shed. Finally, they gave up on the shed and walked back to the landing.

The granite was still damp with clear water puddled in its depressions. The quarry was quiet, the occasional shranking of a blue jay the only sound. The Devil's Club floated beneath the taller derrick and the raft was not to be seen, probably back around the far corner where it seemed always to end up.

The boys stood and looked out across the water and thought of their friend and wondered where he was.

"What's that?" Cavenaugh asked. He shaded his eyes with his hands and squinted at a white shape fifty feet out from where they stood.

"Paper cup?" Alan offered.

"Naw," Roger corrected him, "looks more like a shoe. Sneaker."

"Oh shit — could it be *his?*" Alan asked, almost begging to be proven wrong.

Roger now held his hands above his own eyes. "Nooooo," he drew out the word as he studied the floating object. "It's kinda hard to tell, but it looks like a new one to me. Kurtz's were beat to shit."

"There's its mate." Cavenaugh moved away from them as he spoke. He walked along the landing toward the ledge and the abandoned railroad engine. In the cattails by the shallows the other sneaker floated. Cavenaugh stabbed at it with a long stick and finally succeeded in entangling the stick in the laces. He raised the dripping shoe and brought it back to the ledge. Green slime dripped from it and a polka dotting of algae washed off with the falling water. In spite of the mess, it was obvious that the shoe had only recently found its way into the water. The white sides still gleamed where they were not stained. The soles were perfect and the laces had glossy tips. Even the bright blue ankle disc was unscuffed.

Cavenaugh picked it up. "Right size, wrong shoe."

Roger was now beside him. "Do you think it's a reject dumped by American Tech?"

American Shoe Company was the largest employer in the area. And it was known as a dead-end job. If you didn't go to college and especially if you didn't finish high school, you went to 'American Technical School'. They were rumored to be holding a job just for Junior.

They were also known to dump poorly made shoes in the woods and sand quarries in the area. 'The Midnight Express' was the name the local kids gave to any American Shoe truck which was on the road after dark.

Cavenaugh examined the shoe closely and then handed it to Roger, saying, "Looks like a perfectly good shoe to me. Those poor suckers at American Tech usually sew the tongue to the sole or put too many rivet air holes in the side. I saw one that looked like it was shot by a 22 caliber machine gun."

Roger laughed and held the shoe by its laces. It twirled akilter.

Alan looked at the sneaker and the more he looked at it the sadder he became. "I've got a real bad feeling, you guys."

"Yeh, me too," agreed Roger. He set the shoe gently down on the granite.

The three stared at it.

Cavenaugh looked up at the taller tower. "Let's go up there and sneak around the machinery shed once. You never know."

Beth was having an argument with her grandmother.

"I told you Grandma, I don't have any idea where Louise might be. She's kind of crazy. And then again she's pretty smart. Just quit asking me, please!"

The elderly lady sat in the stuffed chair and chewed on her gums. "Why, Beth, there's no reason to be so upset. Now, that little girl isn't anywhere to be found, and that child's mother is fit to be tied. You wait until you have little ones of your own. Sometimes you think they'll just worry you to death." She blew her nose into a tissue and then tucked it up her sleeve.

"Your father ran away when he was just a teeny lad and I thought I'd die. I cried all night and paced the living room all day. Your grandfather thought I had taken sick in the head. 'Sit down, Florence,' he said, 'before you wear out that new Sears rug.'

"Well I wouldn't sit and I couldn't sleep until Sam Gale drove up later that afternoon, as big as you please. Walked right up to the door and says, 'You missin' somethin', Florence? Somethin' little-like?'

"Well, I ran right by him and there on the front seat of his car was your father. Dirty! Why he didn't have an inch of clean on him. . . ."

Beth tried to think of a way to escape. If she heard one more time about her father's scraped knees she thought she might run away, herself.

"Excuse me, Grandma, I'm going to walk down to Louise's house and see if they've heard anything yet."

She was up and nearly out the door before her grandmother slackened her story.

"Beth!"

But Beth closed the door behind her and left the old lady alone in the living room.

"Well he was a sight!" she finished and smiled to herself. "His knees was skun to beat the band." She dabbed her eyes with a different tissue and stuck it in the top of her slip.

Alan saw the doll at the back door to the machinery shed as Cavenaugh heard Will's sedan pull in at the other side of the quarry.

The older boy called to Roger and Alan, "Come on, the other guys are here."

Roger ran off behind Cavenaugh but Alan stood frozen in the shadow of the building. There was a doll. Against the stone wall. Mutilated.

"Oh, shit," Alan whispered to himself.

He took a small step forward and then turned to see if Roger was near.

He was alone. He ran quickly up to the doll, snatched it away and ran after Cavenaugh and Roger, holding the broken doll at arm's length.

There were diagonal slash marks all across its face and one of the pudgy arms was severed. Some of its tightly curled hair was torn free and the dress it wore was ripped at the shoulders.

"Holy shit," he said again when he noticed the marks where a knife had punctured the front of the doll's dress in a line leading from its neck to between its legs.

Alan ran and held the doll away from him, fearful the violence it had suffered might somehow be visited upon him. Because he ran with his arms outstretched, his speed was significantly less than that of his friends. They were all the way back to the other side of the quarry and standing beside Will's car before he caught up with them.

Freddy noticed him running up and saw the advancing doll.

"Attack of the Flying Dolls," he said with no humor in his voice.

Alan threw the doll down when he reached them. "I found it at The Doll Man's door. He's sick. He's really sick. I think he did it." Alan wasn't certain if he meant the doll or the disappearance of his friend.

Will nudged the doll with his toe. "I hope this wasn't his favorite," he said, the side of his mouth curled with distaste.

Cavenaugh looked and then shook his head. "Our world is getting real complex, you guys. "

Alan asked, "Did you tell them about the bike? And the shoe?" "Shoes," he corrected.

Will picked up the doll by its loose arm. "Louise's bike. Are you guys sure? I mean, a girl's bike is a girl's bike."

"With red, white, and blue streamers?"

Alan didn't like his own tone. It was too sure, too pat, considering that his best friend was missing. "I'm worried, you guys. I can't think of why Kurtz would want to go with his sister and Junior."

Will bridled. "Maybe he didn't *want* to go. Maybe *she* didn't *want* to go. Who says they weren't *forced* to go? If you ask me, Junior's a pervert. I think we should tell the police about the bike."

"And the shoes. And the doll." Alan added.

Freddy disagreed. "I think they'd laugh about the doll. It's just like kids to think a doll is important. They'd think we were regular Hardy Boys."

"Yeh, forget about telling them anything else." Cavenaugh settled it for him. Alan would argue with Will and Freddy and Roger, but he almost always agreed with Cavenaugh.

Will thought about Louise — Louise with Junior — and lost himself and booted the doll toward the quarry.

"Fuck Junior," he said every time he kicked the tumbling doll. "Fuck Junior. Fuck Junior. Fuck Junior." and finally the battered toy sailed into the air above the quarry and dropped to the stained waters below.

All of the boys stood at the edge of the quarry. Will was close to crying. He didn't fear that Louise was hurt. In his heart he believed she had taken off with Junior for California. Probably rode her bike out to meet him. Her brother? Who knew. He was a wise kid. Probably took off from home. Had an argument with his parents. Whatever. It was Louise who mattered to him and she was gone. Gone.

All of them watched the doll sail downward, her arms and legs bent backwards. She fell slowly and hit the water with scarcely a splash. Into the circle of gasoline.

It was Roger who noticed it. He dropped to his hands and knees and squinted. The others thought his interest was in the floating doll. "Look at this," he said and Will and Cavenaugh kneeled beside him.

The water glistened in an irregular iridescent circle.

Freddy recognized it. "Gasoline. Leaking gasoline."

Alan crawled to the lip. "Now we *have* to tell the police."

Cavenaugh disagreed. "Alan, I know you mean well, but the police in this town, Mr. Lathram especially, seem to have a special hatred for kids. We'd be the Hardy Boys for sure. Plus, what if the gas is from Phillip's coupe — who wants to explain that?"

They were silent.

"There's definitely something going on around here," Will said at last, beginning to have doubts about his Louise and Junior theory.

"Now we *got* to get a camera rigged," Alan barely whispered.

"Bingo!" Roger said. "I almost forgot, we've *got* an underwater camera. My dad and I finished it last night. It's a beauty and I bet it works."

Cavenaugh sat on the stone. "What about the glass? What did you use?"

Roger rolled his eyes upward. "Oh man, we have got to be *so* careful. If we damage it my butt is cooked. My dad let me use an unground lense for a telescope he's going make. He's had it for years. But it's perfect. "It's like three inches thick and really clear. There's just a little curve to it but there shouldn't be too much distortion. And he let me use his camera."

"Holy shit," Alan added.

"Yes," Roger agreed and went on, "if we screw his stuff up we're all gonna be paying until we're eighty. Agreed?" He looked at the others.

As abbreviated and cryptic as it was, each boy knew that if he said, 'yes', he was solemnly promising, on his honor, to help buy Roger's father a new camera and a new lense for his telescope if they lost or broke them.

"Agreed."

"Agreed."

"Gotcha."

Alan thought of working for his parents forever without an allowance to show for it. "Agreed."

Roger turned to Will. "It's at my dad's shop. If we leave now we can get it and start right away.

Will looked at Freddy. "Why not?"

They climbed into Will's sedan and bounced back out the road. Alan couldn't keep his eyes from Louise's bike as they passed it.

"Do you think our bikes will be okay out here?" Alan asked.

Will turned back and answered as he drove, "Alan, I don't have the faintest idea what's safe anymore."

Freddy settled low into his seat. "You can say that again." Then he turned back to Alan. "Say, is Beth okay? I mean, have you seen her today?"

Alan felt his stomach drop to his shoes. *Beth in trouble. Beth gone.* "Yes," he mumbled, determined to kill Phillip if anything happened to his sister.

Phillip and Old Man Horvath worked on separate vehicles all day. Several times Phillip had nearly gone to his boss and told him that Junior knew about the money too, but each time he stopped himself, determined to speak with Junior first. It had to have been him. He'd kill the son-of-a-bitch with his own hands. But he'd get the money back first. Whatever was still left.

He imagined Junior pulling up in a new car. And then he imagined Junior on his way to Hollywood; in a new car, Louise tucked in beside him, prattling away about how she was going to be a movie star.

The second it was four o'clock he was determined to hop in the coupe — he nearly choked on *that* thought — he was going to *run* to Junior's.

"I'll bust his fuckin' chops," he mumbled and then swore as he torqued a nut, broke it off, and slammed his grease covered fist onto a sharp hunk of metal. "Son of a *bitch!*" he yelled.

Old Man Horvath looked up from the radiator he was draining. Phillip saw him and they stared at one another without speaking.

Mr. Horvath went back to his work.

The boys gingerly carried the contraption out to Will's car. It was large and it was ungainly and it was heavy. A ton of metal and a foreign car battery, and a camera and a bunch of gears and levers. And a glass lense that was *very* expensive.

Will took an old quilt out of the corner of his trunk and wrapped it around Roger's invention.

Roger tucked the protective covering around it.

Roger's father waved to them as they drove off. He called out, "I want to see those pictures!" but no one heard him.

They pooled their money and stopped at Destin's Feed and Hardware Store and bought 400 feet of heavy rope and a matching length of lighter line. Next they bought three rolls of high speed black and white film and a carton of Pepsi-Cola©.

By the time they had completed their provisioning it was well into the afternoon.

"Are we going to have enough time today?" Freddy asked, thinking of the availability of light.

Roger laughed. "You forget, Freddy, where that camera's going there isn't any light, anyway. We're sending lights down with it."

"What about us?" Alan asked, his heart sinking.

Each of the boys thought about floating around on the raft at night. It had limited appeal. But no one else wished to admit it.

Roger surprised them all. "Guys, we're not doing this for a merit badge. We're talking about our friends."

Reluctantly, each agreed. No one even thought of Junior. It was Louise and Kurtz they were looking for.

"We camp out," Cavenaugh stated.

Alan tried to swallow but the lump in his throat stayed lodged where it was.

Will remembered his dive and the horror he had experienced.

The others tried to think of pleasant things.

Will and Freddy stopped in front of each boy's house as he ran in, convinced his parents, and then ran back out with sleeping bag, flashlight, and invariably, an improvised weapon.

Finally Will ran up to the bank, got in to see Mr. Lathram in his capacity as town constable, told him about Louise's bicycle and couldn't get out soon enough.

"I'm telling you, you think The Doll Man's weird — that Lathram character gives me the creeps. He just watched me when I talked. Raised his eyebrow when I said about Louise's bike out by the quarry, then just sat there. Finally he said, 'Let the adults take care of this,' and had me *ushered* out of his office. Like I was trespassing!"

They drove back to the quarry.

By the time Phillip rounded the last corner to Junior's house he was winded. And surprised. There were two cars parked in front — the town squad car and Chief Lathram's.

"Oh Jesus!" Phillip swore and tried to regain his breath and decide if he should go to the house or not. He had an inbred distaste for traveling toward police. And now he had a double fear. What if Mr. Horvath had called them?

"Then they wouldn't be *here*, would they, stupid?" he said to himself.

Phillip made his decision and cut through the back yard adjacent to Junior's.

"I'll be damned," he said when he saw that Junior had gotten the old wreck running. *But can he keep it going?* he wondered as he turned and headed toward Beth's.

Roger loaded the camera as Will drove. When they reached the quarry, Will went past the lower derrick, down the road, and over to the landing, bouncing over the potholes and rocks.

"Hey! Take it easy, man, we're going to own that camera before we even get to the water!" Roger's concern and anger carried with his voice.

Will gave him a dirty look in the mirror and obediently slowed the sedan to a crawl. Still the old car bobbed and tilted as they moved ahead.

"You guys ever get seasick in this thing?" Cavenaugh asked.

Because it was Cavenaugh, Freddy laughed. Will groaned and muttered, "So funny, I forgot to laugh," and pulled up to the quarry edge. Alan looked out the side window and thought about his friend, praying he wasn't in the dark waters. He brushed a tear away from his eye and averted his face from the others as he climbed out.

He knew they had to be Kurtz's shoes. Probably new school shoes, but he couldn't tell the others because that would make it too true, too real.

Roger's father had welded a series of steel bars which protruded from the cylinder, two to a side, which the boys could use to carry the heavy apparatus. Both ends of the tube seemed to be secured by a myriad of wing nuts on threaded studs.

Roger took a strange looking piece of metal out of his back pocket.

"It's a wrench we made — for the nuts. Makes them easier to take off or tighten." He bent to the front end of the cylinder and started loosening the nuts. "You use it like so — hey, if I get them loose will a couple of you guys take them off the rest of the way?"

Freddy and Alan moved to the granite beside Roger and twisted the wing nuts.

When the last nuts were off, Roger slid the metal end off. In its center was the thick glass disc. It was mounted in such a fashion that water pressure on the lense would actually force it more tightly onto its rubber gasket, thus tightening the seal as it went deeper.

There was a large round gasket which remained on the cylinder.

Alan touched it with the end of one finger. "This looks like a car inner tube."

"Close," Roger answered, "we cut it from a truck tube."

Will smirked. "You sure say 'we' a lot. I bet you handed your dad the tools while he built it."

He was close to the truth.

Roger mounted the camera in the brackets inside of the tube, lining up various points on the camera with levers and arms inside the contraption.

"*If* it stays dry and if we get it down there, how are we gonna get it to take pictures?" Will asked.

Roger pointed generally to the mechanism above the camera. "Well, the plan is that these little guys in here either push the button to take a picture or move this lever to advance the film when we pull on this thing here." He now indicated a see-saw like affair on top if the cylinder. One end touched a tiny rubber circle. "We wanted to avoid any holes in the casing, so the lever here has to push the lever *on the other side of the rubber, inside the tube.*" Roger smiled.

He was proud of his father just as his father was proud of him. Had they lived in the Midwest, Roger's father would have built him the fastest soap box racer in the country — and claimed his son had done it.

The boys watched as Roger refitted the front and replaced the wing nuts.

"What about the back — does it come off, too?" Freddy asked.

"It can come off, but there's no need to take it apart now. It leads to a separate compartment with the car battery — from an Izetta — tiny foreign job. It powers the lights."

Thick wires protruded from the back of the cylinder and ran to a pair of head lights mounted on short outriggers at the business end of the camera.

"They're already hooked up inside, I just connect them right here before we lower it. We should have at least and hour's worth of juice to keep them running. Then we have to recharge the battery off of Will's car. I brought jumper cables."

"Mighty slick, Roger, I have to admit it," Cavenaugh said standing above him, his arms crossed across his chest. "Let's hook up the ropes and get this thing working."

"Well now, shit!"

It was Alan.

The others looked at him.

"What about the raft?"

It was not in sight.

All of the boys swore and then set about getting it back from around the corner by the taller derrick. By the time they had the raft at the landing they were well into evening.

The camera was loaded onto the craft, the coiled rope was set beside it, and the boys saw an unanticipated problem.

"That thing's not going to float with all of us on it," Freddy noted.

There followed a vigorous argument; for while no boy was anxious to ply the quarry waters at night; under the circumstances, being left on the shore was even less appealing.

Will settled the dispute by telling them who would do what. "Roger goes — he knows how to work the camera. Alan stays — he's too little to help with the heavy stuff. Freddy and I go — we're the biggest. Cavenaugh stays with Alan — because — he's a dumb shit." He slugged Cavenaugh's arm as he finished.

"Fuck you." Cavenaugh responded.

"You guys keep an eye out for cars, you never know who's going to show up out here," Will called back from the raft.

It was late in the day when Fox arrived at the turn-off for the cabin. He had driven out the western side of Maine and had headed northwest on a series of undeveloped roads. After three hours he was traveling on what was not much more than a pair of parallel ruts.

Kurtz bounced and banged around in the trunk. He had a killer appetite and he was cramped from being tied.

And Kurtz was mad. He wasn't angry, he was mad, nearly insane with rage at what had happened. He would not allow himself to think of Louise. Not Louise. If he did that he would lose all control. He knew because when he had first regained consciousness he had gone back to her touch in the water and for over an hour he had sobbed and wracked his body with the pain of her loss.

His bladder had changed him, for as he cried he became aware of the pressure and with the passing time the nagging need increased.

And then Kurtz really thought about it and it didn't matter. He released the warm water and it soaked him and it only made him focus on what he was going to do.

Somehow he was going to kill the men who were driving the car.

There had to be a reason that they hadn't killed him and that reason would give him the time to do it.

With every bump he knew with increasing certainty that the kid in the trunk was going to take the lives of the adults in the front.

It was twilight when the car lurched to a stop. Kurtz had been dozing but the lack of movement awoke him immediately. He closed his eyes again and waited. He heard a door open and then slam.

Fox walked through the dim light to the back door of the cabin. He took the screwdriver from his back pocket and unscrewed the fasteners holding the plank door snuggly to the side of the cabin. At last he pulled free the last screw and swung the door open. He unlatched the screen door and entered the cabin. On the table to his right was a kerosene lamp and a box of kitchen matches.

Fox cranked the wick down and then turned it up again. He raised the glass chimney, struck a match, and lighted the wick. The orange glow increased and then a yellowish light filled the cabin room, illuminating the iron stove and the small wooden table.

Kurtz heard the screen door slam. There was a scratching at the trunk lock and then it was opened.

Fox leaned in and roughly seized the boy. He levered him out of the trunk and them hefted him onto his shoulder like an enlarged sack of potatoes. For a small man, Fox was no slouch.

The infantile desire to have saved his urine so he could now release it passed through Kurtz's mind and then he became very angry with himself. *Keep thinkin' like a kid, asshole, and something tells me you're gonna die like one.*

The thought of dying did not bother him in the least. The thought of dying before he got those who — before he got them — was totally unacceptable. Kurtz had never given much thought to the future, to what he wished to be, but he now had his goal.

He would be a killer.

He was dumped onto the floor. It jarred him sufficiently that he involuntarily opened his eyes.

Fox watched him as he hit.

"I thought so," he said and walked over to the sink. He took the coffee can off of the top of the pump and then lifted the metal lid from the bucket. He filled the can with water and then poured it gently into the top of the pump, working the handle as he did.

The plunger squeaked and screamed as it was worked. Gradually the gasket softened and Fox was drawing suction and at last water as he pumped.

He looked over at the boy on the floor. "Priming the pump. You never prime a pump?"

Kurtz looked away. *This guy drops my ass on the floor from five feet and then wonders if I've ever primed a fuckin' pump?*

He would not allow himself to think of the other.

"I think we ought to get some food in us." He surveyed the shelves of canned goods as he spoke. "We've got a lot to talk about and it won't do to do it hungry."

*This guy's nuts,* Kurtz thought. *He's fuckin' nuts.* And then he wondered about the other one.

"Where's your friend?" It couldn't hurt to ask.

Fox stopped and turned.

He weighed the boy and his tone before he answered.

"I think we should understand some things. *I* ask the questions. I ask *all* of the questions. And when I do, *you* have a choice. And I guarantee you, you'll do one or the other." He paused to make certain the boy had absorbed what had been said and then he continued, "You may answer my questions. Or you may scream in pain."

Kurtz had been concentrating on hurting *them.* This was a new twist.

The raft and the boys and the camera nearly tipped over into the water as they attempted to get the camera to the side. Twice they tried and each time they nearly lost it all. Finally Roger said, "We've got a hammer and some nails back at the forge shed. We've got to go back."

Cavenaugh and Alan squinted through the increasing darkness and watched the antics of their friends. Each time the boys on the raft attempted to move the camera to a side, the opposite end of the raft lifted out of the water and Alan would whisper to Cavenaugh, "Oh, shit! There they go,

Cavenaugh didn't comment but he could tell Alan was concerned. Finally, during a quiet moment down on the water, the older boy looked at Alan and said, "You miss him don't you. He was really a good shit."

Alan could not answer at first. He fought back his tears, barely keeping them under control. He bit his lip until he knew it was bleeding and then with the wash of pain he was able to drive Kurtz, dead, from the certainty of his thoughts.

Cavenaugh realized he had said the wrong thing. "I'm sorry," he said quietly and then Alan answered,

"Can we maybe not talk about it yet?"

Alan felt Cavenaugh's arm pass over him. The older boy squeezed his shoulder twice.

"Yes, I suppose we ought to spend our time figuring this out."

When they heard the boys on the raft paddling back to the landing, the two at the top of the quarry rose to follow.

Cavenaugh led them past the bull wheel of the lower derrick and Alan kept close behind him. It was now black in the bushes and neither boy could see where he was putting his feet.

"Watch the cables," Cavenaugh said as he stepped over a slack bunch which ran from the derrick, around the upper perimeter of the quarry and into the machinery shed. Alan stepped over the invisible object and in so doing, missed stepping on the bundle of money which Kurtz had dropped.

Before they went to the landing shed they arced around the lower derrick and walked out along the parking area. Cavenaugh stood in the previous paths of the van and Junior's car. Alan walked slightly to the side and when he did he kicked something metallic on the granite shelf.

"What was that?" Alan asked and bent to the stone. He ran his hand along it until it brushed against the blade of Junior's knife. He recognized it as a knife and gingerly walked his fingers to the handle.

"It's a knife, Cavenaugh, I just found a knife."

The boys tried to examine in it the gloom but they could tell nothing about it. Cavenaugh folded the blade and put it in his pocket. "Let's look at it in the light and see if the others recognize it."

"Kurtz's knife was really little," Alan said quietly to the unasked question.

By the time they got to the landing, the raft was being modified.

"We're taking out the two center boards and then we're going to lay them perpendicular to the others," Roger instructed. "That way there'll be a hole in the middle of the raft that we can lower the camera through. Trying to get it over the side was a suicidal bitch."

Cavenaugh asked, "You guys didn't hurt the camera, did you?"

Roger laughed. "Hurt the camera? Naw, that things pretty sturdy. I think Will and Freddy almost got ruptured though."

"The knife!" Alan interrupted.

Cavenaugh took it out and they examined it in the light of three flashlights. Will opened the blade and closed it several times and each time they all peered as closely as it as six converging heads would allow.

"I don't see any blood," Freddy noted.

"Woulda washed off in last night's rain, is my guess," said Roger.

They agreed that they had never seen it but that it was probably somehow involved in what was going on.

"Unless some night fisherman lost it," Alan volunteered. There were occasional locals who spent a night drinking beer and drowning worms from one of the quarry walls.

The boys went back to the work on the raft, securing the new boards, loading the camera back on, and setting out again to photograph the depths.

They were ten feet out from the landing when Alan called after them, "Hey, can we have one of your flashlights? You've got *three*."

"Sorry," Will answered for the others, "I think we're gonna need them. It gets dicey out here in the dark."

"Hold each other's hand," Freddy joked to the boys on shore, "and you'll be okay."

There was a nervous chuckle which came back from the disappearing raft. Then a light shone from the waters to Alan's eyes.

"Does that help?"

It was Freddy again.

Then Alan heard Will. "Don't joke around. If that thing had got to you when you were swimming, I guarantee you wouldn't be joking now."

The light went out.

The idea of holding Cavenaugh's hand when they walked back up the road to the lower derrick was anything but ridiculous to Alan. He was relieved when he felt an arm on his shoulder.

"You okay?" the older boy asked.

"Yes, I'm just peachy," came the unconvincing reply.

Phillip was nearly hopping from foot to foot as he waited for someone to answer Beth's door. *Five people live here and only one would be pleased to see me,* he thought. *I'm some kind of great guy.*

To his incredible relief, Beth opened the door. When she saw who it was she didn't say a word. She quickly slipped out the door and closed it silently behind her.

"Hi," she said as she pulled him away from her house.

Phillip followed, trying to decide where to start with the many things he had to tell her *this* evening.

She beat him to it.

"Louise and her little brother and Junior are gone. Do you think they left?"

He understood that she meant Hollywood.

"Yeh, that's my guess, too, but I didn't know the kid went. Are you sure?"

They each discussed what they knew.

Phillip thought for a while about Junior and then added, "There's no way he would have let her take her little brother. Somethin's wrong, Beth."

They stood in silence at the end of her block.

"Where's *your* little brother?"

Beth had heard the argument between her grandmother and Alan; the old lady insisting that he stay home that night and Alan actually saying 'no,' and when she remembered it she became frightened for him.

"He's at the quarry with the others."

It sounded terrible when she said it.

"I'm worried, Phillip. I'm scared."

He was moved to see Beth's concern. "Hey, let's go out. They don't have to know we're even there. Let's just go out and kinda check up on them."

Beth turned and hugged Phillip. She wrapped her arms around him and he felt her breasts on his stomach and he could feel that she was trembling.

Then he laughed.

"What's so funny," Beth asked without releasing him.

"Have you got a spare bike?"

She thought of his coupe and what had happened to it and then she laughed, too.

"Well, Mr. Bigshot, (she was teasing, but it hurt him when she did) we've got my bike. I'm sure Alan has his at the quarry, and we've also got the bike-for-two my parents bought for themselves. I don't think its ever been ridden. Once I guess. They tried it after they got on a 'Sing Along With Mitch' kick, but I think my dad ran them into some bushes."

They sneaked back to her house and then into the garage. The bicycle was against the back wall.

Both tires were flat.

"Just need air," Phillip pronounced, "You got a pump?"

He brought the air pressure up in the tires while Beth wiped off the dusty seats and handle grips.

"This should be an adventure," he said as he pushed it out of the garage. At first they took up all of the road as they pedaled, but as they got out of town they stayed basically in one lane and soon after that, Phillip kept them at the side of the road.

It was a cloudy night but the air was warm. They pedaled down the dark lanes, the tires occasionally nipping rocks which they sent off into the woods. Beth leaned forward and spoke close to Phillip's ear as they whooshed through the night.

*This is actually fun*, Phillip thought, *Is this what normal people do?* His beer and cigarettes and pick-up girls seemed cheap to him.

"How do I convince him that I didn't take his money?" Phillip turned his head.

"I think he knows you didn't, Phillip, or you wouldn't have told him you knew where he hid his money. But I think he knows you know who did. So you're still responsible in his book."

"Great. I pay for my slimy friends."

"I think that's how it works," she whispered near his ear.

"I guess it is," he answered.

Kurtz passed out after Fox cut off his first finger. *Kids*, the brother thought as he bound the inert boy's stump.

He had been gentle and polite at first and the boy had stared straight into his eyes. "Just tell me a few things," Fox had said. "Who were those people?"

Kurtz stared.

Fox then went to the table by the front window. He brought a long narrow stick, roughly the width of a thick pencil, from the kindling box. He reached for his knife, felt the empty sheath, and stopped dead. His mind raced back to the quarry, settling on his encounter with the floating stump.

Were Fox one to curse he would have done so then.

He had to go back to get his knife. Soon. It was one of the few things he and his brother owned which linked them with their past. With their glory and honor and their place in the shifting drama of their country. Their lost country. He broke the stick then into four pieces and drove them into the crack between two of the table's boards. He then took a hatchet from the wood box and pounded them down with the blunt end. When he was finished, a few inches of each peg stood above the level of the table.

Kurtz watched, fascinated. Four pegs. An inch apart.

Fox walked to where the boy now sat and manhandled him over to a chair in front of the table.

After a professional flurry of movements Kurtz found himself bound to the chair, his right arm outstretched and tied to the table. The four pegs protruded from the gap between each of his fingers. He could not raise his hand and he could not withdraw it.

Fox then lay the remainder of the stick he had broken — a piece barely two inches long — in the center of the table.

"I have asked you politely. I have deferred to your age and been much more patient than normal. But you have told me nothing."

He picked up the hatchet.

"I shall do more than talk, my little friend."

He arranged the stick so that it was parallel to Kurtz's fingers but a foot away.

"Let's neither you nor I look at that little stick. Let us look at each other."

Kurtz, determined to show no fear, did as he was told and locked his eyes on those of the man. At the periphery he knew he had raised the hatchet. The man didn't look at what he was doing. He didn't even glance toward the stick on the table.

"I can do more than ask questions," he said, "especially when I get no answers, especially when it appears I am wasting my time."

As he finished his sentence the hatchet flashed through the air and whacked into the table. The pieces of the stick skittered away and dropped lightly onto the floor.

Kurtz moved his eyes obliquely to where the stick had been.

Fox rocked the hatchet out of the table.

"Two things — if you are smart you will spread your fingers very far (my aim is not always perfect) — and I ask you again, who were those people?"

He saw from the boy's set mouth and unmoving face that once again he wasn't going to answer.

Kurtz heard the hatchet more than be saw it, and when it severed his first finger he saw the twitching digit roll to the side like a wounded earthworm in no way related to his hand. He didn't feel a thing. A millisecond before his synapses relayed their horrible news, his eyes transmitted the same shocking information and he passed out. His head thumped onto the table.

*I can't believe I left the knife,* Fox thought.

Will and Freddy played out the twin ropes as Roger shined his light on the descending lines. The older boys' arms ached from their task. Even with the buoyancy of the water, it was a heavy, tedious, job.

"It's almost there," Roger noted. "Slow down, we don't want it to crash onto the bottom."

They arrested the descent for a moment.

"I've gotta rest my arms," Freddy complained.

Will agreed. "Yeh, me too. Does that thing get heavier as it gets deeper?"

"Roger thought a minute. "No, but you keep adding the weight of additional rope, plus your muscles are fatiguing."

Will snorted. "*Fatiguing* — is that what's happening? I thought I was getting pooped."

A young voice called down from above them. "YOU GUYS TAKIN' PICTURES YET?"

Roger answered Alan. "NOT YET — SOON THOUGH. SAY, CAN YOU GUYS SEE THE LIGHTS FROM UP THERE? WE CAN'T ANYMORE."

Just before they began lowering the camera housing, Roger had connected the lights. Freddy had been unfortunate enough to have been looking at one of them when it came on.

"Holy shit, I'm blind," he had protested. It took him at least fifteen minutes to regain his night vision.

Will and Roger had worked together to lower the camera while Freddy complained about his eyes.

The twin lights shone clearly through the water and then as the apparatus went deeper they became hazier and smaller. At last they were a tiny light blur and then Roger and Will and Freddy couldn't see anything below them.

"NO, WE LOST THEM A COUPLE MINUTES AGO," Cavenaugh answered. "THINK THEY BROKE OR SOMETHING?"

Roger checked into the water again. "I DON'T THINK SO," he yelled up the quarry wall, his voice echoing with its lack of conviction.

Will and Freddy began lowering again, this time with great care. Neither was anxious to pay anything to Roger's father.

As a starting point they had chosen a spot twenty feet out from the wall and below the spot where Alan had found the knife.

"Looks like a logical place to me," Will had said trying to impress Roger and then wishing to kick himself for trying to show off to a kid.

"We're there;" Will whispered, "my line's slack."

"Mine too."

Roger shined his light on the loose ropes. "Okay you guys, this is the tense part. It could get tangled on anything down there. Slide under some rubble, anything. So now we gotta carefully lift it off the bottom. Carefully. Bring it up about five feet then stop. Freddy, you've got the light line. You just keep the slack out of it."

Freddy obediently pulled lightly on the rope. "We take pictures with this line?" he asked.

"You just did," Roger answered. "Every time we tug on that line from here on out, it moves a mechanism which first hits the shutter button, then on the next pull, advances the film. Pull after that it takes another picture, and on and on until we use up the film. Thirty-six pictures. Seventy-two pulls."

"I think we're at five feet," Will announced, the dripping rope laying across his legs.

"Let me do this," Roger told Freddy, taking the thin rope from him. He pulled up on the rope until it tightened. "Advanced." he said.

"Smile, little monster," Freddy interrupted.

Roger pulled on the line again. "Say cheese."

They spent the next hour pulling in line and swinging the camera from side to side with the trigger rope. They remained in the vicinity of the lower derrick and took three pictures toward the quarry wall for every one they took facing in a different direction.

"I SEE THE LIGHT AGAIN," Alan shouted down to them.

"'That's my little brother," Beth told Phillip. They had left the bicycle at the quarry entrance. "He's a good kid," she added. "I think you two would have been pals if you were the same age."

Phillip thought about it. "I guess."

Beth stopped and turned to him. "Hey, Mr. Tough-guy, you don't always have to grunt your answers when you disagree."

He thought about that.

"Yes," and then he realized he had just done it again. "I mean, yes, why yes, I do that sometimes and I should quit. Doing that."

"Ugh," Beth grunted and then laughed softly.

Alan and Cavenaugh froze instantly.

"I heard noises," Alan hissed. "Somebody's here."

Cavenaugh scrambled to the edge and tossed down a small rock. After he heard it hit he hoarsely called down, "Somebody's here — cool it," and he moved back to Alan.

Will had one hand down in the water to retrieve more rope. He stopped. Roger turned slowly on the gently rocking raft. Freddy rose carefully to his feet and tried to see the top of the quarry wall.

The stars were obscured by clouds and the boys could have been anywhere. The job of maneuvering the camera had occupied them sufficiently to keep their fears at bay, but now, in the quiet, after a warning, they felt suffocatingly vulnerable.

Will went back to the thing in the water. And he remembered where his hand was. He nearly released the rope but he remembered in the nick of time. He yanked his hand and the length of rope out.

"Knock it off," Freddy warned him. "Gheez, you're noisy."

The raft rocked again and Roger cautioned, "Careful you guys. We can't screw stuff up now — we're almost out of film. Two more pictures left. I think."

Phillip stopped Beth. "Do you hear them?"

After what seemed to be a lifetime of waiting, Ezechial could stand it no longer. He struck the match and set it under the paper and kindling.

Alan picked up a large, sharp-edged piece of granite. He crouched beside Cavenaugh near the road. Someone was coming. Actually, it sounded like two persons. Alan did not begin to hope that one of them might be his friend. He was gone, that was for certain.

Cavenaugh squeezed his arm twice. Alan brought his face close to the older boy's. "If — they — come — near — us, — nail — them," Cavenaugh half mouthed, half whispered and then brought his own rock close enough so Alan could see it. Alan nodded and Cavenaugh added, "Don't — mess — around — aim — for — their — heads."

Again, the young boy nodded. *I'll kill them,* he thought.

Phillip slowed Beth. He indicated the lower tower with his hand, pointing toward the bushes where Alan and Cavenaugh crouched. Beth saw Phillip raise his finger to his lips. Phillip stooped and picked up a rock.

He pitched it underhand into the bushes beside the boys.

All hell broke loose.

Alan screamed and chucked his shard of granite at the spot where Phillip's stone had landed. Cavenaugh whaled his projectile at the sound of Alan's.

Beth recognized Alan's scream as she saw Phillip prepare to heave another rock.

"Alan!" she called.

Alan was sweating bullets trying to find another rock in the dark. He had brought a ball bat to the quarry with him but had forgotten it down by the landing. In the middle of his insane search for something to throw he heard his sister calling him.

*This is really crazy!* he thought. *How could Beth be here?* He heard himself answer, "Yes?"

Cavenaugh stood and walked out of the bushes. He recognized Phillip and then Alan's sister. "You guys out for a midnight stroll?" he asked and then said, "Hi, Beth."

Alan untangled himself from the briars he had found. "You shouldn't be here," he called out to his sister. "Does Grandma know you're here?" he asked, trying to cover his embarrassment and assume the attitude of sibling-in-command.

"Alan Wasterly," she settled into lecturing, "you are not my mother or my father, so knock it off. And by the way, Grandma says you are to come home immediately," she added, lying for spite.

Chastened, Alan turned away from his sister and Phillip. He made his way back to the quarry lip and told the others what was going on.

"It's Beth and. . . ." he couldn't say Phillip's name. It was too humiliating. And then he remembered the coupe. "Oh, shit," he whispered to himself.

Phillip gave Cavenaugh the once over.

All brass, Cavenaugh asked, "How did you guys get out here?"

Phillip laughed, surprising the others and then said, "Well, we didn't drive the coupe and we didn't walk."

Beth answered, "We took my parents' bicycle-for-two."

It was Cavenaugh's turn to laugh. Even Alan smiled to himself briefly.

Will and Freddy yelled through the night, their voices laced with macabre echoes.

"WHO'S UP THERE?"

"MEET US AT THE LANDING!"

Alan went over to his sister. "What did Grandma *really* say? Will she tell Mom and Dad when they get home?"

"Alan, she didn't say anything after you left. She thinks there's a murder-rapist-monster on the loose and he has his sights on us. And the answer to your second question is, 'yes, Grandma will surely tell Mom and Dad,' and the answer to your unasked question is, 'Mom and Dad will be very, very, angry and I bet we'll both be grounded for a month.'"

Cavenaugh and Phillip stood to the side ignoring the brother-sister exchange. Both were uncomfortable in the other's presence but Phillip broke the barrier.

"I used to be afraid to jump into the quarry. I got to tell you, drivin' in is no picnic."

Cavenaugh laughed nervously. "I bet," and then added, "We didn't really want to hurt you guys."

Phillip dug his hands into his pockets and shrugged his shoulders. "It could have turned out to be a pretty bad stunt, but the way I see things these days, you guys have got a lot more time to grow up than me. I think I'm kinda overdue."

Beth was talking to her brother but listening to the others. She reached through the darkness and took Phillip's arm.

As she and Phillip started back to the landing they saw a flash of light from the quarry waters.

Ezechial added larger sticks to the fire. He could feel the warmth coming off of it and it was his elixir. Carefully he gathered the chips of coal and fed them one by one to the hottest flames.

It was later than he had intended, but Ezechial had taken the time to check everything again. It was very dark outside. He had stepped out earlier to relieve himself and he could smell the rain in the air. Now he was in the machinery shed, the doors closed, the windows shuttered. Nothing would stop him now.

He sat on the wooden stool before the open fire box door and watched the life being restored to his machines. The kindling snapped and occasionally fiery twigs shot out onto the floor. He ground them out in succession, his attention only momentarily wavering from the pyre before him.

Phillip and Alan stood together at the landing while Will and Freddy held Roger's camera housing. He was intent on loading new film into the camera, his work illuminated by the flashlights aimed by Beth and Cavenaugh.

Roger looked up at Alan. He pulled a shiny cannister from his shirt pocket and said, "We've got one load, kid, so far, so good."

Alan smiled weakly. He saw that the lights on the camera had been disconnected.

"Is the battery okay? Does it need charged or anything?"

Roger smiled at him. Alan had been the only one of the boys who had thought to remind Roger.

"No, the lights were really bright when we brought it to the surface. I think we can do at least one more roll before we have to hook up to the car."

He closed the camera and mounted it back in the housing. Phillip bent and watched, nearly obscuring Roger's view.

"Back a little, if you don't mind."

Phillip stepped back and responded, "Say, that's really slick. Did you make it?"

Roger couldn't help himself. "Well, my father and I did." And then he went on to describe every detail of the apparatus. Phillip listened, impressed both with the construction and Roger's knowledge of it, and jealous of the relationship between Roger and his father.

"Your dad do stuff like this for you all the time?"

Roger couldn't place the tone of Phillip's question. "Yes, if I ask him to he does. I mean if it's a reasonable request." He looked over at Phillip. "Why?"

Phillip took another step away from Roger. "Oh, uh, I was just wondering'."

Beth moved the flashlight so that Phillip's face was in the border of its cone of light. She was saddened by what she saw.

Roger turned to Beth. "Light. I need the light here."

Phillip helped to thread the wing nuts back on the cover and Roger torqued them with the special wrench.

"Slick. Very slick." Phillip said when Roger let him examine the tool.

Will interrupted the exchange. He held out the knife they had found. "Say, Phillip, does this look familiar to you?"

Phillip didn't need to look closely to confirm whose it was, but he did. He tossed the knife lightly in his hand.

"Where'd you find it?"

Freddy told him and Phillip looked through the dark toward the lower derrick and then followed an imaginary path to the water. He pointed out to where the boys had been working from the raft.

"Is that where you've been lowering the camera?"

Several boys answered.

Phillip squeezed the knife in his hand. "I think you might be seein' Junior soon. When are you developing the pictures?"

"I'm doin' it," Will answered. "I've got the school newspaper equipment in my basement. I'll have 'em done in about an hour after I get home."

"I'd like to help you. Could I?" Phillip asked.

Will didn't get a chance to answer because Beth asked Phillip, "Junior's?" And when Phillip nodded the boys felt their stomach's drop as one.

Beth thought of Louise and she started to cry quietly.

They were loading the camera back on the raft when Cavenaugh saw the headlights approaching the machinery shed.

"We've got company!"

The others stopped as if frozen.

Ezechial put several more sticks of wood and a few larger lumps of coal into the building fire. The heat was increasing to the point that soon he would need to use the short-handled shovel.

The fire popped several times in succession. There was another series of sounds and Ezechial realized that the noise was coming from behind him. Someone was pounding on the side door.

*The boy again,* he thought and then he remembered the old lady and hoped it would be her. There was one can left in the carton.

A part of the old man wanted to ignore the intruder and another part was anxious to rise and see who was visiting him so late. At last he pushed himself to his feet and shuffled toward the door.

The boys broke from their trances and scrambled toward the various weapons they had scattered about the granite of the landing. Ball bats clunked on stone, rocks were retrieved and boys bumped into each other. It was for Phillip to bring order to the Chinese fire drill.

"Hey! Calm down!"

The boys gathered around him. It was the voice of someone older — a voice they needed to hear.

Phillip surveyed them.

"Beth, you stay here with Alan. The rest of you guys — let's sneak up there and see what's goin' on. Now be quiet."

Phillip led the others off in a crouch. When they got to the wooded edge, Cavenaugh took Phillip by the arm and whispered, "I'll lead, you don't know your way through here."

Phillip let the boy pass.

# Dead Man's Quarry

Beth and Alan came silently behind the group. She held Alan's hand and Alan was glad she did.

Freddy, who trailed the first group, heard the two followers. He stepped to the side of the path and waited for them. As Beth was abreast him he stepped in front of her.

"Where do you think you're going?" he hissed.

Beth was startled and Alan nearly had a heart attack.

"If he thinks we're waiting alone down there, he's crazy," she said, referring to Phillip.

Freddy thought she should stay at the landing too, but he was loath to side with his nemesis.

"Well, you've got to stay back some and be quiet. And if there's a problem," he turned to Alan, "you get her out of here."

Alan nodded. Before Freddy ran ahead to catch up with the others, he put his hand on Beth's arm. He was about to say something, but he stopped himself.

"He really likes you," Alan whispered to his sister and felt as if he were betraying Phillip when he did.

The Widow Orlap stood awash in the light from inside the machinery shed. She carried a cardboard carton in front of her.

Ezechial tried to take the box from her but she brushed him aside and entered the room with the huge machines.

She smelled the fire. "You be careful with your fires, Ezechial," she said as if addressing a child. She walked over to the base of the stairs and slid the carton onto a greasy table top.

Ezechial stepped outside and was blinded by the headlights of the automobile. He ducked back into the shed and swung the big door shut.

"That's Orsen, Ezechial. He had to drive me out here. I've not been well."

The widow sat on the stool Ezechial had been using. Her breath rattled in her lungs and the fire outlined every wrinkle on her face. She did not look well.

Ezechial wondered if perhaps she weren't the mother of the other lady who used to come. He had never seen this old woman before. But she spoke as if she knew him.

"That's Orsen, out there in the car; I can't seem to drive anymore and he told me he'd bring me out. Wanted to come out in the day but I told him it wouldn't do. Just wouldn't do."

The old lady started to cough and she couldn't seem to stop. At last she brought a stained handkerchief to her mouth and coughed into it. Her thin chest heaved and she closed her eyes.

Ezechial looked from her to the fire and back to her again.

The boys hid in the bushes near the shed. The car lights were on and they couldn't tell if anyone was in it.

Cavenaugh whispered, "We can see through the shutter cracks on the side window. Follow me."

He went off hunched over. The others hunkered behind him.

Cavenaugh reached the window and put his eye to one of the cracks. Will and Phillip found escaping light and did the same.

"He's got a fire goin' in there!" As he said it, Will realized that he could smell the wood and coal burning.

"That's weird," Freddy said. He was standing a little away from the others, keeping his eye on the car and watching for Beth and Alan.

"There's an old lady in there!" Cavenaugh exclaimed.

Beth heard him as she and her brother left the bushes. She went over to Will and tapped. his shoulder. "Let me see."

Surprised, he stepped aside. Phillip heard her too and turned and smiled.

"That's The Widow Orlap," she said, "I know her, she's really nice," and Beth left the window and walked around toward the side door. "She wouldn't hurt anybody," she said to the astonished others.

She walked through the glare of the headlights, hit the door twice and then pushed it open. "Hello? Hello? Mrs. Orlap?"

The big machines blocked her view but Beth felt the wave of heat as she stepped into the building.

The boys and Phillip crowded in behind her as if afraid to be left outside in the dark. They tripped over each other as they progressed behind Beth. Phillip and Roger roamed in awe of the machinery.

Orsen saw the group crowd the door. "What the?" he asked himself as he reached down for the tire iron beside his seat. He opened the door and climbed out of the car. He lumbered forward carefully, his arm flexed.

The Widow blinked at Beth.

Ezechial retreated to a shadow cast by the boiler.

"Mrs. Orlap, it's Beth Wasterly — I talked to you with my Sunday School class — you go to our church."

The old lady wiped her lips with the cloth and then let her hand drop to her lap. She blinked once more and then squinted toward the girl.

"Yesssss," she drew out slowly. And then her face lighted as if she had just seen a beautiful dress in the front row at Easter. "Why yes, child! How are your parents? And that cute little brother? Alvin, is that his name?"

Alan hated her instantly. But when she started to cough again he forgave her.

Beth moved to the widow and tentatively put her hand on the coughing woman's back. She was shocked by the feel of the old lady; it was as if her hand rested on the side of a shaking bag of bones loosely knitted together.

"It's too hot. Far too hot in here!" she croaked. "Ezechial, we're going upstairs."

The old man instinctively brought his good hand to his unkempt beard. He wanted to protest, to stop all these people from entering his life, but they already had and he didn't know what to do next. He watched dumbly as The Widow Orlap struggled to her feet and then went to the stairs.

She and Beth climbed them together. The boys turned to one another and one by one began to follow. Phillip hung behind, examining the machines and skirting the old man.

Ezechial furtively took a stick and threw it through the fire box door.

Phillip recognized the boiler for what it was.

"Sweet Jesus, you're gonna fire that bastard!"

The crudeness of the words took the old man back. *Was it the Boston Boiler Man? Could it really be?*

And he accepted him, again.

Orsen pushed the door open without knocking. He advanced around several machines and confronted Phillip and Ezechial working together to stoke the boiler fire.

"What kind of god-awful party is this? The Widow never told me this was no midnight picnic."

He relaxed the arm carrying the tire tool and walked over to the two at the fire.

"I think we're going to suck some steam from this rivet-studded bitch." Phillip said, indicating the massive boiler.

Ezechial listened to the texture of the words and warmed further to Phillip.

"Can't says I've seen one 'farred' since I was a young man" Orsen added and moved gladly toward the coal heap.

The widow sat in Ezechial's chair by the window. Will had seen her walking to it and had hustled ahead and pulled it out from the alcove. Beth sat on the edge of the bed and Will and Freddy and Cavenaugh and Alan found places on the floor.

"Mrs. Orlap," Beth started, "some terrible things have been happening here."

The old lady sat as if absorbing the very breath which came with the young girl's words. She chewed absently on her gums for a moment and then said, "That does not surprise me, my dear. Do not mistake me — I am sorry to hear that it has started again — but I had always feared it would begin sooner."

The children sat in silence in the dusty room, the bare bulb casting harsh shadows into each lonely corner. There were dolls everywhere, propped against shelves, wedged in corners, seemingly crawling onto the bed on which Beth sat and listened to the widow's tale.

"There are terrible stories that I could tell you, but it is too late for most of them to be of importance. They would serve only to frighten you." She cleared her raspy throat and continued, "but you should know the truth of Ezechial; a gentle and sad man, really, and of the other; for he is powerful and evil."

She turned and looked at each child individually, measuring their goodness and their soul and when she finished she was satisfied.

"Many years ago, after the celebrations of the passing of the last century, changes came to our town and to the quarry. . . ."

Phillip glanced at the rising needles on the gauges. He watched as The Doll Man did the same and they both were fascinated by the creeping movements propelled by the building fire. They shovel-fed coal into the beast's now-raging maw.

The big guy — 'Orsen', he had told Phillip — was having a lark of it. Phillip did not mention the things which had happened recently, so enthralled was he by Ezechial and his awakening machines. He considered it at first, but the big man in the bib overalls didn't encourage confidences. In fact, he had barely said two words after he said his name.

And The Doll Man — he hadn't said anything. He nodded to Phillip familiarly a time or two, but he didn't speak. The young man got the impression that Ezechial thought he knew him, so comfortable did he seem with his presence. At first he thought it was because of his visit of the other night, but the more Phillip studied the old man, the more he saw a friendship or some sort of fawning kinship being wordlessly expressed.

The old guy shuffled back and forth between the machines miming obscure directions but it wasn't until they had gone on for over an hour that Phillip came to understand that the old man was showing him — Phillip — that he — The Doll Man — understood the machines. He was acting like an apprentice to Phillip-the-master.

As confusing as it was, Phillip found himself learning. He came to understand the nature of the different machines and their interconnections by the various levers and valves.

The big spools of greased cable obviously ran to the derricks, and the water pipes leading in from outside must have led to the old water tower. The big dual-flywheeled compressor had at first stymied the real student, but it finally dawned on him that it was not an engine in the sense that it produced power — no, those were live steam lines which ran *to* the barrel-sized cylinders — it compressed air and then drove it out through the pipes to the quarry.

Phillip ran his hand over the warming cast metal of the wheels and he saw The Doll Man flinch and them smile a crooked smile of approval.

"This son of a bitch is a *beauty*. She must shake the shit out of this place when she spins to life!"

Orsen looked up from shoveling another load of coal into the firebox. He was about to respond to Phillip's statement when he saw that the old guy and the kid were talking to each other — well, communicating somehow — so he went back to his own pleasant work. He had broken a man's sweat and as always, he sported it proudly.

"Did a little stokin' in my own day," he said to no one, "when I was just a kid." He wiped some of the grime from his forehead with the back of his broad hand, thinking that he could drink the heat of the furnace all day ('honest heat', he called it) — until he remembered that it was the middle of the night.

"Some strange," he said to himself, careful to be unheard.

The old lady held the children with the strength of her knowledge of things they had begun to recognize as more than legends and tales.

"They were raising the third derrick; would have been the tallest in the state — it's at the quarry bottom now — when one team of horses took a fright. They bolted and pulled the other team in, pulled them right over the side and both horses and the folks tending them fell to the bottom."

She rested and remembered the day. The children glanced at each other, unsure as to the relevance of what she was saying.

"They had hit with a horrible sound. The sound of life escaping and busting bones, and when they got to them, the only one alive was the boy.

"Young Ezechial, his sister, and his father, stacked right up on the horses like a cord of wood. Ezechial come out of it — somehow — he was never right after that and he seemed always to blame himself."

The widow had a coughing fit again and the children darted more looks to one another. Different looks than before. *She was talking about The Doll Man!*

She stopped and Will saw the blood on her handkerchief before she fumbled with her thin fingers to hide it.

Beth asked quietly, "What happened then. I mean, how did he end up here? Owning the quarry."

Mrs. Orlap looked surprised with the tail of Beth's question.

"'Ezechial owns the quarry' — I never really thought of it that way. I suppose he must. I always thought of this place owning him. It is all he has. I sometimes think the only reason he stayed alive was for his machines."

They sat in silence briefly.

"Mrs. Orlap," Will asked finally, voicing what had been on his mind continually for three days, "what is in the quarry water? What is it? I know something's there; it touched me."

She stared at him. "It is there?" she asked.

*"Something's there,"* Will reinforced.

"This place, this ridge, has always been the place of evil," she said, and the children were confused when she called it a 'ridge'.

She saw that they were not following her. "It was a ridge, a majestic, evil, ridge, before the white men came and cut it up and sold it. And now it is a hole in the earth and beneath the waters which fill it is the mother of the spirit of evil."

"It touched me! I felt it!" Will exclaimed and told her about his dive.

The widow did not respond at first and then she smiled thinly.

"I am glad. It is good to know."

*That's easy for you to say,* Will thought, remembering his encounter.

The Widow continued, "There are good spirits which do what they can to protect us. It is why we are not overwhelmed. What you felt," and as she said it she held Will's gaze, "was good. It would do no harm to any of you. The evil," she looked at them all, "is beneath the water and also in our town. One man. . . ."

As she said the latter her words were punctuated by sounds from downstairs. There was a hiss of escaping steam.

Again she was taken by her coughing and this time it was apparent that she was in pain. Beth moved to her side. There was an odor to the old woman and it was repulsive to Beth. She had to force herself to stay near.

The woman waved her away with her free hand, the little color she had draining from her features as she continued her wracking cough.

At last she sucked in a few minor draughts of air. She steadied herself and sat upright, her eyes still closed, and just when the children thought she was going to open them and continue, she dozed off, her head falling until it rested on the side of the tattered chair.

They heard more clanking downstairs.

"Is she dead?" Alan whispered.

Will studied her chest. He shook his head from side to side.

"What do we do now?" Freddy whispered across to Beth.

She raised her finger to her lips.

The children sat in Ezechial's room and waited for The Widow Orlap to awaken. There was no way they were going to move until they learned who the widow spoke of when she said that some one in town was evil.

Phillip sensed the old man's excitement and matched it with his own. Ezechial had twisted open three large valves and now he hovered above a set of levers. The largest had a grip and a handle on it and The Doll Man wrapped his good hand around it and compressed the release.

Gently he nudged the lever forward.

There was a whoosh from the compressor behind Phillip and Orson. They both jumped and then laughed nervously. Next there came a languorous hiss and the giant flywheel rocked a fraction of an inch. Pipes clanked with their fresh heat.

Ezechial smiled.

He caressed the lever and urged it again.

The big wheel — slightly taller than Orsen and almost as wide — rocked once more and then returned, and then rocked again and progressed through the beginnings of an arc.

Phillip didn't know whether to reach for the flywheel and try to urge it through by throwing his weight behind it, or to back well away, against the stone wall. It was alluring and frightening at the same time.

Ezechial compounded the wheel's movement by clacking the lever forward a few more notches and with that the wheel went into a full, and at first, loping, revolution.

There was another whoosh, more full this time and a clattering of little mechanical tappets and then the thrung of the rods raising and lowering in heavy metal syncopation at the compressor's side. There were moist sounds of sucking oil and flowing steam.

At first the floor vibrated and then it pulsed and Phillip noticed the second flywheel at the other end of the axle, on the shadowed side of the machine. It spun with it's brother. Phillip came to feel that the whole shed was moving, that this huge marvelous machine was propelling the entire building into the night, into space.

A few more notches forward and the rushing air from the spoked wheel bathed Phillip in dampness. The noise in the machinery shed was rising to a level where Phillip could no longer identify individual sources of sound. He was in the midst of a howling, mechanical cacophony.

Excess steam escaped around joints and huffed through pipes into the night. The bellows in the boiler raked the fire across the red coals and the door clattered as Orsen opened and then closed it after each measured shovelful of fuel.

The men felt the power in their thumping chests and in the rhythmic pounding of the floor beneath their feet.

Alive at last, Ezechial limped across the room to the shuttered windows facing the quarry. He forced the window up and then unlatched and pushed out the board shutters.

Out there in the darkness was the quarry. The light from the shed cast itself to the feet of the larger derrick.

Ezechial stared through the night as if making a decision — as if choosing.

He looked back at Phillip and the boy knew he was being asked to come forward. Ezechial moved to the side and eyed the different drums of cable. Each had a brace of gears at each side, and a pair of levers, both of which had the shiny, metal, squeeze-grip handles.

Phillip looked out the window and then at the row of cabled spools. He looked out the window again.

*He's going to work the derricks. He's going to operate the booms!* A new flush of excitement flowed through Phillip.

"The far boom — the derrick across the quarry — work that one — swing it out to the quarry!" Phillip exclaimed, pointing and settling into giving orders.

Ezechial listened, concentrating on the words the man was shouting. *The old derrick. He wants me to operate the old derrick.*

He took the levers in his hands and stepped back from them. He leaned into the one on the left and pushed it all the way forward and then he compressed the handle on the right-hand lever and pulled it back to a stop.

With a dangerous whirl, a wrapped spool began to slowly wind in more cable.

Phillip traced the entering cable to the floor in front of the winch and out through the shadowed hole into the night.

The cable whipped slightly as it took up the slack and then it snapped taut and the apparatus strained at its stay-bolts.

Phillip heard it through the window. He heard it over the bass machinery noises in the shed. There was a screaming outdoors, the screeching sound of metal grudgingly twisting in the dark.

Phillip needed to see. He had to see the movement. He bolted out the side door of the shed and ran across the front of the building. He could hear the cables moving through the steadying pulleys around the quarry lip.

And then in the distant shadows he saw the outlined derrick and he saw the rising boom. And then he heard a different set of cables called and the slack was taken up in them and a different noise rose above the others.

The big tower of the derrick pivoted and the raised boom swung above the trees and out over the quarry. It screamed and screeched, and its power and size seized Phillip like a maniacal religion.

"My god," he said in awe.

"My god," he repeated and tried to absorb the sounds of the swiveling derrick and boom and the smell of the coal fire, and the throbbing power that was the machinery shed.

The derrick's noises pierced the upper room of the machinery shed. The Widow Orlap's eyes shot open as if she had heard the valkyries coming for her. Her eyes raped the room in a sad, desperate search for escape and then she saw the children.

She rose and staggered toward the stairs.

Freddy jumped to his feet and put his hand under The Widow's arm.

Beth watched until the old lady turned to her.

"Who is evil?" the young girl asked and The Widow took a step toward her.

The derrick shrieked again and the old lady tried to bring her quivering hands to her ears.

"Lathram!" she shouted to Beth. "It is Phineas! He is the devil himself!"

She made it to the stairs before the cables and the tower protested again. There was blood at the corner of her mouth and a line of phlegm and blood extending to her chin. "Not *your* devil — *ours*," she amended to the girl who was now beside her. *"The spirit-devil,"* she spat.

Phillip was coming back to the side door when Orsen and the old lady brushed past him. The big man had scooped up The Widow and was carrying her hurriedly to his car.

Phillip burst through the door as Beth and the others were bunching just inside of it.

"What's the matter?" Phillip demanded. "What happened?"

He had seen The Widow collapse beside the big man, and Ezechial had been at a loss as to whether to go to her or do something with his machines. Before he could decide she was lifted and carried away.

He insanely hurried around his machines, closing valves, throwing levers, and venting steam.

It was night when Kurtz awoke. The pain in his finger was so intense that he thought he had lost his hand. He was in a cold sweat and he was shaking and he was still bound to the chair. He didn't think of revenge and he could barely think of his sister. Kurtz thought only of escaping, of getting away from this monster who could so casually mutilate a child's body.

The only respite he had was when he found himself wondering about the location of his missing finger.

Kurtz was barely able to control himself when he found that was looking into the eyes of the man who had hurt him.

The lantern flame guttered.

The sound of the outboard motor of a night fisherman passed in the distance.

The boat surprised Fox. He turned away from the boy for a moment, speaking as he did.

"We must continue, it seems."

He turned back to Kurtz.

The boy felt nausea sweep over him as a renewed wave of pain coincided with the man's gripping the hatchet.

Fox lifted it from the table.

"You realize, don't you, that we can do this nine more times."

He moved his eyes to the young boy's crotch. "Ten, actually."

Kurtz was in so much pain and so profoundly in the embrace of mortal fear that he did not catch his tormentor's allusion. All he understood was that the weapon was again off of the table. He wished to vomit, to purge himself of everything that was inside. He wished to be in his bed or at the kitchen table or at a theater. He wished his finger back onto his hand.

He had never dreamed the world could be so crazy. And then the pain became even more intense and he could do nothing more but sob and grieve for his broken body. There was no storming Iwo Jima or tossing grenades at bad guys. There were no flesh wounds which the good guy ignored. There was only his vulnerable body at the mercy of a madman.

"Who were those people?" Fox asked, breaking through the boy's flight from reality. Then Fox corrected himself. "Never mind them. What did you do with the money?"

Kurtz only heard the word, 'money', and it was as if it had been shouted at the end of a very long tunnel. *Money? What the hell was money?*

*Dear God, he is raising the hatchet!*

"Where is the package?"

*Package? There was a package. Yes, there was!*

The boy took heart in the fact that the man was making sense. *There had been a package!*

The hatchet was once more in the air above Kurtz's hand.

His mind screamed for him to stop the other. His body begged him.

*Package. Package. What about a package?* And then he remembered the word 'where'.

The hatchet was poised and he could not move his remaining fingers.

WHERE!! the voice screamed in his mind.

"I DROPPED IT! I DROPPED IT! I DROPPED IT!" Kurtz heard himself cry, but it was really barely more than a whisper.

The hatchet hung in the air.

"Where?" the voice repeated — the man's voice this time.

*Where? Where?* rattled through his tenor. *Oh God, tell him where. Tell me where!*

And then he remembered. And when he did he did not flirt for one fraction of a second with withholding the information.

"At the derrick. I dropped it when I climbed the derrick!"

Kurtz was sobbing so badly that his last sentence was not intelligible. But Fox had understood the earlier response.

It was at the base of the derrick.

The hatchet was still in the air.

"I am going to look soon, and if it is not there I'll come back and I'll kill you."

Fox had his face inches from Kurtz. The boy blinked through his tears. The pain became unbearable again.

Fox pushed himself away from the boy and hesitated. The hatchet whacked into the table again and another of the boy's fingers rolled free.

Ezechial had lost himself in the process of shutting down the machines — he neither heard nor saw the others. The children came down the steps in a file and wended their way around his movements. Phillip stayed with The Doll Man, as absorbed in closing valves as he had been with their opening.

And when Ezechial went to the fire door and opened it and took up the long metal rake and started pulling the fire out from the box, dumping the burning coals onto the granite floor, Phillip grabbed his arm and stopped him. .

"No! No!" Phillip said directly into Ezechial's face. "Don't do that now! Leave the fire. We'll run these son's of bitches again tomorrow!"

Ezechial understood the excitement and the lust for machines he saw in the man's eyes. He saw it in Phillip and they shared the moment.

The Doll Man swung the door shut with the rake and then dragged the smoking coals to a stone shoot which led outside. He then went to the piled coal and pulled out nugget-sized pieces and began to move them toward the firebox.

The heat was incredible and it was delicious to Phillip. He knew his face had to be black from the soot and smoke.

He turned away from Ezechial and said to Freddy. "Let's get out of here for now — we've got lots more to do."

Claude had spent the morning fishing in the stream behind the motel. It didn't matter at all to him that it was overcast and appeared there would be more rain any moment.

The owner had come out several times, once with cold beer, and the two of them had exchanged tall tales.

Before noon Claude changed clothes and walked up the road from the motel. He walked for several miles and then hitchhiked to the next town. There he sauntered into a yard with several older cars and a few pickup trucks with prices shoe polished on their windshields.

He drove a sedan out of the lot, gassed it at the first station, bought a beer and a sandwich wrapped in waxed paper, and cruised back to the motel.

There he idled away the rest of the day fishing.

He felt certain his brother would return soon, if not that night, at least by morning. He never doubted that they would recover the money. Things had surely gone wrong at the quarry, but they could be righted.

There couldn't be a problem with the police.

"What now?" Freddy asked.

"Why don't you take Beth home," Phillip said, surprising at least three of them.

She started to argue, but Will said, "Yeh, you'd better — here's the keys," and held them out.

Freddy hesitated, trying to figure out Phillip's angle.

Roger resolved it by assuming it to be a fait accompli.

He polished the glass on the front of the apparatus. "I want to take at least one more roll of film. We can play around with the film in the dark room — black and white has a pretty wide range, but I want to shoot some more at a different f stop."

Cavenaugh said, "Yeh, me too," and felt stupid for it.

Beth walked about five steps with Freddy and then stopped and turned around.

"Alan, I'm only going to tell you what I think. You can do what you think is right, but I think you should come home with Freddy and me. You can get back out here first thing in the morning. You'll avoid a lot of problems at home that way, and I think things are getting too rough for you to be out here at night."

She waited for her brother's reply.

Freddy had his flashlight shining on Alan. The young boy waved the beam aside.

"You're right, Beth," he said and was saddened when he saw the relief on his sister's face. She was assuming the wrong thing.

"I mean you're right that I should do what I think is right — I'm staying."

Phillip smiled and turned his head so Beth wouldn't see him.

She walked off. After a few steps she stopped again.

"You be careful, Alan."

Then she added, "All of you."

"Yeh, we can handle it," Roger said. "We pretty much have the knack of it."

# Dead Man's Quarry 249

He and Will and Cavenaugh paddled the raft away from the landing. Phillip and Alan stood and watched them disappear into the darkness.

"Feels like rain," Alan said uncomfortably.

Phillip was ill at ease, also. He looked up at the sky as if he could see things. He held his hand out, palm up. "I don't know about rain, but it sure as hell feels like 'dark' to me. Real dark."

Alan laughed politely.

Phillip punched Alan lightly on the shoulder. "Let's go back up to the derrick and keep an eye on the guys."

"Yeh, okay," Alan said, thinking about Phillip's referring to Will and Roger and Cavenaugh as 'the guys'. At first he felt a little angry about it and then he didn't.

"You ever have any friends besides Junior?" Alan asked.

Phillip was surprised to hear Junior referred to as a 'friend'. When he answered Alan, he spoke critically of Junior, but he used the tone folks use when they speak of someone who is dead.

"Well, you know, Junior and I did a lot of things together. I mean we 'hung out', 'cruised around', stuff like that. But it was never like we were really friends. It was almost like we were stuck with each other. I needed somebody to bullshit and he needed a ride. Perfect match."

He was facing Alan when he spoke. The fact that he did, thawed the young boy's reserve.

Phillip went on, "It's like, if my back was ever against a wall — you know, like if I ever really needed somebody — I can't tell you that he would of been there for me."

They walked a few more feet.

"You see, it's funny — it's really important to know you've got a buddy who'll be there for you. Kinda like Beth says you and your friends are. Kurtz and all. And I've never had that. My own damn fault if you want to know the truth."

They walked up the road to the derrick and Phillip found himself telling Alan the same things he had told Beth.

He talked just about non-stop for over an hour. Alan listened to Phillip and tried to understand what the trio in the quarry were saying when their voices echoed up.

Phillip seemed finally to have finished. He and Alan sat with their legs over the quarry edge, something Alan would never have done were he not with Phillip.

Phillip braced his hands on his knees and leaned forward. "HEY, YOU GUYS. . . ."

Will's "WHAT?" reached them.

"WILL YOU DO ME A FAVOR IF YOU GET A CHANCE?"

There was a long pause by those on the water. Finally Roger answered, "LIKE WHAT?"

Alan heard Phillip chuckle.

"IF YOU GUYS GET OVER THERE A LITTLE FARTHER, WILL YOU SEE IF YOU CAN TAKE A COUPLE PICTURES OF THE COUPE? I NEVER TOOK ANY."

Alan laughed with his friends on the raft.

Cavenaugh said, "YEH, WE'LL DO THAT IF WE GET A CHANCE."

Will added, "ANY SPECIAL ANGLE YOU'RE LOOKIN' FOR?"

"WHEELS DOWN, HOPEFULLY," Phillip answered.

Within the hour Roger shot another roll of film.

"WE'RE HEADIN' BACK," he yelled up to Alan and Phillip, although the dawn was close enough that the sagging observers on the quarry cliff could now see their actions.

Freddy had brought the sedan back earlier. He drove it past the lower derrick and parked it down by the landing. Alan called to him to join him and Phillip, but Freddy declined, saying he was going to sit alone for awhile.

Alan didn't say it, but he felt sorry for Freddy. He wouldn't have believed it a day earlier, but he had also begun to understood why his sister preferred Phillip.

Ezechial husbanded the fire beneath the boiler. *Two days! He was going to keep it going for two days!* And in his mind it was because The Boston Boiler Man had told him to. He was just doing what he had been told. He checked the fire once more and hobbled back to the stairs, thinking of the carton of food which awaited him in his room.

He had forgotten about the children and The Widow, but he had not forgotten the fellow who helped stoke the fire. He was a good worker. Like Ezechial. He knew that tomorrow, when they started the machines again, he would be there. And The Boston Boiler Man.

Beth was greeted at the door by a hysterical grandmother.

"I called the police! I called them four times, and every time they said the same thing — they're working on it — they're working on it. They wouldn't believe me when I told them you and Alan were missing too."

The old lady looked around.

"Where is Alan? Where is little Alan?"

Beth collapsed onto the living room chair. She rubbed her eyes with her hand. "He's staying with a friend tonight, Grandma. He's with Phillip; he'll be fine."

She closed her eyes. Images of Phillip and The Widow and her brother and Freddy passed each other in spinning eccentric circles.

"He should be here, Beth Marie, with his family. If anything happens to him I'll never be able to forgive myself. And your parents won't either." She paused. "What's the phone number of this Phillip. I want to call and see if Alan's alright. Estella Brinks has been right all along. This town isn't safe anymore. Not like it used to be when your grandfather was alive — children didn't just turn up missing." She thought of her friend, Estella. "And the elderly aren't attacked in their own back yards."

The last words Beth heard her say were, "If you ask me, Phineas Lathram hasn't done one good thing for this town. . . ."

"Goodnight, Grandma," Beth said and pulled her feet up off of the floor, tucking them close to her chest. She reached out and turned off the reading lamp.

DAY SEVEN

---

Fox waited until just before first light before he left the cabin. The boy had spent the night alternately crying and calling to his mother, and Fox had been unable to get adequate rest. It was not a good way to start the day but he figured that after a cool drive and a big breakfast he would feel much better. There were many things to be done within the next twenty-four hours.

He placed the box of weapons on the floor and backed the car around. The boy wasn't going anywhere until he and Claude got back. He was sure of that.

The boys loaded the trunk with the camera and then piled into Will's sedan. Phillip climbed into the back with Alan and Roger. Alan was asleep with his head against Phillip before Will had his key in the ignition.

Phillip absently opened and closed Junior's knife.

Will cranked the sedan through but it wouldn't catch. He turned to the back seat.

"I never said I was perfect," Phillip said defensively. "But I did say I'll tune this thing so she runs like new. I said that, and I will. Mark my words. Now, try it again."

"Mark his words," Will mumbled to Freddy and tried the engine again. This time it sputtered a few times and then coughed to life. Blue smoke rolled over it and Will drove back up the road, past the lower derrick and out of the quarry.

Ezechial watched the car pull out. He checked the fire one more time and went upstairs to sleep.

"You want to catch a little sleep at my house and then help me develop this film?" Will asked Roger.

"I'd like to sleep a whole lot and then develop the film but I don't think I have that choice do I?"

Will weaved up Old Quarry Road toward town.

"We're getting a little seasick back here," Roger protested, but no one in the front heard. Both Freddy and Cavenaugh were asleep.

"You awake up there?" Phillip asked Will.

Will adjusted his mirror and looked back at Phillip. He ignored the question but took the opportunity to ask his own. "What do you think's goin' on at the quarry?"

Phillip closed Junior's knife. "I don't know for sure what happened, but I do know one thing."

"Yeh, what's that?"

Alan cracked an eye open.

Phillip opened the blade to the knife again, testing its sharpness. "Junior and Louise aren't going to make it to Hollywood."

He didn't say it as a joke.

Will thought about Louise. "Boy, she was sure crazy."

"Yeh," Phillip agreed sadly, "that she was."

They drove the rest of the way in silence. Will made a circuit and Alan and Cavenaugh tumbled out individually in front of their homes. "Catch you later," Will mumbled to each of them.

When he turned toward Horvath's Garage, Phillip asked, "You guys mind if I go with you to check out the pictures?"

"Thinkin' about the coupe?" Will asked.

"No, not really. I was just wonderin' about the kids."

Junior and Kurtz and Louise. The kids. Oddly enough, it sounded right.

Alan walked to the backyard like a zombie, petted Blacky briefly, and then went in and curled up on the couch. Beth was still asleep in the chair, her mouth open, her arm outstretched to the side.

Will and Roger, and Phillip and Freddy collapsed across various rugs and the two beds in Will's bedroom.

"Wake me for breakfast," Roger wheezed with his last breath.

Freddy hugged a pillow and was out.

Phillip briefly marveled at the furniture in Will's room and then fell asleep.

Will covered his head and tried to remember if he had all of the chemicals to develop the pictures. Before he could decide, he was snoring.

For the second day in a row, the morning broke grey with cloudy skies. A light drizzle started with daybreak, and the milk truck's tires seared across the wet streets. Dairy bottles clanked in carried metal holders, newspapers skidded through the air and front doors opened to bathrobed sleepwalkers.

Phillip groaned and scratched himself and Will chewed noisily through the vestiges of his sleep. Roger sat up in his bed.

"Did we sleep? What time is it?"

He reached to his window sill and grabbed his alarm clock.

"Shoot!"

"What time is it?" Phillip asked.

"I don't know, I forgot to wind this thing."

Will wound the clock and set it back on the ledge. "How come you don't have a watch?" he challenged.

Phillip rubbed his wrist. "Never had one that would last. Always whacked it onto a generator or something. Anyway, the coupe had the best clock around. Came from a Cadillac."

Freddy opened his eyes and watched the exchange.

"What makes you think we were involved with your car?" Will asked.

Phillip laughed to himself and then said, "Well, Will, everybody else who's mad at me isn't clever enough to pull a stunt like that. And if they were, they'd be too scared that somebody'd get really hurt. It had to be you guys — sedan that wouldn't start and all, blocking my way."

"You mad about it?" Roger asked. "Going to get us back?"

"Well, I know one thing; you kids could never dream how much money I had sunk in that car."

Freddy and Phillip chuckled at 'sunk'.

Phillip continued, "Everything I ever earned, pretty much. And everything I got ripping off people. So I guess I got what I deserved." He stopped and thought about the car. "'That was one fine coupe though. Nothing could touch it. Fastest rod around," he added, exaggerating.

Will propped himself up on his elbow. "You know, I bet you could pull it out with the derrick. Get The Doll Man to help you — you guys seem to get along."

"Yeh, I was thinkin' about that. We'll see. We'd need to hook up using you guys' camera — if it works."

"Which reminds me," Will said. "I don't know if I dreamed this or not — I think I've got all the chemicals, but I might be out of paper to print on."

The boys stretched their sore bodies and searched the littered floor for matching socks and shoes. They filed through the bathroom, washing with handfuls of cold water.

"Where's you parents?" Phillip asked softly.

"Asleep. They always sleep in on Sunday. They won't be up until around noon. They go dancing down in Portland every Saturday night."

"They worried about what's going on?" Phillip continued, unable to resist learning how real families operated.

"I don't think they've heard anything," Will answered and remembered what The Widow had said about the constable.

The boys followed Will down into the basement. He turned on an overhead light. There was a small room off to their left, basically constructed with sheets of cardboard taped to keep out light. Triple pipes ran into it from behind a wringer washing machine.

The boys fled into the tiny room.

Will started adjusting faucets and laying out equipment. He tried to rattle an empty printing paper box. "I don't believe this."

The others waited for him to continue.

"It's one thing to be out of paper, but *today!* There's no place to buy developing paper on Sunday — they're closed."

He moved aside a stack of magazines. There was a crushed, thin box under them. "We've got one, slim, chance."

Will reached around and turned on a red light then switched off the other.

"What the fuck?" Phillip was sorry he swore as soon as he did.

He remembered something about red lights in developing rooms and didn't ask.

"One sheet," Will said with minor relief. "We can use it for a contact sheet. We'll have to choose the pictures carefully from the negatives, and then they'll be tiny once they're printed, but I think it'll be okay for now."

In fact, none of the boys wished the pictures to be large.

"We can blow them up tomorrow when we get paper."

Freddy stood by the closed door and watched quietly.

They were all pretending that what they feared couldn't be true. Each boy secretly hoped for pictures of nothing. Or better yet, the quarry bottom, littered with cans and bottles. Maybe a bald tire. And a coupe.


Beth and Alan's grandmother made them shower and then sit at the breakfast table. The young boy pushed the glutinous eggs around on his plate and his sister nicked away at the corners of her toast.

"I want you children to stay close to home today," she lectured. It's Sunday and your parents should be calling."

Beth and Alan exchanged glances. It wasn't worth arguing about. They knew they would sneak out the second she wasn't looking.

"And no running off!" their grandmother added, wagging her finger. "I'm responsible for you children and I won't have you gallivanting around with things so strange."

The children couldn't explain it, but their grandmother was always more tuned in to what was happening in the town than their parents. It was certain neither their mother nor their father would have heard a word about Louise and Junior and Kurtz. Not for a week, anyway.

But the old people would know. Especially if it had anything to do with hellions like Timothy Kurtz and Albert 'Junior' Swift. Actually, the elderly in the community had already surmised that the three had run off together. With the exception of Mrs. Brinks, they had to be pushed very hard to speculate along the lines of homicide.

Ezechial dreamed about his machines and about Beth. She was his sister and she was alive again and he had another chance. He would not touch her this time; he would stay far from her. But he would watch her.

Cavenaugh awoke, shoveled in half a bowl of cold cereal and told his parents he was sleeping out again with the guys.

"Spend an evening home with us, soon, will you?"

"Yeh, sure," he called through the slamming screen door. Cavenaugh liked his mother and he wished to please her, but there were other things to be done.

He was surprised when he stepped out into the drizzle and was immediately chilled. He darted back up to his room, grabbed a flannel shirt, yelled, "Bye," once more and was halfway down the block before his parents figured out that he had come and gone again.

Beth and Alan's grandmother heard the basement door creak but took too long to figure out what was happening. She was on the telephone to her friend as her grandchildren cleared the back property line and disappeared, taking a shortcut past the Gabeaux's garage.

"Nice weather," Alan said, hunched against the light rain, and was surprised when his sister handed him a long-sleeved shirt.

"Thanks," he said and pulled it on.

Will clipped the strips of dripping film to a string extending the length of the darkroom. Each boy bumped his head into another's as they tried to see.

The film was disappointingly dark to them.

"I can't see anything," Freddy complained.

"Me either," Phillip agreed.

Will switched back on the clear light and held one of the negatives up to the bulb. "I can see something in a couple of these frames," he said and both Freddy and Phillip looked more closely at the hanging strips.

"We'll see better when I print the contact sheets," Will said and switched back off the light, leaving them bathed in red. He took out the sole sheet of photographic paper and laid it on the table.

Will's door was answered by a sleepy woman in a blue flannel bathrobe. "William? I think he had some friends over last night. I thought I heard them down in the basement a little bit ago," she said, opening the door full to Alan and Beth and then motioning toward a door just to the side of the kitchen.

"Go on down," she said and padded back to her bedroom.

Alan and Beth walked quietly down the rough wooden steps, guessing that at least one member of Will's family was probably still asleep. The basement light was on, and at first they thought Will's mother had been wrong, until they heard muffled voices coming from a little room beyond the washing machine.

Beth heard footsteps passing overhead and then water running. Someone was in a bathroom upstairs. Alan saw a pile of old toys in a corner and identified a huge fire engine and pieces of a plastic fort. A toilet flushed and pipes clanked nearby.

Fortunately for Alan, his sister opened the door.

Light flooded in.

Will looked as if he'd been caught with his hand in his pants. He shifted his eyes from the blank sheet of paper to Beth and then back to the paper.

"Let me guess," Phillip started.

Alan saw the red light. "Uh oh," he said.

"Come right in guys!" Will said, piqued. "I think we just finished up in here. Let's go get your friend, Cavenaugh."

As they rode, each of them held a negative against the nearest window and tried to make out the shapes they saw. They stopped in front of Freddy's and he ran in and then came back out with a big magnifying glass and a small one. He climbed into the rear-seat crush and handed the smaller glass to Beth.

When Freddy couldn't make out anything he handed the larger glass to Cavenaugh.

He scanned his row of negatives, told Will to pull over for a minute, and held his eye close to the negative, the magnifying glass poised.

"This is definitely a car — see what you think," Cavenaugh said very seriously and handed the negative and glass forward to Phillip.

Phillip pressed the film against the side window and examined the frames, starting at the top. At the third image he stopped. He squinted at the frame and seemed to hold his breath as he did.

"It's his," he said at last, and everyone's heart dropped.

They sat in the idling car without speaking.

Roger asked, "There should be a little number in the corner — can you read it?"

"Twelve," Phillip replied, then, "I think it is — might be a thirteen."

"That's okay," Roger answered. "Either one, says the same thing. The car in the picture isn't on the quarry floor."

"Huh?" Alan asked involuntarily.

"Must be stacked on something — another car maybe," Roger explained.

"Could be on a ledge," Phillip added.

They sat and examined the remainder of the negatives until the windows steamed.

"Can we get a little air in here?" Cavenaugh begged, squashed between Alan and Beth.

Windows were rolled down. Will was examining his negative with the glass. He was obviously very interested in one of the frames. Finally he handed both to Phillip and asked quietly, "What do you think of this?"

Phillip looked and let out a long breath.

"I don't think too much of it," he said at last.

"What do you see?" Freddy asked, irritated.

Will slumped forward on his steering wheel and started to cry. Everyone sat and waited for him to stop.

"No!" he said and pounded on the steering wheel. "No! No! No!" he repeated.

Phillip turned to Beth. He cleared his throat lightly. "It looks like the top of Junior's car."

He paused.

"And it looks like maybe there's long hair kinda floatin' up from a window." His voice trailed off as he finished. Then he went on, speaking quietly but over Will's renewed sobbing. "It's just a little picture though. It could be anything. Really."

And no one believed him. But they were glad he had tried.

They sat for nearly a half an hour without anyone speaking further. Phillip reached over and turned off the engine. Beth began to cry and so did Alan. Once, Phillip wiped the corner of his eye and looked away from the others and then went through the motions of looking at a house they were parked near.

Fox pulled into the motel lot and parked beside Claude's car. He made a show of taking a fishing rod and a tackle box out of the back seat. The front door to the motel office squeaked open and a man stuck his head out and inquired, "Any luck?"

"Yeh, I think." Fox said and went into the room before his interrogator could pursue the matter further.

Claude looked up.

"It's at the quarry. By the derrick."

Claude put down his book and Fox continued.

"It's been raining or cloudy since we were out there; shouldn't be any kids around. I think we've got a good chance of it still being there. Any action around here?"

Claude shook his head. "I did a fair amount of fishing. Talked to a few folks. Nothing going on. I think we're still okay."

Fox nodded and put down the pole and box.

"Tonight?"

Claude picked up his book again. "I think so. We've got one stop to make before we check the quarry."

"Yes, we do," Fox agreed and laughed somberly.

"The kid?"

Fox didn't answer.

"The kid?" Claude repeated.

Fox had been thinking about him and hadn't heard his brother.

"Lot of pain. I think he told me what he knows. We'll see. I hope for his sake we find the money. I don't mind killing him, but cutting him up took a little out of me." He thought about the hatchet and the boy's fingers.

Fox smiled at his brother. "Not a lot. Just a little."

"Long night," Claude said, speaking of the future and settled back onto the bed.

Fox fluffed the pillow on his bed and reclined.

Phineas Lathram was fit to be tied. He had received more phone calls in the last day than he could remember getting. Something was sure as hell going on, or had gone on, and he wanted to find out what it was all about. He was not as bothered by the extortion by Claude and Fox as he was by the disappearance of a couple of kids. Claude and Fox he could take care of. But the bike thing at the quarry didn't bode well.

*Goddamn kids,* he thought and tried to decide if he was going to drive out to the cabin that day or the next. As smart as the brothers were, he knew they'd still go back to the cabin. *A smart Indian is still pretty dumb,* he reminded himself and decided to wait until the help arrived from New York.

Finally, Roger asked, "What do we do? Go to the police?"

"I, for one, think that's exactly what we should do. We're way over our heads here." Freddy whined.

"Speak for yourself, Freddy, and I don't mean that as a criticism, but I don't feel like its over *my* head," Phillip said. "We've got some tough customers out there, obviously, but I'm not gonna run to the police. Besides, I don't think they'd do us a bit of good. In fact, I think that by the time the cops got around to believing us, whoever did this will have covered his trail so well, Joe Friday couldn't find him."

"Remember what Mrs. Orlap said," Beth reminded, a chill running through her as she thought of the widow's words. "She said the police were the evil in this town."

*"Chief Constable Lathram,"* Will corrected, wiping his burning eyes.

Phillip turned to Beth and asked softly, "What *did* the old lady say? I was downstairs."

Beth told him. After she finished they lapsed back into silence.

Freddy swallowed loudly and Alan thought of Kurtz and nearly lost control. He forced himself to think of baseball and the best hit he'd ever made.

Will tilted his head so he was facing the head liner in the sedan. He traced a water stain and then said, "You know, this isn't the army. Nobody got drafted. It's a matter of choice. I say we get our butts back to the quarry, take every weapon we can get our hands on with us, make a plan, and wait for the bastard. Who's going with me and who's staying."

Surprisingly, Beth answered first.

"I'm going."

Phillip and Alan seemed to race to be next, then Roger and Cavenaugh.

They turned to Freddy. Phillip reached back to open the door for him.

"I'm with you guys," he said at last, hiding his fear as best he could.

"Take me to Caplinger's" Phillip instructed, referring to the Mom and Pop store near the filling station. He went in and emerged with a sack of potatoes and a small bag.

"Cook out?" Freddy taunted.

"Might save your butt," Phillip replied.

They made several more stops and then Will gassed up the sedan and they turned toward the quarry.

"I'd like to say one thing," Phillip said, balancing a potato in his hand.

Roger took his eyes from the potato. "Yeh?"

"If we're going to do this, you guys, we can't go into it already beat. We got to put our feelings and thoughts about Junior and Louise and Kurtz aside. We got to think like we're tough and act like we're tough. Before we get there we gotta be damn sure we believe in ourselves and each other.

"We're going into this together. Each one of us has to know that his ass is covered." He let the group think of what he had said. "And I want to tell you — you can depend on me. I'll be there for you, I swear to God. You guys are all friends, so I expect you to look out for each other. I understand that. But like I said, you look behind you, and you're gonna see me. Pissed as hell and fighting like a mother. You look back, and I'll be there."

Freddy wanted to laugh off the speech but he couldn't.

A giant flywheel of comraderie, esprit de corps, and whatever else, began to revolve.

The remainder of the drive they worked through a variety of plans.

At one point, Cavenaugh pressed a strip of negatives against the glass.

Phillip spoke for the others when he said, "Put 'em away, man. We'll have plenty of time for that later."

Cavenaugh tucked the strip into his shirt pocket and nodded.

Will's sedan rumbled onto the sodden quarry road, slipped along the mud at the top of the hill, and sluiced the rest of the way to the landing.

Roger was adamant that he be able take at least another roll of film. The others in the car were split as to its necessity and wisdom.

"What if you're caught out on the water?" Freddy asked.

"I think that'll be *my* problem," Roger countered and the discussion was over.

Roger, Will, and Cavenaugh prepared the raft, loading on their various weapons also. Roger took a side trip to the dryness of the forge shed where he screwed the adaptor onto his zip- gun, put a cherry bomb in the chamber, and pushed a wrapped bolt down the business end of the barrel. The others followed and watched.

"That bolt will wobble all to hell and go crooked once it's fired, won't it?" Phillip asked.

"It would if I used it from a distance. I have a feeling that won't be the case."

Phillip was impressed. Definitely impressed.

Then Phillip took off his socks and loaded each with a single potato. Beth was the only one who understood their menace. Next he took a potato and grasped it securely in his fist, leaving a slight gap between each finger.

"This little trick you don't actually do until you're absolutely ready to use it. It's kinda like lighting the fuse on Roger's gun — you damn sure better have a target."

He took a small box of razor blades out of the bag. He carefully unwrapped the red paper from one of the blades.

# Dead Man's Quarry

"You use five, but I can show you with one."

So saying, he took the double-edged blade and gingerly inserted it in the potato at one of the gaps left between two fingers.

"Put five of them in, leaving about half of each sticking out." He pointed to the location for each of the blades. "Then you throw this mother at your target."

Alan whooped.

"My plan," Phillip went on, "is to aim for the face. If you're real lucky, your target won't realize what you're doin', and he'll try to catch it." He moved the spud so that it was held between the arc made by his forefinger and thumb. "This beauty will buy you some time. But understand — it won't make you any friends."

Each of the boys smiled and imagined the potato with five protruding razor blades.

Beth looked away.

Phillip removed the blade and put it back in its wrapper.

"I've got plenty of potatoes and I bought a bunch of boxes of blades. Any takers?"

Hands shot forward from all directions.

Roger wrapped waxed paper over the fuse to his gun and put it back into his army satchel.

Freddy picked up a piece of scrap metal the size of a playing card. He stuck it into the breast pocket of his shirt. "Speaking of TV, plenty of good-guys get their butt saved by just such a thing. Bullet-stopper." Phillip went over the different plans. Basically, they had decided to operate in teams at the two entrances to the quarry. Will's car was a back-up for the hospital or ramming if it came to that.

The rain had let up and the cooler air was being replaced by a muggy overlay of hot, dead, air.

"We're primed for a storm," Roger observed. "Let's shoot the roll fast."

Cavenaugh examined the sky and wished he were staying on shore.

Claude and Fox slept.

Ezechial awoke.

The boys on the raft paddled away from their friends. Beth stood beside Phillip and Alan, and Freddy toyed with his baseball bat off to the side.

Phillip called out to the raft, "Hey, what about the car keys, Will — don't you think you ought to leave 'em? We'll put 'em in the ignition."

Will dug into his pocket and pulled out a jangling mass of keys. "It's the hexagonal one beside the chrome one," he yelled and tossed the wad.

Everyone knew what was about to happen as soon as they left his hand.

Alan covered his eyes and waited for the confirming splash.

Phillip lunged as far forward as he dared, but the keys didn't come near his hand. By the time the ones on the landing realized that diving immediately in after them wouldn't have been a bad idea, it was too late.

They were fascinated at how deep they were still able to see the descending keys.

"Nice throw," Freddy said. "Little higher next time," he added, pretending to take a swing at them with the bat.

Alan looked back at Will's sedan. "Can't you hot wire it or something?" he asked Phillip.

"You've been watching too much television, kid. Anyway, I can't do it without tools."

Then he thought of Ezechial up at the machinery shed and made a decision.

The boys on the raft were still watching as if willing the keys to leap back out of the water.

"Go on and get your pictures, guys. We'll take care of things here."

Phillip turned to walk up to see Ezechial and then looked back at the raft. "Hey Will — don't worry about it. That's the breaks." He took a step and then remembered something. "And Will — at least you still have your car. All I've got is a spare set of keys for the coupe. Wanna trade?"

In spite of the mask of attempted humor, things weren't starting off as well as he had hoped.

Phillip tried to figure out an alternate plan. No matter how he worked it, for the short term, he and Beth went up to the machinery shed, and Alan and Freddy went to a high point to watch both entrances. He didn't want to do that to Freddy. It was obvious that the kid was struggling to overcome his feelings for Beth and be a part of the group.

In desperation Phillip said, "Hey, let's all hustle up to the machinery shed together, get Ezechial to get the fire cranking, I'll get some tools, and then we'll divide up and watch the entrances."

"You really think the fire's gonna make any difference?" Freddy asked.

Phillip smiled at him. "Beats the shit out of me. In the worst case we'll have a place to get warm and dry after the storm hits."

Beth and Alan surveyed the darkening sky. Where before there had been an unmoving mat of grey clouds, now there was movement with dark broken areas scudding over their heads. Errant leaves blew by.

"You may be right," Freddy admitted, thinking of Cavenaugh and Roger and Will on the raft. *If they get caught in the rain they'll be soaked to the skin and some miserable.*

Ezechial put the doll back on the shelf. As he passed the carton he took a can of string beans, opened it with the rusted opener, and ate from the can as he went down the stairs. He was nearly at the bottom when he heard The Boston Boiler Man at the door.

Fox brushed his teeth and took a long hot shower. When he came out of the bathroom, the small towel barely circling his waist, his brother was awake and apparently ready to go.

Phineas Lathram walked the circuit through his rambling house and then settled in on a porch chair. There was an electrical storm on the way and there was little that he appreciated more than the wrath of the gods.

Kurtz spent more and more time cognizant of his surroundings. He realized he had been passed out for a very long time.

The man was gone.

The lamp was turned down to the point that the wick burned faintly. It felt to the boy that night was approaching.

And his hand — his hand hurt with a pain so intense that could he have done it, he would have cut the whole thing off. He would have jumped on it if it were possible — he would have slammed it in a door or he would have plunged it into boiling water.

It hurt so much — so goddamned much — that the boy resented its existence.

When he could, in the brief moments of respite which teased him, he tried to think of a way to get free. Everywhere he looked he was stymied.

Until, in the distance, he heard the motorboat.

The Boston Boiler Man didn't push his way past Ezechial as the old man had expected. Then Ezechial saw that he had brought his friends and it made sense that he would be deferential. The Doll Man backed out of their way and then scuttered to the firebox door, opening it to show that the coals were ready — banked but glowing red and orange — and there was a deep mass of them. No kindling necessary — no waiting. They could be coaxed to life instantly.

And the water. The water in the boiler was hot. Just this side of boiling.

The gauges needled to safety and the valves were cranked shut. The levers were oiled and ready.

The thought of starting the engines again — bringing them to life so soon, was almost more than the old man could bear. It was post-coital touching — too intense — painful even.

The Boston Boiler Man smiled and took in the machinery. He was absorbing it, Ezechial could see that. He was a man with oil in his veins and iron in his bones. He was a man cast and cooled in the biggest foundries in the world.

To Ezechial, now stooped and bent in old age, The Boston Boiler Man was as huge, as room filling as he had ever been. He was here to direct things and The Doll Man was ready to please.

Ezechial saw from his eyes that he wished the fire to be brought hotter and Ezechial adjusted the draught.

He had only to glance at the shuttered windows and Ezechial shuffled to them and threw them open.

It was glorious to him to do as he was bid. Serve the machines, serve the power. My god, he had waited alone for so long. He had husbanded the strength of the machinery for so many years, for so many lifetimes it seemed, that Ezechial felt himself at last to be free, soaring out his crippled body, flying back and forth in the confines of the stone building as he suckled his machines. Suckled them to turn them loose. Nurtured them to open the gates and let them free into the world. Hot steam. Pulsing, booming power. Raging fire.

Ezechial came back to The Man. Came back and saw her.

His sister.

Once Roger lowered the camera into the water he felt that he had been ridiculous. The pictures didn't matter now. He wasn't so macabre that he needed details. It was no longer important.

But the camera worked. He was proud of that.

And a storm. A summer storm was building directly over their heads.

Had he an ounce less pride he would have pulled the camera back in and beat a retreat to the landing.

Fox drove behind Claude.

Kurtz lost himself in a prolonged spasm of white pain. He sweated. He cursed through his gag. He thought his hand was strapped to red-hot scrap of jagged metal. He became fascinated with the lantern flame. He watched it, learned it, and felt it was communicating with him. And then he realized it was.

*I can save you,* it murmured.

Barely able to think it through with clarity, Kurtz came to believe that if he could tip the lantern, the oil would spill out — there was plenty of oil — ignite, and he could somehow burn through his bonds.

He jolted the table.

The lantern slowly rocked from side to side, first lifting one side gently, and then the other. It was all half speed, and Kurtz was enraptured.

He watched as the glass vessel finally tipped, the chimney smashing onto the wooden table top, the amber liquid flowing from the base.

The fuel covered the table in gulping tides and ran onto the boy's legs before it ignited.

They parked one behind the other and walked together through the evening shadows. A block before Lathram's house they cut into the wooded area behind the tended lawns.

Will was no use to them. He vacillated between fear of what he might see on the quarry plateau above him, and what might be watching him from below. The old lady had said there was something in the quarry. He had been right. Something which lived in the black water beneath him. A thousand times Will and the boys and the raft were lifted into the air on its back. Any ripple — any sound — and Will felt his heart stop as if were turned to quarry stone.

And just when he conquered his fear of what was in the water, he looked up and was terrorized again. There were shadows up there. There was approaching darkness. There was a storm.

He came close to seeking refuge in the monster.

But not quite.

Cavenaugh lost himself in every detail associated with the underwater camera. He hovered on the periphery of Roger's instructions. *Do this just so. No, a little more that way. Gently. Firmly. Hold it there.*

Anything. Anything he was told, he embraced.

It was when Roger hesitated, when he lost himself in a problem that Cavenaugh felt his fear crawling through him.

Ezechial looked up from shoveling a load of coal into the firebox and saw that he was alone. Had he always been alone? Had he imagined the others?

He saw the open window, smelled the approaching storm, and knew that his friend had only left temporarily. The Boston Boiler Man always returned. You could bet on it. Just let the fire wane. Forget a valve. He'd be back. Roaring.

Ezechial knew he could find nothing wrong now.

The vibration from the previous night had shattered sections of the spider's skeleton. Bits had dropped to the bottom of the gauge leaving an accumulated dusting against the glass. The needle was driving itself into the remaining hull, distorting its curve, sending microscopic, radiant cracks across its surface. Spider webbing it.

The needle moved just a fraction.

Fox and Claude crouched behind the tree. The rustling bushes masked any sound they may have made. Although they made none.

The wind increased and Phineas kicked the chair back when he stood. He walked to the limit of the porch and gripped the railing with his hands. He watched the clouds, observing their dance, their colliding choreography. He could smell the rain. The hot rain would soon fall.

Roger was getting nervous. He wanted to be done but he had three more pictures.

Thunder crashed in the direction of town. He had not noticed the distant flash in the sky so the boom frightened him.

Cavenaugh saw Roger jump. "Just take the last ones quick. Or don't take them at all. Let's haul the camera up and get back to shore."

While Cavenaugh held the larger rope securing the camera, Roger aimed the underwater device with the front, trigger line. He pulled the line toward him. "Just two more," he said after he gave the line a tug to snap the picture and then another to advance the film.

"This thing weighs a ton," Cavenaugh complained, "and I think it's getting heavier."

Roger hesitated and then looked down into the murky water. As he did a trail of bubbles broke the surface.

"Shit!" he exclaimed and both Cavenaugh and Will tried to see what was the matter. Will thought the thing from the quarry depths was surfacing to attack them, regardless of the old lady's assurances to the contrary, and Cavenaugh thought Roger had some sort of knowledge regarding the intruder. The killer.

"Bubbles! Air!" Roger gasped. "It's leaking! Water's getting into the camera! Pull it up! Pull it up!"

He dragged in the light line. Cavenaugh finally understood and began to take up the slack of the heavier rope.

Claude backed his vehicle into Lathram's driveway, tucking the trunk of the car within inches of the closed garage door. The door opened and Fox stepped from inside the garage. He had a key ready which he used to unlock and open the trunk. Claude set the brake and got out to help his brother load the bundled body into the trunk. Claude slammed the trunk shut and then Fox closed the garage door, this time from the outside.

They stopped momentarily at the other vehicle. Fox got out without speaking.

He kept several hundred yards between his vehicle and his brother's as they drove toward the quarry. It was still light out, but it was fading fast, particularly with the approaching storm.

Lathram was dead. His control had so dissipated with the years that only his evil survived.

Phillip and Alan and Freddy and Beth stood at the base of the larger derrick.

Roger yelled up to them, "WE'RE DONE — THE CAMERA'S SCREWED!"

Beth smelled the coal fire and turned back to look at the machinery shed. The window and the shutters were open downstairs. The old man was there, shyly keeping track of their movements. She lifted her hand in a half hearted wave.

Ezechial ducked back behind the wall.

"Can I stick with you?" Alan asked Phillip once Freddy was out of ear-shot.

Beth turned.

"I mean both of you," Alan protested, feeling he had betrayed his sister.

Phillip didn't answer immediately.

"Let's all go over by the lower derrick and then we can talk about it." Phillip said and started walking around the upper lip of the quarry, away from the landing.

He had become the leader. It was, of course, unofficial, but in fact every one of the others looked to him, and Phillip took their trust seriously. He would have to think about what Alan asked. If they were going to split up into two groups, they had to be balanced. Any way you cut it, three kids were still three kids. There was no way he was going to weaken one of the groups unnecessarily. What if that group made the first contact. Three of them gone before you could blink an eye.

He didn't delude himself.

There were two things strengthening each of them: First was the 'Hey, let's get tough and take care of whoever hurt our friends', attitude.

It was mostly immature bluff nurtured by an unhealthy dose of television-reality, but it pumped them up.

Then there was, 'This isn't a game, I could actually die — just like my friends did. We're dealing with a sick, lethal, adult.'

It was a reasonable response.

Roger, Will, Freddy, Cavenaugh, Alan, and Beth each had a different mixture of each assessment. Of the six of them, Beth and Phillip were tied as to who had the most rational fears in place. At the other extreme was Alan. He was going to make somebody pay.

Phillip had to balance psychological strengths along with physical traits. He thought about Alan's request as they walked.

They walked around to the lower derrick and then out to the quarry lip to see if they could locate the raft. It was very dark in the shade of the bushes surrounding the bull wheel. It was as they stepped over the cables that Beth bumped the package. It skidded ahead of her, nudging the heels of Alan. He jumped involuntarily, imagining a monster-rat nipping at his heels.

"Whoa! What was that?"

"I just kicked it, whatever it was," Beth responded.

"Kicked what?" Freddy asked.

Phillip drew out his Zippo©, flicked the wheel and bent to the granite. His first impression was that they had found the bundle of money from the garage. But it was neither wrapped in mechanics' rags nor the correct size. But the weight-to-size ratio seemed just right for money. He stooped and tore the wrappings off.

In the flickering glow of his lighter he drew in his breath and nearly fainted.

A series of reactions washed over him. To his credit, he initially felt relief that he could repay Mr. Horvath. Then he resented that there were others near him, then he was angry with himself for that reaction, and finally he was crushed. "Oh shit," he moaned.

Beth and Alan and Freddy crowded around him when he rose. Phillip had allowed himself an occasional glimmer of hope regarding Kurtz, but with this much money floating around he knew the kid was dead. Very dead.

He leafed through the thick packets of hundred dollar bills. Freddy hesitantly reached out and touched the edge of one of the packets. Beth could not believe her eyes.

Alan smelled the money. He smelled the obnoxious perfume and thought of it as a poison; a poison which had killed his friend.

He grabbed at the pile and tried to wrench it from Phillip's hands. At first the older boy did not understand.

"It killed him! It killed him!" Alan cried and started to hit Phillip.

Beth wrapped her arms around Alan, whispering, "We'll find him, Alan, he's got to be okay. We'll find him."

Alan sank through her arms and sat on the granite, sobbing. He had tried so hard to be an adult, to help find Kurtz, to solve the mystery and make someone pay, but he just couldn't handle it. Phillip handed the money to Beth and sat down beside the crying boy.

Alan knew Phillip was beside him and he found that suddenly he needed him. He needed Phillip's toughness and his strength and his knowledge of the world. Plus, Beth liked him, he could see that, and he didn't sound as much like an asshole as he used to.

"We gotta be tough-guys, Alan. You and me, we gotta figure this out and we've got to do it together. We both care about Beth and I know you're worried about your friend. Kids are gettin' hurt around here, Alan, and I know kids aren't doin' it."

Phillip took a breath and continued, "Hate me when it's all over pal. Kick me in the balls, whatever. But for now, let's you and me form a team and help out your friend. You with me?"

*With him?* Alan wanted to hug him. He wished that just once his father had been there for him, spoken to him like that, man to man. Even an asshole like Phillip was better than nothing, he figured, attempting to hide his weakness.

"Yeh," he answered, "let's find out who's doing this and kick 'em in the balls."

He didn't want to make a joke out of the problems but he was too embarrassed by his crying to stop himself.

Beth held the money grudgingly. When Phillip stood again she couldn't give him the money fast enough.

Phillip wrapped it as it had been. "I think we're pretty much guaranteed to have a visitor, now. We'd better tell the others."

Freddy stared at him when he spoke. He felt the muscles in his legs liquify.

They hurried past the derrick to meet their friends at the landing.

They were not out of the bushes when Phillip stopped in his tracks. He heard a car pull into the quarry. Two cars possibly. One of the engines was immediately shut off.

Phillip led Alan and Beth and Freddy in a run to the landing.

Fox turned off his car and walked up to Claude.

"We'd better check out the situation first."

"Let's get the money while it's still light enough to find it. Which derrick?"

Fox felt like a fool.

"I didn't ask."

Claude didn't reprimand him or think that it warranted further discussion. "Probably the one near where he appeared. Just in case, and to save time, you check the other one. Do you have a flashlight?"

Fox flicked the switch as an answer and walked off in the direction of the larger derrick.

Claude engaged the gears and drove off to the lower derrick. He had decided to check first to be certain no one was at the quarry, then drive the car with the body off the edge, and then, with the body gone, look for the money. It was a better idea.

They paddled the raft to the landing. Roger was sick and didn't pay any attention to what was happening. The rubber gasket around the lense housing had imploded and water had rushed in and filled the metal tube. His dad's camera was soaked. Maybe it wasn't ruined, he wasn't sure, but he knew they would at least have to pay for a professional to clean the camera and check it out. It wouldn't be cheap.

He was bent over the apparatus while Will and Cavenaugh stood and held the raft to the low granite wall of the landing. All of a sudden Roger saw, out of the corner of his eye, a monstrous dark thing fly off of the quarry ledge by the lower derrick. It was like a pterodactyl, only bigger. But it didn't fly, it just plunged downward. By the time Roger turned full to it, there was a tremendous splash accompanied by rent metal.

"Jesus!" he exclaimed.

Will and Cavenaugh leaped onto the landing before they knew what they had done. "Shit!" both of them cried in wavering voices.

Roger scrambled off of the raft. As he did he kicked the lense housing, toppling it into the water — something he didn't remember doing until much later.

Phillip heard the descending car's engine and then the splash accompanied by the screams from the quarry.

Alan tripped and Beth stumbled over him.

Phillip discarded the package and helped Freddy get them back to their feet.

They raced to the landing.

"Weapons! Weapons! Weapons!" Phillip shouted as they approached the others.

Roger ran in a complete circle before he could convince himself to jump back down to the raft to get his zip-gun bag. Just as he landed on the craft, a big wave from the car caught the raft. It hit as Roger was awkwardly leaning and bending.

He fell.

"Throw up my club! Throw up my club!" Cavenaugh yelled to him.

They hurriedly jammed potatoes into their pockets.

Phillip grabbed Beth. He thought whoever was up there was coming from the lower derrick. "Run up to the machinery shed. Lock yourself in with the old man. Push out the upper window and yell to us if there's something we don't see."

Beth started to protest but Phillip shook her very hard by the shoulders. "Do it! We may need you!"

"Cavenaugh! Will! Freddy! Haul your asses up there with Beth. Check out that side of the quarry. If nobody came in that entrance, hustle your butts back to the landing. If we're not back here, we'll be at the lower derrick! Now move!"

They ran off in a group.

Phillip turned to Roger and Alan. He was panting from the excitement. As he spoke he started seating razor blades in the potato he held. "I heard two cars — up the road," he motioned with his eyes toward the lower derrick. "They've gotta be looking for the money now. If they didn't hear the guys at the raft we can surprise 'em. Let's see if we can get a look at how many we're dealin' with before we let ourselves be known."

He turned to Alan. "You ready champ? Stay behind me. I mean it!" He ran half bent toward the tower, Alan and Roger doing the same.

Roger wondered, but did not ask, *What money?*

Phillip stopped them before they started up the hill. Roger was fumbling with a box of matches. He had the zip gun tucked under his arm-pit and the satchel over his shoulder. Alan carried a rock and a kid-sized baseball bat.

Phillip asked Roger, "Think you can use that thing?"

Roger nodded.

Once again Phillip led them off toward the derrick.

Will and Freddy and Cavenaugh, and finally, Beth, burst from the bushes near the larger derrick, and ran toward the machinery shed.

Fox looked up. He was on his hands and knees under the bull wheel of the derrick. As he saw the approaching, charging, shapes he rolled across the granite, pulled out his revolver and squeezed off a shot at the leading runner. His first impression had been that they were adults attacking him. Instantly he saw his mistake.

Will couldn't believe what was happening. One second he was running forward, the next he was blown backward. He slammed through the giving bushes.

For a heartbeat, the other children skidded to a stop. The three of them locked eyes with the prone figure on the granite.

Freddy dropped his bat, the clattering of hardwood on granite nearly as loud as the pounding of his heart.

Fox had a flash of amusement. He'd been spooked by kids.

Freddy dove into the bushes after Will.

Cavenaugh grabbed Beth, nearly lifting her from the granite, and plunged back the way they had come.

Fox fired twice, his indecision regarding which target to address, telling.

He caught Freddy mid-air, the bullet entering the boy's left buttock. Freddy landed on top of Will. They bunched and then separated to arm's length. Coincidental with the onset of their pain, they started crawling at speed through the underbrush, each helping the other as best he could.

The other bullet missed Cavenaugh.

Claude heard the shots and dropped to the granite. He pulled out his revolver. He crawled quickly to the lip of the granite to see better.

Phillip looked desperately from side to side. He didn't know what to do — whether he should lead the others back around to the opposite side or push ahead and investigate the lower derrick. Somebody *had* to be there searching for the money.

*What if there are several men?*

He felt Alan pushing up against him. Roger was twisting around violently checking every side.

Alan was chanting, "Shit-fuck. Shit-fuck. Shit-fuck."

"Stay here, I'll be right back," Phillip heard himself say.

He didn't advance slowly and he didn't exactly charge the derrick. But he did accidentally kick a stone into the brush.

Claude spun to the side and fired at the sound. *Bad. Bad Bad,* he told himself regarding shooting at sounds. *Calm down!*

Phillip crashed across the jagged rocks of the road. He had heard the bullet ripping through the leaves an instant before he heard the retort.

"Oh sweet Jesus, this is serious shit," he told himself.

He saw blood on his arm and at first thought he had been hit. Then he remembered the potato. It was still in his hand, slightly rotated — just enough.

Claude had heard the stone when it hit the brush at least four feet from Phillip, so he was looking to the right of where the boy lay. The sound of the shot had masked Phillip's dive.

Phillip raised his head a fraction. Through the bushes he saw the profile of Claude's head.

In one motion he rose to a crouch and heaved the potato with all of his strength.

He heard it thunk into the side of the man's face.

Claude felt it hit. It didn't feel too bad, actually. And then the pain flowed in tiny white rivers.

He fired three times into the bushes.

Phillip rolled to one side and then scrambled backwards on his hands and knees. He crashed into Roger, sending him tumbling to the side.

"Shoot the son of a bitch. Shoot him!" Phillip hissed ridiculously and then asked, "What were you doing behind me?" As he spoke he prepared another potato.

Roger was shaking. He's was barely able to speak. "Turn around — I'm there," was all he could manage.

Phillip smiled and hit him lightly on the shoulder. "I'll go around to the other side and try to get his attention." He rolled his eyes as he realized what he was saying.

"Great fucking idea, asshole," Phillip whispered to himself as he made a rapid semicircle, careful to stay low and remain behind a series of bushes.

Claude lay on his side and reloaded. There were three cuts on his cheek and the side of his forehead. They were deep and there was a lot of blood but he knew that face wounds bled profusely. That wasn't the problem.

One razor had slit the corner of his eye and slid across it. Aqueous-humor mixed with the pulsing blood. That was the problem.

Claude was not only blinded in one eye; the pain coursing across that side of his face was intense. He could not stop himself from variously attempting to blink away blood and trying to focus through the rent eye. He controlled the urge to shoot wildly to obscure the pain.

*They aren't police,* he thought, *no guns,* and then he remembered the shots from across the quarry. He was confused. *What is wrong with my eye?* he asked himself. He had never felt anything like it.

There was just too much blood everywhere.

He stuffed the thick cartridges into the gun by feel.

Alan crawled up behind Roger. His pants were wet. He tugged at Roger's foot and Roger nearly jumped over the bushes and into the quarry.

"My god you scared me!" Roger whispered urgently. "Stay down. I've got to concentrate." He had a match against the rough side of the box. He thought a minute and stuffed the box into his mouth, gripping it with his teeth. He took the zip-gun out from under his armpit and then waited, the gun in one hand, the match in the other. He was crouching.

Phillip misjudged Claude's position. He threw a rock and Claude swivelled but did not fire.

He blinked away more blood. He knew the last sound to be a decoy. A wave of pain passed.

Roger heard the rock hit and rose from a crouch. He had the match lighted and moving toward the fuse.

Claude fired twice. The first shot hit Roger in the shoulder and the second tore into his chest. He jolted back onto Alan. He still clutched the zip gun but the match was gone.

Phillip leaped forward when he heard the shots. He ran through the bushes and stumbled over Claude, falling beyond him.

Alan stared at Roger. Little streams of blood ran out of the holes in his shirt.

Roger still had the box of matches in his mouth. He shook his head violently as if trying to clear away the wounds. He jerked a few times and then began to react in earnest to his wounds.

Phillip threw himself back onto Claude before the latter could bring the gun to bear. They wrestled briefly until the bigger brother raised his knee into Phillip's groin.

Phillip drew his knees to his chest and then drove Claude from him. He still had the second potato in his hand.

Claude brought the gun around the same instant Phillip jammed the razor blades into his face. He turned, presenting the already wounded side. Phillip pressed the potato home, grinding it as he did, feeling the thin steel grate against cheekbone and jaw.

Claude screamed in agony. He was able to toss Phillip from him.

Pieces of his face hung down from his cheek. In one place his teeth were exposed, the white porcelain hideous against the gristle and blood and bone.

Phillip was on him again and he managed to grip the wrist of his gun-hand. Claude was still able to force it toward Phillip's chest.

Alan pulled the zip-gun from under Roger. He had rolled over onto it as he rocked in pain. Alan grabbed the box of matches Roger had spit out.

Roger watched him. He kept repeating. "Oh man, the pain. Oh man, the pain."

Alan was almost apologetic as he took the gun and raised himself and ran toward the wrestling sounds of Phillip and the man.

He had a match out by the time he was standing over the two.

Several times Claude and Phillip waved the gun toward Alan. Then it was forced to the side and finally back in the direction of Phillip.

They were tossing from side to side so much that Alan couldn't aim, let alone light the fuse.

"Shoot him, Alan!" Phillip begged, "For God's sake, shoot him!"

Then he caught a full look at the young boy standing terrified above them.

"Run Alan," he gasped, "Run!"

Claude rolled Phillip under him. Phillip's hand was slipping off of Claude's bloody wrist. It was only a matter of time before he lost his grip.

Alan struck a match. It broke in half. He grabbed the nub and tried again. He fumbled it instead of drawing it smoothly across the box. He started to cry.

Phillip's hand was half off of Claude's arm. The gun was coming back to Phillip's head this time.

Alan pushed the drawer of the box open and matches spilled to the ground. It had been inverted. He snatched a match from the rock and forced himself to pause. He drew the match carefully across the black paper. It hissed and smoked as it scraped against the side. It lit.

Phillip lost his grip completely and then was able to grab Claude's arm again. The revolver inched closer to Phillip's face.

Claude was loathsome and he was dripping blood into Phillip's eyes.

The fuse was hissing.

Alan dropped to his knees beside the two. He poked the zip-gun at Claude. He was knocked aside as the two struggled.

The fuse was nearing the hole in the barrel. It would reach the compacted gunpowder of the cherry bomb soon.

Alan threw himself onto Claude and when he did he jammed the zip-gun into Claude's ear. The brother shook his head to the side but Alan compensated for his movement.

Phillip lost his grip again and Claude swung the gun full to Phillip's face.

There was an explosion.

Will and Freddy collapsed against a large block of granite. Both of them were bleeding and in a lot of pain. Each wished to scream out, but the man who shot them was moving cautiously through the bushes near them.

"No! No!" Beth screamed at Cavenaugh. Shots were ringing out from every direction, it seemed.

Cavenaugh stopped pulling Beth. His intention had been to drag her away from the danger but she was fighting him. She shook free of his grip.

"We've got to go back!" she screamed at him. "We can't leave them! He said to stay with our team! We can't just leave them!"

She was nearly hysterical. She flashed at Cavenaugh, grabbed the bat he was carrying, and then turned and ran back toward Freddy and Will.

He watched her run off, stood rooted for a moment, and then went in pursuit of her, scooping a granite rock as he ran.

Fox picked his way carefully through the bushes. He knew the two he shot had to be near; he had heard them crying out earlier. And then they had become silent.

They wormed backward so that they were wedged under a tilting sheet of granite. Will bit his lip and clenched his eyes. It was as if a ragged piece of barbed wire were being used to floss his upper chest. He heard the bushes snap nearby. He moved his hand to Freddy's shoulder and squeezed.

Fox heard Beth and then Cavenaugh run by. He fled the bushes in pursuit.

Beth ran at full speed from the path to the granite. Will and Freddy were gone. She saw that in a flash. She was already swinging the club wildly, hoping once again to get close to the man with the gun before he had time to react.

He was gone. She spun around in a quick circle and remembered what Phillip had told her to do. She ran to the side door of the machinery shed, opening it with difficulty. Once in she hesitated to lock the door and was confused because there was a chance the others might need the sanctuary. Quickly she ran past Ezechial. He had pulled the shutters closed and was squinting through them. He had not heard her.

"Start the fire! Start the fire! Phillip said to get it going!" she ordered as she tore by him and bounded up the stairs. From the upstairs window she hoped to have the view that Phillip had told her to use.

Beth tossed the chair beneath the window aside and opened the shutters. It had started to rain and it was deeply into evening. She could see the derrick at the other side but she could not make out any figures. And then by its base she made out a figure staggering to his feet. He appeared to be clutching his hand or a gun; she could not make out which.

Cavenaugh ran by beneath her. He hesitated on the granite plateau and then turned toward where he had last seen Freddy and Will. He confronted Fox as they were both skirting a high bush. Fox raised his gun as Cavenaugh slammed the rock at him. Fox flinched his head to the side and the rock grazed his neck, superficially cutting him. He fired the gun, missing. Cavenaugh went to tackle the man, at the last instant thought better of it and dove into the bushes, rolling and digging his way deeper into them.

Fox fired again. There were three of them in the bushes evading him. He scanned the area quickly and decided to see if he could make an end run around the building and catch them from the other side where the undergrowth was not as dense.

He ignored the rain.

Beth heard the shot from the bushes. She called out across the quarry for help and then ran back across the room, down the stairs, and through the machinery shed. Ezechial looked up, excited, as she passed. He was stooped before the fire-box door, shoveling coal into the boiler furnace.

She had Cavenaugh's baseball bat clutched with both of her hands, and as she exited the building Fox came around the corner. Beth raised the bat and instinctively swung it at Fox, caught him on his left shoulder and drew back to hit him again. He raised his hand to stop her and she put her weight into the next swing.

The bat caught Fox on his raised forearm. Two bones snapped as they absorbed the weight of the swinging hardwood. Beth heard them break. He staggered, his beaten arm now hanging at his side. He couldn't believe it. A girl had just broken his arm.

Beth went to bring the bat back to swing again when she saw the gun in his hand. He was raising it. She turned and ran around the corner he had rounded, intent on getting out of his field of fire and moving back to Freddy and Will and Cavenaugh if she could. She hoped they might somehow rejoin Phillip and Alan and Roger.

Fox rested against the side of the stone building and drew his breath. *Which way now?* He wished to give the girl with the bat wide birth. Until she was down. And then he wished to be very close. His anger and frustration centered on her.

He remembered his brother. Things were so far out of hand that he believed the wisest course was to find him and work together to extricate themselves from their mess.

He ran wide around the corner of the machinery shed, cradling his useless arm with his gun wielding hand.

Alan stared at his hand. The zip gun had gone off. It had exploded. He opened his fingers and spread them. It looked as if he had a handful of hamburger.

"Oh, shit-fuck. Shit-fuck. Shit-fuck."

The pain flowed.

Phillip worked his way out from under Claude.

The zip-gun had blown apart, but the bolt had also shot out the barrel the same instant. Claude's head was a mess. He still bucked and twitched, but the gun had fallen from his hand.

Phillip gasped and then asked Alan, "Are you okay?"

Alan started to laugh. "Yeh, I'm great." He laughed more. He winced from the pain in his hand. "I'm just peachy."

Phillip searched for Roger.

He was propped against a rock. When he saw Phillip he just followed his movements, not saying anything until Phillip was kneeling by him.

"Boy, this isn't a lot of fun." Roger said through his teeth.

Phillip heard the shot from the machinery shed. He left Roger and ran down the road by the landing. He would join the others. He had run twenty feet when he remembered the gun. He returned, snatched it from the side of the body and ran back down the road.

Alan had been wrapping a torn piece of cloth around his hand.

Phillip saw it was a sock.

He passed the landing and then headed up the path leading to the machinery shed.

The rain was easing again.

Someone was coming. Beth raised the baseball bat and waited.

Phillip ran with his gun hand outstretched.

She swung and hit the gun before she saw Phillip's face.

The pistol sailed into the dark bushes.

Startled, Phillip prepared to attack.

Beth couldn't believe who she had hit.

"Phillip!" she cried. And then, ignoring what she had just done, "Freddy and Will and Cavenaugh are here somewhere. There's a man with a gun up there!" she pointed behind her. I hit his arm. I think I broke it!"

Phillip could believe it. His own hand smarted from the stinging blow to the gun.

They heard Will.

"Shit you guys, shit!" Cavenaugh moaned, his leg had been grazed by a bullet, but he had hurt himself worse when he crashed head-first onto a granite corner.

"The one with the gun — where is he?" Phillip demanded of Beth, momentarily ignoring Will and Cavenaugh.

"I think he went around the top of the quarry. I don't know."

Phillip grabbed Beth and dragged her behind him as he ran to the machinery shed.

Beth was tired of being dragged by various members of the group. She shook his hand free.

"Tell me! Just tell me what you want me to do! You guys! I'm not a dog!"

Phillip answered as soon as be understood. He was having trouble thinking.

"Go up to the window like I told you. Tell me what you see."

Beth didn't want to argue. She had just been there. But she followed him and then they split at the machinery shed. Phillip took her bat and motioned for her to go around to the door at the side.

He ran over to the larger derrick and pulled himself up onto the bull wheel, keeping his body as close to the metal as he could.

Alan had moved over to the edge of the quarry to see if he could see anything. Someone was climbing the derrick tower by the machinery shed. It was Phillip — he could see his white shirt.

Alan went back to the lower derrick. With difficulty he pulled himself through the base of the bull wheel. He rested at the junction between the raised boom and the tower itself. The boom was still extended over the water. It was almost halfway raised, its end pointing to the storm clouds.

And then he saw Fox below him. He was looking from side to side.

Roger groaned.

Fox turned toward the sound. As he approached it he discovered Claude.

*Dead,* he thought and stepped over him. He stood poised, waiting to hear the sound again. Somebody nearby wasn't dead. *Yet.*

Alan saw the man moving toward Roger.

Alan could think of only one plan. He favored his hurt hand, climbing basically with his good hand and the wrist of the other.

Farther and farther out the derrick boom he half crawled and half climbed.

"Shit-fuck. Shit-fuck."

He didn't give his hand a thought. It didn't hurt. It was numb. He just couldn't use it.

He was halfway up the boom. He hoped he blended in with it.

"FUCK YOU, ASSHOLE!" he screamed. "JUST FUCK YOU, YOU MORON-ASSHOLE!"

Fox was two steps from Roger.

Roger had been ready to pass out from fear. He had caught a of glimpse of Fox.

They both heard Alan at once.

Fox spun around and Roger felt a rush off giddy laughter well up inside of him. *Fuck you, moron-asshole?* He wanted to kiss Alan.

Phillip leaned away from the tower at the other side of the quarry.

"ALAN!" he yelled. "WHERE ARE YOU?"

Beth heard the shouts. She saw Phillip but she couldn't locate her brother.

Fox moved cautiously back toward the quarry lip. He passed to the side of the bull wheel. He stopped and listened. *Kids. Kids everywhere,* he thought and then the futility of the situation struck him.

He had to get out of there. Too many shots. Too many people — children. Claude was gone. Fox had to get back to the car and put some fast miles between him and this mess. He turned back to leave.

Alan was watching, his heart roaring in his chest. *Oh Jesus, he's going back for Roger.*

He couldn't let it happen. He pictured the man standing over Roger, shooting him full of bullets.

"FUCK YOU! DON'T LEAVE — FUCK YOU! I KILLED THE OTHER GUY AND I CAN KILL YOU TOO!"

As he finished he knew he had said too much. He didn't want to get the guy that mad. He just wanted him away from Roger.

"Double shit-fuck! Double shit-fuck!"

The sounds were coming from over him. Fox stepped away from the bull wheel and looked up the tower.

Alan decided the best thing was to crawl inside of the webbing of the boom. Fast. As he did he lost his grip.

"SHIT!" he yelled, and below him, back at the base of the tower, Fox caught the movement.

Alan was now thirty or forty feet out on the boom. The wind was blowing and rain had increased again. The derrick was swaying slightly and the boom had settled into a harmonic swinging. It wasn't much. But it was too much.

Fox fired at the shape on the boom. The bullet sparked off of the steel and ricocheted away.

"OH SHIT!"

Alan crawled as fast as his arms and legs would take him. As he got closer to the large wheel at the end of the derrick the swaying was more pronounced. He looked down and could barely make out the quarry water below him.

He could make out the raft. It was almost beneath him. The Devil's Club — where was it? Alan scanned the waters as best he could.

Until he saw it.

Below him.

Directly below.

"Thanks a lot." he mumbled to the gods controlling such things.

He made it to the tip of the boom and huddled against the large wheel. There was no cable over it, its deep v-groove empty. Alan grabbed one of the spokes and tried to snug himself against the wheel's mass, further hiding him. When he did the big wheel revolved slowly. He lost his balance and started to fall.

Alan caught himself. His heart was pumping faster than a model airplane engine.

Phillip had not seen Alan, but he did catch Fox climbing over the bull wheel.

He was over it clumsily. He started to climb the boom.

Then Phillip saw Alan.

"JUMP ALAN! JUMP! HE'S COMING UP THE BOOM!"

"I CAN'T!" Alan replied instantly. "I'LL HIT THE DEVIL'S CLUB!"

The objects in the quarry were a pretty good reason for him not to jump. But they weren't the only reason.

Alan thought of the spirit in the water. *If the old lady is so sure the thing wouldn't hurt good people, then let her jump in. Fat chance.* Alan clutched the boom tip with all of his strength. *Maybe the guy will fall. He doesn't look too steady.*

Alan felt as if he were watching a movie — a drive-in — from way back in a field.

*Time for a Coke©! I gotta pee!*

Fox realized he had been sucked into doing what he had decided not to do. He shouldn't be here, not now. He should be in the car. He thought of what the kid had yelled. Could he have killed Claude? Could he really have done *that* to him?

He thought these things as he worked his way very slowly up the boom. He wasn't enthralled with heights and his arm didn't make things any easier.

Phillip searched the area. There had to be a way.

He saw the boom of the larger derrick extending from where he stood. It was parallel with the edge of the quarry, pointing back to Old Quarry Road and its end rested on a block of granite.

"BETH! BETH!" Phillip yelled, "GET THE DOLL MAN! MAKE HIM SWING THE BOOM OUT! SWING ME OUT TO ALAN! — I'LL CLIMB TO THE END! DO IT, BETH!"

By the time he finished he was shouting to an empty window.

Beth descended the stairs two at a time.

Ezechial looked up and the girl repeated commands, relaying what Phillip had said and as she did she gestured wildly with her arms, pointing to Phillip and then to Alan.

The Doll Man understood roughly half of what she was saying.

Move the boom. He could do that.

Beth ran over to the window by the cable controls. She couldn't get it open fast enough. She struggled with the latches. In a whirlwind of frustration she grabbed the stool Ezechial used and smashed at the window.

Glass and splintered wood and aged planks flew outward from her fury.

The temperature came up fast. The water in the boiler — what there was of it — had already been very hot.

It was strange to Ezechial that his sister was so excited.

Beth could see both derricks from where she stood. She brought Ezechial to her side by force of will and obscure gestures. She pointed to the distant boom extending over the quarry. Then she indicated the closer boom. The rest she explained with her hands, making booms of different fingers and swinging one to meet the other. *Touch* the other, she emphasized.

*Why would she have me do that?* Ezechial wondered, his confusion at last overpowered by his desire to please her.

He went back to the compressor valves. The gauges above them indicated he could open them soon. He went back and checked the levers on the various drums of cable.

Phillip was nearly to the end of the boom. He felt ridiculous because he was running along it, away from Alan. If the old man didn't move it soon there would be disaster for the boy.

*I'll be right behind you,* he heard himself saying to the others. He stood by the wheel at the end of the boom.

"JESUS, BETH, TELL HIM TO HURRY!"

Beth turned back to Ezechial. "NOW! NOW! NOW!" she screamed. She swung her arms around like booms. "DO IT NOW!"

The Doll Man stared at her.

Please his sister. He could please his sister. It was another chance. He could do it now.

He twisted the valves with his good hand.

Steam shushed through the pipes. He pulled the levers and opened different valves. He closed them and then adjusted them again.

The big flywheels on the side of the compressor rocked and stopped. They rocked again.

The fire was raging. Ezechial had left the dampers full open and gusts of air raced across the coals. Here and there patches of iron glowed dull red.

The flywheels rocked again, returned, and then went through a loping full revolution. And then another. And another.

Ezechial opened different valves and machinery started to clatter. Needles danced on a row of gauges.

The floor of the machinery building absorbed a gentle thumping.

The speed of the revolving wheels evened and increased. The needles swung slowly to the right, passing higher and higher numbers.

He vented compressed air to the pistons and gear boxes controlling the cable spools.

Ezechial hobbled quickly back to the compressor and adjusted a lever. Then another.

Fox was two-thirds of the way out the derrick boom.

Phillip saw there was no way Ezechial could get the boom across the quarry in time. He searched Alan's boom for a solution.

Phillip brought his hands to his head. He threw them down.

"BETH! FORGET THIS BOOM! HAVE HIM LOWER ALAN'S! BRING IT DOWN AND OVER TO THE SIDE ROCK!" He pointed to the granite plateau as he shouted.

Beth turned and grabbed Ezechial who was now handling the levers to the cable spools. One had begun to revolve. Slack snapped from the cable.

Phillip was almost jarred loose.

"NO!" he screamed.

Ezechial watched Beth make a different series of motions with her arms. The far derrick. The far boom. He understood. He went to a different set of levers at a different set of cable spools.

Fox was half standing on the boom. He was close enough that he thought he could not miss the boy. He balanced himself on the swaying boom and raised the gun.

Cables were moving. The tension advanced through a series of rusted triple pulleys guiding the cables around the corners of the quarry, to the base of the distant tower.

The derrick and the boom jerked as the cables snapped taught.

Fox lost his balance.

Alan was thrown to the side, the movement at the end several times more severe than where Fox was.

Fox dropped to his knees, banging them painfully on the steel strapping. As he did he grabbed for a handhold. The boom was moving. It had started to swing.

He remembered his gun.

It was gone.

He reached back and touched the sheathed knife. It was there.

It was not the knife of his ancestors, but it would do.

The cables to the far derrick were rusted, burrs and broken wires running their length. A burr and then several protruding strands of twisted wire caught at a pulley. As the cable continued to pass, the wires were stripped back along the cable. A mass of curling orange metal accumulated at the pulley. Then it jammed.

In the machinery shed the cable spool bucked and Ezechial instantly applied more power.

Too much.

The surge ripped the pulley's ancient stay bolts from the granite, pulling one free and then twisting and snapping the others.

The cable, no longer guided around a corner by the pulley, whooshed through the air over the quarry as it was freed. Another pulley let loose and then another.

The drum ran wild taking in the loose cable. The cable snaked back and forth across the drum, tangling over itself until it hung up, a giant bird's nest.

Ezechial had been looking beyond his sister, trying to see the other boom. As he did, the drum fouled and the crystallized gears of the drive mechanism sheered in a flurry of flying cogs. Disconnected power ran amuck.

The old man jammed a lever forward and the mechanism was unpowered.

Beth understood immediately what had happened. She signaled Ezechial to stop, to go back to their original plan.

His reaction centered around gratitude that she was not angry with him. She did not scold. There was still a chance to please his sister. He grabbed the appropriate levers, compressing the release grips.

Phillip saw the boom begin to move and then seize in a spastic halt. He saw that cables were whipping, unfettered in the quarry air. The loose cables which turned the boom had no immediate impact on those who were on it, but the other cables which were now playing wildly to take up slack were responsible for raising and lowering the boom.

It dropped ten feet in the blink of an eye.

Alan's stomach flew into his throat. His heart skipped. The massive swag of cables which ran from the peak of the derrick to the end of the boom where Alan huddled, raced back and forth through a series of four pulleys. Orange rust flew everywhere as the cables passed.

And then the slack was gone.

The boom jarred to a stop and the sudden pressure snapped three of the four bolts securing a different pulley group at a different corner of the quarry.

The boom was being held up by a twisted and slowly stretching bolt.

At first Phillip thought the boom was going to plunge into the quarry below. He saw that the cables to move Alan's boom were fouled. He did not see the pulley which was gradually working loose from the granite.

Before he could turn to Beth to yell to her to change the plan once more, he felt the cables to his boom tighten.

Beth had seen it also.

"HOLD ON!" she screamed to Phillip.

At first the boom began to rise into the air, and coincidental with that motion, it was swinging to the side, toward the quarry. Phillip grabbed the wheel and held, flexing his legs at the knees for stability.

The second boom was moving, Beth could see that. Rescue for her brother was on the way.

Headlights shone from a car turning in at the quarry shed.

Beth ran to the side door and threw the bolt.

The boom was in the air and moving toward its mate.

Fox recovered his balance. He heard the shrieking of the other cables.

Rain now advanced in sheets. Alan looked up to the heavens and let the driving water cleanse his face.

Phillip's boom swung over the water. Cables drew taut and it was raised farther as it pivoted. Phillip grasped a cable and rode toward Alan.

Fox advanced. As he neared the terminus he carefully reached behind him and drew his knife. He climbed after the boy.

Beth used her arms to indicate to Ezechial the relative positions of the booms.

The water boiled further down in the boiler. Less and less was left to address its needs. The needle at the water level indicator crushed more and more of the spider's skeleton. It still indicated an adequate supply.

Phillip was within twenty feet of Alan. They were both above the quarry waters, Phillip some ten feet below. "GET READY, ALAN!" he shouted above the rising wind.

The howl of the boiler and the compressor meshed with the violence of the storm. Great thick rusted cables hummed and the towers themselves vibrated with the wind. The rain pounded and it became difficult to see.

Beth lost track of her brother and Phillip. She tried to calculate where she had last seem them along with the speed of the swinging boom. She hesitated a moment more and then yelled to The Doll Man, "STOP! STOP! IT'S FAR ENOUGH!"

The boom with Phillip swept beneath Alan. It passed him by until with an abrupt jar it halted five feet too far beyond and ten feet below the boy.

Fox slashed his knife at Alan's feet. The boy kicked back at the blade, his ankle severely lacerated in the process. "COME BACK! COME BACK!" he shouted to Phillip.

Phillip tried to see the machinery shed through the downpour. When he continually failed he turned back to Allen. "WE'VE GOT TO DO IT LIKE THIS, ALAN! JUMP TO ME! JUMP!" He stretched out toward the upper boom, one hand wrapped around a spoke in the terminal wheel, the other reaching toward Allen.

The bolt at the quarry corner stretched farther. Fine lines spiraled its length and the mid-section thinned.

The surface of the quarry was a white fury from the rain. Alan rose higher on the boom, but the thought of the drop to the raft or the floating stump restricted his movements.

Beth was beside herself. She couldn't see either boom. There were muffled shouts. When at last she caught a glimpse of their relative positions she shouted to Ezechial and indicated with her arms that he should try to lower the far boom. The gears and apparatus to swing the boom had been violated, she was aware of that. But perhaps it could be lowered. She had seen from the relative positions and angles of revolution, that raising Phillip's boom would actually move him away from Alan if it were moved any more.

Ezechial concentrated on his sister's instructions. She was not nearly as clear as either The Boston Boiler Man or the Chicago Compressor Man. Then he heard banging at the side door to the building. He saw that his sister heard it, also.

*There are more of them!* she thought and then shut them from her mind. The rain hammered onto the granite plateau. She held her arms apart to indicate how far Ezechial was to lower the far boom.

He grabbed two fistful of levers and teased them several times. Cable leaped from the drum in spurts.

It was too much for the failing bolt. It popped and instantly Alan's boom dropped.

"JUMP!!!" Phillip screamed.

Alan flew through the air, pushing as best he could from the falling boom.

Fox lost his balance again. His foothold had dropped away.

The banging on the machinery shed door stopped. Beth heard one of the booms falling. Cables were rattling and growling. Rain was flying diagonally, and thunder was walking closer. Lightning flashed near town and then closer.

A huge man in bib-overalls appeared at Beth's window. It was Orson. He started to climb through and then heard the shouts from the extended boom. He pulled his leg back and turned toward the sounds.

Ezechial saw his stoker and smiled. He checked his gauges again. The water level indicator was pegged past danger and into the faded red quadrant. Ezechial gasped. He reached for the water valve and as he did he heard the shriek of super-heated steam. The crown plate was melting through. In a matter of seconds the remaining water would flood the fire box and the resultant violent build-up of pressure would blow the boiler and the red-hot firebox into thousands of pieces, sending shrapnel and raging steam everywhere, scalding and tearing apart anyone who was near.

*I WILL NOT KILL HER AGAIN!* Ezechial screamed in a rage to himself. *IT WILL NOT HAPPEN AGAIN!*

Alan had Phillip by the wrist. He had grabbed it before his rescuer could come to grips with him.

The boom with Fox plunged to the new limits of the cables and when it reached them it shook through the new restraint, pulling free all of the pulleys and parting some of the old cable.

The boom was headed for the quarry.

As it rapidly angled farther it smashed its underside onto the edge of the quarry, mashing in a section of the boom a quarter of its distance from the bull wheel and pivot. The leverage lifted the derrick, snapping the bolts at its base and ripping free the ring of cables which steadied its apex.

The derrick and boom tumbled forward. A tangle of cables fell toward Roger.

He watched in dumb fascination, the rain on his upturned face.

Fox hit the water at speed. He plunged through it.

The spirit sensed him enter the quarry as an electric shock through its body. It coiled over itself and writhed, excited and anxious to accurately position its prey.
Thick and undulating it rose to meet Fox.

He felt it coming and he knew what it was. He had lost the other knife.

It took him at the waist, a liquid freight train rushing by, roaring to the open air above the water.

Alan's hand ached and it started to slip. He dangled below the boom, Phillip above him with his legs wrapped around the metal bracing, one arm extended, the other attempting to find a way to reach Alan.
  He couldn't hold on much longer. He looked below him to see if there was any way he might hit free water. The derrick was a tangled wreck extending into the water, the boom completely submerged. Cables draped from the quarry sides into the pit.
  There was a chance. Just a chance that he could miss the debris.
  Alan took a deep breath.

Alan saw the thing break out of the water and rise another fifteen feet toward him. Fox was in its mouth and it shook him violently from side to side, his arms and legs those of a flailing doll. And then it arched and headed back to the water, humping in the air over The Devil's Club and diving again past the fallen derrick. In the near darkness its body shone grease-black and after its red eyes the boy could see nothing distinguishing its sliding length until the rasp-like tail passed and disappeared. It surfaced once more, not as high this time, pieces of the Indian falling piecemeal from the gory carcass as it dove back.

Alan watched in awe, his mouth open, forgetting where he was, forgetting his fingers, fatigued to their limit, and forgetting that he was about to release his fading grip on Phillip's wrist.
  The spirit passed, and Alan heard Phillip begging him, "Hold on, Alan. Hold on, please."
  It seemed like a good idea.

Every scintilla of remaining strength, no matter its location in Alan's hanging body, flowed to those fingers. He would hold on. He was certain.

"IT CANNOT HAPPEN AGAIN!" The Doll Man called to his gods.

Beth was at the window when he grabbed her, covering her with his moving body, and propelling her ahead of the steam and flying metal.

They hit the gravel and bushes beyond the window, the bulk of the explosion contained by the machinery shed's thick stone walls. Ezechial's body was light on top of Beth, for he was a little man, but his back was broad enough to have absorbed the steam and power and some of the boiler's side.

He opened his eyes and there was his sister beneath him once more and his dying heart broke again.

Beth moved from beneath the little man and cradled him, holding his torn body to her own.

Ezechial came back briefly, so strong was the love he felt washing through him. He looked and his sister was there, and she had him and he knew that she would not die.

She held him closer and moved her lips to his cheek and he could tell that she was crying.

Ezechial felt his life fading from him, and as it did he was reborn with the knowledge that he had been wrong. He had saved his sister.

He felt her arms tighten around him. *All these years I remembered it wrong.*

With the fury of the explosion and the flying shards of metal, all of the machinery suffered. What was left of the boiler lay on its side, the tubes splayed and spilling from its severed based. The huge compressor had tipped, its mass resting against the wall of the shed. Two of the cable drums were upended, the levers bent to the side, several gears and pieces of driving rods broken and lying on the floor. The arresting dog on the ratchet of one of the other cable drums had been broken loose, allowing the weight of the remaining boom to slowly unwind the cable from its spool.

The sound and the wave of the explosion reached Alan and Phillip coincidentally.

Their boom began to slowly dip toward the water.

Phillip had managed to reach Alan with his other hand. But to do so he had to reach through the boom lacing. He could hold the boy, but there was no way he could raise him.

Alan felt the movement. At first he thought he had let go and was falling. He could make out The Devil's Club below him.

The big man saw the cable moving slowly past him. He looked up and saw what was happening as the boom descended. He was more like a huge jungle cat than a dump truck driver as he easily pulled himself onto the bull wheel and started out the boom. It still had a modicum of up-angle as he scrambled along its length. By the time he reached Phillip the boom was level and modestly picking up speed.

He knew they would all have to move fast now, for when the bottom side of the boom reached the quarry lip it would stop abruptly, certainly shake them loose to fall to the littered quarry water, and possibly break loose the derrick itself as had happened on the other side.

Orsen hung to the side of Phillip and reached a broad hand to the dangling boy's upper arm.

Alan was pulled upward with such force that he thought some different sort of monster had him now.

Phillip released his grip and rolled to the side. He gained his feet as best he could and turned.

"GET OUTTA OUR WAY, BOY!" Orsen roared at him. "WE'RE COMIN' THROUGH!"

Phillip scrambled along the increasingly steep climb. He dove off of the boom, clearing the bull wheel and as he rolled across the granite he remembered hearing a snap coming from the arm he had used in an attempt to cushion his fall.

Orsen had Alan under his arm like a sack of grain. He too hit the granite plateau, but chose to shed his momentum by running flat-footed until he could set his own brakes.

Alan was not entirely sure of what was happening in this new jarring and shaking world.

The underside of the boom hit the stone lip and the internal bracing of the boom bent and absorbed the shock. The derrick swayed within the narrow limits of its cables and then stopped.

Lightning flashed and struck a nearby hill.

One by one and in groups the boys hobbled and crawled to the open area between the machinery shed and the remaining derrick. They sat and lay around Beth, who still held Ezechial.

Orsen went for Roger and brought him gently back, setting the moaning boy near his friends.

As one they lay or sat, and stared at the remaining tower.

A black cloud sent its forked power sizzling through the air.

They saw it and they heard it — the air parting as the blue-white fingered lance sought the derrick top.

CRACK-POW!! The explosion rocked the quarry, shaking the ground and echoing back up from the water.

White-powdered heat raced down the derrick and the cables — dancing, traveling lethal fuzz, hissing as it flowed.

The tower rocked from the impact and the energy of the strike flowed through the rusted cables, super-heating them so that flakes of rust jarred loose and fell in an incandescent orange umbrella above the children.

Two fire-balls danced around the peak of the derrick and then ran down separate cables, one rolling into the woods beyond them, the other moving down the cable, hesitating, moving briefly back up, and then disappearing.

The storm passed and the quarry was still.

# DAY EIGHT

The hospital was small and rural and clean.

Dr. Kemp and his three nurses hovered from child to child, dressing wounds, setting bones, and probing violations to the youngsters' bodies. By dawn it was finished, the doctor washing his hands and shaking his head. His nurses moved on to cluck over their new patients in the domain which was theirs — the children's ward — where doctors visited and nurses ruled.

The wave of parents and other relatives swept through next, bringing with them a mayhem which made the previous night's action seem calm. It continued until Lucille Stitt, nurse superior and mother to any child who happened into a bed in her ward, had enough. She ushered the visitors out, to the number, sending them off to their various breakfasts or catnaps or whatever it was they absolutely needed to calm themselves down.

She would not allow them back to see the children until after lunch. It was just too much with them milling everywhere — asking, scolding, and doing everything short of smothering her exhausted patients.

It wasn't fair to the other children in the ward either.

They all needed to rest.

So the visitors were herded out and the double doors swung shut after them.

Most difficult had been the big farmer in bib overalls who insisted on remaining. The only compromise he permitted was to sit on a metal chair in the hallway opposite the doors. This he did, his big hands folded in his lap, his ears straining to hear what was being said inside, a smile cracking his somber features when he heard his name or some exaggerated description alluding to him.

The children talked quietly, relating what they had seen and heard and done.

They had requited themselves, either through actions or wounds received, and even Freddy, prone on his stomach, his bottom bandaged, was assuaged. Certainly, he would have liked to have rescued Beth or done something brave, but he had faced a dangerous man — one with a loaded gun — and he could not hide in the ignorance of uninitiated youth. He had known curdling fear for his own life and he had heard the screams of those more seriously hurt. It was not a game to the boy and he was thankful to be alive.

Phillip sat in a chair, his arm in a sling, and he watched proudly as the others spoke.

Beth had sneaked in through the back door, the duty nurse more than understanding. She stood at Phillip's side.

Blacky was tied to a tree at the side of the hospital, and Alan, scraped and bruised and favoring a hand sporting more than forty stitches, cried when he looked out and saw his dog.

They were all in one state of shock or another and additionally, they were silently grieving for their lost friends, for each of them had lost someone from their lives.

"I'm sorry about the gun," Roger wheezed, his chest bandaged and the pain very much with him in spite of the drugs.

Alan smiled thinly.

"And what you did, man. . . ." Roger stopped, for the double doors swung open and a peculiar sight appeared.

A new patient, this one swaddled from head to foot in gauze was wheeled in and nested at the end of the row of beds. A bottle of something clear appeared to be draining through a tube leading to the mound of bandages.

The nurse who parked the bed briefly checked the others and then left.

The bandaged visitor made no sounds.

Roger continued, more quietly this time, "You called him away from me. He was comin' for me, and you called him back to you. That's the bravest thing I've ever seen in my life."

They were silent, and then Will turned to Freddy and thanked him too, for his friend had stayed with him when it would have been easy to high-tail it out.

And so it went for some time, the children leaning on one another, thanking, congratulating, and somberly relating their version of the heroism they had witnessed.

It was Alan who noticed that the visitor, the new patient hidden in white, was following the conversation with dark eyes. They moved to each of them as they spoke, skipping from one side of the room to the other.

Cavenaugh, talking haltingly, was becoming extremely emotional, for he was the first to mention outright, those who did not make it.

"And Kurtzy," he said, starting to sob, "that little guy — I bet he put up a helluva fight."

Alan started crying again.

Cavenaugh swallowed and winced with the pain and then continued, "I'm gonna miss him. I'm really gonna miss him."

Not talking clearly, because he spoke through burned lips and a layer of crowding bandages, the visitor shook his head slowly, and groaned, "Stop...." The others turned to him as he rasped, "You're gonna make me puke."

"KURTZY!" they yelled, startling the others in the ward.

And the mound acknowledged it was indeed him but he said little more. It was almost a week before he could tell them his story.

It was sad, of course, at the beginning, and then grisly, and when he came to the part about trying to burn through the ropes by setting the table on fire, and then the whole cabin, and how he had risen, sort of wearing the chair and dragging the table tied to his arm, and smashed through the front door, startling the fisherman who had apparently never seen a burning boy break out of a flaming cabin and take what seemed to be a roomful of furniture with him for a quenching dip in the lake — when Kurtzy got to that part, they knew that the lump of white was really him, and that in spite of his wounds, before too long he'd be giving them the finger again — as best he could.

# EPILOGUE

The United States Navy sent divers up from its Portsmouth, New Hampshire base, and the bodies of Louise and Junior were recovered. They were buried in the cemetery of The First Congregational Church.

Mr. Horvath's money was located and returned.

Ezechial was laid to rest beside his sister and father and mother in the little cemetery behind the shattered machinery shed.

No trace of Fox was ever found.

The imbroglio regarding Phineas Lathram finally subsided and the town elected a new constable. State and Federal police officials traced Lathram back to a death and devil cult which had flourished at the quarry site after the turn of the century. Their findings supported local folklore that evil, rising from the quarry, at one time embroiled the entire town. It was not until an itinerant named Hachaliah Johnson came to the quarry, leading, of all things, a circus elephant, that events precipitating the downfall of the cult were set into motion.

Phineas Lathram was one of the few to survive. He took his small following and sent them across the countryside to do his bidding. Fox and Claude involved themselves in his Death For Hire organization. The others disappeared.

The large bundle of money was impossible to trace and so the town officials grudgingly returned it to the children who had found it. It was kept in trust, of course.

And the knife — Fox's ancestor's knife — it was Phillip who retrieved it from The Devil's Club, and Phillip who used it the following summer in an attempt to save Beth's life.

The Widow Orlap suffered for nearly a month before she died, but before she did she was able to relay to Beth the Indians' legend of the quarry, explaining to her that the spirit had probably gone now and that would not return until evil again threatened.

For the remainder of the summer the only thing worth talking about was what had happened those seven days at Dead Man's Quarry. The new legend lived most vigorously in the tales of Old Lady Brinks; for as she told everyone, the trouble started in her own back yard when those two wicked and dangerous men attacked her with rope and giant knives.

If people had only listened to her.

The End.

Printed in the United States
95240LV00004B/25/A